CURIOUS NEW ENGLAND

CURIOUS

NEW

The

Unconventional

Traveler's Guide

to Eccentric

Destinations

Joseph A. Citro and Diane E. Foulds

ENGLAND

University Press of New England

HANOVER AND LONDON

With great affection
we dedicate this book
to Edith C. Foulds,
the quintessential New Englander.

Published by University Press of New England
One Court Street, Lebanon, NH 03766
www.upne.com

Originally published by University Press of New England in 2003.
Second edition published by University Press of New England in 2004.
Printed in the United States of America 5 4 3 2 1
ISBN 1–58465–359–0

The Library of Congress has cataloged the original edition as follows:
LIBRARY OF CONGRESS CATALOGING-IN-PUBLICATION DATA
Citro, Joseph A.
Curious New England : the unconventional traveler's guide to
eccentric destinations / Joseph A. Citro and Diane E. Foulds.
    p. cm.
Includes index.
ISBN 1–58465–112–1 (pbk. : alk. paper)
1. New England—Guidebooks. 2. Curiosities and wonders—New
England—Guidebooks. I. Foulds, Diane E. II. Title.
F2.3 .C53 2003
917.404'44—dc21   2002014985

Contents

Note to Second Edition

This symbol, when placed at the head of an entry, indicates that this site is either now closed or otherwise not accessible to visitors and exists in memory only.

Preface

This is not a standard travel book.

Each entry could be plotted on a continuum that begins with "Curious" and ends with "Weird." Some entries are stranger than others, but all reflect what we believe to be the classic New Englander's age-old appetite for the extraordinary. It's a quality present in our history, our folklore, our homes, our cemeteries, and in our very landscape.

In this guide we have tried to point out some of the more . . . eccentric destinations that you can visit in all six New England states. True, our list is not comprehensive; that would be impossible—there are simply too many oddities and wonders. We missed some, couldn't find others, rejected a few, failed to hear about more, and sadly, learned that some no longer exist. There were myriad dead ends and disappointments as we tried to ferret out Yankee Unusuals.

One barrier, of course, is that people simply cannot agree on what's weird. It's like pornography: You may not know what it is, but you know it when you see it. In fact, pornography is an apt analogy. There are things out there that are so downright macabre, bizarre, or uncomfortable that museums—who once flaunted them proudly—now refuse them a place on the shelf. Others exhibit some of their oddities with reluctance. But, as one curator said, "We prefer to call the items unusual, not weird."

In an era of political correctness, we repeatedly discovered that many museum administrations are imposing a form of "censorship" upon themselves which has banished to the back room anything considered unduly "curious." (The Vermont Historical Society Museum in Montpelier has a vintage electric chair, but they won't display it.) Some have pulled items off the shelf if a single person questioned their suitability for public view. (The Higgins Armory removed its chastity belt after one patron complained.) Worst of all, some museums have discarded anomalies deemed no longer of value, and in so doing have destroyed forever anyone's chance of seeing them. (One historical society museum threw away the caul that had been taken from the seventh son of a seventh son.)

So what *is* weird, anyway? For the purposes of this volume, let's say it is anything that inexplicably diverges from the norm. Anything mysterious, eccentric, and unexpected. Extreme expressions of individuality, odd juxtapositions, natural wonders . . . and blunders, or anything overtly incongruous, kitschy, imperfect, or just plain silly.

In our efforts to lead you to unconventional destinations, we have looked beyond museums. Many of the sites are not easy to get to. Some may require permission, a bit of exploration, or even an all-out hike. If we direct you to mainstream museums, it in most cases will be because of a specific exhibit inside. We sometimes alert you when a museum has something that may not be currently on display. But some museums themselves are treasure houses, and we've listed a few of those, too. Overall, we've tried to spotlight hidden corners of a region that rivals Old England in its mysteries, miracles, and marvels.

In closing—and before we're confronted with its absence— we should confess that we did a little self-censoring, too. We have omitted entirely what many would consider the epicenter of all New England strangeness—Salem, Massachusetts. To us, listing it would be a little like including Disneyland in a geography text. The town has become so much a theme park that it needs no reference here. They've carnivalized what in fact was a nasty bit of local history. And that may be just as bad as relegating it to the back room.

We invite your feedback. We have included our email address. We welcome all additions, corrections, opinions, comments, and suggestions. Please note that all email addresses and website URLs were up and running at the time this book was written.

So without further ado, let the tour begin . . .

J.A.C. and D.E.F.

CONNECTICUT

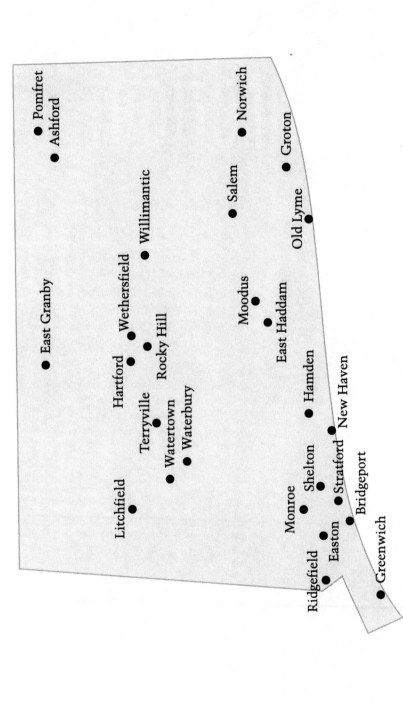

A Pauper's Grave

Lucas Douglass never married. He had no friends and no family. On the cold night of December 5, 1895, the seventy-two-year-old man was found dead, alone and penniless, on the street in Ashford. He had died in utter poverty. Or so people thought, until someone discovered his will. Mr. Douglass had left thousands of dollars to erect a monument to himself. It was to be thirty-four feet high, made of Italian marble, and would include a headstone, carved urns, and a 140-foot stone wall around the entire plot. It bears a portrait of Mr. Douglass, an epitaph—"I have heard Thy call"—and various other inscriptions that he had selected long before the fatal night. Though overlooked in life, each year hundreds of tourists visit Lucas Douglass's elegant monument. Ironic that in death he earned so much more attention and dignity than when he was alive. But maybe he had planned it that way.

Location: The Douglass Monument is in Westford Hill cemetery, located near the Meeting House on Westford Hill. The thirty-four-foot grave is easy to find.

The Barnum Institute of Science and History

Known today as simply "The Barnum Museum," this eccentric architectural edifice encapsulates much of P. T. Barnum's flamboyant spirit. Though a man of great learning, Barnum's uncanny ability to pique the public's curiosity made him rich, famous, and influential. Perhaps best remembered

The Barnum Institute of Science and History, a.k.a. the Barnum Museum, in Bridgeport, Connecticut. Photo: Joe Citro

for "The Greatest Show on Earth," he was without doubt "The Greatest Hoaxer." Clearly Mr. Barnum had a highly developed sense of the weird. The museums he ran in New York City specialized in a mishmash of curiosities and wonders. Though his "odditoriums" are long gone, their ghosts can be summoned here. The true epicure of the odd is advised to skip (or at least defer) the first two floors and go directly to the third where you can experience a sampling of the sorts of hard-core oddities for which Barnum's American Museum was world renowned. There's the mummy of Pa-Ib, an Egyptian priest believed to be twenty-five-hundred years old (with bones and teeth exposed), a giant's finger ring, a human footprint embedded in solid rock, tools belonging to Ulysses, fragments of Noah's Ark, and perhaps weirdest of all, the Feejee Mermaid, who is just as authentic today as she was in Barnum's era. Also, this floor showcases miniature memorabilia from Barnum's greatest human curiosity, the thirty-four-inch superstar, General Tom Thumb, and his tiny world.

The "Feejee mermaid," a mysterious monkey-fish hybrid, in the Barnum Museum.
Photo: Courtesy of the Barnum Museum, Bridgeport, Connecticut, and used by permission

And speaking of miniatures, check out the thousand-square-foot scale model of a five-ring circus. Okay, so it's not Siamese Twins, Borneo Wild Men, or even a Swedish Nightingale, but it's pretty mind-boggling just the same. Its creator, Mr. Brinley, began carving it at age nine, completing it sixty years later.

The Barnum Museum
820 Main St.
Bridgeport, CT 06604

Phone: (203) 331-1104
awestmoreland@barnum-museum.org
www.barnum-museum.org

Location: From I-95 south: Take exit 27, bear right following sign for Lafayette Boulevard. Follow onto Lafayette and take right at State Street. Turn right onto Main Street and The Barnum Museum will be on left, one block down.

From I-95 north: Take exit 27 (Lafayette Boulevard). Continue straight off exit ramp through five lights. Turn left onto Main Street at the fifth light. The museum will be on right past the first stop light.

Hours: Tuesday–Saturday, 10 A.M.–4:30 P.M., Sunday, noon–4:30 P.M. Closed Mondays (except during July and August).

Admission charged.

Wheelchair accessible.

Bridgeport, Connecticut

The First Real Airplane?

When we think about the history of American aviation, the Wright Brothers fly immediately to mind. History says they invented the airplane and, on December 17, 1903, were the first to achieve sustained flights in a powered, heavier-than-air vehicle. But Wright is wrong! Much evidence proves Bridgeport inventor Gustave Whitehead beat the brothers by more than two years. On August 14, 1901 he took off from what's now known as Bridgeport's Sikorsky Airport and remained aloft for half a mile. Because of poor documentation, Mr. Whitehead is ignored by such authorities as the Smithsonian Institution (who, according to William O'Dwyer's book *History By Contract*, is not legally permitted to recognize anyone prior to the Wrights). From photographs and the inventor's plans, the Whitehead Research Society has reconstructed Whitehead's plane. It's appearance is quite different from the Wrights' machine; from above it looks very like a giant moth—but it flies! The modern working replica—and much convincing evidence—is housed in a building at Captain's Cove Seaport.

Location: Captain's Cove is on historic Black Rock Harbor at 1 Bostwick Avenue in Bridgeport, Connecticut. Take I-95 N or S to exit 26 and follow signs.

NOTE: Whitehead's machine is displayed only occasionally. Viewings by appointment only. For information call (203) 335-1433.

Wheelchair accessible.

Bridgeport, Connecticut

Out of Place Parrots

Yes, parrots!

About two thousand of them up and down the Connecticut coast are building huge round stick nests in trees of all species. Some nests contain four or five living compartments, all inhabited by parrot pairs, usually offspring and their mates. They live in their condo-like homes year-round. The parrots are about twelve inches long, a bright apple-green color, with gray on their heads and chests, looking something like a monk's hood. They are bright blue on the underside of their wings, which you can see when they are in flight, and yellow-green lower on their chests. They screech and squawk as they fly—a very vocal bird. And they love iconoclastic nesting places, such as electric poles.

Oddly, the best time of year to see these parrots is in the winter, when the nests aren't hidden by foliage, and the birds' bright green feathers are not camouflaged by green leaves.

As to where they can be seen: The best tree is one in Bridgeport on Beacon Street off of Grover's Avenue. It is loaded down with fourteen large nests—the record as far as we know. Go there at sunrise and spot the birds with your binoculars as they are leaving the nests to start foraging for food. Or go at sunset, when they return home and hang around socializing before retiring into their condos for the night.

Another place to spot them is in Fairfield, on Beach Road off of Route 1. You'll come to a little island where the road divides, and on that island are some trees filled with huge circular nests made of sticks.

Still no luck sighting them? Then head to Stamford. On Cove Island Park is Sound Waters. There's a little museum there, and parrots graze on the ground year-round. They live further west in nests they've built in the huge spotlights of Cummings Park baseball field.

Or try the Woodmont section of Milford where the birds have moved into pine trees along Beach Avenue.

These beautiful birds are actually "Monk Parakeets," a species of parrot native to Argentina, Bolivia, Uruguay, Paraguay, other parts of South America—and now Connecticut. They probably didn't immigrate here on their own. Most likely they were imported as pets in the late 1960s and early '70s, but escaped, reproduced, and adapted to Connecticut's chillier climate. Decorative as they are, they're considered an agricultural pest in Argentina, as they eat crops. But so far, no complaints of that nature have surfaced here.

America's Black Hole

Connecticut's answer to the Tower of London (or maybe the Black Hole of Calcutta), Old New-Gate Prison—named after its dismal counterpart in England—began life as a copper mine (1707) and was transformed into the state's first prison (1773) until it was abandoned in 1827. Since the authorities wanted their "gaol" to be escape proof, they could find no sturdier (or less costly) house of detention than the earth itself: the abandoned Simsbury Copper Mine. Over the years it housed criminals, British soldiers, and British sympathizers. A prisoner was dropped down a twenty-five-foot shaft into a black maze of clammy holes and twisting tunnels. There he would serve out his sentence without ever seeing the light of day. Though considered humane in its day, a visit to the prison might convince you otherwise. Imagine being locked up in these damp, lightless depths. Imagine trying to move around under a rock roof that is only four or five feet high. And imagine being chained in solitary confinement at the bottom of a dead-ended tunnel. With no illumination, it must have seemed more like a grave than a cell. Yet, oddly, people did manage to escape. Apparently they had plenty of motivation.

Old New-Gate Prison and Copper Mine
Newgate Road
East Granby, CT 06026

Phone: (860) 653-3563

Location: From I-91, take exit 40 and follow 20W through East Granby Center. You'll come to a light at Newgate Road. Turn right and drive one mile to the prison.

Hours: Closed until further notice.

Admission charged.

Gillette's Fantastic Fortress

Looming above the Connecticut River is an imposing medieval fortress designed and constructed as the embodiment of a man's eccentricities. Gillette's Castle, as it has been known since construction began in 1913, is entirely the handiwork of William Gillette, who made the role of Sherlock Holmes famous long before anyone had heard of actors Basil Rathbone or Jeremy Brett. Mr. Gillette brought his own peculiarities to the design of the place, filling it with gadgets and gizmos that would make Rube Goldburg envious. There are secret panels, a complex mirror system Gillette used to spy on guests, and forty-seven hand-carved doors, each with an ingenious wooden puzzle that serves as a lock. There is even a room furnished to replicate Holmes's quarters at 221B Baker Street in London. A real showpiece is the trick bar that vanishes and secretly locks in case a Prohibition agent strays too near. There are many more examples of the millionaire's whimsies, more fun to explore than to read about. Two of Mr. Gillette's passions were trains and cats. Outside, he constructed a full-scale, three-mile railway on the grounds. Inside, there are over sixty decorative cat images scattered about and many of the doors contain cat-sized openings to permit Mr. Gillette's pets to roam freely.

Gillette Castle State Park
  River Rd.
  East Haddam, CT 06423

Phone: (860) 526-2336
  www.dep.state.ct.us/stateparks/parks/gillettecastle.htm

Location: Four miles south of East Haddam off Route 82.

Admission charged for castle. Entry to grounds is free.

Hours: Grounds open at 8 A.M. Castle open daily from Memorial Day through

Labor Day, 10 A.M.–5 P.M. Labor Day–Columbus Day, Saturdays and Sundays, 10 A.M.–5 P.M.

Admission charged.

Wheelchair accessible on first floor and terraces only.

The White Lady

She may be the most famous phantom of the century and she resides in what may be America's most haunted cemetery. She's "The White Lady" and, for more than fifty years, she has been appearing in Easton's Union Cemetery. Hundreds of people have confronted her. This out-of-place, out-of-time apparition, with a bonnet and a single braid of hair, wears a white ruffled nightgown. She makes her solitary evening sojourns among the gravestones. Some witnesses have seen dark, shadowy figures grabbing at her. Occasionally she leaves the cemetery. In 1993, she was walking on the road nearby when Glenn Pennell, a local fireman, accidentally slammed into her with his pickup. He went right through her. But Easton's celebrated specter is not alone. Many other apparitions roam these haunted grounds. For decades cemetery visitors have reported conversations with what seem to be people—they look, talk, and act like living human beings—until they vanish into thin air. Those photographically inclined have had some success taking pictures of the phantoms. Developed photos often reveal forms that were not visible when the picture was snapped. If you want to try your luck at meeting the White Lady, we suggest you bring a camera.

Location: Easton is in southwestern Connecticut just south of the spot where Route 136 intersects with Route 59. Union Cemetery is on Route 59, near the Easton Baptist Church.

Greenwich, Connecticut

Cursed House

Whether your appetite is for preternatural curses or good old-fashioned scandal, Dunnellen Hall offers plenty of both. It was built in 1918 by Daniel Grey Reid as a wedding present for his daughter Rhea and her husband, Henry Ropping. This Jacobean behemoth near Long Island Sound may not have been born bad, but, within the last half-century it certainly has picked up an "evil reputation." Supposedly, Dunnellen brings bad luck to anyone who has acquired it since it was first sold by the Roppings' sons in 1950. The first "outsider" to purchase it was steel magnate Loring Washburn (1950). Shortly afterward his money problems began, escalating until 1963 when a finance company took over the property. Perhaps Dunnellen's reputation as a "scary place" grew because it remained vacant for a long time after that. Finally it was bought by the ex-wife of an heir to the Dodge automobile fortune. A former showgirl, she married Daniel Moran, a New York City cop who later shot himself. In 1968, Jack Dick, a financier, bought it for one million dollars. In 1971, he was indicted for stealing 840,000 dollars. Before the case went to trial, Mr. Dick died of a heart attack while being chauffeured home in 1974. When his widow, Lydia, put the house up for sale she articulated what many had suspected: The place was like the Hope Diamond; it brought bad luck to everyone who owned it. Nonetheless, oil merchant Ravi Tikkoo eagerly paid three million dollars to possess the estate. Unforeseen financial problems associated with the mid-seventies oil embargo soon forced Mr. Tikkoo to sell. Then Harry and Leona Helmsley acquired it. Not long afterward—in 1988—the Helmsleys were arrested on federal charges of income tax evasion. In 1989, Leona was convicted and sentenced to prison. One can't help but wonder whether the Ropping boys knew what was coming . . .

Location: From Route 15, turn right onto Round Hill Road, which lies between Riversville Road and Lake Avenue. Dunnellen Hall is well hidden at the end of a curving drive, behind gates and walls, and only a smidgen of it can be glimpsed in the dead of winter when the trees are bare. Round Hill Road is narrow with no places to pull over, so if you go, be careful. Then again, maybe you shouldn't bother. If the place really is cursed, it might be best to avoid it.

Groton, Connecticut

Gungywamp

It seems miraculous that twenty-four acres of Bronze Age ruins could possibly survive within miles of a six-lane highway, but they do. What's even more strange is that the vast majority of motorists cruising by in their SUVs haven't the slightest idea the ruins are there. Were they to turn off at the Groton exit, they would happen upon one of the strangest sites in all of New England, a haunting reminder of just how little we know about the land we inhabit. It is Gungywamp. Though the word may sound Indian, it's actually ancient Gaelic, meaning "Church of the People." This indisputably ancient walled-complex sits atop a steep, thirty-foot cliff, just six miles north of Long Island Sound and two miles east of the Thames River. On a ridge near its center there's a double circle of massive quarried stones laid end to end. Some reveal traces of burning, suggesting the site may have been used as a ritual altar. Excavation has disclosed a stone floor between the circles, and in the 1980s, charcoal was uncovered dating from the first millennium. An oracle? A tomb? It may be more complex. A handful of standing stones and a single slab are positioned along astronomical lines, indicating that Gungywamp could have functioned as a calendar. Part of what makes it so unusual is the variety of structures concentrated at a single site. There are earthen mounds, stone piles, petroglyphs, and four stone chambers not dissimilar to dozens of others scattered throughout New England forests, the largest is eighteen feet long (see our entries for Salem, New Hampshire, Royalton, Vermont, and Goshen, Massachusetts). What's particularly odd is a rock ledge known as the Cliff of Tears. Over time, regulars have noticed that people walking past this area tend to get inexplicably depressive. Some start to weep without understanding why. Others get nosebleeds or bleeding gums. An electromagnetic reading showed wild activity, which may be the most important clue: Gungywamp may be the vortex of some as yet unexplained electromagnetic field. While we may be tempted to chalk this up to a scientific anomaly, the ancients may have come to a different conclusion: It is the seat of God. Tread carefully. They might be right.

Please direct all correspondence to:

The Gungywamp Society
P.O. Box 592
Colchester, CT 06415-0592

NOTE: To sign up for an outing with the Gungywamp Society, write them at least a month in advance. For more information, visit their website, www.gungywamp.com, or contact Jack Rajotte at (860) 405-0844. Outings are limited to twenty people, first-come, first-served.

There is a small charge.

Ghost Cars

An aura of neglect doesn't destroy the eerie effect of the Ghost Cars. And the eye doesn't quite know what to do with them. They seem like three dimensional shadows that almost merge with the parking lot. One conjures the notion of an automotive horror film in which zombie cars push their way up from graves beneath the macadam. Some have partially emerged, others more completely. A few, like blisters, barely bulge the surface. So what is this odd automotive display? *Why is it?* And what could it possibly mean? Conceived in 1978 as a work of art, the twenty Ghost Cars sit like abandoned statues at the edge of Hamden Plaza. Do they express the essence of modern America in which tar and car have become one? Are they an apocalyptic vision in which all motion has stopped? Is their intent to frighten, warn, or comfort? The enigmatic tableau invites each of us to consider the artist's intent and what his creation has come to signify. Certain local speculation is more horrific than aesthetic: perhaps they're the carcasses of cars in which accident victims actually died. Or perhaps the asphalt coating conceals real cadavers within. Whatever they are, this is a one-of-a-kind sight that will lodge itself forever in your memory and imagination.

Location: From Route 10 north take exit 60. Find Hamden Plaza at 2100 Dixwell Avenue. Look for Shaw's Supermarket and Marshall's. The Ghost Cars are easy to spot, not far from a much more animated wind sculpture mobile.

"Cabinet of Curiosities"

Blast into the past. Head straight up the stairs inside Hartford's "Old State House," turn around, and be whisked back to the eighteenth century. Here you enter "Mr. Steward's Hartford Museum," a lovingly faithful reconstruction of a genuine House of Wonder and Curiosity that opened in 1797. Allow yourself plenty of time to ponder the dense displays of hundreds of oddities that made our ancestors stare in open-mouthed amazement or gasp with surprise, outrage, and indignation. Check out the horrific hand (mummified), the largest Bengal tiger ever seen (stuffed) and the baffled-looking calf ("having two perfect heads and one body"). Nearby there's a pig similarly equipped, a unicorn horn, a giant lobster claw, the tusk of a seventy-million-year-old triceratops, a stuffed mongoose killing a stuffed cobra, electrifying machines, an elephant's foot, and many enormous bugs (all dead). And you can be sure these make up only a fraction of the curiosities—natural and unnatural—that you'll witness in Connecticut's first museum. Historically, this delightful depository is the pet project of former State House Executive Director Wilson Faude. With stamina and affection, he rounded up many of the fascinating exhibits that Joseph Steward displayed two hundred years ago. Since Mr. Faude's departure, the museum has lost some of its hyperbolic grandiosity. Among other things, they have pulled from display "authentic" tea from the Boston Tea Party, Egyptian "King Ramses's" hand, and the veiled head of Charles I (which he's apparently lost a second time). Still, the alchemy is perfect: This wonderful museum captures a genuine sense of the past, with all its clutter, arrogance, and dignified naiveté.

Old State House
  800 Main St.
  Hartford, CT 06103–2399

Phone: (860) 522-6766

www.ctosh.org

Location: From I-91 south, IGNORE outdated sign saying "Old State House Visitors Information." Just beyond it take the exit that says State Street exit 31. It will curl around the Hartford Steam Boiler building and drop you onto State Street. You'll see the Old State House with its gold dome. The museum is inside.

From I-84 take the "Downtown Hartford" exit. You will cross the Founders Bridge, come up the hill, and the Old State House will be looking down at you.

Hours: Monday–Friday, 10 A.M.–4 P.M., Saturday, 11 A.M.–4 P.M. Closed Sundays.

Admission free.

Wheelchair accessible.

Hartford, Connecticut

Menczer Museum of Medicine and Dentistry

Though the Hartford Medical Society has existed since 1846, they didn't open the museum until 1974. A good thing, too. Now visitors viewing their collection of antique instruments can try to appreciate today's versions of the same grim tools. There is something fascinating about these unusual but uncomfortably familiar surgical devices—saws, vices, pliers, mallets—that allowed Revolutionary War physicians to compete to see who could most speedily sever a leg. Early dentistry is also represented with such vintage torture instruments as iron "Toothkeys" (1750); the name says it all. If these hors d'oeuvres whet your appetite, examine the authentically reconstructed dental office (1919) and doctor's office (1923). "Alternative medicine" is represented here as well. Electricity has long been touted as a mystical cure-all. What was it like to be treated by some nineteenth-century gizmo like the "Improved Patent Magneto Electric Machine" (1862), the Fleming Battery (1885), or Dr. Elisha Perkins's Galvanic Tractor, fabricated in 1798 from copper, zinc, gold, iron, and silver (it was used to stroke the affected body part to stimulate the nerves)? No doubt a fixture in Dr. Frankenstein's laboratory. We don't know how to classify the 200-year-old Chinese acupuncture set. Or the surreal surveillance provided by the eye trays, from which glass eyeballs—fifty to a case—stare unblinking. The museum might have been called "The Museum of Pain" had it not been for local dentist, Horace Wells, who pioneered the use of surgical anesthesia. On December 11, 1844, he sniffed laughing gas and had a colleague yank out one of his molars—painlessly. Sadly, his fate was no laughing matter, as you will learn during your visit.

Menczer Museum of Medicine and Dentistry
230 Scarborough St.
Hartford, CT 06105

Phone: (860) 236-5613
library.uchc.edu/hms/menczer.html

Location: From I-84 take exit 46 to West Boulevard. Take a right on South Whitney Street. Continue one and a half miles to Scarborough Street. The museum is located on Scarborough Street and Albany Avenue, inside the red brick Hartford Medical Society Building.

Hours: Open Monday–Friday, 10 A.M.–4 P.M. Closed holidays.

Admission charged.

Wheelchair accessible.

Hartford, Connecticut

Walk-In Kaleidoscope

The Science Center of Connecticut is a fascinating place. You can mingle with nearly fifty species of animals, play with "MathMagical Toys," wander through the belly of a whale, or soar into space at the Gengras Planetarium. But forget all that.

What you really want to do is go directly to the "Walk-In Kaleidoscope" and brace yourself for a mind-bending, exhilarating, drug-free thrill-ride. You'll stand at a railing and look down to what seems to be the center of the earth. Then you'll look up and around at a multicolored infinity of mirrors. And when the whirlwind of color commences—with you at the controls—your senses will kick into high gear. No one who experiences the Walk-In Kaleidoscope can escape feeling like the character in *2001: A Space Odyssey* who blasts—thanks to stunning 1968 special effects—through the infamous Star Gate and into . . . what? The future? Another dimension? An alternate reality? When you finish you'll still be back in Hartford, but the trip will be worth it. This is probably the biggest Kaleidoscope on the globe, and the time spent within its colorful corridors is an experience that's out of this world.

Science Center of Connecticut
   950 Trout Brook Dr.
   West Hartford, CT 06119

Phone: (860) 231-2824
   webmaster@sciencecenterct.org
   www.sciencecenterct.org

Location: The museum is at the intersection of Farmington Avenue and Trout Brook Drive.

Hours: Tuesday–Saturday, 10 A.M.–5 P.M., Sunday, noon–5 P.M. Open Mondays during holidays and school vacations. Closed Thanksgiving, Christmas, and Easter.

Admission charged.

Wheelchair accessible.

Litchfield, Connecticut

Lourdes in Litchfield?

Too bad North America doesn't have Europe's numerous religious shrines commemorating miracles, where healings and other mysteries still occur. Places like Fatima, Medjurorje, Lourdes, and the like just aren't part of the American landscape. But since no divine personages have chosen to reveal themselves here, a journey to Litchfield, Connecticut, can save you a trip to France. Back in 1954, the Montfort Missionaries began constructing a replica of the French grotto where, in 1858, the Virgin Mary allegedly appeared to simple country child Bernadette Soubirous. Construction was completed and "Lourdes in Litchfield" opened to the public in 1958, the centenary of the apparition's manifestation at Lourdes. While nothing supernatural is likely to appear to you in Litchfield, the manufactured topography may give you some idea of why every year thousands of people from all around the world make pilgrimages to Lourdes in France. If not, this is a quiet place to rest and meditate.

Lourdes in Litchfield Shrine Grotto
Route 118
Litchfield, CT 06759

Phone: (860) 567-1041
lourdesct@aol.com
www.montfortmissionaries.com/lourdes.phtml

Hours: Open daily dawn to dusk.

Free admission.

Wheelchair accessible.

Monroe, Connecticut

Warren's Occult Museum

During their forty-year career, Ed and Lorraine Warren, New England's most conspicuous demon-chasers, have fought a single-minded campaign against the forces of darkness. Over the years they have built up a one-of-a-kind collection of fascinating curios. There are voodoo and fertility dolls said to have inflicted grievous harm on unsuspecting victims, a cursed string of pearls which strangled its owner, and an organ taken from the haunted Phelps mansion, which sometimes plays all by itself. And if that isn't weird enough, there is a coffin once used by a human vampire and a homicidal Raggedy-Ann doll that supposedly can walk—and kill—on its own. A visit to Warren's Occult Museum can be a terrifying experience. No place in New England can rival this eclectic private collection of occult paraphernalia; the hard-earned spoils of the Warrens' war against evil.

NOTE: By reservation only. Call for appointment and location (203) 268-8255 between hours of 9–11 A.M. and 8–9 P.M. We recently heard that the museum is open only to tour groups of ten or more people.

ALSO NOTE: May not be suitable for folks twelve and under.

Admission charged.

Moodus, Connecticut

The Sounds of Moodus

This is the granddaddy of all New England's unaccountable clamor. The venerable "Moodus noises" have been groaning and grinding for centuries, just as if Mother Nature were in continual gastro-intestinal chaos. Native Americans called the area *Mackimoodus* which translates as something like *place of noises*. Reverend Stephen Hosmer, Haddam's first minister, wrote about the spooky sounds in 1729. He described them as earthquakes, but with this peculiarity: "They seem to have their centre, rise and origin *among us . . .*" Then he added, "Now whether there be any thing diabolical in these things, I know not . . ." And that has been the question ever since. Sometimes likened to thunder, sometimes to artillery fire or falling timber, the noises continue to mystify; beginning somewhere near Mount Tom, and ending near the person perceiving them. The noises occur at unpredictable intervals. Some investigators have concluded they originate near the town of Leesville, from a point known as Cave Hill, the location of a cavern which has never been thoroughly explored because of its noxious air. An abandoned lead mine was also found here. Whether the Moodus Noises are supernatural symphonies or seismic shenanigans, we may never know for sure.

Location: Moodus is twenty-one miles from Hartford. Go southeast on Route 2 to North Westchester, ten miles southwest on Route 149.

New Haven, Connecticut

Judges' Cave

In 1649—long before the revolutionary fuse was fully ignited in this country—the British Parliament convicted King Charles I of treason. The monarch was allowed a short speech, made to lie over a wooden stand, and then, with a swift stroke of an ax, beheaded. Parliament continued to rule for about ten years, but its leadership collapsed, and the king's heir, Charles II, took the throne. His first act was to track down the regicides. Of the fifty-nine "judges" who had signed Charles's death warrant, ten were executed and nineteen imprisoned for life. Twenty-four were already dead—but six had escaped. Of those, at least three hightailed it for the New World, arriving in Massachusetts. Two of these, high-ranking Puritan generals William Goffe and Edward Whalley, were welcomed with open arms by like-minded colonists, who conspired to protect them. It wasn't long before the king's agents showed up, hot on their trail. The judges fled from house to house to evade their pursuers, finally being reduced to taking refuge in this cave. Here they spent a good part of a summer before an angry catamount frightened them away. Judges Goffe and Whalley ended their lives concealed in the bleak basement of a nondescript Hadley, Massachusetts, home. But the cave lives on as a monument to their escape, albeit somewhat shifted over the centuries. If you look closely, you can still make out handwriting left on the side of a wall, a grim reminder of how politics can reduce a man of stature and means to the status of a troglodyte.

Location: The cave is about an hour's trek to the top of West Rock in West Rock Park in the northwestern part of the city, off of Route 15. It is accessible from the Regicides Trail, which can be found in any Connecticut walk book. Ask locals for directions, and look for the huge outcropping of reddish rock.

New Haven, Connecticut

Miracle Tree

About ten years ago a young woman was enjoying a casual evening stroll through New Haven's Columbus Green when she saw a startling sight: a tree transformed into a giant crucifix. Since she had never seen such a thing in the municipal park before, she took a closer look. Although legally blind, the girl was struck with the apparition, instantly becoming convinced it was a symbol from on high. She passed the message along, and soon thousands were gathering at the spot after sundown in order to draw their own religious conclusions. Some thought it a product of the girl's visual impairment. Others saw it as a fantasy of light and darkness, created by a shadow cast by a street lamp, making the tree's vertical trunk and horizontal branches stand out. But the majority burned candles and left flowers, half-convinced they'd witnessed a miracle. The tree is still there, but the crowds are gone. It is a tall sycamore in the center of the park where all the paths come together. Go after dark and circle the area until you see it. This particular park is full of cherry trees, so springtime might be an enjoyable time to go. New Haven's Parks and Recreation Department says the park has not been the scene of muggings, but to play it safe, take someone with you.

Location: The park is open year-round. Fittingly, it's on the corner of Chapel Street and Academy Street. Park your car on Worcester Place, which is on the northeast side. You can call the Park Department's tree division for more information at (203) 496-6971.

New Haven, Connecticut

The Most Mysterious Manuscript in the World

The so-called Voynich Manuscript is a book no one can read. It is an octavo volume, six by nine inches, containing 204 pages of careful, coherent-looking script with tiny, colorful drawings of plants, constellations, and female nudes. But the script is in no known language, the constellations are unrecognizable, and the plants appear nowhere on this earth. The age of the manuscript is another puzzle. It most likely dates from the thirteenth century. We know that for a while it was in the oddity collection of Rudolf II of Prague, who may have acquired it from the Elizabethan magician John Dee. In any event, it found its way into the archives of a monastery in Frascati, Italy where it was discovered by book dealer Wilfred Voynich in 1912. Mr. Voynich passed it along in 1961 to Hans Krass who tried to sell it for 160,000 dollars, hinting it might contain priceless new insights into the nature of man. There were no takers. In 1969 he donated it to Yale. But this much is known for sure: For centuries, teams of the world's most accomplished linguists and code-breakers have been able to learn nothing from the mysterious language (of which there is no other known example) and the puzzling, almost cartoon-like illustrations. The manuscript remains a mystery; no one has been able to figure out what it says, who wrote it, when, where, or why.

Location: The Voynich Manuscript is in the Beinecke Rare Book and Manuscript Library at Yale, located on High and Wall Streets.

Hours: Monday–Thursday, 8:30 A.M.–8 P.M., Friday, 8 A.M.–5 P.M., and Saturday when college is in session, 10 A.M.–5 P.M.

NOTE: The Voynich Manuscript's catalogue number is MS 408. www.voynich.nu

Free admission.

Wheelchair accessible.

New Haven, Connecticut

Skull and Bones Club

This is either a place for Yale frat boys to blow off steam or the cornerstone for power, wealth, and politics in the United States of America. Its membership list reads like a "Who's Who," with Grandpa Bush, Papa Bush, and President George the younger among its distinguished ranks. Each year, so the story goes, fifteen elite members of the club graduate and pick fifteen senior-year replacements. For decades afterward, the older help the younger, and the younger "cooperate" with their elders—a system that perpetuates allegiance and patronage. Frightening initiation rites provide the mortar to this wall of the wealthy. Each has to be immersed naked in mud, then spend a night in a coffin. But perhaps the most bonding scheme is the so-called CB, or "connubial bliss," ritual. The initiate tells the Order all the sordid sexual secrets of his young life. Such disclosures have obvious permanent application in enforcing solidarity among members. (We suspect Junior George's revelations were more entertaining than his father's, but who knows?) Meetings take place every Thursday and Sunday and reunions every year. Who can say what rites are practiced and what deals are cut? Their clubhouse ("no girls allowed") looks exactly like a tomb, its privacy guarded as if it were a state secret. So here our presidents-to-be meet with other wealthy, amoral young men with guaranteed futures of unlimited power over the rest of us. Though few commoners have seen the inside of the Tomb, persistent rumors speak of grisly souvenirs displayed there. One—evidently true—is that they possess Geronimo's skull. And their own records reveal it was secured for them in 1918 by Grandpa Prescott Bush, who personally robbed the noble warrior's grave. So it looks like "the old boys' network" is alive and well. But—you ask—can any of this be true? Most of us will never know . . . and those who will won't tell.

Location: The Skull and Bones "Tomb" can be seen from High Street between Chapel and Elm. You can't go inside, but you can gawk and take pictures. It is made from a kind of brown stone and is windowless. To get to the campus from I-95, connect to I-91 north in New Haven. Take exit 3 (Trumbull Street) and continue until Trumbull Street ends at the fourth traffic light. Turn left onto Prospect Street and go a block until it becomes College Street. Follow College Street for three more blocks, turn right at Chapel Street, and go right at the next light onto High Street. The tomb is almost immediately to your left, just past the Yale University Art Gallery.

New Haven, Connecticut

Treaded Lipstick

What would you do with a twenty-three-foot tube of lipstick? How would you move it around? Both these nagging life-problems seem to have been solved by artist and Yale alumnus

Claes Oldenburg; he donated his giant steel and aluminum sculpture to his alma mater in 1969. Called *Lipstick (Ascending) Caterpillar Tracks,* it caused quite a stir at its secret unveiling at Beinecke Plaza. Administrators panicked, thinking it was a political protest, maybe even a disguised cannon. No department heads wanted this puzzling object in their backyards, so, in the dead of night, the Swedish-born artist took his creation back. Wondering how they could lose a lipstick that big, the college caucused. Now, realizing the depth of their artistic blunder, the academics fell all over themselves trying to set things right. The artist's feathers were eventually smoothed and the lipstick returned. *Lipstick (Ascending) Caterpillar Tracks* now graces Morse College's isolated courtyard. But even after all the commotion, we still don't know what it *means.* War on Revlon? The feminization of the military? A subtle plea for soil conservation? We're stumped. If you figure it out, please let us know.

Location: The Lipstick can be glimpsed through the gate of Morse College at 302–304 York Street on the Yale campus. The courtyard itself is not open to the public, but if you hang around long enough someone will wander through the locked door and let you in.

NOTE: Some of Claes Oldenburg's other works include *Clothespin* in front of the Philadelphia City Hall, a fifty-one-foot long spoon at the Minneapolis Sculpture Garden with its 1,200 pound maraschino cherry, and a *Colossal Ashtray with Fagends* at the Pompidou Centre in Paris . . . in case you're in the neighborhood.

 Norwich, Connecticut

Sanctuary of Love

We don't know what it is about the state of Connecticut that inspires so many offbeat religious displays. Take the "Sanctuary of Love." Since experiencing a miraculous vision some thirty years ago, Sal Verdirome (now over eighty) has devoted his life to single-handedly building a vast outdoor shrine on his steep hillside lot. Though people come from all around to pray here, others may see the sanctuary as an inspired bit of lunacy. At least fifty Madonnas beam beatifically from upended, cast-off bathtubs. Those who don't fancy hygienic virgins may enjoy the scores of other religious brick-a-brack—including hand-painted statues of saints and angels—placed helter-skelter around these peculiar premises. Mr. Verdirome himself may be there to greet you. If so, you'll enjoy your own vision when you behold his long gray hair and Old Testament style beard. Perhaps he'll guide you along the concrete walkways and ramps, which are dappled with stars, crosses, and inspirational sayings. Especially notable—or bizarre, depending on your point of view—is Mr. Verdirome's rendition of the Sea of Glass as prophesied in Revelation. Impossibly huge and decorated with mystical beasts, it may give you the chills . . . at least that's one possible reaction. In the final analysis, the Sanctuary of Love is an amazing accomplishment for a single individual whose unique vision—supernatural or otherwise—has produced a true eccentric masterpiece.

Sanctuary of Love
   62 North Main
   Norwich, CT 06360
   (Look up the slope above the street to see it.)

NOTE: Mr. Verdirome accepts no cash donations. The Sanctuary is his gift to you.
   Closed until further notice.

 Old Lyme, Connecticut

Nut Museum

We hesitate to describe this place as seedy, although the Connecticut Department of Tourism has ignored it for years. It is definitely an *eccentric* spot (though we wouldn't say nutty). It's an entire museum dedicated to—of all things—the common nut. Central to the core experience is artist, entrepreneur, and Nutland ambassador, Elizabeth Tashjian, the so-called "Nut Lady." In 1973, she turned her Victorian mansion into a fantasy world where nuts and nutcrackers coexist in perfect harmony. Since then she has become principal advocate of all the seeds of the world. Her Nut Museum displays nutcrackers, nutty music, nut painting and other nut art, nut jewelry, nuts-in-liquid, nut dishes, nut masks, nut trees (filberts, chestnuts, hazelnuts, and walnuts), but principally nuts—thousands and thousands of mixed nuts—including her pièce de résistance, the largest nut in the world, the slightly X-rated *cocoa-de-mer*, weighing thirty-five pounds. Though the grounds of her nut house are sometimes under siege by squirrels or vandalized by hooligans, Ms. Tashjian's enterprise endures. Despite the cold shoulder from Connecticut Tourism and the embarrassment of municipal prudes, regardless of derision in the media and repeated mockery in guide books such as this, the Nut Lady remains thick-skinned and hard to crack. She should probably be promoted to kernel.

Nut Museum
  303 Ferry Rd.
  Old Lyme, CT 06371

Phone: (203) 434-7636

Location: From I-95, take exit 70 to Connecticut Highway 156 and follow it to Ferry Road. Look carefully for the small sign.

Hours: Closed until further notice.

Admission: One nut (and change).

Bara-Hack

This isolated colony was founded by two Welsh families in 1780. Although it was abandoned in 1890, the sounds of the former inhabitants remain. Children's laughter, singing, mothers calling their husbands and children, barking dogs, mooing cows, and the rumble of wagon wheels can still be heard here. The sounds seem to emerge from a portal in time and float over the ruins of stone cellars and the old cemetery. Investigations carried out in 1971 and 1972 failed to record the sounds, but researchers did encounter the apparition of a bearded man at the cemetery's west wall and the wraith of a small child in an elm tree near the north wall. Some of the apparitions were successfully photographed.

Location: Bara-Hack can be reached from the intersection of U.S. Highway 44 and Highway 97 in Pomfret Township in northeastern Connecticut. Take Highway 97 north to a side road just north and to the left of Mashomoquet Brook. Follow the dirt road about a quarter-mile. When you see the remainder of a stone wall on either side, you'll be entering the ghost town of Bara-Hack.

Cannonballed Pub

If you were a British soldier trying to track down a group of colonial rebels, where would you look first? The pub, of course. And that's just where the King's troops found Ridgefield's renegades in 1777: the Keeler Tavern. Now a museum, it was then known as a meeting place where patriots drank, planned, and secretly manufactured musket balls in the basement. So when the Battle of Ridgefield ignited in April, the Redcoats were quick to fire on the place. Keeler Tavern tour guides—dressed as eighteenth-century townsfolk—will explain what happened next. But we want to tell you the strangest part: By some stroke of luck, a British cannonball fired at the building failed to penetrate the beam in which it securely embedded itself. It is lodged there today, a tiny assault from the Battle of Ridgefield, frozen in time, never reaching its mark. How, we ask, can such a thing happen? Why did providence spare the colonials inside? One possible explanation is that they were bombed already.

The Keeler Tavern
132 Main Street
Ridgefield, CT 06877

Phone: (203) 438-5485
www.keelertavernmuseum.org

Location: The tavern is about three-quarters of a mile south of the commercial center, on the east side of Main Street (Route 35).

Hours: Open year-round, except for the month of January, on Wednesdays, Saturdays, and Sundays, 1 P.M.–4 P.M., with tours every half hour until 3:30 P.M.

Admission charged.

The first floor is wheelchair accessible.

Rocky Hill, Connecticut

Dino Park

There is something just a little unsettlingly incongruous about an ultra-modern geodesic dome (resembling a flying saucer) that's being used to house about five hundred footprints. While the jury is still out as to whether Celts strode these New England hills, it is a fact that dinosaurs did. And the proof—at least some of it—is right here. These tracks are two hundred million years old. They range from ten to sixteen inches in length and are spaced three and a half to four and a half feet apart. In some, clear skin impressions are visible. In all, about two thousand dinosaur tracks were accidentally uncovered in 1966 while excavating for a new state building: Fifteen hundred of them were covered up again. But if you want to see what it feels like to track a dinosaur, there are five hundred footprints left to practice on. And if you don't mind getting a little dirty, you can make a plaster cast of a dino track to take home. Think of the stories you could tell your neighbors. Frankly, we've always found it a little tough to understand exactly how such perfect paw prints could have been made in allegedly soft earth. Why didn't it just ooze in again, or become indistinct around the edges? Well, this is the place to find out. You can also get some insight into what conditions were like back in the Jurassic Period by examining an exciting and colorful life-sized, eighty-foot long dinorama depicting Rocky Hill, Connecticut, as it must have been at the time the tracks were made. Unfortunately, there are no dinosaurs here. In fact, no remains of the dinosaur that made these tracks have ever been found in the Connecticut Valley. Maybe it was just a tourist passing through.

Dinosaur State Park
400 West Street
Rocky Hill, CT 06067–3506

Phone: (860) 529-8423 or (860) 529-5816
www.dinosaurstatepark.org

Location: The park is one mile east of exit 23 (West Street) off I-91, a few miles south of Hartford.

Hours: The Dino Exhibit Center is open Tuesday–Sunday, 9 A.M.–4:30 P.M. The Park is open seven days a week, 9 A.M.–4:30 P.M. Both are closed Thanksgiving, Christmas, and New Year's Day. Trails are open 9 A.M.–4 P.M.

Admission is charged to enter the Exhibit Center, but, like the dinosaurs of old, you can walk the park for free.

Water Music

On certain warm, still summer nights, boatsmen and fishermen on Gardner Lake hear a haunting refrain played on a faraway piano. It is impossible to determine just where the music is coming from, but young folks guess, and old-timers know, it is coming from the water itself. There is an explanation, but it only accounts for part of the mystery. In the past, certain divers have been so convinced the music was coming from the depths that they've investigated wearing scuba gear. Sure enough, on the bottom of the lake, they've discovered a house—and inside there is a piano. How the house and piano got there is simple enough. The last owner of the place hired a contractor to move the whole thing to a beautiful lot he had purchased on the lakeshore. Trouble was, it was on the far side of the water. This was not seen to be a problem. The foreman decided they'd wait until the lake had frozen over, then jack up the house, put it on sleds, and slide it across, furniture and all. Everything went swimmingly, but a little slower than anticipated. By the time night fell they'd dragged it only half-way. Cold and exhausted, they decided to finish in the morning. But when they arrived the next day they were horrified to find the house leaning dangerously, having broken part way through the frozen surface. There was no way to pull it out, so they rescued what furniture they could, and gathered in the spring to watch it sink. No one was killed as it bubbled under, but someone, or something, has caused that mysterious music decade after decade. Those who've investigated are convinced it comes from the old piano, far too heavy to rescue when the house went under.

Location: Gardner Lake can be reached by taking Route 354 southeast from Colchester. There is a boat access on the lake's southern end. Local inquiry should reveal the approximate location of the sunken house.

NOTE: Listen for the music from the shore or from a boat, but please don't attempt a dive unless you are qualified. Exploring underwater structures can be very dangerous. That said, recent descents confirm that much of the furniture inside is still remarkably well preserved.

Ghost Squirrels

People think they're going nuts when they see one, but there really are strange white whatsits scampering across lawns and zipping through the trees of Derby and Shelton. No, they're not animal ghosts. They're squirrels—white squirrels. And there are a lot of them. First off, there's nothing unnatural about them—they're albinos—and identical to the common gray squirrel in every other way. In fact, they are gray squirrels. Their albinism is a genetic condition that doesn't effect their reproduction; their population is soaring. For similar genetic reasons, "Melanistic" or "Black Gray Squirrels" also occur and seem to be just as frequent as albinos in this area. Gray squirrels, white gray squirrels, and black gray squirrels exhibit identical behaviors and can be seen any time of year since they don't migrate or hibernate. A genetics scientist could, with some reasonable assuredness, explain the why of it all. Perhaps the greater questions is, why here? Why are both more prevalent in this geographic region than elsewhere? The answer, we're sure, won't be black and white.

Location: Seeing these natural curiosities might take some perseverance. We're not aware of any public area for white squirrel-watching. There is a neighborhood in Shelton off Howe Avenue (south side of Route 110) just east of Route 8 that has a generous albino population. But that's one of many. Probably the best thing to do is to visit the Stratford-Milford-Shelton-Derby area and ask around.

Eccentric Homestead

Within moments of setting foot on the property you'll know you're in the presence of genuine New England eccentricity. The Boothe Brothers—Stephen and David—were wealthy enough to buy anything they wanted, and parsimonious enough never to throw anything away. The result is this hodge-podge of clutter and art, Yankee ingenuity and outlandish incongruity—a Disneyland for the benignly demented. Look around. You'll see a lighthouse (every New England farm needs one), a windmill, an observatory, a toll booth, a stone arena, and more. Perhaps their most bizarre creation, the "Technocratic Cathedral," is a one-of-a-kind windowless showpiece constructed from California redwood boards laid flat in the manner of stacked lumber. Their most imposing contrivance is arguably the clock tower. The brothers acquired a church steeple which they plopped down on top of their nineteenth-century barn. Carved into its bell is the history of the Boothe clan dating back to 1663. To give you an idea of the Boothes' misplaced sense of competition, check out the peculiar design of their blacksmith shop. Henry Ford's blacksmith shop had four sides, so David Boothe designed his with forty-four sides and forty-four corners. The building interiors are another world altogether. The out-buildings are museums while the main house contains stained glass, secret compartments, amazing "puzzle" floors, and even a ghost who's especially active in the Civil War room. "Psychic discomfort" has seized so many people in this room that guides keep a chair by the door in case anyone feels faint. David Beach Boothe and Stephen Nichols Boothe willed their collection of architectural and personal oddities to the town. Thank God Stratford knew better than to bulldoze it. As of 1985 the homestead was listed on the National Register of Historic Places.

Boothe Memorial Park and Museum
Friends of Boothe Park, Inc.
P.O. Box 902
Stratford, CT 06614

Phone: (203) 381-2046 or (203) 381-2068

Location: From Merritt Parkway, use exit 53. Proceed south on Route 110 to Main Street, Putney, which branches off to the right, immediately south of the Parkway. Ride south on Main Street, Putney six-tenths of a mile to the park.

From Connecticut Turnpike (I-95) westbound, use exit 33. Follow the signs to the Merritt Parkway. Take the Parkway south to exit 53, and follow the instructions above.

From Connecticut Turnpike (I-95) eastbound, use exit 33. Follow Ferry Boulevard, bear left at fork and go under the Turnpike. Bear right onto East Main Street (Route 110). Follow East Main Street to its end at Main Street. Turn right onto Main St. and after the small bridge at the bottom of the hill bear left on Main Street Putney and drive seven-tenths of a mile to the park.

Hours: Museum is open June–September; Tuesday–Friday, 11 A.M.–1 P.M., Saturday–Sunday, 1–4 P.M. The grounds are open and free all year round.

NOTE: The Boothe Brothers' Homestead may well be New England's equivalent to California's Winchester House. For the true connoisseur of the strange, this one is not to be missed.

Admission charged.

Grounds and some buildings are wheelchair accessible.

Terryville, Connecticut

Keep out! The Lock Museum of America

You probably haven't spent a lot of time thinking about locks. They're something one takes for granted. Because of familiarity, they lose their fascination. But an hour spent at the Lock Museum of America may change all that. You'll see locks, security devices, even keys, as you've never seen them before. And you'll get answers to questions you may never have asked, like: How does the time lock on a bank vault work?

What is a cannon ball safe? What does a 4000-year-old Egyptian pin tumbler lock look like? What was the earliest padlock? How did the first panic exit device come into being? There are leg irons, "slave locks," and many variations on the handcuff. Frankly, much of this collection of eighteen thousand locks and keys may be repetitive and dull to all except the enthusiast, but there are exhibits that will captivate even the most tired tourist, like the world's largest and smallest locks (a padlock weighing twenty-nine pounds and an "earring lock") And those with a penchant for the weird will not be disappointed. We'd call your attention to one unusual animated display built around 1920 that shows how a pin tumbler lock works. It's a robot of sorts: A huge animated hand opens a giant lock with its mechanism exposed. And don't overlook the beautiful intricacy of a Spanish Armada safe circa 1580. A *real* treasure chest! There seems to be some question as to whether the lock museum includes a real chastity belt. We've heard it does, but we didn't have the courage to ask.

The Lock Museum of America, Inc.
230 Main St.
Route 6
Terryville, CT 06786–0104

Phone: (860) 589-6359
www.lockmuseum.com

Location: The museum is on Route 6 in downtown Terryville.

Hours: Open every day (except Monday) May–October, 1:30–4:30 P.M.

Admission charged.

Holy Land

We just don't know what's going to happen to the Holy Land. During its heyday it attracted thousands of tourists from all over the world. Today it is sadly neglected, a sprawled lilliputian ruin high atop Pine Hill beneath a sixty-foot stainless steel cross. Holy Land was the product of local lawyer John Greco's religious obsession—or perhaps inspiration. He got it into his head that there were many people who could never visit the real Holy Land, so he decided to bring the Holy Land to them. In 1956, he set to work constructing a seventeen acre village that is like no other in the world—including its namesake. He financed his fantasy with his attorney's fees; his building materials were whatever he could find: car parts, cast-off sinks, old boilers, refrigerators, plywood, chicken wire, and concrete. Yet somehow he fashioned an impressive but primitive work of art that was loved by the community but suspected by the church. Holy Land matured into hundreds of buildings, tombs, grottos, tunnels, catacombs, statues, and tableaus of religious instruction (such as "The Pictorial Life of Christ—From the Cradle to the Cross," an authentic photograph of Jesus, or a replica of the shroud of Turin). John Greco's creation lived while he lived, but at age eighty-eight he could no longer keep up the pace of construction and maintenance. In 1984, Holy Land, U.S.A., closed to visitors. Since then it has waited, sad and forlorn, looking for all the world like an abandoned miniature golf course that's been weather-beaten, graffitied, and vandalized. But like the ruins of any great city, Waterbury's deteriorating marvel still casts a spell, its strangeness perhaps heightened by its atmosphere of eccentricity, naiveté, and neglected devotion. Like the real Holy Land, its future is uncertain: Will it be bulldozed or resurrected?

Location: Holy Land's giant cross is visible from I-84. Take Exit 23. Turn right off ramp. Take first left under tunnel. Come to stop sign; turn right. Take second right up hill. Holy Land, U.S.A., is at the top of Ayers Street. Go up Pleasant, left on Emerald, right on Ayers. Watch for small rusty Holy Land pointers on telephone poles.

NOTE: Though Holy Land is well worth the trip, it is no longer officially open to the public. Its owners, the nuns to whom Mr. Greco willed it, seem not to object to your looking at it . . . but there's no guarantee.

Wheelchair accessible, with effort.

Waterbury, Connecticut

Timexpo

Easter Island! If you see a peculiar elongated stone head, don't panic, it's just another of Waterbury's geographic peculiarities. If Holy Land can be here, why not Easter Island? But a forty-foot head? See for yourself at Timexpo, an all-new, unfailingly unique museum that celebrates "time" in two senses. First, it provides a history of the Timex Company (complete with interactive displays and exciting, Disney-like special effects). And second, it considers the more speculative notion that America was visited long ago by ancient people. No, not Celts this time. Easter Islanders. As divergent as these two themes may seem—Timex and anthropology—they're linked by the "Time Tunnel," a sensory cascade of shifting images, sounds, and video, that propels the visitor back in time. Based on the work of Thor Heyerdahl of "Kon-Tiki" fame, Timexpo explores complicated archaeological puzzles in entertaining ways. Were there long-ago long-distance contacts across vast oceans? How else can we explain striking similarities between apparently unconnected civilizations? Consideration includes Professor Heyerdahl's voyages and the "Water Table," a model of the Pacific Ocean with submerged jets simulating the currents. Here you can launch small boats and try to reach Polynesia by sailing either with, or against, the current. You can ponder the secrets of Easter Island, then try "Putting the Pieces Together," a computer game that explores the island's many mysteries. That forty-foot head outside is just the beginning . . .

The Timexpo Museum
    Brass Mill Commons
    175 Union St.
    Waterbury, CT 06706

Phone: (203) 755-8463 or 1 (800) 225-7742
    www.timexpo.com

Location: Take exit 22 or 23 off I-84 and watch for the head. It's visible from the highway (flood-lit at night). The Timexpo Museum is on Union Street.

Hours: Tuesday–Saturday, 10 A.M.–5 P.M., Sunday, noon–5 P.M. Closed Mondays and major holidays.

Admission charged.

Wheelchair accessible.

Watertown, Connecticut

Leather Man's Cave

This cave is evidence of one of the most mysterious and eccentric men in Connecticut history—the legendary Leather Man. No one ever knew his name; they identified him by the suit he always wore: a crude patchwork of leather scraps and discarded boot tops held together by leather thongs. He was extraordinarily predictable, walking a set circuit of 365 miles every thirty-four days (one for each day of the year, perhaps?), traveling clockwise, never retracing his steps. He was so regular that "housewives could set their clocks by him." After he appeared in the 1860s people began to make small gestures of kindness, offering food or refreshment, even tobacco and matches.

The Leather Man accepted willingly, expressing his appreciation only with gestures because he never spoke. He'd refuse money and alcohol and would never accept accommodation in anyone's home. Instead, he had staked out a series of caves of which this is known to be a remarkable example. Leather Man maintained his punctual pacing and peculiar practices until his death in Ossining, New York, in 1889. There are legends about his identity, and also about the treasures allegedly buried in his caves. Some people even claim to have seen his ghost on his trails and in his caverns. But in truth, all that remains is a mystery: Who was the Leather Man? Where had he come from? Why this solitary life of self-imposed silence? Why this particular route? And ultimately, why did he always dress in leather?

Location: On Route 6 north, after passing the "Watertown Line" sign on the right, drive by one right turn and park at the pull-off under the sign that says "Mattatuck Trail." Follow the blue blazes to the cave.

NOTE: This is a relatively strenuous forty-minute hike, much of it over rock surfaces. Think twice about tackling it in wet weather when the rocks are slippery and dangerous.

ALSO NOTE: There are tributes to Leather Man here and there in Connecticut. You can see his picture displayed in the public libraries of Derby and Bristol.

Wethersfield, Connecticut

The Hole Story

The odds are against it. In fact, they're astronomically against it. But the town of Wethersfield was struck by a meteorite in April of 1971. It ripped through the roof of Paul Cassarino's home, ending up in his living room. This is unusual because the majority of meteors burn up in our atmosphere, splash down at sea, or crash in some remote area. So the odds against the 1971 strike were pretty high. But here's what's weird: In 1982, Wethersfield was hit a second time! This meteorite tore through the roof of Wanda and Robert Donahue's Church Street home, landing in their living room. It would take a Stephen W. Hawking to calculate the odds against that. In fact, Arthur C. Clarke said it was "the most incredible event [he'd] ever heard of." Only four meteorites have been known to hit Connecticut in recorded history, yet these two hit the same town, landing in living rooms less than one and a half miles apart. One has to consider whether it was coincidence or by design. Alas, the remains of the two meteorites are nowhere in Wethersfield to be found; they have been carted off to the Smithsonian Institution and the Peabody Museum. But Wethersfield still has the hole. And if you stop in at the historical society they may show it to you. They preserve part of the roof, plaster, lathe, and other structural material from the Donahues' home through which the space stone crashed.

Wethersfield Historical Society Museum
200 Main St.
Wethersfield, CT 06109

Phone: (860) 529-7656

Location: This stately brick building is on the main thoroughfare in town and easy to find.

Hours: Tuesday–Saturday, 10 A.M.–4 P.M., Sunday, 1–4 P.M. Closed Mondays and major holidays.

Admission charged.

Wheelchair accessible.

Frog Bridge

One dark and dismal July night, during the terrible drought of 1758, the people of Willimantic were awakened by a frightful racket. Hideous cries seemed to come from the sky directly overhead. Many thought it was Indians; others feared a French attack; Puritans guessed it was tortured spirits announcing Judgment Day. Fear heightened when a summons sounded: Names were being called, "Dyer" and "Elderkin." Terrified people rushed from their homes as the horrid caterwauling continued. Those with firearms blasted into the darkness. Others fell to their knees praying as the cacophony resounded through the night with escalating fervor. In the morning someone discovered the awful truth: warring bullfrogs. A local mill pond had dried up. Its dense population of bullfrogs had been battling over what little water remained. Thousands were found dead on both sides of the ditch. Apparently some atmospheric peculiarity had caused their war cries and dying croaks to amplify and permeate the air. Imaginations did the rest. Since then, the townspeople have embraced the source of their eighteenth-century mortification. They depicted a bullfrog on their town seal and, in 1999, outdid themselves by erecting a bridge with behemoth bronze bullfrogs mounted on its four corners. Each Volkswagen-sized amphibian is twelve feet tall and weighs one and a half tons. They are an unusual sight, more magical than menacing—well worth a swing through Willimantic.

Location: Willimantic is part of Windham. From I-84 take Route 32 south to Willimantic. Turn right on Jackson Street. The Frog Bridge is right there.

NOTE: Ask for directions to a boulder that identifies the infamous Frog Pond where a bronze plaque tells the story.

www.threadcity.com/images/files/nytfrog1.jpg

MAINE

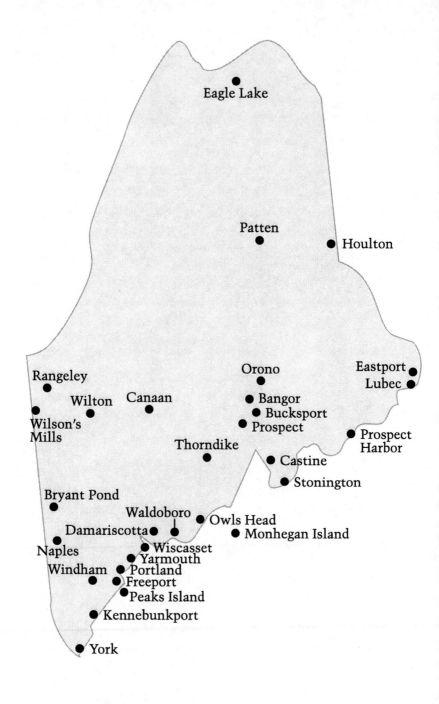

Eagle Lake

Patten

Houlton

Orono

Eastport
Lubec

Rangeley

Wilton   Canaan

Bangor
Bucksport

Wilson's
Mills

Prospect

Prospect
Harbor

Thorndike

Castine

Stonington

Bryant Pond

Waldoboro

Owls Head

Damariscotta

Monhegan Island

Naples

Wiscasset
Yarmouth

Windham   Portland
Freeport
Peaks Island

Kennebunkport

York

Police Museum

The police station is probably not high on your list of places to visit—but Bangor's may be the exception. In the hallway of police headquarters there's a small museum displaying over one hundred historical corrections artifacts from the eighteenth century until today. Display cases hold everything from handcuffs to radar devices, diaries, uniforms, and weapons, all lovingly compiled by former Bangor officer Fred Bryant. One exhibit that stands out is the "tramp chair," a technological improvement on the old-fashioned stocks. This metal contraption clasps itself around you like some medieval instrument of torture. In the old days, wayward individuals were locked inside and rolled out in a sitting position for public display, sometimes for days at a time. Townsfolk could taunt offenders to their heart's content. This one-man jail, made by a man from Maine, is a real rehabilitation rarity. Only three others are known to exist and one of those is in the Smithsonian. It is well worth a look so you can ponder what effect humiliation had on crime control.

We should hasten to add that Bangor is no less law-abiding than any other city, although it does have an unusually colorful past. During the nineteenth century, the town had a vibrant red-light district known as the "Devil's Half Acre." After log drives, lumberjacks descended upon Bangor's hordes of cat houses and taverns, typically in two weeks blowing every cent they had earned over the winter. Though today there's nothing left of this colorful Harlow Street district, there was a time when the industry boomed, despite the police's best efforts to keep it under wraps. In those days, even the possession of prurient paraphernalia could land you in the slammer—or worse yet—in the tramp's chair.

The Police Museum
Bangor Police Department
35 Court St.
Bangor, ME 04401

Phone: (207) 947-7384
pdmuseum@mint.net
www.bairnet.org/municipal/Bangor/police/museum.htm

Location: The police station is in the center of town, a left turn off of Route 2 going east, between Ohio and Harlow streets.

Hours: Open by appointment only, Monday–Friday, 8 A.M.–5 P.M.

Free admission.

Wheelchair accessible.

Bryant Pond, Maine

Three-Story Outhouse

One of the dark secrets of Bryant Pond's Masonic Lodge is that it houses the last working interior three-story outhouse in the state of Maine. Quite a distinction. The lodge, and its retro facilities, were state of the art in the mid-1800s when they were constructed. This skyscraper privy is a simple pine board with a hole in it. Anything dropped through falls two complete stories till it smacks the earth. Venerated by some, abhorred by others, the three-holer was finally supplemented by real indoor plumbing in the year 2000—a flush toilet and everything. But only on the ground floor; the second and third stories remain as they were. You can view them, but can't use them (at least you're not supposed to).

But if it's an emergency, you can go next door to the Grange Hall. They have an outhouse, too, but it's a measly two-story affair. Although it's still in use, you'd better time your emergency well; it's only open the first and third Monday of every month between seven and eight P.M., when the Grange meets.

Location: To view the three-holer, contact Bill Roberts at (207) 875-5890. He'll come and let you in. Bryant Pond is on Route 26 about fifty-four miles north of Portland.

One Foot on the Grave

There are several stories about how it got there, but it's there all right: The silhouette of a foot and part of a leg imprinted on Colonel Buck's tombstone. Supposedly it's the consequence of a curse. Colonel Jonathan Buck, the town's seventeenth-century founder, was responsible for administering local justice. When rumors of witchcraft began working their way up the coast from Salem, the good citizens of Bucksport began eyeing each other with suspicion. Eventually many fingers pointed to an elderly and eccentric recluse. Colonel Buck hauled her in and put the question to her. She denied communing with Satan and all other witchery. Of course, Colonel Buck knew that witches lie, so he applied torture to evoke a more truthful answer. Still the old crone would not confess. Colonel Buck realized that anyone who could endure such sustained agony without confessing must be receiving preternatural assistance. That was proof enough. With the help of eager townspeople, the old woman was marched to the gallows. But before the noose did its work, she cursed her tormentor, promising Colonel Buck that she would return to dance on his grave. The malediction was forgotten long before Colonel Buck had his own rendezvous with the grim reaper. He was buried and a monument was erected—a giant stone obelisk befitting such an important man. Then something seemed to blemish the perfect white marble. An indelible shadow fell across it—a stain. And anyone who saw it recognized the outline of a foot. People began recalling the curse and realizing that somehow that old woman was in fact dancing on the colonel's grave. Suspecting it was the work of a prankster, Colonel Buck's family hired a team of workmen to pumice down the monument, making it as smooth and unblemished as before, but the outline gradually reappeared. They tried more aggressive cleaning techniques, but always the foot would return. Finally the family had the monument replaced. Yet the old woman's dance continued on the new stone, and the family gave up. To this day you can see the stone, the footprint, and an explanatory plaque at the Bucksport Cemetery.

Location: The cemetery is in Bucksport, across from the supermarket, in the tiny graveyard closest to the traffic light.

Bucksport, Maine

Northeast Historic Film

While you're within kicking distance of Colonel Buck's foot, you might be interested to check out this unusual archive. They say they have the "largest collection of home movies in North America," but it's far more than that. From old newsreels, family films, amateur productions, and sources too numerous to mention, they have pieced together a gigantic reference library of moving images that traces much of Maine's—and New England's—history in events monumental and mundane. They collect, preserve, and present films in the old Alamo Theater by showing second run movies, conducting an annual silent film festival (projected at proper speed), and displaying movie-related paraphernalia like peep show machines, flip cards, and other theatrical memorabilia. Then there are the archives themselves . . . While Northeast Historic Film isn't in any sense "weird," it is unique, with 240 collections of amateur movies, a growing selection of commercial films shot in

Maine, and their oldest holding, the epic fifteen-second short called "Drawing a Lobster Pot," from 1901.

Northeast Historic Film
   P.O. Box 900
   85 Main St.
   Bucksport, ME 04416
Phone: (207) 469-0924
   www.oldfilm.org
Location: In the center of town in the old Alamo Theater.
Hours: Open Monday–Friday, 9 A.M.–4 P.M., June–Labor Day, Saturday also.
Fee for screenings only.

Canaan, Maine

A Crate Place To Visit

There's an odd little house on a hillside in Canaan, Maine, but it hasn't always been there. Before that, it was nestled among some pines on the shore of the Blackwater River in Hopkinton, New Hampshire. And prior to that, it was on a nearby Contoocook farm. But this mobile home actually began its wandering in 1927 when it made a transatlantic voyage aboard the U.S.S. *Memphis,* sailing from Paris, France, to America. Look closely and you might get some idea of what its meandering is all about. The house is in fact a big wooden box, the very box that housed the *Spirit of Saint Louis* when it was shipped home after Lucky Lindbergh's historic flight. Since it was originally nailed together it has put on as many miles as Lindbergh's plane. Vice Admiral Guy Burrage purchased it directly from Mr. Lindbergh during the return voyage. He carted the crate to his farm in Contoocook, added a porch to either end, and remodeled it as a house. In the early 1960s his grandson moved it to the Hopkinton riverside, where it was used as a cottage. When the grandson sold the property in 1986, the buyer sold the crate to Larry Ross, who then moved it to his land in Canaan, Maine. Today it sits behind his house and barn facing east—the direction in which Charles Lindbergh set off. Mr. Ross, a flying buff, has restored it and transformed it into a museum containing pictures and letters related to Lindbergh's flight. There's a mockup of the small plane that children can ride, drawn on a 140' cable. The museum is open whenever Mr. Ross is home, which, he says, is most of the year. But be warned; it's not heated in the winter.

Location: Take Route 2 going east into Canaan village. After you see the post office on the right, turn left across from it onto Easy Street (not surprisingly, the sign is often missing). Go 1.1 miles and look for the Mailbox that says "Ross." He usually has a sign up that says "Lindbergh Crate." Turn into his hundred-yard driveway and drive up to the house. The crate is in the back. For info, call Larry at (207) 474-9841 or e-mail him at <larreb@somtel.com>.

NOTE: Please keep in mind that this is private property.

Free admission.

Castine, Maine

Wilson Museum

Castine is the idyllic New England town: scenic, wealthy, tranquil, and well south of the tourist riffraff on Route 1. You can't imagine anyone here being anything but polite, peaceful, and serene. So it comes as a surprise to walk into the elegant town museum and find it brimming with world savagery: Paleolithic weapons, stone axes, spears, knives, swords, daggers, Bali devil masks, a wolf jaw (with teeth still attached) used by Indian shamans, porcupine quill combs, an array of American firearms, and umbilical fetishes. There's even a seventeenth-century helmet worn by one of Oliver Cromwell's soldiers. The Hearse House nearby stores vehicles for both summer and winter use. To be fair, the museum also displays more civilized artifacts, such as decorative arts, native crafts, a collection of rocks and minerals, and some wonderful miniature dioramas with historical themes. It's all the work of John Howard Wilson, an anthropologist and sugar industry heir who, like many of his nineteenth-century peers, felt compelled while abroad to acquire souvenirs reflecting his take on human civilization. Mr. Wilson died in 1936, leaving this beautiful little museum with the dangers and pleasures of the world within its walls. Still, you can't help feeling a certain relief when stepping back onto the street, as if waking from a bad dream to discover that you're safe in your own bed. All the brutality stays locked up tight inside glass cases, where it belongs. That, in the final analysis, may be just what the Castinians like about the place.

The Wilson Museum
   P.O. Box 196
   Perkins St.
   Castine, ME 04421

Phone: (207) 326-9247

Location: It is on the waterfront in the town center.

Hours: The main building is open daily except Mondays, 2–5 P.M., May 27–September 30.

Free admission.

Damariscotta, Maine

Monstrous Middens

Such a lovely sounding name, Damariscotta. You'd never think it translates as "plenty of alewives." Most would suspect another fishy-smelling sea-dweller: the oyster, because that's what you'll find here, oysters—or rather, oyster shells. They're in colossal piles along both banks of the Damariscotta River and they represent thousands of years of Native American feasting. What they discarded resulted in huge chalk-white piles. Known as "middens," or more colloquially "shell heaps," some are thirty feet high and maybe six thousand years old. They include shells that are fourteen inches long! The Glidden Midden on the west bank is the biggest. Exactly why the locals had such a taste for mollusks is unknown, perhaps word was out about their alleged aphrodisiac quality. Anyway, their appetite was voracious; estimates suggest that they must have eaten thirty-five million bushels to create Maine's monstrous middens. There are over one million cubic feet of shells piled up here. Archaeologists divide the shell heaps into three layers. The bottom layer is so old it shows evidence that Maine was once a much warmer place. Apparently, the ancient and mysterious "Red Paint People" contributed to the middle layer. And the upper layer is comparatively new, maybe just two thousand years old. For some unknown reason, the natural oyster population that once supported Maine's early people no longer exists. Maybe the natives, like the walrus and the carpenter, "have eaten every one."

Location: The shell heaps are on both sides of the Damariscotta River below the south side of the bridge off Route 1. To get there, take the Salt Bay Heritage Trail from the kiosk across from Lincoln County Publishing on Mills Road in Newcastle, and follow the signs.

Eagle Lake, Maine

Teleported Trains

Two huge steam locomotives out in the middle of nowhere may look like proof of teleportation. Just the engines, mind you—no freight cars, no tracks, not even a road. So how did they get there? And what are they doing in the depths of some of the most inaccessible country in the entire state?

As puzzling as the sight of stranded steam trains may be, the cause is not nearly as exciting as the effect. Years ago—in an effort worthy of Fitzcarraldo—the two locomotives were hauled in on sleds over land. They serviced a short-line railroad that ran from Eagle Lake to Umbazooksus, a distance of about ten miles. The trains hauled pulp out of the deep woods to where it eventually could be floated, lake to river, all the way downstream to the Bangor paper mills. (The Umbazooksus terminus was a 600- to 700-foot-long wooden trestle that was hauled intact from Canada and installed out into the lake where the pulp cars could dump their loads.)

Things changed. The logging ended. The trains no longer ran. Although the tracks were taken up and recycled, the engines were simply too big to remove. It was far cheaper to abandon them. A half-century ago they were in a shed, but it and neighboring buildings have long since burned. Forest has reclaimed everything but two out-of-place locomotives in the remotest wilds of nowhere.

Location: The best way to see the locomotives is to fly in by float plane or wait until the lake freezes over and go in by snowmobile. Boats can be launched at John's Bridge on the narrows between Churchill and Eagle Lakes. From there it is a five to six mile trip to the trains.

Another possibility is to launch a boat at Chamberlain Bridge at the southern end of Chamberlain Lake on the Telos Road. From there it is about ten miles to the Chamberlain end of the old tramway with about a mile walk through the woods across the narrow strip of land dividing the two lakes.

NOTE: Before planning a trip to see the locomotives, keep in mind how big Maine is. Eagle Lake is way up north, almost in Canada. A train-viewing trip would be a major undertaking. It might be better to simply visit the Lumbermen's Museum in Patten, where you can see pictures of the trains along with many other oddities and reminders of the Northwoods logging life—New England's answer to the wild, wild west.

Old Sow and Her Piglets

Odysseus may have his Scylla and Charybdis, but Maine has its infamous Old Sow, a sea monster known to have chewed up small craft, toppled tankers, and swallowed up entire four-masted schooners. The Old Sow—and her piglets—reside in the western passage of Passamaquoddy Bay, between Deer Island, New Brunswick, and Moose Island in Eastport, Maine. Sometimes she sleeps, but when the moon is right, the winds are strong, and the weather foul, she's the largest whirlpool in the world—or at least in the western hemisphere. Created by the convergence of two powerful tides and a dangerous back-eddy, the Sow's dizzying swirl gives birth to hundreds of smaller whirlpools called "piglets" because of the sucking sounds they make. But beware, this is a dangerous natural phenomenon and perhaps best viewed from a distance. If you wish, you can get a closer look by taking the ferry to Deer Island. And if you're really brave, you may be able to talk some local salt into taking you through the vortex. If the sailor's experienced enough, and if the boat can climb uphill, you'll probably survive. You will then be entitled to join the Old Sow Whirlpool Survivors' Association. But, like Odysseus and the boys, you must actually pass through, not just by, the Old Sow. And you must do it when she is awake. She is, after all, tidal, and therefore active only at certain times. Winds and phases of the moon affect her mood. The use of a tide table is probably a good idea.

NOTE: Although it may be possible to glimpse Old Sow and her brood from the northeastern shore of Moose Island, she's reluctant to disclose her fatal charms from a distance. A better approach is to take the toll ferry that runs from Eastport every half-hour between 9:30 A.M. and 7:30 P.M., June–September. Inquire locally about viewing options or to get the names of local boatmen who can be hired to provide you with close-up observation.

The Desert of Maine

Close to the ocean, but closer still to a thriving tourist community, is a mysterious arid wasteland, a bleak panorama of sun-blasted sand that covers nearly one hundred acres of once fertile soil. There is no question that this Saharan vista was once a flourishing farm: peaks of buildings protrude from wind-driven dunes. Shacks and ancient wagons emerge and vanish as the sand ebbs and flows. Gnarled treetops extend above gritty drifts, where blueberries once grew and cattle grazed. Yet this blighted island is surrounded by perfectly healthy vegetation. Green trees and leafy bushes are visible in every direction. Something obviously happened there . . . something that transformed fertile farmland into the bewildering wilderness now known as the "Desert of Maine." Most geologists will tell you it's the result of bad nineteenth-century farming practices that destroyed the protective layer of grass that kept the dunes at bay. But older stories hint at a darker explanation. They say the down-east desert is the result of deception, betrayal, and ultimately a curse. Whatever the explanation, these sand dunes were abandoned until 1917, when the enterprising Henry Goldrup saw Maine's out-of-place desert and envisioned an oil well. He bought the land and began to exploit its unique characteristics. Today the desert is a sightseer's Mecca complete with escorted tours, picnic tables, and a gift shop. Curse or blessing, the present owners continue the tourist tradition. And the sand dunes—little by little—continue to spread.

Desert of Maine
 95 Desert Road
 Freeport, ME 04032

Phone: (207) 865-6962
 info@desertofmaine.com
 www.desertofmaine.com

Location: Only two miles off Route 95. Take exit 19 and follow the signs on Desert Road in Freeport.

Hours: Open May 15–October 15, 10 A.M.–5 P.M. June 15–Labor Day, 8:30 A.M.–dusk.

Admission charged.

Camping in Maine: Nazi Prisoners of War

One of the last things you'd expect to find in the outer regions of Maine is a Nazi POW camp. But it's there, at least what's left of it. Houlton was an ideal setting for such a place. Positioned on a remote stretch of the Canadian border, it was wild, cold, and black fly-infested; no one would be desperate or foolhardy enough to contemplate escape. Between 1944 and 1946, some three thousand soldiers, most of them Germans, Soviets forced to fight for Germany, and Italians, were imprisoned here behind twelve-foot electrified barbed-wire fences. Would-be escapees were put on bread and water in the camp jail. But for the rest, it wasn't so bad. During the day they were trucked to worksites to cut trees or pick potatoes. At night they bought beer and saltines in the canteen, read the camp's German-language newspaper, watched the occasional movie, or sang patriotic songs.

Houlton's other role in the war effort occurred during the

The old control tower overlooks what remains of Camp Houlton, a World War II–era POW camp for German and Russian soldiers. Photo: Courtesy Kay Bell

so-called "Lend-Lease," when the United States agreed not to fly bombers directly to Europe. Instead, they slipped them over the border at Houlton and shipped them out from Canada. Much of the airport is unchanged. There is a World War II–vintage control tower and an officer's canteen. The foundations of the POW camp barracks are there as well. To find them, poke among the trees on the hill closest to the runway.

Location: Exit Interstate 95 at the Houlton International Airport exit 63 (last exit before Canada), turn right on the off-ramp, and drive straight ahead to the Terminal Building on Terminal drive. Park in the parking lot beside the flag pole.

Hours: The Terminal building is open Monday–Friday, 7 A.M.–5 P.M.

NOTE: A plaster-of-Paris model of the runway believed to have been created by the German prisoners is on view at the airport's Terminal Building.

Free admission.

Wheelchair accessible.

ALSO NOTE: While you're in Houlton, drive up Military Hill toward the airport and see if you can figure out what's going on. At number 314 there is an unusual mask-and-antler-covered compound that may be a UFO landing site, a convention center for Bigfoot, a runway for Santa's sleigh, or, possibly, the colorful creation of a highly individualistic artist who's marching to the beat of a very different drummer. The whole place is a chaotic visual treat but at the same time a puzzle. Suppose his exhibits are not artistic displays at all; suppose instead they're decoys? Is the invasion going to start here?

Directions to UFO site: From I-95, take the Houlton exit and turn right onto North Street. Go through two traffic lights to the stop sign. At the stop sign, turn left onto Military Hill. The UFO house is on the right near the top of the hill.

Kennebunkport, Maine

Blowing Cave

This astounding freak of nature has been pleasing tourists since before there were tourists. Settlers and Indians sought it out and found it fascinating. Alas, today this natural wonder has lost some of its allure, succumbing to more garish attention-getters, like Old Orchard Beach and George Bush. It's called "blowing cave" and if you're there at the right time you can watch it spout like Moby Dick. The magic is worked in a six-by-thirteen-foot seaside cavern. The secret is that it's all done with compressed air. At high tide the sea repeatedly bashes the opening, compressing and eventually trapping air inside. When the tide starts to reverse, the pressure eases, and the air lets go, blasting skyward a spectacular spout of water and mist. This volcanic waterspout can shoot upward a good thirty feet. When the tide is entirely out, things become strangely tranquil. You can walk into the cave and never be the wiser unless you surmised something was up by its surprisingly smooth rock walls.

Location: Leave Route 9 and take Ocean Avenue. Look for Sandy Cove, between Walker Point and Cape Arundel.

Lubec, Maine

Gold Accumulator

We can only speculate about what the good people of Lubec, Maine, must have thought when that odd crew moved in. They bought up the old Comstick grist mill, surrounded it with a ten-foot board fence topped with barbed wire, then posted armed guards to keep people away. Locals tolerated the mystery, though, because new construction was putting six hundred people to work. In time word got out: A minister named Prescott F. Jernegan, from one of the best and oldest families on Martha's Vineyard (and an honors graduate of Brown University and Newton Theological School, to boot), had received divine inspiration in a dream. He had been told how to extract gold from sea water. For years people had known that every ton of seawater contains a small amount of gold, but no one knew how to get it out. Surprisingly, Reverend Jernegan's method worked. Somehow he had fabricated an apparently simple contraption in which mercury was combined with a "secret compound." This "accumulator" was then lowered into the water while a small electrical current ran through it. The next day, when the device was hauled up like a lobster trap, it was crusted with thin flakes of gold. Jernegan and company had come to Lubec to build accumulators on a grand scale, at least a thousand of them. The venture was backed by a group of dignified investors, including the scrupulously honest and very successful Middletown, Connecticut, jeweler Arthur Ryan. Shares in the "Electrolytic Marine Salts Company" were sold publicly: 350,000 shares rose from one dollar to fifty dollars each as New Englanders rushed to get in on the action—mining gold from the sea. To this day no one knows what Reverend Jernegan's "secret ingredient" was. Perhaps it was Charles E. Fisher, the clergyman's silent (and invisible) partner. A trained diver, Mr. Fisher would sneak in at night and salt the traps, so to speak. They didn't really trap gold, but they ensnared lots of investors. When Jernegan and Fisher vanished, so did the money and what might have been Lubec's biggest industry.

The "Electrolytic Marine Salts Company" has been gone since the turn of the twentieth century, but some of the accumulators are still kicking around. Lubec resident Bernard Ross has reconstructed the process using an authentic accumulator in modern mountings. It is as close to the original as he could fathom and is on display in the yard of the Lubec Historical Society.

The Lubec Historical Society
    P.O. Box 5
    Main Street
    Lubec, ME 04652
Phone: (207) 733-4696

Location: The accumulator is next to the Historical Society, on the water side of Main Street across from the cemetery.

Hours: Open Mondays, Wednesdays, and Fridays, 9 A.M.–3 P.M., mid-June–Labor Day or by appointment.

Admission: a donation (not an investment).

Wheelchair accessible.

Monhegan Island, Maine

Fairy Houses

If you are susceptible to the charms of island living, you might find your way to Monhegan without our suggestion. This tiny pin-prick of an island, only about one mile square and ten miles out to sea, offers varied pleasures. There are six hundred species of wildflowers; old, wind-battered buildings; quaint streets without pavement and cars; and clusters of artists presenting their works. Or maybe your taste runs more toward the shipwrecks on the beaches; the lighthouse; or the ghosts that prowl at night. But there is one attraction that is easy to overlook, though once seen, difficult to forget. It's the work of fairies. If you walk along the web of paths that follow the tops of cliffs and crisscross Cathedral Woods, you might discover some of these miniature domains. Look carefully, they're tough to spot, but searching for the fairy houses is more fun than an Easter Egg Hunt, and much less caloric. And who knows, maybe you'll find a fairy, too.

Location: Monhegan Island is accessible only by boat. You may not take your car, but parking is available at the dock for a daily fee. Boat trips on the "Laura B" Mail Boat run year round, but the number of daily trips varies with the season. For info and reservations contact Monhegan Boat Line, P.O. Box 238, Port Clyde, Maine 04855, call (207) 372-8848, or e-mail <barstow@monheganboat.com>.

Cursed Idol

Sort of a down east version of the trouble at King Tut's tomb—a tale of high adventure, treasure, and malediction that unfolded in rural Maine—Charles and Ruben Hill were ship owners and merchants engaged in the China tea trade during the late 1800s. Amid the chaos of the Boxer Rebellion, they stole three golden idols from a Buddhist temple and brought them home to Naples, Maine. They discovered a fortune in jewels in one of the statues and used it to build a grand sixteen-room, three-story mansion on Long Lake. In the center of the hallway they displayed the biggest statue, a curious seven-foot grotesquery. But their good luck soon ended when the curse clicked in. The statue seemed to radiate an aura of evil. First the brothers died so suspiciously that their heirs threw two of the idols into the lake, and the big statue disappeared. Bad luck, unhappiness, and premature death stalked future homeowners. The next owner's son was murdered; a subsequent owner hanged himself. Another burned to death in a fire; his wife perished shortly afterward in a mental hospital. When a religious group took possession of the house, the pastor absconded with church funds. As recently as 1998 the place was used as a business, but the manager's son died mysteriously and once again the ineptly named "Serenity Hill" was up for sale. The submerged idols in Long Lake have never been recovered, but the third materialized at Boston's Museum of Fine Arts. Naples Historical Society Museum curator Robert J. Dingley was able to reclaim it. The impressive seven-foot, wood, plaster, and gold leaf statue is now deteriorating in the little museum behind the church. It may be of great value, but nobody has stolen it. They know better.

Naples Historical Society
Route 302
Village Green
Naples, ME 04055
Mailing Address: P.O. Box 1757, Naples, ME 04055

Phone: (207) 693-4297
nhs@pivot.net

Location: The museum is behind the Methodist Church on the village green, which is just off the causeway.

Hours: Open Fridays, 10 A.M.–noon, or by appointment, Memorial Day–Labor Day.

Free admission.

Wheelchair accessible.

Orono, Maine

Mexican Tomb Figures

It's amazing, the oddities you can find squirreled away in rural Maine. Take The Hudson Museum at UMaine in Orono, whose collections include some mighty strange stuff. Like what, you ask? An assortment of whaling implements? Artifacts of the Red Paint People? Exhibits demonstrating the evolving sophistication of logging tools? No, none of the above. We're talking about the largest collection of ancient West Mexican tomb figures in the United States. About 550 in all, dating from around 200 B.C. to 300 A.D. These bizarre ceramic effigies were placed in graves to accompany the dead into the afterlife. So how did they emerge from the tomb and find their way here? Well, initially they must have been extracted by grave robbers, but that's the unsavory part of their journey. Between 1965 and 1970, William P. Palmer III, a rather eccentric alumnus of the University, collected them at his home in Falmouth Foreside, Maine, where he exhibited hundreds of them. When

Mr. Palmer died in 1982, his collection of tomb figures—along with other interesting ancient relics from Mexico and Central America—was bequeathed to the museum.

The figurines—from terrifying to nearly comic—are highly colorful, stylized, and dynamic. Art historian Barbara Braun suggests certain animal figures may have inspired Disney artists in the 1930s. Apparently Alfred Hitchcock took note of them, too. A figure from Nayarit played an important role in his classic *North by Northwest*. Even marketers saw the power of these effigies. During the early 1990s, Kahlúa liqueur—which is produced in Mexico—used tomb figures in the background of their advertisements. Who knows what impact the figures might have had on the work of Stephen King if he had been here while they were.

Hudson Museum
> University of Maine
> 5746 Maine Center for the Arts
> Orono, ME 04469-5746

Phone: (207) 581-1901
> hudsonmuseum@umit.maine.edu
> www.umaine.edu/hudsonmuseum/default.htm

Location: The Hudson Museum is in the Maine Center for the Arts building. Once on campus there are many brown and white signs pointing to both the Maine Center for the Arts and the Hudson Museum. If there is some confusion, anyone on campus should be able to point out the route to the buildings.

Hours: Tuesday–Friday, 9 A.M.–4 P.M.; Saturday, noon–4 P.M.; closed Sundays.

Free admission.

Wheelchair accessible.

Transportation Museum

There is something here for everyone, but, admittedly, more for some than others. If you have even a smidgen of interest in pioneer-era airplanes, automobiles, bicycles, motorcycles, horseless carriages, even engines, you'll find much to keep you entertained. There are twenty-eight examples of aircraft dating from 1804 to 1946 including a working replica of Sir George Cayley's 1804 glider, the first man-made machine to fly. They also have the world's only flying replica of a 1913 *Etrich Taube,* a plane that looks more like a bird than an aircraft. And there are fifty automobiles from 1885 to 1980, nine motorcycles (1913 to 1953), including the one-of-a-kind Bi-Autogo featured in *Ripley's Believe It or Not* as the world's largest motorcycle (complete with landing gear). Examine petroleum-powered cars, steam-powered cars, early electrical cars (like the one owned by one-legged Ned Green, son of the infamous Hetty). You're guaranteed to see vehicles you've never seen before, gadgets you've never even imagined. And the true connoisseur of curiosities will not be disappointed. Check out John Domenjoz's 1930 *Sailing Glider* (an airplane built to generate its propulsive power by sails) and an original 1900 *Ornithopter,* an early attempt at manned flight using mechanical flapping wings (it didn't fly). Our favorite oddity was the *Elliot Cricket III;* it alone made our visit worthwhile. Dubbed "the car of the future" in 1938, this wonderful contraption looks exactly like one of the clunky rocketships from the old Flash Gordon serials.

Owls Head Transportation Museum
P.O. Box 277
Owls Head, ME 04854

Phone: (207) 594-4418
info@ohtm.org
www.ohtm.org

Location: From Route 1, follow Route 73 from either Thomaston or Rockland. Watch for the signs.

Hours: Open daily April–October, 10 A.M.–5 P.M., and November–March, 10 A.M.–4 P.M.

Admission charged.

Wheelchair accessible.

Lumbermen's Museum

For over 160 years, thousands of lumbermen made the trek up Shin Pond Road, with horses and supplies in tow, heading into the depths of the North Woods. Today you can make that same trip, albeit much faster, and stop at the Lumbermen's Museum where, in any of nine buildings, you can take a peek into the past. One major oddity is a replica of a complete logging camp as it would have been in 1820—built without using a single nail. Not one! Amid the dingles, loghaulers, water carts, and snubbing machines are some items that suggest how stark the logging life must have been. There are "bog shoes" that function as snowshoes for horses and oxen, prized tree burls measuring over a foot in diameter, and a goblet made completely out of pine needles.

Some especially poignant exhibits date back only to 1944, when three thousand German prisoners of war were put to work chopping wood. They knew their chances of escape were nil, but that didn't stop them from trying. Few remember these escape attempts, and tangible memorabilia is scarcer still. But there is something here: a pair of hastily made snowshoes woven on the sly out of twigs and branches, sturdy enough to endure a single epic trek. That they've been preserved at all suggests that the breakout failed.

American loggers and POWs both had tragedies to tell, but as every item in this museum suggests, art and ingenuity never deserted them.

The Patten Lumbermen's Museum
P.O. Box 300
Shin Pond Rd.
Patten, ME 04765

Phone: (207) 528-2650
elliott.hersey.55@alum.dartmouth.org
www.lumbermensmuseum.org

Location: It is just west of the town of Patten on Route 159, which is Shin Pond Road.

Hours: Open Memorial Day–June 30, Friday–Sunday, 10 A.M.–4 P.M.; July 1– August 31, Tuesday–Sunday, 10 A.M.–4 P.M.; September–Columbus Day, Friday–Sunday, 10 A.M.–4 P.M.; and holiday Mondays, 10 A.M.–4 P.M.

Admission charged.

Partly wheelchair accessible.

Peaks Island, Maine

The Cover Story

Could there be anything more esoteric than an umbrella museum? Sure. How about an umbrella *cover* museum. You know, those little nylon slip-on sleeves that most people immediately lose. Perhaps all the lost ones ended up here, along with over 250 others dangling from panels and strings. Though umbrella cover art has long been underappreciated, museum creator, curator, and principal visionary, Nancy 3. Hoffman, finds beauty in such mundane wonders. Some years ago she launched her unique collection by swiping its first exhibit from a store display. Subsequent specimens were discovered lying around the house or were donated by interested acquaintances—most of whom had lost the accompanying umbrellas.

Some of the more outstanding examples were created just for the museum, but you can see native umbrella sleeves from seventeen countries, including exhibits called "People and Their Covers" and "New Umbrella Cover Fashions." (A "special exhibit" features several items that are not covers, although what they are is not clear.) A number of one-of-a-kind items are sure to make your trip memorable, including an umbrella cover made of bulletproof kevlar and another fabricated from gum wrappers, contact paper, glue, and chewed gum. But—you might ask—what does it all mean? That you can't judge an umbrella by its cover? That there's beauty in the most mundane creations? That there really is a constructive application for gum wrapper chains? Who can say? Greater minds than ours have pondered the question.

Umbrella Cover Museum
62-B Island Ave.
Peaks Island, ME 04108

Phone: (207) 766-4496
ucm1@aol.com
www.umbrellacovermuseum.org

Location: From I-295, take exit 7 (Franklin) to the end, which is Commercial Street. Park at the ferry terminal or on the street. Take the Casco Bay Lines ferry to Peaks Island, a twenty-minute trip. Ferries run every hour, 6 A.M.–11:30 P.M. (For ferry rates and schedules, call (207) 774-7871.) From the ferry dock, walk up the hill, turn left on the first street, called Island Avenue, and the museum is the third house on the left. Look for the sign with the umbrella over a white clapboard house.

Hours: Open May–December. Call for hours or appointment.

NOTE: Ms. Hoffman, who changed her middle name to the number 3, is also director of the Maine Squeeze accordion ensemble.

Admission charged.

Not handicapped accessible.

Giant Eyeball

This is Renaissance technology in modern Maine—and one of the city's best kept secrets. The mystical, whimsical aspects of the *camera obscura* are described in the "Norwich, Vermont" entry—but here we find serious science: a full-function *camera obscura* with top-quality Eastman Kodak optical equipment. This big-city version of its Vermont country-cousin demonstrates all the potential of this old-fashioned optical oddity. The *camera obscura* acts as a giant eyeball, providing a panoramic view of the city. Let your inner-voyeur come alive as you watch people, cars, birds, and boats move in hypnotic silence across the forty-two-inch viewing table. There is something covert about it all: seeing without being seen, jumping invisibly from location to location, spying from the sky. Children like it, but adults find it absolutely fascinating. This elaborate system of lens, mirror, and turret is housed in the cupola on top of the museum building. The optics are so good that even on a wet and gloomy day the image will be clear and well-defined. On a sunny day, it is mesmerizing.

The Children's Museum of Maine
142 Free St.,
P.O. Box 4041
Portland, ME 04101

Phone: (207) 828-1234
www.childrensmuseumofme.org

Location: The museum is right next to the Portland Museum of Art. The *camera obscura* is on the third floor.

Hours: Open Labor Day–Memorial Day, Tuesday–Saturday, 10 A.M.–5 P.M., Sunday, noon–5 P.M. Memorial Day–Labor Day, Monday–Saturday, 10 A.M.–5 P.M., Sunday, noon–5 P.M. Open Monday and Tuesday during school vacations.

NOTE: See also *A Glimpse of Fairyland* in Norwich, Vermont.

Admission charged.

Wheelchair accessible.

Living with Monsters

It's an unassuming two-story house on a quiet residential street. But what's that on the porch? A life-size cutout of Bigfoot. The anomalies multiply as you step inside. You've just entered the International Museum of Cryptozoology, also the home of one of the world's most respected cryptozoologists Loren Coleman. Known for multiple books, articles, and media appearances, Mr. Coleman is new to the curating business.

This snoozing what-is-it resides among other oddities at Portland's Cryptozoology Museum.
Photo: Joe Citro

Over the years his private collection of curious artifacts just got so big that he had no place to store them. His solution was cohabitation. Now his roommates include a full-sized, anatomically correct coelacanth (a six-foot fish presumed to have been extinct for sixty-five million years, but reappeared crawling on the deck of an African fishing trawler in 1938), a Feejee mermaid that co-starred in a movie about P. T. Barnum, replicas of such oddities as the Dover Demon, Mothman, and various aquatic conundrums like the Loch Ness Monster with his American cousin, Champ. And of course, Bigfoot, that large hairy hominid that has been seen, fleetingly, in every American state and almost every country of the world. Mr. Coleman displays its hair samples and enough authentic casts of Bigfootprints to lead any cryptozoologist on a merry chase.

Though everything is presented with Mr. Coleman's unfailing good humor, the Cryptozoology Museum is no joke. Some of these unknown animals may really be out there and

Mr. Coleman's museum provides a place to centralize data and discussion and introduce curious people to an unusual science that will pique curiosity and wonder. The whole place is a feast for the eyes and the imagination.

Watch for the chupacabras, mystery cats, jackalopes, the infamous furred trout, and the museum-quality skulls: Gigantopithecus, Paranthropus, Australopithecus, Panthera atrox, gorilla, chimp, lion, cougar, and much more. (If you don't know what any of these are, this is the place to find out.)

International Cryptozoology Museum
P.O. Box 360
Portland, ME 04112

NOTE: The museum, like many of its inhabitants, remains hidden. For now you can visit, but by appointment only. Tours are free. Contact Loren Coleman at the above address or e-mail him at <museummail@lorencoleman.com>. For more information, go to <www.lorencoleman.com>.

Portland, Maine

Observatory

When you're spying through the *camera obscura*, or while you're driving around the city, a tall wooden tower may catch your eye. Don't be quick to dismiss it as yet another of Maine's many lighthouses—that's not what it is. An eight-sided wooden edifice, the Portland Observatory has been a popular local landmark since Captain Lemuel Moody constructed it in 1908. He built it as a commercial enterprise and was hired by the city's merchants to signal the moment their ships were spotted on the horizon. Since then it has stood while its peers in other cities have succumbed to weather, age, and the wrecking ball. Today the Portland Observatory is unique, the only remaining signal tower of its kind in the country. It was closed for a while, deemed unsafe due to an insect infestation, but, because of its popularity, hundreds of people leaped to its financial rescue. Thanks to a 1.2 million dollar restoration, it's up and running again. A quick trip up the 103 steps to the top (if such a thing is possible) and a few minutes on the outdoor observation deck, are a good way to see how Maine's biggest city developed. You'll also see why the Portland Observatory has so many fans. In fact, you'll probably join them.

Portland Observatory
   138 Congress St.
   Portland, ME 04101

Phone: (207) 774-5561
   www.portlandlandmarks.org
   info@portlandlandmarks.org

Location: The tower is at 138 Congress Street at the top of Munjoy Hill. It's easy to spot.

Hours: Open daily May 24–October 13, 10 A.M.–5 P.M., closed July 4.

NOTE: Take a tour—they're inexpensive—so you don't miss any of the historic graffiti or fascinating stories about the tower's past.

Admission charged.

Prospect, Maine

Fort Knox

Perhaps it's more for the kids, but adults can derive a chill or a thrill from this massive nineteenth-century fortress. Commissioned in 1839 and built on a promontory over the Penobscot River, this creepy old bastion may be as close as America gets to a European castle. It's gigantic, full of dark tunnels, vaulted brick ceilings, secret passageways, circular stairways, lofty parapets, huge cannons, and walkable walls— all the things that make young pulses quicken. It was constructed at a time when the boundary between the United States and Canada was somewhere in the wilds of the north-country and more than a little hazy. The Americans were worried that Great Britain might attack via river and seize Bangor, then the lumber capital of the world. The attack never came. Since then the fort has been used only twice for military activity: Union volunteers were trained here during the Civil War; and in 1890, five hundred Connecticut troops were stationed here for the Spanish-American War. No combat round was ever actually fired at Fort Knox. Still, it remains an engineering delight and an intriguing place to explore. It extends 252 by 146 feet over two levels and provides magnificent views of the Penobscot River. But don't come here expecting to see the nation's gold supply. That's the other Fort Knox.

Fort Knox State Historic Site
R.R. #1
Box 1316
Stockton Springs, ME 04981

Phone: (207) 469-7719
fortknox.maineguide.com/

Also . . .

The Friends of Fort Knox
P.O. Box 456
Bucksport, ME 04416

Phone: (207) 469-6553
FOFK1@aol.com

Location: From U.S. Route 1, turn onto Route 174 on the side of the Waldo-Hancock County suspension bridge opposite Bucksport. Fort Knox will be approximately one quarter mile up on your right.

Hours: Open May 1–November 1, 9 A.M. till sunset. Guided tours available.

NOTE: One impressive feature is the fifteen-inch Rodman cannon which required about seven people to load and fire. A shell weighed about 315 pounds, had a charge of 50 pounds, and could shoot over two miles. Don't forget a flashlight for the tunnels.

Admission charged.

Partly wheelchair accessible.

Perry's Nuts

So that you won't be as disappointed as we were when we discovered that our beloved Perry's Nut House in Belfast has become an antiseptic shadow of its former self, we offer you a bit of consolation. When the owner of the time-warp tourist trap (founded in 1927) decided to call it quits, his overgrown accumulation of taxidermied animals, Man-Killer Clams, and delightfully outdated oddities was auctioned off. His fabled nut collection—the world's largest—went to Al DiMarco, a realtor from Prospect Harbor, a town further up the Maine coast. Al had no real affinity for nuts, but he couldn't bear to see Maine lose the infamous collection. When the auctioneer hollered "sold!" Al says he silently panicked, wondering what he would do with ten thousand of the wrinkled things. But before he could negotiate with a rival bidder, cameras were flashing, reporters were swarming, and the next day his picture was all over the news. Al has now settled in with his new family of nuts, which includes every botanical species known to man. The star of the group is the gigantic Seychelles nut from the Indian Ocean islands, and the smallest . . . well, to tell the truth, he doesn't know. But among the multitudes is a rather odd turtle—an amalgamation of mixed nuts with an ivory head. He also fancies some of the ivory nuts from India that have been converted into buttons. The collection, in its entirety, is still in its original glass cases in Mr. DiMarco's antique shop, adjacent to his realty office. Alas, we don't know what became of Mr. Perry's stuffed albatross.

Perry's Nut Collection
Coastal Antiques/DiMarco Realty
P.O. Box 124
Main St.
Prospect Harbor, ME 04669

Phone: (207) 963-5540
dimarco@acadia.net

Location: Mr. DiMarco's shop is at the intersection of Routes 195 and 186 on Corea Road in Prospect Harbor, which is across the bay from Acadia National Park.

Hours: Open 9 A.M.–5 P.M., Wednesday–Sunday, or by appointment.

NOTE: We hear the giant elephant and its baby that once greeted visitors at Perry's door now reside at the Colonial Theater in Belfast. And for the hopelessly nostalgic, you can probably look longingly at the mixed nuts at their concession counter.

Free admission.

Wheelchair accessible.

Rangeley, Maine

The Orgone Energy Museum and Observatory

What did Dr. Wilhelm Reich do to get the government so angry at him? A student of Freud and practicing psychiatrist, Dr. Reich believed his newly discovered "Orgone Energy" influenced human health and behavior, and if properly channeled, could even change the weather. Trouble is, the energy source was sex (Orgone takes its name from "orgasm") and the 1950s were repressed times. The government thought Dr. Reich was a quack. In a dramatic display of bureaucratic bullying, the Food and Drug Administration burned his books, destroyed his machinery, and eventually threw him into jail, where he died in 1956. He is buried here at the complex he named Orgonon, where he experimented with his "Orgone Accumulator" and built his "Cloud Busters," which look very much like anti-aircraft guns. Many people treated with his "Accumulator" claim to have been helped, and he is credited with ending the drought of 1953 with his Cloud Buster, causing rain and thus saving the state's blueberry crop. Today, visitors to Dr. Reich's museum can examine the evidence and decide for themselves: was he a brilliant healer far ahead of his time, a mad scientist, or just a charming charlatan?

Wilhelm Reich Museum
P. O. Box 687
Dodge Pond Road
Rangeley, ME 04970

Phone: (207) 864-5156
wreich@rangeley.org
www.wilhelmreichmuseum.org

Hours: Observatory: Open July and August, Wednesday–Sunday, 1–5 P.M., September, Sundays only, 1–5 P.M.

Conference center: Open year-round, Monday–Friday, 9 A.M.–2 P.M. For information call: (207) 864-3443.

Admission charged for the observatory.

Stonington, Maine

Tiny Town

There ought to be enough room for everybody in the vast reaches of Maine, but for some unfathomable reason the citizens of Stonington have packed themselves into the village, a decision perhaps influenced by the sardine industry. Here it's obvious: Smaller is better. Some of the houses are so crammed together that it's hard to tell where one ends and the next begins.

As if to underscore this urge to compact, residents have filled a tiny park with miniature houses—a lilliputian replica of their already tiny town. There's a barn half-full of hay, a bride and groom taking their wedding vows in a white-steepled church, an inn with thimble-sized cups on saucers filling the tabletop, and countless other houses, some occupied, some not, many packed with pint-sized paraphernalia.

These diminutive domains were the work of the late Everett Knowlton, a local who built them at the rate of about a house a year. The better ones are sheltered during the winter in nearby homes, and put out again come spring.

But if Mr. Knowlton's houses are still not small enough for you, head to the Granite Museum on the waterfront. There you'll find a delightfully detailed eight-by-fifteen-foot three-dimensional model of the whole town and nearby Crotch Island as they looked circa 1900. The replica—full of fist-sized houses, ribbon-roadways, and people the size of paperclips—depicts the granite-cutting era, which put Stonington on the map. Push a button and the whole thing comes alive! As a sixteen-minute narration plays, tiny horses, people, and wagons go about their day's work. You'll see stonecutters riding a horsecart to work and a boat the size of a bar of Ivory soap chugs over to Crotch Island. Quarries are dynamited, cranes move granite slabs, trains huff along the tracks. The detail is impressive, and it can't get much smaller than this.

The Deer Isle Granite Museum
> Box 469
> Main St.
> Stonington, ME 04681

Phone: (207) 367-6331

Location: Stonington is on the southernmost tip of Deer Isle on Route 15. Heading south, the miniature park is on the right just as you make the right-hand curve into the town center. The museum is only a few steps away.

Hours: Memorial Day–Labor Day, Monday–Saturday, 9 A.M.–5 P.M., Sunday 12 –5 P.M., or by appointment.

Free admission.

Wheelchair accessible. A ramp is at the side of the building.

Bryant Stove Museum

Bea and Joe Bryant have been restoring and selling old stoves since 1970. They opened their "Stove Museum" to preserve and display rare, beautiful, and ingenious woodburners. Since their facilities are so modest, it would be easy to pass them by without taking a second look, but that would be a big mistake. Sure, the beautifully restored antique stoves are something in themselves—clever, ornate, often ingenious signposts pointing to a lost America—but to the fantasist, the real draws here are the unique creations of Mr. Joseph Bryant himself. A man blessed with a highly developed sense of whimsy and an innate mechanical genius, he has taken a simple stove works and moved it into the magical kingdom of Oz.

If you choose you can quickly bypass the scores of stoves along with some antique trucks and Model-T's. The real fun starts with a vast variety of working nickelodeons, player pianos, and hurdy-gurdies, all restored by the intuitive skills of Mr. Bryant. Some have rinky-tink mechanisms, tambourines, drums, triangles, and accordions that you can watch as they hammer out an oom-pa-pa tune orchestrated by paper player rolls.

It sounds as if the circus is coming . . . and it is!

Mr. Bryant's "Doll Circus" is not a restoration but rather his original creation. It is a colorful extravaganza of spinning and twirling Barbies, teddy bear trapeze artists, and puppet tightrope walkers, complete with a miniature Ferris wheel made from a bicycle wheel, each seat occupied by a tiny doll. It is all homemade, all self-designed. There's nothing slick, corporate, or pre-fab about it. The Bryants flick the switch and colored lights flash, the music starts, and everything starts spinning, twirling, and toppling.

Something like this can only come from the imagination of someone like Joe Bryant. That's why this place is unique—a highly eccentric, vastly entertaining, one-of-a-kind thrill-ride for the child in each of us.

Bryant Stove Museum
  Stovepipe Alley
  Thorndike, ME 04986

Phone: (207) 568-3665

Location: The museum is in Thorndike at the intersection of Routes 139 and 220 on Rich Road.

Hours: Open Monday–Saturday, 8 A.M.–4:30 P.M., but call first.

Free admission.

Wheelchair accessible.

Waldoboro, Maine

Monument to Deception and Disappointment

Maine's earliest settlers included a fair number of German immigrants, many of whom were cultivated city folk. In the early eighteenth century, starting from scratch in the American wilderness was not an appealing concept unless you were fleeing religious persecution or, perhaps, the law. To attract newcomers, colonial authorities had to create sophisticated marketing strategies (in other words, lies). The extent of their fabrications comes painfully to light in this small community whose founders had the last say. And etched it in stone. A marker in the back of the German cemetery is one of the most bitter arrival announcements possible: "This town was settled in 1718 by Germans who emigrated to this place with the promise and expectation of finding a populous city, instead of which they found nothing but a wilderness; for the first few years they suffered to a great extent by Indian wars and starvation." It goes on from there. Many Waldoboro residents are descendants of these Germans and still have German names, although the language and culture have all but vanished. Even the gravestones are written in English. The town did however manage to conserve the original German church built in 1772. It's one of Maine's three oldest churches. It is a steeple-less yellow edifice on a hill adjacent to the cemetery. Inside you'll find straight, unpainted wooden pews and framed portraits of the town's founders on the walls. The original communion table is still there, and a cabinet holds German mementos.

The Old German Church and Cemetery
    Maine Hwy. 32
    Waldoboro, ME 04572

Phone: (207) 832-5100

Location: From Route 1, take Route 32 south toward Bremen and pass under a blinking light. The church is on a hill about half a mile on the right behind two stone gates. The marker with the historic inscription is on the left side of the cemetery at the back, the tallest white obelisk without an urn on the top. The inscription faces the rear.

Hours: The church is open 1–4 P.M. daily during July and August.

Wilson's Mills, Maine

Buried In Forest

It's as weird as any episode of the *The X-Files*. And, if you're interested in exploring and treasure hunting, this little-known but most intriguing gravesite may be right up your alley. It's hidden somewhere on the slopes of Deer Mountain, not far from Wilson's Mills. Author Richard Pinette describes the unusual entombment as "especially bizarre . . . !" So what's weird about it? First, the remote location, deep in the Northwoods. Second, its size—that tomb is gigantic! And finally, what it contains is almost unbelievable—an entire B-17 Flying Fortress, a colossal World War II bomber. Back in 1944, it took off with a full crew on its way to England. Its flight path took it just north of Wilson's Mills. But as it approached Deer Mountain, something happened. It lost altitude and crashed. No one survived. A military team went into the dense woods to retrieve the bodies. The plane itself was far too big to haul out. So they commandeered a giant bulldozer from a nearby logging operation, excavated a huge trench, pushed the bomber's remains into the hole and covered it. But perhaps they worked too quickly. Even today elderly residents of Wilson's Mills claim they hiked to the scene after the military left. They found unused parachutes, metal scraps, tubing. Then someone made a sickening discovery—a severed limb . . . and another. The outcry provoked a second, more thorough cleanup. But the bulk of the huge craft is still there, buried, overgrown, waiting like an undiscovered time capsule since that tragic day in the Northlands forest in 1944.

Location: The buried bomber is somewhere on Deer Mountain on the side facing the Wilson's Mills and the Aziscoos Dam.

Wilton, Maine

The Maine Giantess

The Farm and Home Museum in downtown Wilton is a big structure. Good thing, because it houses oversized memorabilia—the belongings of the Maine Giantess, Sylvia Hardy. Though largely forgotten today, Ms. Hardy was a wonder of her era. She traveled with P. T. Barnum, was best friends with Mrs. Tom Thumb, and got to see much of the world from an elevated viewpoint. Billed the "Tallest Lady in the World," Ms. Hardy was seven feet ten and a half inches tall and weighed over four hundred pounds at the time of her death in 1888. When introducing her to a crowd, Barnum's huckster would never fail to mention that:

Miss Hardy is a very large and well-proportioned woman, rather lean than fleshy, weighs 330 pounds, and is one of a pair of twins that weighed only 3 pounds at birth. Her parents were both below the medium size. Her complexion is fair, her eyes blue, and the very modest and mild expression of her countenance is a true index to her character. She is unable to pass ordinary doors without stooping a good deal, and it is said that for convenience she usually puts her thimble and other little articles upon the casing over the door instead of upon any lower object as a table or desk. Formerly employed as a nurse, she never took an infant in her arms, but always held it in her hand. Placing the head upon the end of her fingers, its feet extend toward the wrist, and with the thumb and little finger elevated, she forms an ample and admirable cradle—the length of her hand being quite equal to the whole length of an infant.

Sylvia would then demonstrate how she could conceal a newspaper beneath her spread hands. When she retired from show business she returned home to Wilton, where she was well liked. She spent her later years alone, developing a great interest in spiritualism. She was supposedly a fine medium. Perhaps her spirit occasionally visits the museum, where, among other things, you can see a life-sized figure of her and a gown she wore measuring six feet eight inches. She is buried in Wilton's Lakeview Cemetery in an eight-foot coffin.

Wilton Historical Society
P.O. Box 33
Wilton, ME 04294

Phone: (207) 645-2091, (207) 645-4353, (207) 645-3436

Location: The museum is in the big white building in back of Mario's restaurant. The main entrance is on the street behind the Key Bank.

Hours: Open Saturdays in July and August, 1–4 P.M. Additional tours for small groups may be arranged.

Admission: a donation.

Stairway to Nowhere

No matter how you explain or describe it, this is a peculiar site. You could simply say, "On a rocky bluff, in the middle of nowhere, there is a twenty-five-foot flight of stairs carved into rock—beginning nowhere and ending nowhere." Since the mysterious steps were firmly in place before the first settlers arrived, there has been ongoing discussion about who made them. Why there? And what was their purpose? Settlers blamed the Indians, dubbing the site, "The Indian Steps," but prior to the European intrusion, local natives were equally puzzled: They didn't make the steps, either. And they had been there as long as anyone could remember. Much speculation resulted about a vastly ancient civilization predating the Native Americans. For years the whole thing was a wonderful puzzle. Then geologists stepped in and spoiled the fun. They said

The mysterious "Indian Steps" lay hidden in the forests of Windham, Maine. Photo: Joe Citro

the builder was Mother Nature and she made them some two hundred million years ago. In fact, they said, Windham's so-called "Indian Steps" are a naturally occurring formation known as a basalt dike. Well, maybe so. But we like the puzzle more.

Location: From the intersection of Routes 302 and 202, go north on 202, past the rotary heading toward Gray. Turn right at the blinking lights onto Falmouth Road, and take the second right onto Albion Road. On the left is a sign that says "Grandpa's Village." Just before that, on the right, take the dirt road leading through the trees. The last (newly built) house on the left sits closest to the stairs.

NOTE: "Indian Steps" is on private property. Please seek permission before you explore.

WARNING: Wear a hat, socks, long pants, and insect repellent. The ticks here carry Lyme disease.

Wiscasset, Maine

Mummy, Dearest

Terry Lewis is a clever salesman, but some things are just a tough sell. Take his mummy, for instance. He tells of the people who have offered him thirty-five thousand dollars and more for it, yet it stays and stays. You see, some things can't be measured in money. The mummy greets you as you walk into his antiques store, its blackened arms crossed over its chest. The exposed head and limbs are stiff and dark, its eye sockets are empty, and ever since bugs started their pilgrimage into the glass case, it has shown disturbing signs of decay. But what do you expect from a three-thousand-year-old corpse? At one time the cadaver belonged to the collections of New Hampshire's lamented Morse Museum; part of a gold mine of nineteenth-century exotica that was auctioned off when it closed. Mr. Lewis got the mummy for eight thousand dollars. Egyptologist Peter Lacovara of Boston's Museum of Fine Arts determined it had been an Egyptian male (Mr. Lewis had thought it was a woman) of average height, around age forty, possibly a temple priest. Lacking a coffin and pedigree, however, he deemed it of little cultural value. Up until then, Mr. Lewis had battled the Egyptian government and U.S. Customs to prevent its seizure, but the mummy prevailed and has now become a permanent fixture in the shop. In keeping with the theme, Mr. Lewis bought out the inventory of the 1920-era Coombs Funeral Home in nearby Belfast: coffins, bottled embalming fluids, and antique crematory urns. Strange bedfellows, you say? Not really. He also carries a collection of colorful dolls crafted from the body shrouds of robbed Peruvian graves, picked up for a song during his thirty years at sea. You're welcome to come in and browse, but if you're in the market for a mummy, forget it. It's not for sale.

Nonesuch House of Antiques
   1 Middle St.
   Wiscasset, ME 04578

Phone: (207) 882-6768

Location: The Nonesuch House is on Middle Street, a right turn off Route 1 just over the bridge as you drive south through the center of town.

Hours: Open daily, 10 A.M.–5 P.M., May–Columbus Day, or by appointment. *Wheelchair accessible.*

Wiscasset, Maine

Old Jail Graffiti

A Hollywood horror film couldn't depict a more sinister dungeon. The dread prisoners must have felt upon entering this escape-proof edifice is still palpable, radiating coldly from the walls. This nightmarish man-made cave is constructed from massive granite slabs that threaten at any moment to collapse, crushing any cowering wretch within. Its few windows are mere slits bisected with iron bars. A bucket in each cell was the only plumbing; heat was virtually nonexistent and thick, solid stone doors, set in granite walls, lock with a ten-inch key. There was a pecking order, of course. The worst offenders stayed below on the (literally) ground floor. Rowdies and drunkards lived one flight up, and the top was for debtors, women, and the mentally ill. Sailors were frequent guests due to Wiscasset's deep-water port. Of the thousands who were incarcerated here between 1811 to 1913, only one escaped. This clever German, appearing to be well-behaved, was given temporary liberty to pace the corridor between cells. When the jailer was momentarily out of site, the sailor cast off. He broke through a door, leaped the stairwell, and crashed out a second-story window. He was never seen again. After 1913, the Lincoln County Jail lay dormant for half a century. When historians reopened it in the 1960s they discovered a time capsule of prison life that's unchanged to this day. Nineteenth-century graffiti still covers the walls. Not today's rude bathroom-door variety, but graceful lines of poetry, a clipper ship scratched out in full sail, and cave-like depictions of suffering human forms. A tour through this place might make Leavenworth look good.

The Old Lincoln County Jail and Museum
Route 218
Wiscassett, ME 04578

Phone: (207) 882-6817

Location: Going east on Route 1, turn left onto Route 218 and go 1.2 miles. The jail is on your right.

Hours: Open Saturdays, 10 A.M.–4 P.M., and Sundays, noon–4 P.M., June–September. Open Tuesday–Saturday, 10 A.M.–4 P.M., Sundays, noon–4 P.M., July–Labor Day. Closed Mondays.

NOTE: Don't miss the small police display in the jail stairwell, with its archetypal tin cup, badges, brass knuckles, handcuffs, nightsticks, and more.

Admission charged.

Sounds of the Past — The Musical Wonder House

In an age of the Walkman and personal CD players, we may never stop to wonder how music was reproduced before there was electricity. The Musical Wonder House will show you— and wonders they are. The variety of ingenious mechanisms is staggering: candy dishes, door chimes, coin operated boxes with animated figures, a magic musical mirror . . . You really can't imagine the scope and variety.

There are deceptively simple gadgets like windup jewelry boxes. There are gags, like musical snuff or cigarette boxes, inkwells, trivets for the table, even a Swiss hand-carved bust of St. Bernard who'll serenade you with two German folk songs. Some of the musical wonders are full-sized pieces of furniture that would be a delight to own even if they had no musical aptitude. There's a round-topped hand-crafted Louis XV type table, circa 1895. Open it and discover a twenty-inch metal disk that, through technology we can't seem to understand, will play beautiful melodies with an unbelievably rich sound. Then there's the ingeniously engineered "Shifter" that actually plays and changes twenty-inch metal disks, just like your record player used to (remember them?).

We took special delight in animated creations, like the 1895 musical candy dispenser, with its drum, bells, moving figures, and dancing dolls. And the French bird cage with three mechanical singing birds. The oldest automaton is a French derinette bird organ from 1740. It seems like magic. How did they do it?

All these wonders are housed in a nineteenth-century mansion. It's the home of curator, founder, and chief tour guide Danilo Konvalinka, whose personal animation is an engaging part of the show. He will introduce you to music machines of every era, all working as well as the day they were made. It is hard to believe all this musical magic is created with gears, springs, perforated metal disks, and combs.

Musical Wonder House
   18 High St.
   Wiscasset, ME 04578

Phone: (207) 882-7163
   musicbox@musicalwonderhouse.com
   www.musicalwonderhouse.com

Location: Take Route 1 into Wiscasset an follow the signs.

Hours: Open daily, Memorial Day–October 15, 10 A.M.–6 P.M. Guided tours until 5 P.M.

NOTE: It was no surprise to learn a place that keeps the past so vibrantly alive should have a ghost. It is said to be a shadowy young man in his late teens or early twenties. He has been seen on the "Flying Staircase," sitting on a couch, and in the kitchen. No one seems to know who it is . . . or was.

Admission charged. You can choose among three different tours at different prices.

Not wheelchair accessible.

Wiscasset, Maine

Time Warp House

Many historic homes try to replicate life in the nineteenth century, but in Wiscasset, Castle Tucker does one better. It *is* the nineteenth century, a home left virtually untouched since the 1890s. This 1807 Federal-style mansion was built when Wiscasset was the busiest seaport east of Boston. It passed through several hands until wealthy shipping scion Captain Richard Tucker moved in with his young bride in 1858. They refurnished it top to bottom in quintessential Victoriana: stuffed birds, ornate parquet flooring, steel engravings, tapestry-like wallpaper, and dozens of moody oil paintings. In the billiard room the captain proudly displayed souvenirs from his foreign travels: gaucho spurs, a ceremonial adze from Fiji, a tortoise shell kava bowl, and more. After the captain's death, his youngest daughter, Jane, stayed on alone. Her niece from Boston, another Jane, visited her frequently throughout the 1950s. The two Janes kept it as it appeared one hundred years ago. Lack of money meant that nothing significant was changed. When Aunt Jane died, Jane the younger and her sister inherited the house. They considered selling it, but neither could bear to see it emptied of its treasures. So in 1972, Jane bought her sister's half and turned it into a private museum. Somehow she kept it pieced together and running. Like her aunt, she left everything undisturbed—a time capsule of nineteenth-century life. In 1997, when she could no longer maintain the place, she donated it to the Boston-based Society for the Preservation of New England Antiquities (SPNEA), which, thankfully, is leaving it be.

Castle Tucker
> Lee St. at High St.
> Wiscasset, ME 04578

Phone: (207) 882-7364
> www.spnea.org/visit/homes/castle.htm

Location: Take exit 22 from I-95 to Route 1, Brunswick. Follow Route 1 to the junction with Route 218 at Wiscasset. Turn right onto Lee Street. Castle Tucker is on the corner of Lee and High Streets.

Hours: Open June 1–October 15. Tours given Friday through Sunday on the hour starting at 11 A.M. and ending at 4 P.M.

Admission charged.

Yarmouth, Maine

War of the Worlds

Many people will argue that Babson College in Wellesley, Massachusetts, has the largest globe in the world (twenty-eight-foot diameter). Others insist it's the thirty-three-foot sphere in Apecchi, Italy. But if you check the *Guinness Book of World Records*, you'll find that the winner is here in Yarmouth, Maine. Eartha—as it has been dubbed—is one mother of an earth. At over 41 feet in diameter, it has a circumference of 130.91 feet and a surface area of 2,727.52 square feet. This six thousand pound orb is mounted on a specially designed cantilever arm so, driven by two computer-controlled electric motors, it can revolve and rotate every two minutes. In fact, every aspect of Eartha was developed with computer technology. The database used to design its surface is mind-boggling—about 140 gigabytes, or 214 CD-ROMs. As you watch it rotate, a hundred CD-ROMs worth of data passes by every minute (that's a lot when you consider that the average person reads only about one CD-ROM's worth of text in a lifetime). Maine's globe of globes—tilted at 23.5 degrees, just like Earth—has a scale of 1:1,000,000. One inch equals nearly sixteen miles. So California is three and a half feet tall! This whole surreal masterwork was the brainchild of David DeLorme, of map publishing fame. Though it seems almost big enough to support life, Eartha took a good deal longer than seven days to create.

DeLorme
P.O. Box 298
2 DeLorme Dr.
Yarmouth, ME 04096

Phone: (207) 846-7000
info@delorme.com
www.delorme.com

Location: Eartha is squeezed into a three-story glass atrium at the DeLorme Map Company headquarters. Take exit 17 off I-95 going either direction. Get on Route 1 and take second right onto DeLorme Drive.

Hours: Open Monday–Saturday, 8:30 A.M.–6:00 P.M. and Sundays, 9:30 A.M.–5:00 P.M.

Free admission.

Wheelchair accessible.

The Old Gaol

Parts of this creepy, slightly barn-like structure represent the oldest existing jail in America. Built as a wooden structure in 1653, it soon became apparent that something stronger was needed for the Gaol. Timbers were reconfigured, huge stones were added, and by 1719 Mainers had themselves a prison worthy of the Province of Maine. Since little about the cells and dungeons has changed, you can get a pretty good idea what it must have been like to be incarcerated here. People were separated according to the severity of their crime, rather than by gender, age, or class. The upstairs housed the real bad ones: murderers, arsonists, and so forth. Downstairs was for lesser evils: profanity, intoxication, gossip, lying, or failing to keep the Sabbath. Most of the criminals were debtors. Strictly speaking, people were not punished here, they were simply

The Old Gaol in York, Maine, is one of New England's earliest.
Photo: Joe Citro

held until trial, which, depending on the crime and timing, could be up to a year away. Punishment came after being found guilty: hanging for the bad guys, public humiliation for the rest. Ancient graffiti still shows how one former inmate marked the passing of the days.

An additional level of weirdness comes with the stories of a haunting. Certain modern-day workers refuse to be in the jail alone. Though the specter's identity is not known, many suspect it may be Patience Boston, a wild, wicked, and wanton native American who had committed crimes against the local minister. He'd tried to Christianize Patience; she retaliated by drowning his son and trying to poison him and his wife. From all reports she was a pretty menacing character who arrived pregnant. Patience was incarcerated for almost two years, but after her son was born and weaned, she was hanged. Presumably she would have been kept upstairs among the dangerous inmates, and it is there that many spirit confrontations are said to occur.

The Old Gaol
Old York Historical Society
P.O. Box 312
207 York St.
York, ME 03909

Phone: (207) 363-4974
oyhs@oldyork.org
www.oldyork.org/visiting-pages/goal.htm

Hours: Tuesday–Saturday, 10 A.M.–5 P.M., Sunday, 1–5 P.M.

Admission charged.

MASSACHUSETTS

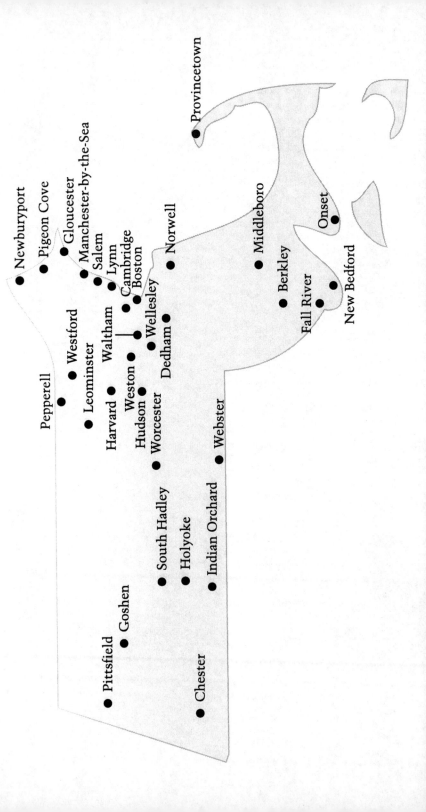

Puzzle Rock

Dighton Rock, at the mouth of the Taunton River, is a forty-ton boulder that has been puzzling people since it was first observed and sketched by Dr. John Danforth in 1680. It was a mystery then, as now, because its westward-facing, ten foot by four foot sandstone face is covered with unfathomable petroglyphs of ancient and uncertain origin. Apparently it's the oldest known inscribed rock in North America. Cotton Mather became fascinated with it in 1712, calling it one of his American *Curiosa*. Since then, countless scholars have taken a crack at deciphering the rock's odd hieroglyphics. For various reasons the markings have been attributed to Native Americans, English settlers, the Scythians, the Viking Leif Erikson, the Portuguese Miguel Corte Real, the Italian Verrazano, nameless Phoenician explorers, and hoaxers. Or it could be the work of all of the above. Perhaps, like a graffiti-covered boulder along a highway, every passing pre-Columbian explorer left his mark. To protect these mysterious messages from further graffiti artists, and the destructive forces of erosion, the State of Massachusetts moved Dighton Rock in 1974 and set aside the surrounding area as a park. Today the rock is installed in a small museum along with other exhibits and several explanations of the carvings. You can try your hand at decoding them, or simply marvel at a mystery that may never be solved.

Location: It is on the east side of Taunton River off Bay View Avenue in Berkley. Take Route 24 south to exit 10 west. Take a right at the end of ramp onto North Main Street. Go left on Friends Street. Follow signs.

Hours: Dighton Rock State Park is open Memorial Day–Labor Day, 11 A.M.–5 P.M. The museum is open by appointment in the summer. For information, call: (508) 644-5522.

Free admission.

Wheelchair accessible.

Devil's Eye View of the World

Suppose hell really were at the center of the earth. And suppose the devil really was down there, sitting on his throne, looking up at the world. "The Mapparium" is what he would see. This is a giant, hollow, brilliantly colored stained-glass globe. And, like an arrow through an apple, a thirty-foot glass walkway known as the "crystal bridge," runs through its middle. You can step into the earth (by plunging into the Indian Ocean), stand at its center, and look all around at the beautifully backlit countries of the world, configured as they were when this optical oddity was manufactured around 1932. But before you leave (surfacing in the South Pacific) check out an unusual aural phenomenon: If you stand on one end of the glass walkway and whisper, someone at the opposite end will hear you as clearly as if you were whispering into their ear. (So watch your language.) To keep this glass world out of the devil's clutches, it is safely housed within the Christian Science Publishing Society building. This unique sphere is constructed from 608 concave pieces of glass held together by a bronze frame. Each panel, covering ten degrees of latitude and longitude, is externally illuminated. Clocks circle the globe so you can compare time zones. Considered an original work of art, the "Mapparium" was designed by Chester Lindsay Churchill, architect of the building that contains it. The "why" of this colorful curiosity is a little elusive, but we might say the same about the world it represents.

Christian Science Center
175 Huntington Ave.
Boston, MA 02115

Phone: (617) 450-3793, ext. 7000, or (617) 450-7330
www.tfccs.com/GV/TMC/TOURS/Mapparium.html

Hours: Tuesday–Saturday, 10 A.M.–9 P.M., Sunday, 11:30 A.M.–4 P.M. Closed holidays.

NOTE: While you're on the premises, why not tour the rest of the Publishing Society and visit The Mother Church, The First Church of Christ, Scientist, in Boston, built in 1894. It contains one of the world's largest pipe organs made out of 13,595 pipes. The large reflecting pool in the plaza outside the church is a pleasant spot to sit and collect your thoughts.

Free admission.

Wheelchair accessible.

Boston, Massachusetts

Ether Dome

Most of us have never been in a room like this. If we've seen such a place, it was probably in one of the old Hammer horror films—something about diabolical medical experimentation or the terrible trio of Burke, Hare, and Dr. Knox. But here—in this dome atop the Bulfinch Building at Massachusetts General Hospital—a medical miracle happened: Anesthesia was used in surgery for the first time. And pain was conquered. Prior to that day in 1846—when the best surgeons were the fastest—operations had indeed been the stuff of horror movies. More like the Spanish Inquisition than medicine, surgery involved unendurable pain so it was always kept as a last, desperate resort. But this chamber has been in use since 1821; its acoustically contoured walls have heard many screams. Between 1821 and 1868, more than eight thousand operations were performed here. Today the hospital has restored the Ether Dome to the way it was, an early nineteenth-century operating theater. By design it was placed at the top of the building for unobstructed sunlight. The steep, multi-tiered rows of seats were to facilitate observation. On display you'll see an array of antique medical instruments—including a saw and a selection of products from the

American Cystoscope Makers—that will make you glad to be part of the twenty-first century. Incongruously, and for reasons we cannot fathom, also displayed is a statue of Apollo crafted in the Louvre, and, of all things, an Egyptian mummy (with exposed head) complete with sarcophagus. You can't miss the graphic—some might say grisly—painting of the memorable operation on the wall. And of course there's a skeleton. Visiting the Ether Dome is a very atmospheric experience. It's like stepping back two hundred years . . . or into a horror film.

Bulfinch Building
Massachusetts General Hospital
55 Fruit St.
Boston, MA 02114

Phone: (617) 726-2861
neurosurgery.mgh.harvard.edu/bulfinch.htm

Location: The Ether Dome is at the very top of the historic Bulfinch Building, which is part of the main hospital. Once you're inside, just follow the signs. To arrive by subway, get off at "Government Center." Exit the station onto Cambridge Street. Turn left, going north on Cambridge Street. Mass General is a ten-minute walk. When you reach North Grove Street, turn left.

Free admission.

Wheelchair accessible.

Boston, Massachusetts

A Hole Man

In 1848, Phineas Gage, a respected railroad foreman in Cavendish, Vermont, met with a ghastly accident. While packing some blasting powder into the hole in a rock ledge, the powder ignited, blowing the three-foot, thirteen-pound tamping rod into his skull. It penetrated his cheek, passed through the roof of his mouth, burst out the top of his head, and rocketed fifty feet into the air. Co-workers thought Mr. Gage was a goner for sure. Miraculously, he wasn't even knocked out. His crew carried him to the doctor's office where the wound was cleaned of tissue and bone. The prognosis wasn't good: No one could survive such damage to the skull and brain. Another miracle: Mr. Gage lived, though his left eye was irreparably damaged. But he had changed. He turned from a well-liked and reliable railroad employee into an impulsive, foul-mouthed, and combative reprobate. Now virtually unemployable, he supported himself by joining P. T. Barnum's freak show. Then he moved to Chile to drive a stagecoach. He died at his mother's home in San Francisco twelve years after the accident. Since his death, Phineas Gage has become renowned in scientific circles because his injury proved that the connection between brain and behavior is, in fact, physical. You can view his death mask, the tamping rod, and the poor man's skull at the Warren Anatomical Museum of Harvard University.

NOTE: Additional information about Phineas Gage may be found at the Phineas Gage Information page by Malcolm Macmillan at <www.deakin.edu.au/hbs/gagepage>.

Dr. Warren's Museum

Phineas is our favorite resident of the Warren Anatomical Museum, which houses more than a few of our favorite things. It all began in the late eighteenth century with Dr. John Warren instructing young physicians at his home in Boston. He'd demonstrate surgical techniques on cadavers, tossing limbs here and there, turning the ground floor of his residence into a veritable charnel house. But human remains were not always available, so he began to assemble a variety of healthy and diseased body parts to use as teaching tools. For a while his acquisitions filled a whole building on Boylston Street; his museum may have been the greatest curiosity on the east coast. Eventually, it even included a box containing Dr. Warren's own skeleton, though only his family was permitted to see it. The entire collection still exists, but for reasons we can only surmise, most of it is in storage and may stay there for as long as New England remains Puritan. Its emaciated remains may be seen in several display cases referred to as "The Warren Exhibition Gallery" on the fifth floor of the Countway Library of Medicine. Among the odd, uncommon, and even disturbing medical and anatomical exotica you can see: chilling Civil War–era surgical equipment in decorative cases, trephining equipment and a trephined encephalitic skull, a watercolor of an arm with gangrene, a dried arm with hand, several types of anatomical models made of various materials including papier-mâché and wax, a selection of French model-eyes showing various afflictions, the skeletons of conjoined (Siamese) twins, a sailor's skull with a small cannonball lodged in it, the deformed skeleton of a woman who had rickets, a twelve-week old fetal skeleton in a glass dome, and a swatch of human skin with a clipper ship tattooed on it. None of this is weird, the librarian assures us. They prefer the term "unusual." Maybe the weird stuff is still in storage.

Warren Anatomical Museum
 Countway Library of Medicine
 Rare Books and Special Collections
 10 Shattuck St.
 Boston, MA 02115

Phone: (617) 432-6196
 www.countway.harvard.edu
 www.countway.med.harvard.edu/rarebooks/warren_museum/warren.html

Location: The Warren Museum is on the fifth floor of the Countway Library of Medicine. Its entrance is at the end of Shattuck Street. The nearest MBTA "T" stop is at Brigham Circle on the Green line "E" Train. From there, cross Huntington Avenue toward the Kresge School of Public Health and walk down the short flight of stairs leading to a large plaza. The library is on the left.

Hours: Monday–Friday, 9 A.M.–5 P.M.

Free admission.

Wheelchair accessible.

Marble Phantoms

Who would look for riddles in the Massachusetts State House? But there, in the Hall of Flags and elsewhere, a series of bewildering ghosts and apparitions has been appearing for years, apparently all on their own. Visitors can readily see spectral portraits emerging from veins of Italian marble on pillars and panels. The figures are uncannily lifelike and completely recognizable. There's a life-sized likeness of "The Bride in White" with raised arms and a veil covering her long hair. "The Athlete" stands just outside the Hall of Flags, his muscles tense and ready for action. We wonder if that pair is somehow responsible for the "Naked Baby" who's not far away. Like Iago lurking nearby, we find the romantic "Kissing Cavalier" and a likeness of poet and abolitionist William Cullen Bryant. There is a ghostly menagerie that includes an English bulldog with a studded collar and protruding teeth, a mule, a pig, a rabbit, and a little hen with a chick underneath her wing. The strange figures were first observed by Henry G. Weston, a Civil War veteran who worked for many years as a State House guide. Neither he nor anyone else has been able to explain them or why such a concentration of anomalous apparitions should appear in one place.

Location: The Massachusetts State House is on Beacon Street at the head of Park Street (Subway stop: Park Street). Look for the large golden dome.

Phone: (617) 727-3676
www.iboston.org./buildings/card/statehouse.htm

Hours: Open Monday–Friday, 10 A.M.–4 P.M.

Free admission.

Wheelchair accessible.

Museum of Dirt

It may come as no surprise that Boston has a museum of dirt—and we don't mean pornography. The idea took root after founder and multimedia designer Glenn Johanson visited the Liberace museum in Las Vegas. Surprised that he couldn't find a decent souvenir, he still wanted some sort of memento. So he did the logical thing: took some soil from the parking lot. Now he's the proud owner of an avalanche—a whole roomful of earthy specimens: dust from Pearl Harbor, lava from Mount St. Helens, compost from Julia Child's garden, and more. Over forty samples of foreign soils are represented here, including bits from the Berlin Wall, sand from Australia's Great Barrier Reef, elephant dung from Kenya, ash from Mount Fuji, and debris from the Great Wall of China. Each is neatly contained in little glass jars and displayed around the lobby of Mr. Johanson's company, Planet Interactive. He has a unique way of getting the dirt on celebrities: He writes and asks them for it. Contributions have come in from the likes of Bob Hope, Ted Turner, and Vanna White, the smiling letter-spinner on *Wheel of Fortune.* Sadly, Prince Charles declined, saying he didn't have any. Donations of interesting dirt are heartily welcomed, but Mr. Johanson is getting selective. At this point the only soil Planet Interactive lacks may be extraterrestrial.

NOTE: The Museum of Dirt is closed until further notice.

Science Museum

Boston's state-of-the-art Science Museum is a mecca for kids, who swarm through its turnstiles in a cacophony of mega-decibel shrieks. Two of its top attractions are the virtual fish tank, where you can use computers to create your own fish, and the anatomical room on the second floor, where you can contemplate your own innards in a playroom full of toy-like body parts. It's all good clean fun and just what you'd expect in a kid-friendly environment: educational, non-toxic, upbeat, politically perfect. So we were more than a little surprised to look into a glass case near the anatomy room and discover a parade of ghastly birth defects. Poised in life-like plaster models was a hand missing a finger, a hand with six fingers (the math seems to work), a middle finger split in two, stunted fingers, and a hand with a "floating thumb" sprouting out of the wrist. An illustrated panel treated the subject of webbed fingers and clubbed hands, and how the wonders of medical science can now repair them through surgery. These developmental nightmares were exhibited in plain sight, some of them too awful to contemplate. And in a museum for sweet, innocent kids! Here we'd come to a children's paradise, only to be assaulted with this brutal anatomical display. You'd think the kids would be clustered around, gawking at the exhibits right along with us. But no, not a single one was there. They were all too deeply absorbed in something far more menacing—computers.

The Museum of Science
Science Park
Boston, MA 02114

Phone: (617) 723-2500
information@mos.org
www.mos.org

Location: From I-93 south, take exit 26A (28 North, Leverett Circle and Cambridge). Go left off the ramp at the traffic light. At the next light, turn right onto O'Brien Highway. The Museum will be on your left. The parking garage is at the far end of the building. By subway, take the Lechmere Green line train to the Science Park stop. The Museum is two hundred yards from Science Park station, but the station itself is not wheelchair accessible.

Hours: Open daily except Thanksgiving and Christmas, 9 A.M.–5 P.M. (On Christmas Eve it closes at 2 P.M.) July 5–Labor Day, hours are extended to 7 P.M., 9 P.M. on Fridays. Occasionally the museum closes without warning for special events, so call to double-check.

NOTE: To avoid traffic disruptions caused by the Big Dig, you might call the museum at (617) 723-2500 for updated directions.

Admission charged.

Wheelchair accessible.

Boston, Massachusetts

Skinny House

City living can get cramped, but this is ridiculous. At 44 Hull Street in Boston's historic north end is a house so skinny that it might be called anorexic. At just ten feet wide and thirty feet deep, it is Boston's tiniest wooden house. And if you think ten feet is skinny, walk to the back, where it tapers to a mere thirty-six inches. Looking from the street, you might wonder how to enter. Well, the door is at the front of the house, which is in the narrow alleyway at left. With real estate priced the way it is, squished property is better than none at all. But space wasn't this scarce in the eighteenth century, so why so thin? According to one legend, it all boils down to spite. In colonial times, Joseph Eustus is said to have inherited the land from his father. Trouble was, his brother inherited more, and had a sizable homestead built while Joseph was away. The meager strip left over was hardly enough to bother with, so he assumed Joseph would lose interest and forget it. But he assumed wrong.

Joseph erected four stories, enough to efficiently eclipse his deceitful brother's view of Boston Harbor. The four floors are connected by a narrow, steep staircase, and ceilings are low, just six feet four inches on the top floor. Today that floor is the master bedroom. It holds a queen-sized bed, because that is the largest that would fit. The bed was too big to haul up the stairs, so its frame was sawed in half, hoisted through the back window, and permanently reassembled. There on the top floor overlooking the old graveyard, it has found its final resting place, and for a very good reason: It's stuck.

Location: The skinny house is at 44 Hull Street, almost directly across from the entrance gate to Copp's Hill Burying Ground on the Freedom Trail. The burying ground is Boston's second-oldest (1659), open daily 9 A.M.–5 P.M. (until 3 P.M. in winter).

NOTE: The skinny house is a skinny private home, so please keep your distance.

Boston, Massachusetts

Skinny Tome

The very dignified Boston Athenaeum Library holds one of the most curious treasures in all of New England, though we suspect they are not eager to talk about it. According to one of their own publications (*Athenaeum Items* February 1944), "it looks as innocent as a Book of Psalms." But there is nothing innocent about this inconspicuous little volume. It is the autobiography of a notorious highwayman named George Walton (A.K.A. James Allen, A.K.A. Jonas Pierce, A.K.A. James H. York, A.K.A. Burley Grove, etc.). It's bound in what appears to be a grayish leather, but is in fact human skin. Stranger still, it's the skin of its author. The Athenaeum fact sheet notes, "These gruesome facts relating to the outside of the book are matched by its lurid contents."

Mr. Walton, "a Jamaica mulatto," earned his bad reputation from a career as a burglar, bank robber, horse thief, and highwayman. But it all came to an end in 1833 when he made the mistake of attacking John Fenno Jr. of Springfield, Massachusetts. Mr. Fenno was shot during the struggle, but fortunately survived, leading to George Walton's arrest. In prison Mr. Walton penned his infamous tome. To recognize Mr. Fenno's bravery, he requested that Mr. Fenno be given a copy of "The Highwayman" bound in the author's skin.

Mr. Walton died on July 17, 1837. His body was transported to Massachusetts General Hospital for anatomical study. There his gruesome wish was honored. They removed skin from his back and cured it to resemble gray deerskin. Bookbinder Peter Low had no idea what he was working with. By the time the deed was done, however, Mr. Low was experiencing extreme distress and, his grandson reported, "nightmares filled the night that followed."

The book was donated to the Athenaeum by a descendant of John Fenno, where it remains the most bizarre of their 500,000-plus volumes.

According to Head of Reference Stephen Z. Nonack, "This curiosity is not normally available to visitors and I do not know if there are plans to exhibit it [in the future]."

The Boston Athenaeum
  10½ Beacon Street
  Boston, MA 02108

Phone: (617) 227-0270
  info@bostonathenaeum.org
  www.bostonathenaeum.org/

Hours: Monday 9 A.M.–7 P.M., Tuesday–Friday, 9 A.M.–5 P.M., Saturday 9 A.M.–2 P.M.

Free admission.

Wheelchair accessible.

Steeple Flyer

Who flew first? The Wright Brothers at Kitty Hawk? Gustave Whitehead of Bridgeport, Connecticut? Or some unknown aviation pioneer? Whoever it was, we assume it happened around the turn of the twentieth century. So what are we to make of a puzzling plaque mounted on a brick wall near the Old North Church in Boston? It says, "Here on September 13, 1757, John Childs—who had given public notice of his intention to fly from the steeple of Dr. Cutler's church—performed it to the satisfaction of a great number of spectators." The plaque is there for anyone to see. What it conspicuously fails to mention is that the next day, September 14, Mr. Childs did it again—two more times. Writer James Chenoweth researched the event in Boston newspapers. According to a September 1757 issue of the *Boston News Letter*, a reporter, who apparently witnessed the second day's event, claims Mr. Childs "set off with two pistols loaded, one of which he discharged in his descent; the other missing fire, he cocked and snapped again before he reached the Place prepared to receive him." The *News Letter* said Mr. Childs landed on a slope about seven hundred feet from the steeple. Each flight took approximately sixteen to eighteen seconds. But the most important of the newspaper's omissions is this: It doesn't say *how* Mr. Childs accomplished his astonishing feat. The colonial aviator subsequently seems to have soared right out of New England history, leaving us with an interesting puzzle. Remember, this all took place about twenty years before the American Revolution. So, presuming Mr. Childs wasn't an angel, just how could he, a man in the America of 1757, take to the air . . . and fly?

Old North Church
193 Salem St.
Boston, MA 02113

Phone: (617) 523-6676
    church@oldnorth.com
    www.oldnorth.com

Location: The plaque is the third one from the left on a brick wall facing the church to the left of its main entrance. The church is at the Haymarket subway stop on the Green or Orange line. It is at the east end of Hull Street.

Hours: Open daily, 9 A.M.–5 P.M.

NOTE: The Old North Church itself is an oddity when you consider that over eleven hundred bodies are buried in the cellar, including the nameless victims of colonial shipwrecks.

Admission: a donation.

Wheelchair accessible.

Cambridge, Massachusetts

Ant Collection

When you talk about insectomania probably nothing surpasses Harvard's Museum of Comparative Zoology, which boasts the world's largest collection of ants. More than a million of the tiny (and not so tiny) critters are glued onto diminutive white display triangles or preserved in alcohol. Some thirteen thousand species have been identified by Edmund O. Wilson and his students, assistants, and predecessors. One species was named in his honor, the Lepto thorax wilsoni, found only on New Hampshire's Mount Monadnock. The longest in the collection is the Indonesian Carpenter Ant, at almost three inches. The smallest is the Atomicus, at less than half a millimeter. Dr. Wilson discovered several species encased in Miocene Dominican amber. North America is still being scoured by antophiles bent on discovering new types of Formicidae to bear their names (as if thirteen thousand species weren't enough).

The Harvard Museum of Comparative Zoology
    26 Oxford St.
    Cambridge, MA 02138

Phone: (617) 495-3045
   hmnh@oeb.harvard.edu
   www.mcz.harvard.edu/

Location: The museum is housed in Harvard's Museum of Natural History, where the Blaschka glass flowers are. Entrances are at 26 Oxford Street and 11 Divinity Avenue. (Subway stop: Harvard.)

Hours: The ant collection can only be viewed by appointment. The Museum is open daily 9 A.M.–5 P.M., closed January 1, July 4, Thanksgiving Day, and December 25.

Admission charged.

Wheelchair accessible.

Cambridge, Massachusetts

The Glass Garden

In a special climate-controlled room of this large museum you'll find a real international oddity: case upon case upon case of intricate botanical specimens. The flowers, plants, insects, and fruits—even the rotted, disease-ridden figs—are created entirely from glass. Yet nothing about them looks "glassy," and that's the wonder of it; if you didn't know better you'd swear they were real, somehow magically flourishing without soil or water. A closer look and you'll realize that each labeled piece is extraordinarily complex, usually life-sized but in some cases magnified hundreds of times. A speck of pollen is the size of a golf ball. An oversized sprig of sage is invaded by a brobdingnagian bumble bee who looks like a terrifying mutant from a sci-fi film. Who on earth would devote the time, patience, and nearly superhuman skill it must have taken to create such things? And so many of them! A display in an adjoining room explains the mystery, at least in part. It turns out the models—over three thousand in all—were the work of a nineteenth-century father and son team, Leopold and Rudolph Blaschka, master Bohemian glassmakers working near Dresden, Germany. Harvard had commissioned the glass replicas as study aids in the days before photography, and they're still used as such. What the museum can't tell you is how they were made. It seems that Rudolph and his father, having spent their entire lives creating these glass wonders, went to their graves without ever revealing the technique.

Blaschka Glass Flower Collection
Harvard Museum of Natural History
26 Oxford St.
Cambridge, MA 02138

Phone: (617) 495-3045
emccourt@oeb.harvard.edu
www.hmnh.harvard.edu

Location: The flowers are on the second floor in a separate room of the red brick museum building.

Hours: Open Monday–Sunday, 9 A.M.–5 P.M. Closed holidays.

NOTE: The glass reproductions of stricken fruits and monstrous bugs with lethal stingers should not be missed, but may be displayed separately. If you don't see them, ask. Also, many people don't realize that the Blaschkas' first Harvard project was the creation of glass models of marine invertebrates for the neighboring Museum of Comparative Zoology. The marine models, too, are on public display and are well worth checking out. In fact, they inspired the commission for the flowers. What's really staggering is to contemplate the sheer number of models these men created.

ALSO NOTE: This is not a place for small kids. They'll be bored. One of the flowers was shattered by a sonic boom, so imagine the impact a distracted youngster could have.

Admission charged.

Cambridge, Massachusetts

MIT's Wonder Museum

The Massachusetts Institute of Technology's museum is a wonder of special effects and twenty-first-century gadgetry—

but who would expect anything less? At the time of our visit there was a display of kinetic sculptures by Arthur Ganson, a visiting professor. Each is a moving machine, whimsical and inventive, expressing the articulate humor of a scientific genius. In one, a walking wishbone pulls a metal contraption along a conveyer belt, step by laborious step. Are we watching a metaphor of the human condition? Many of the pieces require you to step on a pedal or turn a crank, suggesting humanity is in charge (but don't bet on it). This, however, is just a warm-up. In the next room is "The Shadow Wall," a magical device that allows you to walk away from your own shadow, then watch it fade into nothingness. You'll also see Harold Edgerton's split-second photography, which is on permanent display. The late MIT scientist used a stroboscopic flash to produce mesmerizing stills of matter hurling through space; his badminton birdie piercing an apple is just a sampling. If you're not yet on overload, don't miss the wonders of the world's largest and most comprehensive hologram collection, showing early pieces from the late 1940s through today's mind-boggling sci-fi effects. The holograms' three-dimensional subjects look so real they could almost bite you. In "Kiss I," a 180-degree multiplex, a woman watches you, gestures, and puckers up for a kiss. "Tigirl" is an unsettling animated hybrid of girl and tiger. And "The Lindow Man" is the corpse of a two-thousand-year-old man discovered in a bog in England. This three-dimensional image makes you feel as if you're standing at the autopsy table. The MIT Museum just doesn't hold back, which is why it's irresistible.

The MIT Museum
Main Exhibition Center
265 Massachusetts Ave.
Cambridge, MA 02139–4307

Phone: (617) 253-4444
museum@mit.edu
web.mit.edu/museum

Location: It is in Cambridge, north of Boston, where Central Square intersects with Front Street. From Boston, take the number 1 bus to the NECCO Factory stop. By subway, take the Red line to Central Square and walk down Massachusetts Avenue toward the center of Boston for about seven minutes. The museum is on the left.

Hours: Open Tuesday–Friday, 10 A.M.–5 P.M., Saturdays and Sundays, noon– 5 P.M.

Admission charged.

Wheelchair accessible.

Cambridge, Massachusetts

Useless Research

What do you do when a recognized scientist produces research that stinks? If you're the Massachusetts Institute of Technology, you chuck it—into the Archives of Useless Research. Since about 1940, when it received the file as a donation, MIT's Hayden Library has kept six file boxes full of what appears to be rambling nonsense. The treatises of Seabury Doane Brewer, for example, include the startling revelation "that temperature, with its variations, is one of the most wonderful things, and is always present everywhere," and "that physicians should be compelled to destroy all unfit specimens of humanity immediately upon their birth." (What about unfit scientists?) Instead of contributing to the existing body of knowledge, most of the rants simply attack previous breakthroughs. One of them is a paper issued in 1929 by George F. Gillette, "Orthod Oxen of Science." There is "no ox so dumb as the orthodox," he writes. These "built up favorites of publishers" are "the reverse of true scientists, . . . cramped with Homoplania, ignorant of ultimotically related sub and supraplanias." The paper characterizes Einstein's theory of relativity as the "moronic brain child of mental colic," and proceeds to set the record straight on physics: "In all the cosmos there is naught but straight-flying bumping, caroming and again straight flying. Phenomena are but lumps, jumps, and bumps. A mass unit's career is but lumping, jumping, bumping, rejumping, rebumping, and finally unlumping." Kathy Marquis, the former reference archivist who actually read some of the papers, noticed that most of them fall into one of three categories: an uncomfortable attempt to mix science with religion, indignant criticism of a successful peer, or a misguided effort to solve the world's problems in a single generalization. The documents date from 1900, but MIT put a stop to the collection in 1965. They probably just ran out of space.

The Archive of Useless Research
MIT Institute Archives and Special Collections
Hayden Library, Room 14N-118
77 Massachusetts Ave.
Cambridge, MA 02139-4307

Phone: (617) 253-5136
mithistory@mit.edu
libraries.mit.edu/archives/

Location: The file is in the Special Collections of Hayden Library, although stored off-site. It is collection number MC187, which is not accessible online. To see it, go in person and ask for the "finding aid" listing its contents.

Hours: Open Monday–Friday, 11 A.M.–4:30 P.M., except holidays. Morning hours by appointment.

Wheelchair accessible.

Chester, Massachusetts

Hiram's Tomb

As it says in an old account, "A certain farmer of the region, Hiram Smith by name, did not take kindly to the idea of being buried in the ground . . . " His specific reasons may be lost to history, but one can imagine: insects, worms, grave robbers, whatever. One story holds that Mr. Smith saw his parents' graves get washed away during a terrible flooding of the West-field River; he was determined his corpse would suffer no sim-ilar fate. To put his mind at ease, Mr. Smith had a very special tomb commissioned. First, he discovered a large boulder high on a ridge, well away from any flood water. It's the size of a cabin, roughly ten feet high by thirty feet wide. Then he had its face smoothed on one side and had two coffin-sized cavities hewn into the solid rock. When his time came, Mr. Smith's stone sepulcher was sealed up with slabs of the original stone. And there you may read the original inscriptions: Hiram Smith, died 1873; Sarah Toogood, died 1869. We're not sure if Ms. Toogood was Hiram's wife or sister, but we're just happy to know he won't be spending eternity trapped in that rock alone.

Location: The site is on Maynard Hill Road in Chester, Massachusetts. From the intersection of Crane Road take Maynard Hill Road four-tenths of a mile and you will see a logging road on the right. The trail to the tomb branches off in a southerly direction. It is roughly a ten-minute walk. The Hiram Smith tombstone is right on the trail.

Dedham, Massachusetts

Museum of Bad Art

What is the punishment for bad art? For some it's perma-nent obscurity, for others, perhaps, it's eternal banishment to this garish gallery of "art too bad to be ignored." Located downstairs in a somewhat ramshackle movie theater, this mu-seum seeks to preserve what many would like to abolish. In fact, their seminal piece, "Lucy in the Field with Flowers," was rescued from a trash can. Since then the museum has grown—or make that "groan." We understand their art for art's sake philosophy, but perhaps it's overkill that you have to enter via the theater's men's room. The immediate olfactory impression speaks eloquently of things to come. Each of the one hundred or so pieces is bad in a unique way. While some are clearly the work of disturbed personalities, others simply demonstrate the efforts of people whose skills are losing a race with their vision. Others, though devoid of competence altogether, have a certain *je ne sais quoi*. Techniques range from the sophisticated "pointillistic" (thousands of tiny dots—a style acquired, perhaps, from watching too much TV) to the flamboyant and aggressive crayon on canvas. One favorite seems to be *Sunday on the Pot With George*, a portrait of a middle-aged, moderately distinguished-looking man wearing BVDs and crouching. We can't determine just what he's doing, but we can imagine if we must. Another is *Faith in Numbers*, a board with a phone book stuck to it. Perhaps the next artist was possessed by the spirit of a Picasso wannabe to render such an oddity as *Pablo Presley:* It shows a Latin-looking Elvis in a green lounge-lizard jacket. And there's *The Athlete*, a crayon-on-canvas celebration of the naked male form, adorned with discus, white socks, and wingtips. At this point not all of MOBA's acquisitions are coming from trash cans, flea markets, and dumpsters. People are submitting work for consideration and most of it is rejected. Imagine the indignity! It's not enough to say these paintings are bad, you really have to see them for yourself. And—art critics that we are—we say it is worth the trip.

Museum of Bad Art
580 High St.
Dedham, MA 02026
Mailing Address: 10 Vogel St., Boston, MA 02132

Phone: (617) 325-8224
moba@world.std.com
www.glyphs.com/moba

Location: Once you've attained downtown Dedham, the museum is easy to find. Look for the Dedham Community Theater and follow your nose to the Men's Room.

Hours: Open Monday–Friday, 6:30–10:30 P.M., and 1:30–10:30 P.M. on Saturday, Sunday, and holidays.

Free admission.

Fall River, Massachusetts

Lizzie Borden

Lizzie's House

The local Chamber of Commerce might not agree, but the best reason to visit Fall River is Lizzie Borden—or at least what remains of her. Can anyone not know the story of this thirty-two-year-old spinster accused of ax-murdering her parents on August 4, 1892? Her guilt—and the number of whacks—is still disputed, but you can visit the crime scene and speculate for yourself. The actual house where the Borden bashing took place is now lovingly restored to its 1892 splendor, complete but for the blood stains. Bizarre as it may sound, the proprietors run it as a Bed and Breakfast. You can sleep (maybe) in Lizzie's room or in the room where Lizzie's stepmother was butchered. Or you can simply take one of the tours of their small museum where you'll see, among other things, artifacts that belonged to the Borden family and the dress Elizabeth Montgomery wore in the movie *The Legend of Lizzie Borden*. It is no surprise that this haunted house is said to have a ghost; he (or she) stomps around and messes with doors and lights. Be sure to ask your hosts, Martha McGinn and Simone J. Evans, so you won't miss any of the other murder memorabilia in town.

The Lizzie Borden Bed and Breakfast/Museum
92 Second St.
Fall River, MA 02721

Phone: (508) 675-7333
lizziebnb@lizzie-borden.com
www.lizzie-borden.com

NOTE: There's also a gift shop where you can acquire such heirloom quality items as an authentic brick from the Borden home chimney, a sweatshirt with Lizzie's face on it, an ax key chain (engraved "Lizzie"), a copy of Lizzie's will, a custom-made replica of the Borden House, even a comic book of the Borden tragedy. Do your Christmas shopping early.

Fall River Historical Society

Not tired of Lizzie? Want more gore? Check out—in fact don't miss—the bloody Borden bonanza at the local historical society. It's the world's largest collection of artifacts relating to the life and trial of Miss Lizzie A. Borden. Like one of the jurors in the 1893 courtroom, you can consider actual physical evidence from the trial, such as a bloodstained camisole, a blood-splattered bedspread, and "hairs taken from hatchet." Or if these seem too grisly, examine Mr. Borden's skull (he was buried headless), and the hatchet said to have smashed it. If all this is not antiseptic enough, perhaps you'd like to confine yourself to just the crime scene photos, including Mrs. Borden dead on her bed and Mr. Borden faceless on the couch. If this doesn't motivate you to spend a night at the Lizzie Borden Bed and Breakfast, nothing will.

The Fall River Historical Society
451 Rock St.
Fall River, MA 02720

Phone: (508) 679-1071
www.lizzieborden.org/

Location: Find President Avenue and follow it until it turns onto Rock Street. The museum is a granite building with a wrought-iron fence.

Hours: April–mid-November, Tuesday–Friday, 9 A.M.–4:30 P.M. Tour hours: 9, 10, 11, 1, 2, 3. Saturday and Sunday, 1–5 P.M. Tour hours: 1, 2, 3, 4. Open Mondays in December. Closed Mondays, holidays, and the months of January, February, and March.

NOTE: "The Mourning Room" offers a look at nineteenth-century practices of mourning the dead. There's a wide range of cheerless artifacts, from clothing, needlework, and jewelry to postmortem photographs, portraits, and other memorial pieces.

Admission charged.

More Lizzie

—Lizzie was born July 19, 1860, at her grandfather's house at 12 Ferry Street. It is no longer there.

—She was a member in good standing of the First Congregational Church at 282 Rock Street, not far from her home.

—Lizzie was held for ten months at the Taunton Jail until her acquittal, June 20, 1893, at which time she was free to enjoy her substantial inheritance.

—She purchased a mansion that she named "Maplecroft." It is at 306 French Street. She lived there until she died. Now, too, it is a bed and breakfast.

—The whole Borden clan is reunited at the Oak Grove Cemetery at 765 Prospect Street. Lizzie's father, Andrew Borden, lies headless under a stone that says simply, "A.J.B." Lizzie's birth mother, Sarah, rests on one side of him, Abby (also headless) on the other. Lizzie is there too. She died at age sixty-eight on June 2, 1927. Her entire body lies under the stone marked "Lizbeth."

—And the heads? Andrew and Abby Borden's heads were removed by the coroner and shipped off to Harvard for examination. Mr. Borden's skull may be seen at the historical society. Mrs. Borden seems to have lost hers.

—And for those of you with a yen for the immensely trivial, Lizzie's dogs are buried in Pine Ridge Cemetery, 238 Pine Street, Dedham, Massachusetts. Named Laddie Miller, Royal Nelson, and Donald Stewart, they're all buried in a single grave with a stone bearing the their names and the words "Sleeping Awhile."

Maplecroft Bed and Breakfast and Museum
(Home of Lizzie Borden, 1893–1927)
306 French St.
Fall River, MA 02720

Phone: (508) 673-8088

Hours: Tours daily 11 A.M.–3 P.M. or by appointment.

Fall River, Massachusetts

Mini Titanic

If you can't get enough of the *Titanic*, a quick stop at this Marine Museum is probably in order. They exhibit a large selection of the Titanic Historical Society's extensive collection. Much of it is exactly as you'd imagine—a wooden chaise lounge, a life ring, a section of deck railing, and other waterlogged wonders. But the thing that will make your visit worthwhile is the twenty-eight-foot, one-ton replica that was created in exact detail by Twentieth Century Fox for the 1953 film *Titanic*. It is thirty-seven inches wide and seven feet high and it is designed to sink, whereas its prototype was designed not to (the model went down twenty-two times). When you're finished pondering pre-computer generated special effects, there are a few other novelties to check out: about 150 scale-model ships, including a replica of the *Bounty* on loan from Ted Turner, a thirty-nine-inch version of the *Andrea Doria*, and some nasty shipboard peacekeeping devices, among them a metal whip, brass knuckles, blackjacks, leg shackles, and hand-cuffs. There's something about it all that may put you off ocean voyages. (See also *Titanic Museum*, Springfield, Massachusetts.)

The Marine Museum
  70 Water St.
  Battleship Cove

Phone: (508) 674-3533
  staff@marinemuseum.org
  www.marinemuseum.org/

Location: The museum is on the waterfront. From the town of Fall River, try to get on Davol Street and follow it to Battleship Cove. There are small blue and white directional signs to help you find your way.

Hours: Monday–Friday, 9 A.M.–5 P.M., Saturday, noon–5 P.M., Sunday, noon–4 P.M.

Admission charged.

Wheelchair accessible.

Gloucester, Massachusetts

Abbadia Mare

Wealthy, brilliant, and more than a tad strange, John Hays Hammond indulged a life-long fantasy and, in 1929, built himself a castle. More than that, really, he built himself a world. Here he lived, worked, and entertained. Christened *Abbadia Mare*, his medieval monument on Cape Ann's rugged coast is full of eccentric gadgetry, visual jokes, and historical oddities. For example, he displays the skull of one of Christopher Columbus's mariners and has a wall constructed from ancient Roman tombstones. In true world-builder fashion, he was able to control the weather in his indoor courtyard with a subtly concealed system of pipes. He could create rain, from an eerie mist to a torrential downpour. An adjustable lighting system determines the time of day, from pale moonlight to blistering sunshine. Mr. Hammond made his fortune as an inventor, specializing in wireless communication devices. And, perhaps oddly for a scientist, he was fascinated with Spiritualism. One wonders if these two interests merged within the gothic confines of his castle. The place is said to be haunted. This question is often asked, "Did he invent some way to communicate from beyond the grave?" Perhaps not, but he is present just the same in his whispering gallery, his vanishing doorways, and the gigantic pipe organ eight stories high. There is even a statue of Mr. Hammond himself, in the nude, keeping an eye on things.

Hammond Castle
    80 Hesperus Ave.
    Gloucester, MA 01930

Phone: (978) 283-7673
    www.hammondcastle.org

Location: From Route 128, take exit 14 onto Route 133 east (Essex Avenue) toward Gloucester. At Gloucester Harbor, turn right onto Route 127 south (Western Avenue), then bear left onto Hesperus Avenue.

Hours: Year round, Monday–Friday, 10 A.M.–6 P.M., Saturday and Sunday, 10 A.M.–3 P.M.

Admission charged.

Gloucester, Massachusetts

Dogtown

Anyone who has enjoyed Sherlock Holmes stories may remember Sir Arthur Conan Doyle's vivid descriptions of the desolate Grimpen Mire from *The Hound of the Baskervilles*. It was a bleak, scary place—a place to be shunned. Perhaps the closest thing to it that New England has to offer is a section of Gloucester known as "Dogtown." This wild lonely heath with its numerous geological monstrosities evokes a sense of evil and mystery. It is one of the few New England places where werewolves have been reported. And to this day, monsters are still seen. In older, more prosperous times, Dogtown was a village called Cape Ann Common. After the American Revolution it was abandoned. Deserted buildings were taken over by penniless squatters: widows with children, disabled veterans, the elderly, the homeless, and the fallen. Some were said to be witches, like the elderly Lucy George, who would threaten to hex passing oxen in order to extract a toll from their drivers, and Old Peg Wesson, who claimed she could transform herself into a crow. And there was Black Neil Finson, who lived for years in a cellar hole believing pirates had hidden gold there. In time these colorful characters died off or moved on, leaving the decrepit houses to collapse. Soon all that was left were former guard dogs running wild, the namesakes of Dogtown. In later years Roger Babson, self-made millionaire and founder of Babson College, took an interest in the place and tried to change its character. Rather than writing the traditional autobiography, Mr. Babson conveyed his message to mankind in inspirational slogans carved on rocks. They can still be discovered. And while you're exploring this ghost town, see if you can determine the strange fate of James Merry, who died there on September 10, 1892, under very unusual circumstances . . .

Location: Dogtown is big—3,600 acres—so it is easy to get lost unless you have a map (readily available). There are several entrance points. To read Mr. Babson's "Stone Book," take Route 128 from Gloucester to Blackburn Circle. Get off at the "Industrial Park" exit. Proceed a half-mile to the end of the park. Park by the broadcast tower on the left. Walk back behind the tower along the cart-road. Keep to the right where the path forks into an open field. Descend through the trees. A large boulder will instruct you to "Get a Job." This begins the "Babson Boulder Trail."

Sleeper House

John Hays Hammond wasn't the only eccentric to build a castle on Cape Ann. Across the cove that separates Hammond's stone chateau from the town of Gloucester, maverick interior designer Henry Davis Sleeper bought a parcel of land in 1907. He started by building a quaint summer cottage, but as his fortunes grew, so did his architectural ambition. Over the next quarter century his "humble cottage" evolved into a gabled and turreted labyrinth. He enjoyed staying home, where he allowed the decor to follow his whimsy. He salvaged old timbers from historic houses and acquired nautical memorabilia for his in-house maritime museum. His library was a two-story stone edifice called the Norman Book Tower. Rooms were designed around famous writers and historical figures, but it was the secret nooks, crannies, and hidden surprises that made Beauport an eccentric's masterpiece. Two secret staircases allowed him to wave to guests from upstairs, then magically appear on the ground floor among them. During a gathering, he could lean against a spring-loaded door and suddenly vanish from the room. And he enjoyed telling dinner guests that they were dining on a Chinese funeral table. In the Lord Nelson bedroom he startled guests with a concealed mirror, and he surprised visiting actress Helen Hayes by turning her bedroom's windowsill into a miniature stage. From his back porch, which emulated the pilot's cabin of a schooner, he could look across the harbor at the battlements of John Hays Hammond's castle. Ideal neighbors, they would greet each other by blasting classical music over the water at top volume. By the time Henry Davis Sleeper died in 1934 at age fifty-six, his Byzantine abode had grown to forty rooms, twenty-six of which are open to the public.

Beauport—The Sleeper-McCann House
75 Eastern Point Blvd.
Gloucester, MA 01930

Phone: (978) 283-0800
www.spnea.org
www.cape-ann.com/beauport.html

Location: Follow I-95/128 North to end; follow sign for East Gloucester, then go one and a half miles to Eastern Point Boulevard, a private road open only during museum hours. Continue the half mile to the house and park on the left.

Hours: Tours on the hour May 15–September 15, Monday–Friday, 10 A.M.–4 P.M., and September 16–October 15, Monday–Friday, 10 A.M.–4 P.M., Saturday–Sunday 1–4 P.M. Closed Memorial Day, July 4, Labor Day, October 16–May 14, and on summer weekends. Last tour at 4 P.M.

Admission charged.

Goshen, Massachusetts

The Goshen Mystery

Not one of Goshen's one thousand residents can tell you what it is. It has been a mystery since it was discovered, "sodded over," in the late 1800s. Its function and the identity of its builders have left archeologists scratching their heads for almost two centuries. The Goshen Mystery is a sophisticated underground stone structure, a tunnel, constructed without mortar. The main shaft, three and a half feet wide, goes straight down for fifteen feet—but it's not a well. It contains no water, is dug in dense "clay hardpan" soil, and perhaps most vexing, it has horizontal tunnels radiating from the sides. One, flush with the bottom of the main shaft and leading eastward, is about three feet wide, two and a half feet high, and seventy-five feet long! The upper tunnel, which is about waist-level if standing on the bottom, is larger, extending west for about fifteen feet. It may once have been longer, but has since caved in.

In the days of hand-tools, this huge structure containing many tons of stones would have required a phenomenal amount of slow, backbreaking labor. It could never have been created without the first settlers taking note. Yet it is nowhere written about, nor is it mentioned in the area's oral history—even among descendants of the first families. In fact, no one has ever claimed knowledge of its origin or purpose. So what was it? A "den of thieves"? An underground railroad stop? A root cellar? A hideout from the Indians? An abandoned treasure pit? It doesn't seem similar to New England's controversial "ancient Celtic" sites. Whatever it is, or was, locals say "it's always been there."

Location: Goshen is about thirteen miles northwest of Northampton on Route 9. The structure is built into the side of a hill a short distance west of the Goshen Cemetery. Alas, for reasons of safety it has been covered with a large rock, which will help you spot its location but keep you from seeing (or entering) the tunnel. But take heart: There's an exhibit, including pictures, documentation, and a video, at the Goshen town museum, on the main drag, at 13 Main Street.

Hours: Memorial day–Labor day, but only Sundays, 2–4 P.M.

Free admission.

Wheelchair accessible.

Harvard, Massachusetts

Fruitlands Knife Antlers

The Fruitlands Museums are a cluster of historic houses in a scenic part of the Massachusetts countryside, including a Shaker home, a collection of Indian artifacts, and an exhibit about a nineteenth-century Transcendentalist commune whose approach to farming—and just about everything else—was unconventional, to say the least. All three are worth visiting, but if you're short on time and would enjoy a puzzle, go straight to the Indian Museum for what may be the oddest sight of all. What its use or purpose was remains a mystery. It is a set of antlers, probably elk, with each point sharpened into a five- or six–inch knife. If it's a weapon, it would be rather unsettling to watch it hurling towards you. If it's a ritual item, it's probably bogus, as no Indian tribe has recognized it as anything familiar. Most people look at it and scratch their heads. Fruitlands curator Michael Volmar has no idea what it is, but wouldn't dispense with it as it is simply too bizarre. He suspects it's a hoax, one of many counterfeit "Indian artifacts" fabricated during the Depression when certain people would do almost anything to make a buck. There are other fake artifacts in the Indian collection that fall into that category, he says, but don't ask to see them: They're consigned permanently to the back room.

The Fruitlands Museums
   102 Prospect Hill Rd.
   Harvard, MA 01451

Phone: (978) 456-3924
   www.fruitlands.org/

Location: It is about forty miles west of Boston on Route 2.

Hours: Mid-May–mid-October, weekdays, 11 A.M.–4 P.M.; weekends, 11 A.M.–5 P.M.

NOTE: The knife antlers, for lack of a better name, is not always on display, but will be brought out upon request.

Admission charged.

The Indian museum is wheelchair accessible.

Haverhill, Massachusetts

Hannah Duston

This is the city from which Hannah Duston, on March 15, 1697, was abducted by Indians and marched toward Canada and

Colonial heroine Hannah Duston is memorialized in downtown Haverhill, Massachusetts.

Photo: Diane Foulds

eventual slavery. Encamped temporarily on an island in the Merrimack River near Concord, New Hampshire, Mrs. Duston planned her escape. Understandably grief-stricken after the Indians had murdered her infant daughter, and fearing the horrors that awaited her in Canada, Mrs. Duston, her midwife, and fellow captive Samuel Lennardson turned the tables on their captors. While the Indians slept, Mrs. Duston and company dispatched ten of them with tomahawks and removed their scalps. The trio then returned to Haverhill to receive a fifty-pound bounty for the scalps, generous tokens from friends and townspeople, and an audience with Cotton Mather, who recorded the tale. In downtown Haverhill you can see a statue of the town's favored daughter. Its base illustrates four scenes from the ordeal: the capture, Mr. Duston's defense, dispatching the Indians, and the canoe trip home. More intimate mementos of the tale may be viewed at the Haverhill Historical Society, including a piece of Hannah's clothing, a ring, the fatal tomahawk, and the scalping knife.

Haverhill Historical Society
240 Water St.
Haverhill, MA 01830

Phone: (508) 374-4626

Location: Take I-495 to exit 52 Haverhill/Bradford. Take Route 110 west toward Haverhill. Continue 1.7 miles to the first set of lights. Take a left, then an immediate right. Continue one mile to a set of lights, turn left onto Water Street and take the second left, John Ward Avenue. The museum is on the right.

Hours: Winter: Wednesday, Thursday, Saturday and Sunday, 1–4:30 PM. Summer: Hours are subject to change. Call for information.

Location of the statue: Travel on I-495 to exit 50. Turn east on Route 97 (Broadway Street). Continue for about one mile, passing through a small rotary that surrounds a statue of Lafayette. A few blocks later you'll arrive at the Haverhill Common/GAR Park. The statue is on the eastern end, facing the Haverhill Public Library. (See also the *Hannah Duston Memorial* in Boscawen, New Hampshire.)

Admission charged.

Wheelchair accessible.

Holyoke, Massachusetts

Tracking Dinosaurs

A dinosaur just went by! That's the way it looks, anyway; these tracks seem so fresh and clear. Actually they're over 190 million years old. The largest, about thirteen inches long, was probably made by a carnivorous critter around fifteen feet tall, and twenty feet long. For some reason packs of these seemingly social beasts commuted along the riverbank, from where and to where is a mystery. But they've left 134 fossilized footprints for dino enthusiasts to marvel at. Apparently the tracks were left by three types of two-legged beasts, all dating from the late Triassic and early Jurassic periods. The suspects are Eubrontes giganteus, Anchisauripus sillimani, and Grallator cuneatus.

Dinosaur Footprints
   Route 5
   Holyoke, MA

Phone: (413) 684-0148 or (413) 298-3239
   westregion@ttor.org
   www.thetrustees.org (Then do a search for "dinosaur.")

Location: You'll find them on Route 5 along the west bank of the Connecticut River. Going north on I-91, take exit 17A (which is Route 141 east) toward Holyoke. Turn north onto Route 5 and go 2.2 miles. The entrance is on the right. Park off the roadside at the turnout. Going south on I-91, take exit 18 (Route 5) toward Holyoke. Turn south onto Route 5 and go 5.2 miles. Entrance and parking on left. Walk the quarter-mile trail over the boardwalk to the footprints.

Hours: These footprints are accessible April 1–November 30, daily, sunrise–sunset.

NOTE: The area is jointly managed by the Trustees of Reservations, a conservation group, and the Massachusetts Department of Environmental Management. They ask that we all respect these ancient and fragile footprints so future generations may enjoy them, too.

Free admission.

Hudson, Massachusetts

Tiny Church

If you've overdosed on grand churches and colossal cathedrals, the town of Hudson may provide an acceptable antidote—quite possibly the smallest church in the world. It is a real church, all right, with a steeple and bell and everything. Marriages have even been performed there. But its congregation is, by necessity, small. It will hold only four adults. One suspects it was built by a minister lacking ambition (or more likely as a novelty or tourist attraction). Anyway, churches, like souls, can be saved. Apparently this tiny temple had been neglected in recent years, so the First Federated Church moved it to their property where today it may be visited, photographed, and pondered.

Location: Off I-95 west of Boston, follow Route 62 north through town. Where the road splits at a flashing light, bear right onto Central Street. Watch on the left for the First Federated Church. Its adopted sibling is under the trees at the rear of the parking lot.

Indian Orchard, Massachusetts

Titanic Museum

There is nothing titanic about the display space—it's just the back room of Henry's Jewelry Store. It'll only accommodate about six people at a time. But this minuscule museum contains one of the biggest and best private collections of *Titanic* memorabilia in the world. There is probably enough flotsam and jetsam from the *Titanic* to supply a number of museums for a long time, but a lot of the best stuff has washed up here. And nowhere will you find a more appreciative curator. It all grew out of Ed Kamuda's all-consuming interest. In 1958 as a seventeen-year-old boy, he saw the movie *A Night to Remember* and never forgot it. Because his father owned a movie theater, young Ed was privy to a list of *Titanic* survivors, along with contact information. The producers' idea was to get the survivors into theaters to help promote the film. But Ed put his list to better use; he wrote and told them of his passion. Soon people were contributing things to his museum—what else were they going to do with them? In his cramped display quarters you can see tickets, menus with the fatal date on them, telegrams sent from the ship, chairs, bells, diaries, letters from people who survived, letters from people who didn't survive. He even has the telegram warning the *Titanic* about the lethal iceberg. There is carpeting, clothing, signal flags, an original *Titanic* blueprint, and the pièce de résistance, the life vest worn by John Jacob Astor's wife, Madeleine. And don't forget, most of this stuff is "pre-discovery," before the submerged liner was found and excavated. Mr. Kamuda has become a world-class authority on the disaster. If you too are fascinated by the story of the *Titanic* and her era, this museum is a great place to network and trade stories. Even James Cameron conferred with Mr. Kamuda about Cameron's 1997 film, *Titanic*.

The Titanic Museum
208 Main St.
Indian Orchard, MA 01151

Phone: (413) 543-4770
titanicinfo@titanic1.org
www.titanic1.org/

Location: The museum is 7 miles northeast of the center of Springfield. You enter through the front door of Henry's Jewelry Store at 208 Main Street, Indian Orchard, across from the Grand Theater.

Hours: Open Monday–Friday, 10 A.M.–4 P.M., Saturday, 10 A.M.–3 P.M., 11 A.M.–2 P.M. during July and August. Closed Sundays and holidays.

NOTE: Mr. Kamuda is also the founder of the Titanic Historical Society, which has about eight thousand members worldwide. The museum has information about the society and its newsletter. (See also the entry *Mini Titanic* in Fall River, Massachusetts.)

Admission charged.

Wheelchair accessible.

Leominster, Massachusetts

Magic Hill

There is something weird on Lowe Street. For years it has had a reputation for possessing some odd "magnetic" power that will pull an automobile uphill. This mysterious attribute was discovered around 1939 by a salesman who had parked his car near what was then R. W. Hapgood's estate. The salesman shut off the engine, but failed to leave the vehicle in gear or apply the brake. When he returned, he saw his car moving all by itself. Uphill! It climbed about fifty feet and stopped. When the salesman told his strange tale, many others wanted to see for themselves. Sure enough, it was true. Word spread in the press and crowds followed. While Lowe Street's Magnetic Hill caused quite a stir in its day, now the phenomenon seems largely forgotten. Opinions vary as to the cause—magnetism, magic, or misperception—but we may never find out for sure. Today the anti-gravity spot is difficult to find. Our research disclosed a number of references to it, but our road trip failed to locate what may be Leominster's lost legend.

Location: The magic hill is just south of the town center. Go east on West Street, passing the Leominster Public Library on your left. Take your first right and go two blocks. Stay right and pass the old brick schoolhouse, then follow it to the left, where it becomes Pleasant Street. Take the first right onto Lowe Street. The magnetic spot is after the first hill, in the dip before the road climbs another hill.

NOTE: While you're in town, drop by the Leominster Historical Society Museum on 17 School Street, which boasts the world's largest collection of combs. It's open Tuesday, Thursday, and Saturday mornings and by appointment. Call (978) 537-5424 or e-mail <LCris5745@aol.com> for information.

You might also want to take a peek inside E. J. Marrone's, a restaurant whose owner displays a colossal personal collection of JFK kitsch, some of which is authentic memorabilia. Ask a local for the address, or call E. J. Marrone's at (978) 537-6029.

Leominster, Massachusetts

Mr. Palmer's Beard

If you enter Leominster's Evergreen Cemetery, chances are you'll stop short at one of the first graves you see—a handsome bearded face carved in white marble. The face is cartoon-like, seemingly happy, with neatly combed hair and a long, well-groomed beard. Below, there's a surprising caption: "Persecuted for wearing a beard." In the mid-1800s the grave's occupant, Joseph Palmer, went against fashion by growing facial hair. The act was considered unsociable, even sinful. So the clean-shaven majority took it upon themselves to taunt him. Children pitched rocks at him, women avoided him on the street, even his clergyman ignored Mr. Palmer at the communion rail. After being verbally attacked from the pulpit, Mr. Palmer was then physically attacked in the street. But it was the assailed, not the assailants, who was thrown into jail. The charge: "Disturbing the peace by wearing a beard." Behind bars, the principled Palmer still refused to shave. When his time was up, he refused to leave, demanding an official proclamation assuring his right to wear a beard. In 1831—after more than a year behind bars—he was tied to a chair and carried from the building. By then, thanks to the *Worcester Spy* and other newspapers, public opinion had shifted. Today, in presumably more enlightened times, the whole unsavory incident is recalled in marble on Mr. Palmer's grave.

Location: Take Route 12 north past the post office. Turn right onto Route 13. Watch for "Evergreen Cemetery." Take the first cemetery entrance and follow the lane that's parallel with the road. Palmer's grave is near the stone wall.

Lynn, Massachusetts

Rev. Frankenstein

Perhaps the weirdest event in Massachusetts history took place in the High Rock section of Lynn, a spot long considered charged with spiritual energy. Jesse Hutchinson, a well-known nineteenth-century singer, bought the land and built a house and tower (the house remains; the tower has been replaced). A devoted spiritualist, he made his property available to Reverend John Murray Spear, whose bizarre experiments would blend science and religion in a manner never dreamed of in the gothic imagination. During dialogues with a "high society of angels," Reverend Spear was directed to create . . . dare we say it? . . . life! And the weird thing is, some people say he succeeded. The grotesque process included infusing life force into a mechanical contraption constructed from metal balls, magnets, pulleys, and more. A human mother participated, suffering nine-months with all the pains and indignities of pregnancy and childbirth. Everyone expected the machine, or "New Motive Power," would become the world's new messiah. The results were much disputed. Boston's "New Era" newspaper proclaimed, "THE THING MOVES!" But perhaps another commentator summed it up best: "The new motor would not move to any purpose," he said. "This was the only drawback in its great benefits to mankind." Eventually Reverend Spear's machine was destroyed by a group of angry villagers, but the house, a tower, and the high rocks themselves are there to observe.

Location: From Western Avenue (which is Route 107 through Lynn), turn onto Lawton Avenue and drive east toward the sea. Turn left onto High Rock Street, then take your first right onto Circuit Avenue, which will take you right up to the tower.

Lynn, Massachusetts

Treasure Tunnel

Of all the mysterious places in New England, none is weirder than Lynn's "Dungeon Rock." There, in the early 1600s, pirate Thomas Veal is said to have concealed his treasure. Pirate and prize were sealed-up forever in his underground hideout by the 1658 earthquake. About two hundred years later, Hiram Marble, aided by a Spiritualist medium, contacted Veal's ghost who revealed the whereabouts of the loot. So Hiram started digging all by himself—day after day chipping away at unyielding stone, progressing about one foot every thirty days. His savings ran out in 1856, when he was fifty-three years old, but his faith never wavered. By 1864—with the spirits still cheering him on—his serpentine passageway through solid rock had reached the astonishing depth of 135 feet! It was about seven feet wide and seven feet high. Yet Hiram, joined by his son Edwin, persevered, financing the effort by selling admissions to curiosity seekers. By November 1868, father and son had burrowed to a depth of two hundred feet but still came up empty-handed. Hiram Marble died that year. Edwin continued until he too expired in 1880. Both are buried nearby. Massachusetts's original "Big Dig" is still there and can be visited. Strange lights and apparitions are occasionally reported. Perhaps it's Veal trying to mislead another victim, or maybe it's the Marbles warning them away.

Location: Dungeon Rock is within the Lynn Woods Reservation. From Route 1 take Walnut Street, driving toward the sea. Walnut Street hugs the side of Lynn Woods. Enter the park at the entrance on the left labeled Penny Brook Road. You'll soon come to Dungeon Rock Road, take it to Dungeon Rock. Entering the Park from 129 on the other side, take a right turn onto Great Woods Road and follow it around to Dungeon Rock Road.

Manchester-by-the-Sea, Massachusetts

Sonorous Sand

It really works, but nobody seems to know why. For centuries the puzzling phenomenon of "Singing Sand" has excited scientists and enchanted everyone else. The "Singing Beach" at Manchester-by-the-Sea is a modest natural wonder, supposedly the only one of its kind in North America. And we have to admit we had our doubts; we did not think it would sing to us. But, with patience and perseverance—and much surprise—when we stepped just-so on a patch of dry sand, it did respond. Was it really music? We guess that's in the ear of the beholder. To us it was more of a yip or a bark, perhaps the sound a seal might make if you tromped on its flipper. But the point is, it did "speak," and sand really shouldn't make any sound at all.

Location: "Singing Sand Beach" is a busy public park about one mile southeast of the village. Follow the crowd or ask someone to point you in the right direction.

Free admission.

Middleboro, Massachusetts

A Small Exhibit

Though much of Middleboro has degenerated into twentieth-century sprawl, there's a historic section with a wonderful museum. Its focus is the life and memorabilia of one of Middleboro's native daughters, Lavinia Warren Bump, and the man she married. A visit to this quiet treasure is a trip back to a time before today's stifling political correctness. Here we get a feel for what it must have been like to associate with that master showman, P. T. Barnum. In 1862, Mr. Barnum journeyed to Middleboro to persuade Lavinia's parents to let her travel and perform. He saw her, quite literally, as a living doll—just thirty-two inches tall, weighing a mere thirty pounds. Yet, she was a perfectly formed adult—intelligent, witty and talented. All the world soon fell in love with her, as did Barnum's diminutive superstar, General Tom Thumb. Tom and Lavinia married and toured the world. They had a mansion constructed—all to scale—back home in Middleboro, and eventually retired there.

Tom Thumb and his wife Lavinia Bump retired to a Middleboro home pictured in this old postcard. The tiny couple lived in the big house; the small building on the right was for carriages.
Photo: Courtesy Middleborough Historical Association, Middleboro, Massachusetts

Now, a century after their deaths, the lilliputian lovers live on at the Historical Society Museum. Through photographs, exhibits, and minuscule memorabilia, you almost get to know them and the lost world they lived in. Tom's walking stick is less that a foot long. Lavinia's elegant gloves have fingers about an inch in length. Her sewing thimble is no bigger than a pencil eraser. There is a lot more to see, but it is all very small.

Middleborough Historical Museum
  18 Jackson St.
  Middleboro, MA 02346

Phone: (508) 947-1969

Location: It is across the street from the Robbins Museum of Archaeology off the town's main thoroughfare, Main Street.

Hours: Open June–October, Wednesdays and Saturdays from 1 to 4 P.M. At other times, by appointment only.

NOTE: There are portraits of Tom, Lavinia, and her sister on the wall in the reading rooms of the town library. For information call: (508) 946-2470. Open June–October, Wednesdays and Saturdays, 1–4 P.M. At other times, open by appointment only.

Admission charged.

Giants of the Sea

Have you ever wanted to feel larger than life? Or wondered how it might feel to be a giant? You can find out by visiting the Whaling Museum in New Bedford. They have a spectacular whaling bark called Lagoda that was constructed by shipbuilders in 1915. But here's the magic: It was constructed to half-scale. Step aboard and you double your size! At eighty-nine feet long, it is the world's largest ship model. Its sails are set, its gear rigged, and it's ready to chase the whales. You can tromp around the deck, inspect the hold, and bark orders at your imaginary crew. But before you start feeling too big for your britches, check out the sixty-six-foot skeleton of a rare male blue whale. Spectacular in size, it will put everything back in perspective. Funds to construct the Lagoda were donated by Emily Bourne to commemorate her seafaring father. It marks the passing of the great days of sperm whaling, as well. The blue whale was accidentally killed by a tanker in March 1998 and brought ashore in Rhode Island.

New Bedford Whaling Museum
18 Johnny Cake Hill
New Bedford, MA 02740-6398

Phone: (508) 997-0046 or (508) 997-0018
info@whalingmuseum.org
www.whalingmuseum.org/

Location: The Whaling Museum is downtown in the New Bedford Historic District. Turn right on Elm Street and take the second left, Bethel Street, which becomes Johnny Cake Hill. The museum is on the second block and has a whale in the window.

Hours: Open daily, 9 A.M.–5 P.M., and until 9 P.M. on the second Thursday of each month. Closed Thanksgiving, Christmas, and New Year's Day.

NOTE: Recently, the collection of the Kendall Whaling Museum was given to the New Bedford Whaling Museum. Please call the number above for any information. To read more about the former collection at the Kendall Whaling Museum, please see pages 151–152 here.

Admission charged.

Mostly wheelchair accessible.

The Queen of Cupidity

Was she truly the most wicked woman in the world, or merely a misunderstood eccentric? Did she really allow her son's gangrenous leg to be amputated just because she couldn't find him a free clinic? Or was there a kinder, gentler side of Hetty Green, the "Wicked Witch of Wall Street"? One thing's for sure: She was the richest woman in the world at a time when women weren't allowed to vote and men dominated most everything—especially the world of finance. Whatever she was, we have the city of New Bedford to thank for her. She was born here in 1835 to a wealthy Quaker family. But kindness and generosity were never among her strong points. She tricked relatives out of their money, forced her husband into the poorhouse (where he died), and put her daughter in a convent—simply because they didn't charge room and board. But neither was she self-indulgent; she wore secondhand clothes, did without plumbing in her mansion, used newspaper to insulate her clothes in winter, and took cold oatmeal for lunch at her Wall Street office. All in all, Hetty seems like the sort of person we'd like to forget. But they remember her in her old hometown at the Hetty Green Museum, which owner Edith Nichols calls the "Very Frugal Woman's Museum." Here you'll get the real scoop on Ms. Hetty Howland Robinson Green, you'll view the largest collection of Hetty memorabilia anywhere (put together without a single cent of taxpayer money!), see a short film about her life, and meet a delightful woman—Edie Nichols—who probably knows more about Hetty than anyone else alive.

Frugal Woman's Museum
  52 Union St.
  New Bedford, MA 02740

Phone: (888) 55-HETTY
  www.hettygreen.com/

Location: In New Bedford, from the Seamen's Bethel on Johnnycake Hill, proceed to Union Street at the foot of the hill. Turn left and go one block toward the waterfront, where 52 Union Street will be on your right.

Hours: Tuesday–Sunday, 1–4 P.M. Closed Mondays.

Admission charged, but occasionally offers free admission to anyone bearing a Hetty Green newspaper article or memento.

Newburyport, Massachusetts

Lord Timothy Dexter (Part I)

Lord Timothy—known to some as the Newburyport Nut—commissioned a statue of himself and had it inscribed, "I am the first in the East, the first in the West and the greatest philosopher in the Western World." To illustrate, he published his philosophy in a little book called *A Pickle for the Knowing Ones*. It was the story of his life and a summary of his opinions—mostly negative—on politics, religion, his contemporaries, and other "Plain Truths in a Homespun Dress." Its rambling, outlandishly spelled, and unpunctuated prose—appearing to be just one long sentence—brought criticism from all who saw it. In response, Lord Dexter added two pages to subsequent editions, containing nothing but punctuation marks and explained, "The Nowing ones complane of my book the fust edition had no stops I put in A nuf here and they may solt and peper it as they please."

"Pickle" won the reputation of being one of the greatest curiosities of American letters and its author is truly one of America's greatest eccentrics.

To sum up Lord Dexter's unusual life would require an entire volume. Briefly, he was born poor in 1747, but made his fortune from impossible twists of fate during wacky business dealings. For example, he literally shipped coal to Newcastle—luckily, he did it during a miners' strike and made a killing. He also shipped warming pans and cats to the West Indies. The pans sold quickly as molasses-dippers; the cats arrived just in time to end a plague of mice.

But respect did not accompany his growing fortune as he felt it should. New England's High Society continued to snub him. Worse, everyone in Newburyport refused to address him by his title, "Lord." In 1797, he picked up and moved to Chester, New Hampshire, where he stayed until he was soundly beaten by a local judge. At that point he returned his kingdom to Newburyport.

Here he bought a grand mansion in Newburyport's "best" neighborhood and had it decorated with forty life-sized wooden statues of famous people, including Adam and Eve, Napoleon, King George, Venus, and of course the greatest of them all, Lord Timothy Dexter. His intention was to create a new wonder of the world, called Lord Dexter's "Mouseum." People came, just as he'd hoped, but instead of respect, his museum won only laughter.

Lord Dexter's funeral took place in 1806. Today the greatest philosopher in the western world lies buried in the town's Old Burying Ground, where his grave may be seen. His mansion still stands on Newburyport's High Street, but unfortunately, the ornate statues are gone. By visiting the local historical society you can see one of them, his Pickle, and other colorful memorabilia of "the first Lord in the younited States of Amercary." (For Part II, *The King of Chester*, see Chester, New Hampshire.)

Historical Society of Old Newbury
  Cushing House Museum and Garden
  98 High St.
  Newburyport, MA 01950

Phone: (978) 462-2681
  hson@greennet.net
  www.newburyhist.com

Hours: Open May 1–October 31, Tuesday–Friday, 10 A.M.–4 P.M. Saturday,
  11 A.M.–2 P.M. Open by appointment, Tuesday–Friday, November 1–April
  30. Closed Sunday, Monday, and holidays.

NOTE: While you're in town, stop by the Custom House Maritime Museum at
  25 Water Street. Its exhibits include a preacher carved from a cow vertebra,
  a ship model crafted from bones and human hair, and other nineteenth-
  century oddities brought back from Burma and Calcutta. The museum is
  open May 1–mid-December, 10 A.M.–4 P.M. Monday–Saturday, Sundays, 1–
  4 P.M. Other times by appointment.

Admission charged. Phone: (978) 462–8681.

Norwell, Massachusetts

Success Cymbal

There's not much to see here. You can drive by the building,
of course, but there is no point going in. They have no show
room, no display cases, no official tours, and everyone is too
busy for questions. But the next time you're at a rock concert
or any musical event where there is a drummer, pay careful attention to the cymbals and you'll see—and hear—all that you
need to. They are probably Zildjian, and if so, they were made
here. This is America's oldest family business, and, according
to *Family Business* magazine, one of the nation's 102 hardiest
companies. They make ninety percent of the cymbals used in
the world today. So what is their secret to success? What kind
of magic do they practice that allows them to produce the finest cymbals in the world? A little history reveals all: The Zildjian Cymbal Company was founded in Turkey in 1623 when an

alchemist named Avedis created a secret formulation of metal alloys that—if made into cymbals—would produce a clear, perfect sound. This carefully guarded secret formula has been handed down through fourteen generations of the Zildjian family. In 1929, they came to the United States to practice their art in Massachusetts. But their secret, that alchemical formula, is as mysterious today as it was in Byzantium. In fact, a team of scientists from MIT tried to analyze the cymbals in order to reproduce the alchemist's formula, but they were not able to duplicate a Zildjian cymbal or its sound. Even in this modern world, magic can still hold its own against science.

Avedis Zildjian Company
22 Longwater Dr.
Norwell, MA 02061
Phone: (781) 871-2200
www.zildjian.com/

Onset, Massachusetts

Thermometer Man

The question is WHY. Why would anyone want to collect thermometers at all, much less amass the largest collection in the world—totaling some three thousand? Perhaps retired science teacher Richard T. Porter just didn't have enough degrees. Anyway, Onset's "Thermometer Man" has traveled the world and come back with . . . thermometers. And maybe he's journeyed even farther; somehow he managed to acquire the backup to the instrument that traveled to the moon on *Apollo 9*. Featured in *Ripley's Believe It or Not* and *The Guinness Book of World Records*, Mr. Porter's obsession has put Onset on the map; it's the Thermometer Capitol of the world! And Mr. Porter boasts the biggest (and only) such collection on the planet. In the organized clutter of his basement museum in his seemingly ordinary home—where thermometers hang from the ceiling like stalactites—you can witness such wonders as the Marilyn Monroe *Some Like It Hot* thermometer (which tends to read a little high). Its polar opposite, an apparatus from the Yukon calibrated all the way down to minus 100. There's an earring thermometer, one rescued from a 1650 whaling ship, and a pill sized thermometer like the one swallowed by John Glenn in his 1998 space flight. Or check out his "Swiss Weather House." It tells the temperature and predicts the future, signaling fair or foul weather with tiny figures of Little Red Riding Hood and the wolf. Some thermometers are even media celebrities. Eight of his antique devices appeared in Oliver Stone's 1997 movie, *U-turn*. And there are many more examples to see—2,985 in fact. A visit here will quickly demonstrate why the big names in thermometers are Galilei, Fahrenheit, Celcius, and Porter.

Porter Thermometer Museum
   49 Zarahemla Rd.
   Onset, MA 02558

Phone: (508) 295-5504
   members.aol.com/thermometerman/index.html

Hours: Open 365 days a year, twenty-four hours a day.

NOTE: Mr. Porter's motto: "Always open and always FREE, with over three thousand to see!" Call for directions.

Free admission.

Pepperell, Massachusetts

Signs or Shrines?

In the yard of a kindly old man in Pepperell, Massachusetts, there are some controversial structures. Not ancient ruins of indeterminate origin, but brand new paintings. Described by some as works of art and others as eyesores, the creations have a lofty purpose, and, according to property owner Noel Dube, they were divinely inspired. Mr. Dube believes that the Virgin Mary spoke directly to him, requesting that he build a community shrine. Since he was just as unaccustomed to religious visitations as the rest of us, he didn't know how to go about getting started. So he commissioned an artist and put him to work. The product can never be described as subtle. In shrieking, almost comic book colors, giant scenes have materialized. There is a twenty-two-by-sixty-foot mural depicting the holy visions experienced in Fatima, Portugal in 1917. You can see the sun—or is it a flying saucer?—zigzagging through an electric-blue sky. On the far end of the property stands a thirty-by-twelve-foot, gold-framed mural of Jesus. Mr. Dube also commissioned fourteen stations of the cross where the horrific side of Calvary is depicted in unrestrained, gory detail. This shrine might not be to everyone's taste. In fact, taste might not even apply. But it sure is big, and it sure is bold, and it sure is colorful. Although it attracts pilgrims of varying persuasions, it hasn't brought the everlasting peace Mr. Dube intended. His nearest neighbor objected to the shrine, saying it negatively affected her property value. She insisted that the pictures were billboards and therefore illegal. Mr. Dube—conforming to a higher authority—says they are not signs; they're religious paintings. And in Massachusetts, land used for religious purposes is exempt from zoning regulations. In the end, perhaps another miracle occurred. His neighbor sold her property and peace has been restored to Our Lady of Fatima Community Shrine.

Mr. Noel Dube
   47 Heald St.
   Pepperell, MA 01463

Phone: (978) 433-9332

Location: Mr. Dube's house and religious murals are just south of Nashua. From Route 3, go west onto 113 (Kendall Road) towards Pepperell. That becomes Main Street, and leads to five corners. Your closest right is Park Street, but take the next right, which is Heald Street. Mr. Dube's place is on the corner of Heald and Sheffield. Park inside the tall hedge. He's used to visitors.

Hours: The shrine is open during daylight hours.

Free admission.

Wheelchair accessible.

Pigeon Cove, Massachusetts

Paper House

Except for the shingled roof, this cottage is constructed almost completely from newspapers. Builder Elis F. Stenman was a Swedish immigrant who read half a dozen papers a day. He had to do something with them, so in 1920, he and his family began this odd ode to recycling, which took twenty years to complete. They rolled and pasted some one hundred thousand tribunes and tabloids to form walls and ceilings. Exterior walls are made of 215 layers of paper, under two tons of pressure. Then they went about furnishing their paper paradise with more paper. There's a paper grandfather clock, writing desk, and even a lamp made of newsprint. Everything is assembled with historic articles showing. You can read about Charles Lindbergh's famed trans-Atlantic flight on the desk or skim Herbert Hoover's 1928 presidential campaign on the radio cabinet. The "why" of this peculiar paper monument remains a mystery. Maybe Mr. Stenman just wanted to be in the paper.

Paper House
   52 Pigeon Hill St.
   Rockport, MA 01966

Phone: (978) 546-2629
   www.rockportusa.com/paperhouse/

Location: It is a little hard to find as the signs are easily missed. It's in the town of Pigeon Cove, which is north of Rockport. On entering Rockport, follow 127 to Pigeon Cove. After the Yankee Clipper Inn take the second left (Curtis Street), then another left onto Pigeon Hill Street, to number 52 (it's on your right).

Hours: Open daily, July–August, 10 A.M.–5 P.M. Also open weekends and selected weeks during the fall and winter.

Admission charged.

The Berkshire Battery

The jury is still out on the technological attainments of ancient science. But there is pretty good evidence that electrical batteries were used about two thousand years ago in ancient Baghdad. This prospect may be startling for anyone who equates the "birth" of electricity with Ben Franklin and his kite. But back in 1936, an Iraqi museum discovered among its more prosaic holdings a peculiar clay jar about five-and-one-half inches high. Traces of asphaltum, a common sealing material of the Parthian period were around its mouth. Inside was a copper cylinder, which contained an eroded iron rod held in place by an asphaltum plug at the top of the cylinder; the cylinder's bottom was a neatly soldered insulated copper disc. Scientists had no idea what it could have been if it *was not* an electrical battery. So what does all this have to do with New England? Around 1974 Willard Gray, an engineer at GE in Pittsfield, heard about the "battery" and decided to test it. He assembled components that would have been available two thousand years ago, except the electrolyte. Mr. Gray reasoned that a copper sulfate solution would surely have been available in Parthian days. To make a long story short, he tried it and it worked. The battery put out a tiny amount of current. But mystery still abounds: If it was a battery, what was it used for? Mr.

Gray speculated that it might have been part of an apparatus used for electroplating gold, or possibly to power some primitive sort of "electric semaphore" for communication between temples. Willard Gray's reconstruction of the Baghdad Battery is still in the holdings of Pittsfield's Berkshire Museum. It's not on display, but may be viewed by appointment.

The Berkshire Museum
  Route 7
  39 South St.
  Pittsfield, MA 01201

Phone: (413) 443-7171
  info@berkshiremuseum.org
  www.berkshiremuseum.org/

Provincetown, Massachusetts

Pirate Parts

In 1997, Barry Clifford and his hi-tech crew found the *Whydah* (pronounced Whih-dah), a sunken vessel once captained by the infamous pirate Sam Bellamy. From an undisclosed spot near Wellfleet, Cape Cod, they recovered thousands of gold coins and ingots, priceless ancient African "Akan" gold jewelry, Spanish gold doubloons, and a fascinating collection of everyday objects that date back to 1717—the year the ship went down in a tempest. All sorts of pirate paraphernalia is on display at the Expedition Whydah Museum. There are elegant pistols, nautical instruments, and more prosaic stuff, like a buccaneer's stocking, a leather pouch, and a boot. The pirates' life stories are described, and a few exhibits suggest just how loathsome they were, such as a teapot with a human shoulder bone stuck in it. But Bellamy's crew got its comeuppance in the end. You can see the torso of one them encased in a concretion formed by sand, salt, and the action of the sea over the last three hundred years. The museum's staff is still chipping away at other mysterious encrustations. Visitors can watch as they uncover more riches—or body parts.

Expedition Whydah
16 MacMillan Wharf
P.O. Box 493
Provincetown, MA 02657

Phone: (508) 487-8899
www.whydah.com
whydahinfo@whydah.com

Location: The museum is on MacMillan wharf, which is on Provincetown's southern shore where Commercial and Standish Streets meet.

Hours: Open Memorial Day weekend through Labor Day weekend, daily, 10 A.M.–7 P.M.; weekends only in September and October.

Admission charged.

Salem, Massachusetts

Cabinet of Curiosities

The Peabody Essex Museum houses an old-fashioned cabinet of curiosities created by a nineteenth-century trading society whose members traveled the world ferreting out oddities and exotica for a joint collection. Perhaps some of their acquisitions seemed stranger then than now: scrimshaw, Asian artwork, Fijian spears, African shields crafted from rhinoceros hide, male earrings, and wooden clubs from the Pacific islands; but there are stranger things to be seen. The museum possesses, though rarely exhibits, shrunken heads, a Fiji "mermaid" (fabricated from fish and monkey parts), numerous talismans containing human hair, and paraphernalia from the witch trials. Sublimely weird is Blackbeard's skull, silver-plated and said to be cursed. Of more recent vintage, there's

Robert Wadlow's size 37 shoes. (In 1940, Mr. Wadlow was the tallest man in the world, standing at eight feet eleven inches).

In the East India Marine Room on the second floor, a cabinet displays items sea captains used in the 1880s to maintain discipline aboard ship: a lanyard, brass knuckles, slingshots, and whips. Another cabinet shows a long wooden bat that James Drown used in 1804 to mark the days and weeks he spent castaway after a shipwreck.

A side room scene is devoted to "Cleopatra's Barge," America's first pleasure yacht, perhaps the most luxurious ever made. To fully appreciate the extent of self-indulgence one need only remember what a grim, puritanical place Salem was when the ship was built there in 1816 by wealthy eudaemonist George Crowninshield. Step aboard; you'll see the place looks more like an ornate mansion than a vessel. Mr. Crowninshield dispensed with nautical nomenclature, calling things as he saw them: a drawing room, a hall, a master bedroom.

Objects from his own collection include relics from his hero, Napoleon: a few locks of hair and the imperial black leather boots, which the emperor found to be too tight.

Founded in 1799, the Peabody Essex is the oldest continuously operating museum in the country, so you can be sure there is plenty of other weird stuff hidden away.

Peabody Essex Museum
East India Square
Salem, MA 01970–3783

Phone: (978) 745-9500, or (866) 745-1876
pem@pem.org
www.pem.org

Location: The main entrance is on Essex Street, a pedestrian walkway, at the intersection of New Liberty Street in the center of historic Salem.

Hours: Daily, 10 A.M.–5 P.M.; Thursday, 10 A.M.–9 P.M. Closed Christmas Day, Thanksgiving, and New Year's Day.

Admission charged.

Wheelchair accessible.

Whale's Eyeball

Moby Dick may have prevailed at sea, but here in Sharon, the human race is supreme. As if to flaunt our mastery, the Kendall museum has set up a vast collection of whale-killing artifacts and severed body parts. Many woebegone specimens sit soaking in jars of formaldehyde. For example, there's the eye of a sperm whale looking out at you from its murky main. It measures over two inches—the size of a cow's eye—and seems rather stunted for such a gigantic animal. "To the eye of a whale," begins the introduction to an 1837 poem on the label, "accidentally discovered, shriveled and shrunken to a shapeless mass, in a long, unvisited drawer of a cabinet . . ." Other choice specimens include an assortment of diseased and misshapen whale teeth in a case next to a slightly incongruous fossilized mastodon incisor. There are numerous harpoons; spears; whaling guns; and a huge collection of scrimshaw, those politically taboo, minutely detailed pictures that idle seafarers carved on whatever they could find: an emu egg, a cow horn, a whale's tooth, whatever. They'd carve up the mammal, then carve up its parts; the examples are staggering. There's a whalebone bird cage, a banjo, a yarn winder, a scrimshawed ship in a bottle—even a twenty-three pound whalebone chair. The pièce de résistance, however, is an encyclopedic South Seas whaling scene engraved onto an oversized jawbone slab, dating from about 1835. Straying a bit from whales, whaling, and dismemberment, the museum tries to be eclectic. Note the sizable collection of African, American Indian, and Pacific Island exotica. Among our favorites is an elegant cannibal fork that upper-crust Fijians used to ingest their favorite enemies. But Europeans aren't completely exempt: Look closely and you'll find the tooth of Major John Andre, a British officer captured in upstate New York during the American Revolution. It hasn't been carved upon, but that's only because this museum is so far from the sea; the whales have no opportunity to return the favor.

UPDATE: This entire collection was donated to the New Bedford Whaling Museum; please contact them for location and other information (and see pages 138–139).

South Hadley, Massachusetts

Dinosaur Land

In 1939, Carlton Nash opened an unheard of business—a quarry for mining dinosaur tracks. About one hundred million years ago—give or take a decade—giant monsters preceded tourists up and down the Connecticut River and left their tracks in the malleable mud. Growing up in the area, Carlton discovered the ancient imprints, kept mum about them, hatched an idea, and years later purchased two acres of apparently worthless land. He then started mining and selling the fossils. You can follow Carlton's tracks to gardens, foundations, and fireplaces all over the world. Museums and schools—like the University of Arkansas, Augustana College, the Kyoto Imperial Museum in Japan, even San Francisco's Golden Gate Park—display dinosaur footprints from Carlton's quarry. When he opened the place to tourists, he launched an institution. Those of us who visited Dino Land in the good old days recall an animated, possibly eccentric man in a cluttered environment full of colorfully crude signs and arrows and awkward statuary.

There was a primitive humor about the place that can never be forgotten. For example, back when dino tracks were plentiful, Carlton covered the sides of his gift shop with fossilized imprinted slabs and called it The World's Oldest Building. But today, more than sixty years along, this business on the rocks is on the verge of extinction. Mr. Nash died a few years ago and the supply of fossil tracks that kept the place afloat is virtually depleted. Still, Dino Land is very much worth a visit, not for what it is but for what it was. Like the dinosaurs themselves, these once plentiful old-time attractions are dying fast. Soon, we fear, this unique bit of Americana will be gone forever.

Nash Dinosaur Land
Route 116
South Hadley, MA 01075

Phone: (413) 467-9566

Location: From Holyoke head east on 202 toward South Hadley. At the circle, where 202 intersects with Route 116, go left and watch for Dino Land signs.

Hours: Open Memorial Day–Labor Day, Monday–Friday, 8:30 A.M.–5 P.M. Saturday–Sunday, 10 A.M.–5 P.M. Open weekends and by appointment, April–Memorial Day, and Labor Day until the first snow. Closed December 23–mid-March.

Admission charged.

Waltham, Massachusetts

Sounds Weird

The sound of this unusual instrument has been said to cause trances, convulsions, combativeness, premature births, illness, insanity, and even death. Surprisingly, it is not a weapon of war; it's a musical instrument with a sound so sweet and pure that it seems celestial, almost divine. The glass harmonica is a series of nesting crystal bowls mounted along a central axis. The glass assembly revolves horizontally like a lathe. It is played by wetting your fingers in water and touching the edge of the spinning bowls, a process similar to running a finger around the rim of a wine glass. In fact, sonic wine glasses originally inspired the instrument. It was invented and named by Benjamin Franklin around 1762 and enjoyed a brief popularity until people became afraid of it, apparently because dogs reacted poorly to its sound and a woman once died during a concert. Today the only American manufacturer of the unusual instrument is a company founded by German-born master glassblower Gerhard Finkenbeiner. This fragile instrument with its delicate, haunting tones has to be heard to be believed. Then again, maybe it does exert some sort of negative power as Mr. Finkenbeiner, its maker and champion, seems to have disappeared.

G. Finkenbeiner Inc.
33 Rumford Ave.
Waltham, MA 02453

Phone: (781) 899-3138
gfiglass@erols.com
www.finkenbeiner.com/

NOTE: Since there is no formal showroom, those interested in seeing and hearing the glass harmonica would be well advised to phone ahead, Monday–Friday, 8:30 A.M.–4:30 P.M.

Webster, Massachusetts

Lake Charcogg-etc.-maugg

Undoubtedly the most extraordinary, if not the weirdest example of Native American wordsmithing comes to us as the name of Lake Chargoggagoggmanchauggauggagoggchaubunagungamaugg, in Webster. At forty-nine letters, it is the longest lake name anywhere and supposedly the fifth-longest word in the world. Looking at its syllabic repetitiveness, one might think it's some kind of put-on, but Harvard's great Indian scholar, Professor Horsford, assures us that it is a perfectly legitimate Indian name. He says it has to do with fishing boundaries (or as our favorite linguist, Bill Bryson, translates, "You fish on that side, we'll fish on this side, and nobody will fish in the middle"). The name even appears, in its entirety, on some maps. Of course it is exactly the sort of linguistic tongue-twister that would interest Robert Ripley, but—believe it or not—he misspelled it. In his defense we must say that there are probably few who can spell it accurately, and fewer if anyone who can pronounce it. Sometimes it is written simply as Lake Charcogg-etc.-maugg and locals have anglicized it to "Junker-mug." To make things easy on everybody—and to save the municipality a fortune in sign money—Lake Chargoggagogg-manchauggauggagoggchaubunagungamaugg is now generally referred to as Webster Lake. It seems to lose a little something in the translation—like about forty-two letters.

Location: Webster and Lake Chargoggagoggmanchauggauggagoggchaubuna-gungamaugg are on Route 395, right on the Connecticut border. A green sign bearing its full name is on Thompson Road by the hospital on Route 193 toward Connecticut.

www.net1plus.com/users/websterpd/webster_lake.htm

Wellesley, Massachusetts

World's Biggest Outdoor Globe

Want to feel like an astronaut without leaving the ground? Check out the largest outdoor globe on the planet. It represents the earth as it looks from five thousand miles out in space. Seeing this twenty-eight-foot rotating wonder is an authentically surreal experience, like something from a science fiction movie. The idea for a grand globe was conceived in 1947 by Roger Webber, grandson of the college's founder. It took seven years to construct and was cobbled together from 578 enameled panels. Although it weighed twenty-five tons, it could rotate on its axis. In the 1980s it started to fall apart, and for a while seemed to be a dying planet. But today it's a new world, and viewing it proves that planetary restoration may indeed be possible.

Babson College
Wellesley, MA 02181

Phone: (781) 253-1200

Location: From Route 16 in Wellesley, turn onto Forrest Street, it will take you to the college. Take the first of two entrances to campus called College Drive. Turn left onto Map Hill Drive. Coleman Hall is up the hill and on the right. The globe is in front of Coleman. You can't miss it.

Free admission.

Wheelchair accessible.

Westford, Massachusetts

Knight on a Rock

Here we'll find another pre-Columbian claim to North America. This time, from Scotland! If you look very closely at a certain rock ledge, you will perceive a pattern of punched holes, a sort of megalithic follow-the-dots. Though they're extremely weather-worn, someone occasionally connects them with paint, making the life-sized, five and a half foot figure more discernible. Holes, lines, discoloration, and a little imagination merge to reveal a Scottish nobleman in full fourteenth-century military garb—including the twenty-inch handle, hilt and pommel, of a huge broadsword. There is no question that it's manmade. But who was the artist? And who does his handiwork depict? A certain contingent of enthusiasts have studied the figure and are convinced of his identity. They say Westford's knight is Prince Henry Sinclair, a Scottish nobleman who arrived here in 1398. Others examining the shield have recognized what they believe to be a coat of arms: the Gunn family insignia. Why Sinclair or Gunn should be depicted here just adds to the mystery. Perhaps the stone knight marks one of their graves. More creative examiners have identified many other figures in the stone, from falcons to Masonic emblems— though most people probably toss the whole thing off as the work of schoolboys, or a bored Indian "dot-pecking" with his tomahawk. Frankly, we found it impossible to see how anyone could perceive anything at all in this much romanticized rock. Take a look and decide for yourself.

Location: Westford is ten miles southwest of Lowell, off I-495. The image is on Main Street, a half-mile north of the Fletcher Library at Westford Center. On the right, look for a chain on a stone, then park at the Abbot School just up the road. It's an easy walk back to the chain.

NOTE: There's an entire file about the knight at the reference desk of the library. In their basement they have displayed the controversial "boat rock," a small boulder with an apparently prehistoric etching of a ship on its surface. A nearby glass case shows photos of other Massachusetts mystery sites, many said to date from 10,000 B.C. to 1399 A.D.

Library hours: Monday–Thursday, 10 A.M.–9 P.M., Friday, 1–5 P.M., Saturday, 10 A.M.–5 P.M.

Free admission.

Wheelchair accessible.

Weston, Massachusetts

Norumbega

Many people believe the Vikings visited America long before Columbus arrived. If so, New England is a likely spot for them to have landed. And there is a lot of ambiguous evidence suggesting that they did. Eben Norton Horsford, the Harvard professor who invented baking powder, was absolutely convinced Vikings had not only landed, but had actually settled the Charles River Basin by about 1000 A.D. There, Professor Horsford discovered what he thought was evidence of a Viking fort, so he named it Fort Norumbega and, in 1889, built a Viking-like structure to commemorate it. This impressive monument, a replica of what might have been there, contains a stone Professor Horsford believed Vikings used to grind grain. As if that weren't enough proof, he published his findings in a series of elaborate books containing maps, photographs and theories. Though most specialists dismiss him as an imaginative amateur—if not an out-and-out crackpot—Professor Horsford's final argument, made of mortar and stone, has outlived him and continues to argue his point rather convincingly—especially if you can read the fine print.

Location: Professor Horsford's tower is at the Charles River Reservation in Weston. It is constructed at a spot where the towns of Weston, Waltham, and Newton come together, roughly at the intersection of Routes 128 and 30. One way of access is to take the park road connecting South Street in Waltham with the Charles River Duck Feeding Area. Norumbega tower is nearby.

NOTE: Oddly, this general area has long been known locally as "Norumbega." Most people figured it was an Indian word, but Professor Horsford suggested it was the Indians' pronunciation of *Norbega*, an ancient form of *Norvega*, or Norway. For more information on his fascinating theories see if your library can get a copy of his book *Discovery of the Ancient City of Norumbega.*

Worcester, Massachusetts

Bancroft Tower

If you happen to be in Worcester, take a drive to Bancroft Tower. The creepy looking monument was erected in 1900 to honor the memory of George Bancroft, who was born at the foot of the tower's hill in 1800. Before his death in 1891, this ambitious native son rose to become Secretary of the Navy, U.S. Minister to Great Britain and Germany, and founder of the U.S. Naval Academy at Annapolis, Maryland. A plaque on the hilltop explains all this—but that's not what we're interested in. The site has a gothic atmosphere and a bit of a mystery that has puzzled Worcesterites for a long while. There are two "half-compasses" mounted in the earth before and behind the tower. They are marked as if they are directing your attention to . . . something. A cursory glance would suggest they are pointing at the so-called "Seven Hills of Worcester." But closer examination reveals that is not the case at all. In fact, no one is quite sure what they are pointing at, so all sorts of theories have cropped up, from misalignment, to buried treasure, to ley lines that intersect beneath the tower.

Location: From downtown Worcester, follow Route 122A going North. When it takes a right turn from Madison Street onto Park Street, start watching on your left. You'll soon see the tower. Take a left onto Institute Street, then right onto Farnum. Follow it up to Salisbury Park. The tower is at the top of Bancroft Hill.

www.eyrie.net/~gryphon/Worc/bancroft.html

Worcester, Massachusetts

Higgins Armory

The whole thing is weird. It's wildly incongruous, positioned as it is in the middle of Worcester, Massachusetts. The odd riveted steel and glass four-story edifice that houses it is fantastically retro-modern. The outsized suit of armor dangling over the roof is the crowning touch. But the interior, that's the strangest thing of all. Here John Woodman Higgins, the wealthy

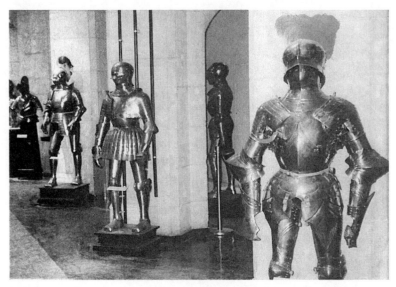

Knights in shining armor are among the incongruous finds in the Higgins Armory in Worcester, Massachusetts. Photo: Diane Foulds

founder of Worcester Pressed Steel, displayed his peculiar passion—an incredible collection of armor and weaponry. It's the only museum in the western hemisphere dedicated solely to the accumulation and exhibition of arms and armor. Never mind the first two floors. Go directly to the third where you'll plunge from twenty-first century America into the great hall of a medieval European fortress. You'll confront life-size steeds beneath jousting knights and tireless warriors frozen in eternal sword-to-sword combat. There is an army of suits of armor, standing around like antique robots. You'll see armor for knights, horses, and dogs—even training armor for kids. Then move on to savor the array of remarkably inventive ways to kill and maim people, from headsman's axes and pikes to primitive tooth extractors, firearms and fantastic contrivances like a gentleman's gun-cane and a nasty mechanism to discourage grave robbery. You'll see maces, mauls, machetes, and more. And who knows what visiting exhibits may be on display? We saw the earth-encrusted remains of a Roman soldier in a mail shirt, complete with skeleton protruding. The exhibits are fascinating and extremely well done, not to mention bizarre, curious, and macabre. Rumor has it that they even have a chastity belt, but refuse to display it because someone complained. You'd think in an edifice devoted to courage and valor they'd be gutsy enough to show it.

Anyway, the Armory's holdings include nearly six thousand pieces. The European collection holds over three thousand armors, one thousand weapons, five hundred swords, one hundred firearms, plus other medieval memorabilia. The remainder holds over one thousand African, Islamic, Indian, and Japanese defenses and arms. In short, there's something for everyone. Kids will love it. Historians will have a field day. Goths will gather. But for the true connoisseur of the eccentric, it's not far from Valhalla.

Higgins Armory Museum
100 Barber Ave.
Worcester, MA 01606

Phone: (508) 853-6015
higgins@higgins.org
www.higgins.org/

Hours: Open year round. Tuesday–Saturday, 10 A.M.–4 P.M., Sunday, noon–4 P.M. Closed Mondays and select holidays.

Location: From the East: Take I-495 to I-290 W; to exit 19, I-190 N; take exit onto Route 12 N (West Boylston Street); go past the Greendale Mall and over the green bridge; take next right onto one way access road; then right again onto Barber Avenue. The Museum, a tall steel and glass structure with flags on the roof, is a quarter mile ahead.

From the South or West: Take the Mass Pike to exit 10 onto I-290 E; take exit 19 onto I-190 N; take exit 1 onto Route 12 N and follow directions above.

From the North: take exit 1 off of I-190 S; follow Route 12 S a few yards to Route 12 N. Turnaround on left and follow directions above.

Public Bus: Number 30 stops at Barber Avenue, then it's a five-minute walk to the museum.

Admission charged.

Wheelchair accessible.

Worcester, Massachusetts

Shrine to Sanitation

Maybe it's not at the top of your vacation itinerary, and certainly not the place to escort potential paramours—yet an essential fact of life for everyone. Ever wonder about the history and evolution of . . . plumbing: the toilet, the faucet, the urinal, even the dishwasher? Ever wonder how we got along before them? Here's the place to find out. You'll see all things unmentionable beautifully showcased in this fascinating gallery of the art of water acquisition and disposal. Wander through rows of toilets and urinals displayed like fine statuary. Contemplate an array of shower heads blooming like sunflowers. Examine an antique "water closet," essentially an indoor outhouse. They were decorative, like furniture, until the owner lifted the lid or inhaled the bouquet. Then there are bathtubs in evolutionary formation, old and new prison toilets (the challenge is how to keep them from becoming weapons), even a rare early American dishwasher, developed around 1920. As always, the last thing to take care of is the paperwork. Toilet paper, a staple of the American bathroom, is comparatively modern, replacing such unsavory precursors as reusable sponges, corn cobs, sea shells, leaves, newspapers, and catalogs. Check out examples before you leave. All too easily overlooked, the American Sanitary Plumbing Museum is an unexpectedly interesting, informative excursion. Founded in 1979,

Worcester's shrine to sanitation is the brainchild of Charles Manoog, whose successful plumbing business inspired this tribute to the industry.

American Sanitary Plumbing Museum
    39 Piedmont St.
    Worcester, MA 01610

Phone: (508) 754-9453

Location: Take I-290 west to exit 13. Follow Route 122 west (Madison Street). Cross railroad tracks and stay on Madison. Piedmont Street will soon be coming up on the left.

Hours: Tuesday and Thursday, 10 A.M.–2 P.M. Closed July and August.

Admission charged.

NEW HAMPSHIRE

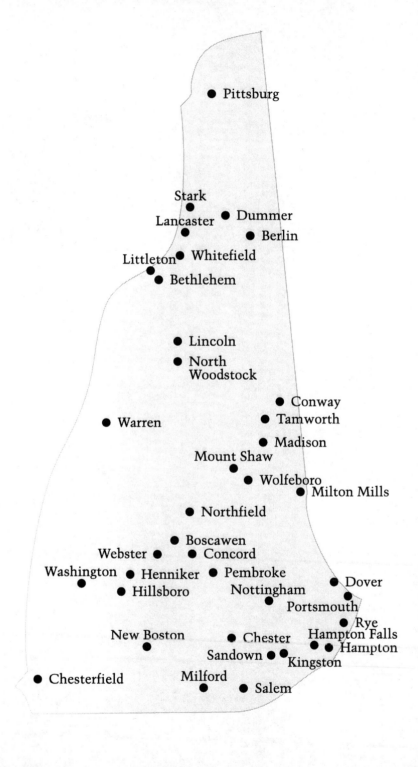

Bleeding Cross

The headlines were real. "Crucifix Draws Blood . . . and a Crowd." On June 1, 2000, somebody reported to Father Richard Roberge, the priest at St. Joseph's Catholic Church, that the crucifix on the wall of the sanctuary was "oozing blood." Soon word got out. By that weekend, crowds had gathered, convinced there had been a modern miracle at St. Joe's. If true, its implications could be staggering. Berlin has been a city in decline for several decades. Of the four Catholic churches, St. Joseph's was one of three scheduled to be closed. A legitimate Bible-style miracle had the potential to keep the church alive and restore vitality to the city. The crucifix in question had been on the wall for forty years with no prior hemophilic history. Though red paint highlighted the wounds on the image, the priests doubted the presence of miraculous blood. They took a sample of "a red substance" from the wall behind the crucifix and had it tested at the Androscoggin Valley Hospital. Sure enough, it wasn't blood. But whatever it was, church attendance rose greatly. Catholics from as far away as Pittsburg, New Hampshire, came to the morning mass. Curiosity seekers came at all hours. Can divine intervention save St. Joe's? Was the bleeding crucifix a miracle or a misperception? We—like all the faithful and faithless—will have to judge for ourselves.

St. Joseph's Roman Catholic Church
633 Third Ave.
Berlin, NH 03570

Location: The church is at the top of the hill as you come south on Route 16. It is next to the Preservation of Mary Convent.

Crossroads of America

At first glance this place may be nothing like you expected. It doesn't even look like a museum. And the sign on the door— "Never mind the Dog, Beware of Owner"—might discourage you. But tough it out, you're looking for the unconventional, right? This homemade museum in a former boarding house is well worth a visit. Here you'll find preadolescent preoccupation gone wild, a vast collection of collections. A boy's bedroom gone ballistic with hundreds and hundreds of models: cars, trucks, planes, ships, and—for some reason—over forty antique outboard motors. Most striking, of course, is the model railroad. It covers the whole third floor of the building, an old dance hall. Trainmaster Roger Hinds says he possesses the largest 3/16 scale model railroad in the world. Of course, he's referring to the *real* world, not the world he has created to house his entertaining assortment of somewhat eccentric acquisitions. Don't expect to find your childhood Lionel train set neatly displayed behind a sparkling glass case. No, here we have working replicas intricately populating a manmade landscape of twists, turns, tunnels, mountains, and tiny towns—not unlike Bethlehem itself. Besides the five moving trains (with rarely a collision), there are animated scenes and rustic tableaus that add fascinating detail to this monument to monomania. The detail is amazing. So much is going on you'll find it difficult to keep track of it all.

Crossroads of America
  6 Trudeau Rd.
  Bethlehem, NH 03574

Phone: (603) 869-3919
  www.fortunecity.com/meltingpot/gregory/1016/cofa/cofaxmypage.html

Location: It is at the intersection of Route 302 and Trudeau Road.

Hours: Tuesday–Sunday, 9 A.M.–5 P.M. (tours every half hour).

Admission charged.

Hannah Duston Memorial

In 1697, Hannah Duston hacked out a place for herself in New England horror when she somehow got the drop on her Indian captors. While they were sleeping she took a tomahawk and killed all ten of them, then headed home to Haverhill, Massachusetts. Before she got too far she recalled that Massachusetts paid a bounty on Indian scalps, so she returned to the scene of the slaughter and scalped the corpses. The grisly event is commemorated by this larger-than-life statue showing Hannah, tomahawk in one hand, scalps in the other, with an interesting décolletage in the center. Occasionally, no doubt in the interest of historical accuracy, some stickler for detail paints things red.

Location: The Hannah Duston monument is north of Concord on Route 3 in Boscawen. About a half-mile south of town you'll find a park-and-ride parking area beside the Merrimack River. Park here and look carefully for the historical marker. At the west end of the lot there's a path leading downhill toward the river. Follow it over a disused railroad bridge to the island. The statue can't be missed, though we're sure some people would like to see it disappear.

Grave Smiles and Frowns

There is much of note in the Chester Village Cemetery. It is of tremendous historical interest because of the Revolutionary era graves. But we'd like to point out some carvings. First, for those interested in near-death experiences, there's the grave of Lydia A. Webster, who died in 1862 at age thirty. She seemed to offer circumstantial evidence, etched in stone, of an experience described by many who have returned from death's door. Her tomb bears her actual last words, "It is all light now." The other curiosity is the number of pre-1800 tombstones with faces carved upon them. Some of the faces are smiling, some wear conspicuous frowns. Exactly what determined who got a smile and who got a frown has long been the subject of conjecture. One story is that the town's only stone-carver was in the habit of creating happy-faced effigies. But when he suddenly "got religion," none of his neighbors would convert. In a huff, he picked up and moved away. The Chesterites still required his services as a gravestone carver, but from then on all his faces wore disapproving frowns. A second explanation involves the work of *two* carvers, the brothers Abel and Stephen Webster. Supposedly they carved a smiling or frowning effigy depending on what they thought of that person's chances of achieving eternal salvation. While both explanations make interesting stories, the truth seems to be that all Abel's effigies are smiling while all Stephen's frown. The why of it is still a mystery. But if the frowning faces do predict damnation, they are of insufficient number to disprove what the town's Father Nathan W. Morse (1830–1902) had to say about the place, "Chester is like a hill of potatoes—the best part is underground."

Location: The cemetery is on Chester Street, the town's main thoroughfare, across from the public library.

Chester, New Hampshire

The King of Chester (Part II)

It was here that Timothy Dexter retreated after practical jokes and aristocratic snubs drove him from Newburyport, Massachusetts, where everyone refused to address him as "Lord."

When he arrived in Chester with his retinue—an African servant, a dwarf, cooks, kitchen maids, laundresses, waitresses, hostelers, gardeners, and a personal poet laureate, each wearing a shield with "$5" on it—people willingly indulged him with his self-awarded title, especially after they learned he would pay them to do so.

He purchased a beautiful Georgian-style house on Chester Street where he lived grandly, deciding to make Chester his kingdom. Still, he was never confident of anyone's allegiance or respect. To test his popularity, Lord Dexter faked his own death to see who'd come to his funeral. He observed everything from a hiding place and afterward beat his wife because she had not appeared properly aggrieved. To further punish her, he had his poet compose her epitaph. After that, Mrs. Dexter was known as his "gost" (ghost) and he treated her as if she were dead.

Lord Dexter departed Chester suddenly in 1796. It may have had to do with his efforts to replace his gost with a unwilling local girl, or it may have been the consequence of a feud with a local judge who horsewhipped him unmercifully until his "poor face looked like beefsteak fresh from the grill."

NOTE: Not much remains of Lord Dexter in Chester. New occupants have labored to restore the home that once was his castle. For memorabilia and monuments, you'll have to follow his Lordship and head for Newburyport. (See Part I in Newburyport, Massachusetts.)

Chesterfield, New Hampshire

Madame Sherri's Castle

An eccentric, out-of-place, though highly dramatic, ruin of a castle is all that is left of this famous (or infamous) local celebrity, Madame Antoinette Sherri. Once associated with

Paris music halls and later the Ziegfeld Follies, "Madame" commissioned the construction in 1931 of a building unlike anything southern New Hampshire had ever seen. There, much to the chagrin of locals, she conducted wild parties and unseemly goings-on. Some even whispered that she was running a brothel, a notion easy to imagine with flirtatious flappers and long lines of black cars with cigar-chomping occupants wending their way north from New York City for a weekend at "Madame's." She continually scandalized the good people of nearby Brattleboro, Vermont, with her propensity for younger men, her pet monkey, and her habit of driving around wearing nothing but a fur coat and a bright smile. Eventually circumstances caught up with her and she had to abandon her castle. Over the years it fell to neglect and vandals, all the while solidifying its reputation as a haunted place. On October 18, 1962, the castle was gutted by a fire, leaving only the castle-like foundation, graceful arches, chimneys, and grand stone staircase winding to nowhere. This magnificent ruin, once overgrown and nearly lost to the forest, can still pique curiosity and provoke a chill or two. But fortunately—or, perhaps, unfortunately—the building and grounds have been donated to the Society for the Preservation of New Hampshire Forests. Thus, Madame Sherri's Castle has gained attention at the expense of atmosphere. Madame died in 1964 at age eighty-four, a penniless ward of the town. But she is still occasionally encountered, young and beautiful, gliding down the stone stairway from a boudoir long gone.

Madame Sherri's Castle
   The Madame Sherri Forest
   The Conservation Commission
   Chesterfield Town Offices
   Chesterfield, NH 03443

Phone: (603) 363-4624
   www.chesterfieldoutdoors.com/plands/sherri.html

Location: From Route 9 take Route 63 south through Chesterfield Village. Turn right onto Stage Road, then make a quick left on to Castle Road. Castle Road joins Gulf Road and continues to the Madame Sherri Forest. The castle can be seen on a side trail close to the forest entrance. *Free admission.*

Concord, New Hampshire

The Mystery Stone

Of all the strange objects that have been found in New England, none is more puzzling than the "Mystery Stone." It was unearthed in 1872 by workmen digging a ditch in Meredith, New Hampshire, not far from Lake Winnipesaukee. Seneca Ladd, a collector of Indian relics, happened by and noticed an odd-looking clump of earth about three feet down in the hole. When he picked it up he realized it concealed something. After cleaning away the earthen crust, he found a smooth, greenish-black, egg-shaped stone decorated with finely cut designs. It was about four inches long and weighed just eighteen ounces. Running through the center, top to bottom, was a tapered hole, roughly a quarter inch wide, tapering to about an eighth of an inch. The surface was covered by ten different designs, etched or carved with extraordinary precision. Within a small perfect circle—possibly representing the sun or moon—were images of a bird (or bumblebee) in flight, a deer's leg, and what might be a bear's paw (or possibly a tooth). Above the circle there was a three-sided Indian teepee and an artfully etched ear of corn with seventeen kernels to the row. There was also a delicate spiral and a perfect, eight-pointed star. Four arrows, or maybe spears, were crossed, seeming to form the letter "M." The stone's most puzzling feature covered one complete side—a human face that was definitely not Native

American. The features seem to be Aztec, Eskimo, or possibly Polynesian. Seneca Ladd kept the stone until his death, when it was purchased by D. V. Coe. In 1927 his widow donated it to the New Hampshire Historical Society, where it rests today. Uncertainties surrounding the Mystery Stone remain. Do its odd images have some coded meaning? Who made it and for what purpose? When was it created? How was it carved? What method was used to drill that strange tapering hole through its center? And why would anyone take the time to do all that intricate carving only to abandon his handiwork in a wild, untraveled part of the New Hampshire countryside? Thanks to the Museum of New Hampshire History you can examine the Mystery Stone and form your own opinion.

Museum of New Hampshire History
  7 Eagle Sq.
  Concord, NH 03301–6384

Phone: (603) 226-3189
  visit@nhhistory.org
  www.nhhistory.org

Location: In downtown Concord at 6 Eagle Square, across the street from the state house.

Hours: Open Tuesday–Saturday, 9:30 A.M.–5 P.M., Thursday evening till 8:30 P.M., Sunday, noon–5 P.M. Also open Monday, 9:30 A.M.–5 P.M. in December and July–August 15.

Admission charged; Thursday evenings free admission.

Free parking.

Wheelchair accessible.

Conway, New Hampshire

Cuff Link Museum

"Remember Nikita Khrushchev at the UN, banging his shoe on the table? Yes, he was wearing cuff links," says Claude

Jeanloz, who has amassed the world's largest collection of the little sleeve fasteners. This exercise in extreme excess started, well, off the cuff. He developed a passion for them over thirty-five years ago after receiving his first pair at confirmation. They proliferated, and in 1995 he joined the American Cuff Link Society, where he hatched the idea of a museum. Now the Executive Director of Yield House Industries, a home furnishings company, Mr. Jeanloz boasts seventy thousand pairs and counting, all beautifully displayed in 221 handsome wooden cases lined with black velvet. The collection is a microcosm of maleness in two-by-two formation, as if awaiting some jeweler's ark. For first-timers, the sight of so many cuff links under one roof is almost disabling. There's no way to see everything. We suggest you make it a treasure hunt and try to find some of our favorites: eyeballs, minuscule cameras, big-eyed alien heads, cigars and cigar butts, even brassieres. But you can also discover functioning clocks, compasses, and thermometers. And there are weapons: pistols, rifles, cannons, bullets, jackknives and bejeweled monstrosities big enough to brain someone with. There are buildings, from ivory-carved igloos, to Eiffel Towers, to Empire State Buildings, and more. There are transportation themes: cowboy boots, cars, Corvettes, hot-air balloons, trains, and of course airplanes, since Mr. Jeanloz is a licensed pilot. While we like the quirky ones, you're sure to discover favorites of your own. Mr. Jeanloz likes those with precious gems. We had assumed his intent was to preserve this near extinct species of masculine attire, but we were wrong. As it turns out, cuff links are back in style.

The Cuff Link Museum
Yield House
71 Hobbs St.
Conway, NH 03818

Phone: (603) 447-8500
www.enamelcufflinks.com

Location: Take Route 16 north until you come to the high school on your right. Turn left there and go half a mile to the Ham Arena skating rink. You'll see the Yield House and Renovators sign on the left. The museum is on the third floor of Yield House Industries.

Hours: Open Monday–Friday, 9 A.M.–4 P.M.

Free admission.

Wheelchair accessible.

Dover, New Hampshire

Woodman Institute

If you've ever explored a huge, cluttered attic, you know how it feels to walk through the Woodman Institute. Though the displays in its three buildings are labeled and orderly, you know that at any moment you might happen upon something spectacular. The feeling starts at the front door, where you're greeted by a rearing Siberian polar bear frozen in mid-attack. To be truthful, "frozen" might be a good description of the whole museum, a mixture of natural history, military history, local history, colonial history, and just about every other kind of history. The mineral room has been left untouched since the 1930s; the bird room is equally untouched and even older. With its woebegone animals, the mammal display would be a taxidermist's delight (or terror). Name it, and it's here: a stuffed manatee, a coyote, an armadillo, a crocodile, a mongoose battling a cobra, and much more. Upstairs is a saddle that belonged to Abraham Lincoln, and confederate currency that didn't. The war room features artifacts from ancient Rome alongside World War II souvenirs like the Nazi helmet and armband emblazoned with swastikas. The pride of the zoological specimens is the tiny two-headed snake. Contenders include a bevy of discolored frogs in liquid, a four-legged chicken, and myriad canning jars filled with more unappetizing oddities.

Then there's the mystery of the six-foot iguana found dead on a roadside near Dover in 1937. Too much of a puzzle? Then check out the white building in back. It's deceptive; it's not really a building, but a building within a building. The facade encloses an authentic 1675 garrison, a fortress-style log cabin where the settlers holed up during Indian attacks. But the best exhibits are arguably next door in the 1813 John Parker Hale house. There's something for everyone. Interested in a silver voice trumpet? A leather water bucket? A quill toothpick? How about the blackjack used in the 1897 murder of a local cashier? The medieval suit of Japanese armor struck our fancy. It was hauled here in the nineteenth century by a local sea captain, and that's the whole point. The draw of this community-owned museum is its wild eclecticism. Like a family attic, it is a repository of Dover detritus, an archaeological dig of a New England community and its puzzling acquisitions.

The Woodman Institute
182 Central Avenue
Dover, NH 03821

Phone: (603) 742-1038

Location: The institute is in downtown Dover. From I-95, follow Spaulding Turnpike, taking exit 7 to Central Avenue.

Hours: Open Wednesday–Sunday, 12:30–4:30 P.M. In December and January, open Saturday and Sunday. Closed holidays. Closed February 1–March 31.

Admission charged.

Dolls of Dummer

It has been like this for at least ten years. And if it was weird at the start, it's getting weirder by the minute. This, simply speaking, is lawn decoration from hell. Fat ladies bending over flower gardens and virgins in bathtubs are old-hat compared to this exercise in aesthetic abnormality. All sorts of figures populate the lawn of Mildred Smith's mobile home. They are ghostly, mildly mysterious, occasionally monstrous. What you'll see are dressed effigies arrested in the middle of some manic random movement. In the eerie stillness, one gets the impression of something apocalyptic, the atmosphere of something subtly disturbing. There are terrifying tots in hard-hats, adult-sized mannequins bending under the weight of unseen pressures, masked scarecrow-like figures that could be paralyzed extras from a Freddy Kruger movie. Immobile zombies. Demonic dolls. We can imagine the seizure of terror one might experience upon stumbling onto this display by accident, at just about sundown. What on earth can it be? A burial ground without graves? An outdoor catacomb? One wonders at the apparent lack of point, the evasiveness of meaning. Only the creator, the artist, knows for sure. She may not see it as strange, but for the rest of us this remarkable display is likely to prove irresistibly haunting.

NOTE: At last visit, the dolls were no longer there.

Hampton, New Hampshire

Thorvald's Rock

It may look like a circular stone well, but it's actually the third resting place of "Thorvald's Rock." Thorvald's own resting place, however, is a bit of a mystery. For years many people—especially tourism types, realtors, and developers—have argued that Thorvald, son of Eric the Red, brother of Leif Eriksson, was killed by Indians and buried under this rock somewhere in Hampton. Runic markings cover its surface, so, they reason, it must have been carved by Vikings. The leap from etched rock to Thorvald may be a little hard to follow, but you can view the stone and try to puzzle it out. This marked stone is always on display and constantly exposed to the elements. It is crisscrossed with metal bars intended to protect it from tourist-erosion and theft. And it's just one of myriad bits of evidence—pseudo or real—used to argue that Vikings got here first. Before the Puritans. Before Columbus. Before the Beatles. While the specific evidence may be bogus, the conclusion is probably valid. And it's certainly as accurate to say the Vikings landed at Thorvald's Rock as it is to say the Pilgrims landed at Plymouth Rock. Quite frankly, it might be more fun to be descended from Vikings than Puritans, but calling New England New Iceland would take a bit of adjusting.

Tuck Museum
    Hampton Historical Society
    40 Park Ave.
    Hampton, NH 03842
    Mailing address: P.O. Box 1601, Hampton, NH 03843-1601

Phone: (603) 929-0781
    hhs@nh.ultranet.com
    www.hamptonhistoricalsociety.org

Hours: The rock is always on display. The museum is open June–September, Tuesday–Friday and Sunday, 1–4 P.M. Open year round by appointment.

Free admission.

Hampton Falls, New Hampshire

High Spirits

It's easy to miss it if someone doesn't point it out to you. But once you've seen it, what will you make of it? Look way up at the top of the steeple on the First Baptist Church in Hampton Falls. Use binoculars just to be sure. Then take this short quiz:

1. Is something unusual really up there?
2. Is it a five-and-a-half-foot-tall beer bottle?
3. What in the world is it doing on a church steeple? Especially a *Baptist* church steeple?

As with all such oddities, there are several competing explanations. The most popular seems to be that in the mid-nineteenth century a Portsmouth brewery offered to donate the funds necessary to construct a new steeple. But there was a catch: A likeness of their product had to be displayed at the top where everyone could see it. Well, certainly there are far worse products that might be up there. At least this, like a traditional steeple-top adornment, is promoting spirits. Then again, the raised-high bottle could simply be the parish's way of toasting their maker, "This Bud's for You!"

First Baptist Church
  3 Lincoln Ave.
  Hampton Falls, NH 03844
Phone: (603) 926-3724

NOTE: We've heard there is something odd about the clock face, too. While your binoculars are out, why not have a look?

Henniker, New Hampshire

Ocean-Born Mary House

The only "Henniker" in the world has the most famous haunted house in the country—though the owners are doing all they can to keep it from looking that way. The saga of "Ocean-Born Mary's" house comes equipped with high-adventure, pirates, lost treasure, murder, and of course ghosts. The historical part of the tale, which appears to be true, involves a boat load of Irish emigrants on their way to the new world, among them James Wilson and his wife, the very pregnant Elizabeth. On July 28, 1720, their daughter was born at sea; shortly afterward their vessel was seized by a pirate band led by the bloodthirsty Captain Don Pedro. Just before he gave the order to have everybody killed and tossed overboard, his heart was softened by the cries of a new-born baby. He then made the mother an offer she couldn't refuse: If she would name the baby after his own dear mother, Mary, he would spare the lives of all aboard. When she readily agreed, he presented the family with a bolt of green silk cloth. This, he explained, would be for the baby's wedding dress. Mary continued to Londonderry, New Hampshire, where she grew, married (in her green silk gown), and had sons of her own.

Here our romantic tale comes to a crossroads. One route says that after Mary's husband died the wicked Captain Don Pedro retired from the sea, moved to Henniker, had his ship carpenters build a house, and invited Mary and her sons to live with him. He buried his plunder somewhere on the grounds and was later murdered by an unidentified scoundrel bent on finding it. Mary had the captain's body buried under the three-ton fireplace hearthstone, where his skeleton remains to this day. In an alternate telling, Mary's son Robert built the house and there the family lived ever after, happily and pirate-free. The legends converge again after Mary's death in 1814. Supposedly she loved the house so much that her six-foot, red-headed, beautiful ghost stuck around to protect it. Many stories—most of them told by Louis Roy, a former owner—support the idea that there is a phantom on the premises.

Today the house has been gentrified beyond belief, but it can never be free of Mary's specter, real or imagined. You can view the house, then go to the local historical society to see Mary memorabilia and get the *real* scoop on the ghost stories. Afterward, head to the town library and ask to see an authentic fragment of Mary's wedding gown. You can even visit her grave at the local cemetery. If all this ghost chasing is too much, just check into the Henniker House bed and breakfast; host Anita Lavigne is a bit of an expert on Henniker's fabled haunt.

Henniker Historical Society
Academy Hall
5A Maple St.
P.O. Box 674
Henniker, NH 03242

Phone: (603) 428-6267
society@hennikerhistory.org
www.henniker.org/obmary.htm

Hours: Open Thursdays and Saturdays, 10 A.M.–2 P.M., year round.

The Ocean-Born Mary House

Location: Cross the river onto Depot Hill Road. Follow it until Depot Hill Road intersects with Bear Hill Road. Stay on Bear Hill Road for about one mile. The Ocean-Born Mary House is on the right, a big brown colonial house with two chimneys. The windows are white; the doors are red.

NOTE: It is a private residence. Apparently visitors are not encouraged. Best viewed from the road.

The Henniker Library

Location: It is right in downtown Henniker and easy to find.

Hillsboro, New Hampshire

Dick Kemp's Truck Farm

It is hard to guess what his neighbors might be whispering, but extreme-collector Dick Kemp's peculiar preoccupation is there for all to see right in the center of downtown Hillsboro. He collects trucks—Not toy trucks, not models, not pickups—great big Mack Trucks. His dooryard is brimming with over six hundred tons of rusted rigs. At last count he had 134, all lined up pretty as you please. His collection, which surrounds the family homestead, has been growing for forty-eight years, with specimens dating back to his 1926 AB Mack. How does he explain his urge to collect such conspicuous metal behemoths? "I like to see the trucks" is all he'll say. And that's all the rationale he needs to add another gem to his lot. Though his fondness for the big rigs dates all the way back to when he was in grade school, one can't help but wonder why anyone would want to live in the middle of what some might call a junkyard. Mr. Kemp has a logical explanation, "I can just come out here in the yard and look at it, and there it is." But maybe a noble mission lurks behind it all. "If I don't save them," Mr. Kemp asks in his distinct New Hampshire accent, "who's going to?" Good question.

Location: Take highway 149 into Hillsboro. Turn left onto Bridge Street and then another quick left onto Mill Street. You won't need a street address; the trucks are in plain view.

NOTE: Dick Kemp's truck farm is not—strictly speaking—a tourist attraction. But before stopping by you might note the sign on his door: "We shoot every 3rd bullshitter. The *second just left."*

Kingston, New Hampshire

Hobo Hotel

The small brick building's origins are a little uncertain. Local folks even call it a mystery. No one seems to know when the Tramp House was put up or who built it. The best guess it that it was constructed as a jail. Situated at the rear of the Town Hall, it is a small, sturdy brick structure with a concrete floor and a wooden roof. Inside, it's furnished with two metal cages, six and a half feet tall. Within the cages are frames for bunk beds. There is a hasp on the door where a padlock could have secured it. But Mr. Arthur H. Reynolds, keeper of the keys, says there was never any lock. In fact, no one was ever imprisoned there. Its principal use, apparently, was to shelter those homeless souls who roamed hills and highways during the Great Depression. When tramps needed a place to stay they could find a meal and a bed there. A man living across the street was paid by the town to bring them supper and breakfast, and wood for the stove. Before leaving these wayward souls would scrawl "18" on the outside of the building or somewhere nearby. It was a coded signal for the next to arrive. It meant, "I ate."

Location: It is a small brick building behind Kingston Town Hall. The sign on door says, "Tramp House."

Hours: Open only on "Kingston Days," August 4 and 5.

NOTE: For more information call Museum committee member Daniel Luparello at (603) 642-8838.

Lancaster, New Hampshire

Wooded Bliss

There is no way to tell what kind of a relationship John and Abigail Bergin had during life, but if their postmortem circumstances are any indication, they had a habit of letting odd things come between them. John and Abigail were among the earliest settlers of Coos County. He had been an officer in the Revolutionary War. She, judging from the lengthy poetic inscription on her tombstone, was a properly pious woman. They died in 1828 and 1826, respectively, and were buried side by side in Wilder Cemetery on a hillside overlooking Lancaster's Main Street. There they should have rested peacefully for all eternity. But, unbeknownst to anyone, there was an intruder in their midst. A seedling rested inconspicuously between their headstones. As the years passed it grew and became a sapling. One hundred years later it filled the three-foot space between their stones. As the twentieth century progressed, it grew, widened, and pushed against the sides of the stone markers, cracking them and eventually swallowing them up. You can see what remains of the Bergins' stones in the Wilder Cemetery. They're the ones partially embedded in the wooden trunk, joined—or separated—for all eternity by a huge evergreen tree.

Location: Lancaster is on the Connecticut River in northern New Hampshire. The village is on Route 3. Wilder Cemetery is on a hill overlooking Main Street.

Lincoln, New Hampshire

Clark's Trading Post

Roger Babson spent years trying to harness anti-gravity, all to no avail. Why didn't anybody send him to Clark's Trading Post? Within its vaguely Disney-like walls is Merlin's Mystical Mansion and the Mysterious Tuttle House, two addresses where gravity is turned on its head. Merlin, an eccentric magician, mesmerizes you in his dreamy Victorian parlor until—zap—reality starts to shift, you feel weightless, and—well, we don't want to spoil the surprise. The ruse is brilliant, contrived by Eddie Clark Jr. and other family members using a combination of motors, computers, trompe l'oeil, and sheer trickery. The Tuttle House is a geezers' home that somehow breaks the laws of physics: everything is a little off kilter. But there's more! Just outside is a black cage which was once the town jail. If you've never understood why they call prison "the pen," you will now. The performing bears they keep a short distance away have more space than this. Nearby is a gray museum containing some good old-fashioned sensationalism: a calf with four hind legs, another with two heads, and two mutoscopes. Insert a dime, crank the handle, and pictures flap by. These "moving picture" devices in fact were the forerunners of contemporary film. The green one on the right plays a strip-tease a la 1920. As much as we love Disney World, there's something irresistible about this home-spun amusement park. You really get the feeling that it's run by people who know the value of fun and the importance of the unusual.

Clark's Trading Post
> Box 1
> Route 3
> Lincoln, NH 03251

Phone: (603) 745-8913
> info@clarkstradingpost.com
> www.clarkstradingpost.com

Location: Clark's Trading Post is on Route 3. Huge billboards point the way, making it hard to miss. Don't be put off by the kitschy gift shop or its somewhat garish facade.

Hours: Open 10 A.M.–5 P.M., weekends only, Memorial Day–June. Open daily 10 A.M.–5 P.M., June 24–Labor Day. Open weekends only, Labor Day–mid-October.

Admission charged.

Some sites wheelchair accessible.

Littleton, New Hampshire

Hair Today

Sometimes the oddest things can be discovered in the most out-of-the-way places. Tiny historical society museums, the kind staffed by good-natured volunteers and open only a few hours a week, can hide tantalizing treasures. Take the Littleton Area Historical Society Museum. They display a curio that is sure to catch the eye of any weirdness buff: a "hair wreath." And it's exactly what you think it is: a wreath made of human hair. Though they have fallen out of popularity, and may be perceived as a trifle grisly, decorative hair was quite a trend in the nineteenth century. Supposedly people who attended a wake would leave a lock of hair for the dearly departed. Someone would gather them up and construct a multicolored memorial from them. Though such a thing seems morbid, recent research suggests that making hair wreaths and hair jewelry were simply crafts practiced by nineteenth-century women, like quilt-making, tatting, or crocheting. But it is difficult to imagine how anyone could enjoy working with something as unforgiving and tiny as hair. Littleton's sizable specimen was made circa 1865 by Mary Ann Burley for her brother Frank, a rural mailman. If it was given to him during life, it has outlasted him and now serves as a memorial.

While visiting the museum, there are a few more oddities not to be overlooked:

1. Two stuffed one-week-old bear cubs. Their mother was shot and they died shortly afterwards. What else was the hunter supposed to do with them?

2. A druggist's logo from the 1900s that proves pop art was ahead of its time. It's an electrified trade sign—a three-dimensional mortar and pestle—consisting of over 200 "glass jewels" that sparkle brightly when the current is turned on. Garish but great.

3. And don't forget, Littleton is the land of the Stereoscope, a magical and nearly forgotten entertainment industry from our pre-movie past. It was here that the Kilburn Brothers ran their Stereoscopic View factory from 1867 to 1909. The Historical Society Museum has thousands of three-dimensional pictures (stereographs) in their library, with many fine pieces on display. Our favorite is a machine in which black and white three-dimensional images magically turn to color, an early special effect that still has the power to fascinate.

Littleton Area Historical Society Museum
   1 Cottage St.
   Littleton, NH 03561

Phone: (603) 444-6435
   www.museumusa.org/data/museums/nh/114708.htm

Location: in the old fire station, part of the Town Hall and Opera House at the center of town.

Hours: Open April–November, Wednesdays, 9 A.M.–4 P.M.

Admission free.

Wheelchair accessible.

Madison, New Hampshire

Shock Rock

You have to see it to believe it!

This is the sort of oddity that attracted our ancestors long before movies, television, and automobiles. Today's tourists are ready to be unimpressed. They look around, trying to spot this "wonder of nature," but they're standing right next to it. They don't see it because they think it's a mountain. The Madison Boulder is a so-called "glacial erratic." It's the biggest boulder in New England and one of the largest in the world. It glacier-surfed to its present location over twenty-five thousand years ago and nothing has moved it since. Reports of its size and weight vary. One says the Madison Boulder is thirty-eight feet high, ninety feet long and forty feet wide, weighing approximately 4,700 tons. Another authority puts its weight at 7,650 tons. But no matter how you look at it, it's huge! It was "discovered" by geologists in 1887. When word got out, the boulder caught on among "city boarders" from the many local inns and boarding houses. Sightseers and picnickers loved it. Men liked to climb to the top. Some energetic local genius installed iron rods (since removed) to make the dangerous climb easier.

The Madison Boulder is unique, not just to New Hampshire, but to the whole continent. It's one of those things that may not sound all that interesting, but it is! The sheer magnitude of this single stone cannot be truly appreciated until it is seen.

Location: Head south from Conway on Route 113. Go approximately four miles and watch for signs. The Madison Boulder is at the end of a dirt road.

The Baptist Murder

Milford, New Hampshire, called "The Granite Town," has one of its darkest tales immortalized on a slab of marble in the Elm Street Cemetery. Known as the "Old Graveyard," this one-acre burying ground is unusual because all the graves are oriented so their inscriptions face west. More unusual, however, is the marker erected by Dr. Calvin Cutter for his wife Caroline. In words chiseled in stone, he records forever the great wrong committed against his family. So inflammatory was the content, that Dr. Cutter erected the stone at night by lantern light. His 140 word saga is a tale of pettiness, greed, small town politics, and death. It begins, "Caroline H., wife of Calvin Cutter, M.D., murdered by the Baptist Ministry of the Baptist Church as follows . . ." Then he goes on to tell the tale. Though local reaction is not recorded in the 1978 town history, we may presume the powers-that-be were aptly shamed, or infinitely tolerant, for the stone still stands.

Location: From Route 101, turn east onto 101A (Elm Street) and head toward the center of Milford. The Elm Street Cemetery is behind a Korean War memorial, near the corner of Elm and Cottage Streets. The Cutter plot is on the east side—the far right when facing the cemetery from the road.

God's Hand

In 1871 and 1872, local people built the Milton Mills's Methodist Church using only donated materials. By the end of the first summer, most of the crew had wearied of the task. They decided to stop and begin again come spring. However, Aratus B. Shaw, the church founder who'd directed the construction, was *not* ready to quit. He worked through fall and winter, determined to finish the job—alone if he had to. After solitarily building and positioning the pews, he began decorating the exterior. When he was all but finished, he decided he needed to create a grand finale. From a solid block of wood he carved—carefully to scale—a giant closed fist with its forefinger pointing upward. The wrist is twenty inches in circumference, the knuckles thirty-four inches, and the thumb eight inches. The whole thing is about forty-four inches tall. The finger itself is eleven inches long. Using a half-bushel wicker basket, Mr. Shaw carried his creation up to the dizzying top of the steeple. The hand is easy to see, but over the years there has been a lot of speculation about exactly what it means. The obvious message is that the finger points the way to Heaven. But some say Mr. Shaw carved it to show who had given him the courage, strength, and endurance to see the project through. Maybe he just wanted to give God a hand or show everyone he'd done the work . . . single-handedly.

Location: Milton Mills is almost on the Maine border where Route 109 and Willey Road come together. The Finger-Church is obvious.

The Gravity Shield

Perhaps the weirdest historical marker in all of New England stands in the middle of a traffic island on Route 13, right in the center of New Boston. It's a small granite monument unnoticed by thousands of people who drive by it every year without stopping to take a look. But read it.

Okay, at first it may look like a joke . . . but keep reading.

In 1929, statistician Roger Ward Babson correctly predicted the drop in stock prices that lead to the infamous stock market crash. Less well known is that he also predicted that he could make things rise—not stock prices, but metal, transportation devices, even people. In other words, anti-gravity. The New Boston marker, funded by Mr. Babson, is there to commemorate his efforts to create "anti-gravity and a partial gravity insulator."

Yes, this is the same Babson who founded Babson College and commissioned the biggest globe in the world. He picked New Boston for his gravity research because he thought it would be safe from an atomic attack. In 1948, he bought up much of the town and established a research institute in what is now the Molly Stark Tavern. The institute had three main purposes: to set up an information center and library of gravity-related papers and books, to conduct an annual conference, and to award prizes each year for essays pertaining to innovative research of gravity.

Sounds knuckle-headed, we know, but scientists as renowned as Albert Einstein took it seriously. Thomas Edison was fascinated with the prospect. And other big-name visionaries like Igor Sikorsky, inventor of the helicopter, and Clarence Birdseye, of frozen food fame, attended the annual meetings. Stephen Hawking, the physicist who wrote *A Brief History of Time*, won Mr. Babson's annual prize several times.

Things shut down—or maybe floated off—around 1963, with Newton's laws still firmly in place. Today there is little to see, just the odd marker and perhaps some scattered memorabilia at the New Boston Historical Society, including a Gravity Research Foundation pamphlet.

Location: The marker is on a traffic island on Route 13 in downtown New Boston.

North Woodstock, New Hampshire

Rock of Ages Church

There is not a lot to say about this particular oddity, but perhaps that's as it should be, because it is very small. The symbolism is obvious—a church perched upon a sturdy rock—but the church itself is less obvious because it is so easy to miss. It measures a mere eleven- by eleven-feet and is said to accommodate twelve and a half people when it's fully packed. We curiously looked around to find that half person. Anyway, it is a *real* church in the sense that services are occasionally held there—weddings and such. There is a steeple, an altar, a cross, wide windows welcoming in the sun. It is always open, as a real church should be. You'll note signs like "Rock of Ages," "A wee, free kirk," and "Via Dolorosa" stenciled on the rock. Apparently at one time somebody had big plans for the little place. Alas, now there is a subtle air of neglect about it, possibly attributable to the junk cars that are abandoned in front of it or the all-seasons Woolworth-style Nativity that seems about to be crushed by the rock itself. Rock of Ages Church is definitely worth a look, especially if you, like us, are on an eternal search for the world's tiniest house of worship.

Location: The church is about two miles south of town on Route 3 after Parker Ledge Road. It's on your right. Look quickly; it's easy to miss.

Hours: Always open.

Free Admission.

Tilton's Arch

There aren't too many arch enemies in Tilton or Northfield. Most people are quite proud of their hilltop curiosity, one that's easily mistaken for a replica of the Arc de Triomphe. Actually

Tilton's Arch towers over Northfield, New Hampshire, as a reminder of one man's folly. Photo: Joe Citro

patterned after the Arch of Titus in Rome, it was to have marked the grave of local merchant and millionaire Charles Elliott Tilton. In 1882, he erected the fifty-five-foot monument to himself and placed it where he could keep an eye on things for eternity. However, that part of Tilton town became Northfield, which he refused to use as his final resting place. He had also neglected another detail: The arch wasn't constructed in a graveyard, so he couldn't be buried there anyway. All this leaves an elaborate but empty sarcophagus adorned with a fifty-ton lion serving no purpose but to inspire curious questions and the nickname "Tilton's Folly." The place is rife with local rumors.

Some say there is a tunnel connecting the interior with a nearby house. Some say a ladder, recently removed, gave anyone access to the top and an excellent vantage point for sightseeing. But the arch itself is a sight to be seen, and it is visible from anywhere around. Built for a cost of fifty thousand dollars—far more than Mr. Tilton's nearby mansion—it is one of the most imposing and least known mega-structures in all New England. Mr. Tilton's real grave is worth a look, too, though no one can guarantee he's there, either. Also see the mansion he used to occupy, now the Tilton School library; check out the weird markings on the wall of the main reading room.

Locations: The arch—in Northfield—is obvious and easy to find.

The Tilton School Library—in Tilton—is up the hill from the town center. Just follow the signs.

Park Cemetery is south on Route 3 about a half mile out of Tilton on the left. His current residence is toward the back and conspicuous—but it is a real comedown from the palatial memorial in which he'd planned to spend eternity.

Nottingham, New Hampshire

Rock Group

One of New England's most astonishing natural wonders is hidden deep within a dense forest. It's a cluster of "gray giants"—house-sized boulders that a glacier plucked from North Mountain and dumped, like tombstones for giants, on its southeastern flank. Churchill Rock is the largest, measuring some sixty by forty by forty feet and weighing in at an estimated six thousand tons. According to legend, it was named after a demented man who'd escaped his keepers and climbed to its top, a spot so precarious that no one in his right mind would dare follow. Chase Rock is the next largest, at forty by forty by thirty feet. It commemorates three generations of Chases who farmed around it in the early 1800s. Eventually— like so many determined pioneers—the Chases were overcome by death and the elements. Their grim burial patch is visible nearby, on what remains of the family farm. The other eight or so boulders are about two-thirds the size of the Chase block, all of them made of syenite, a course-grained stone that looks like granite but is much darker. A cluster of the boulders litters North Mountain's eastern edge beside a cliff that rises verti- cally like the sheer wall of a four-story building. Slices have fal- len away to reveal deep mysterious crevasses, inspiring the name "Devil's Den." It is a steep, forbidding place. And it's eerie, reminding one of how formidable a foe nature must have been for so many vanished settlers.

Pawtuckaway State Park Boulder Field
128 Mountain Rd.
Nottingham, NH 03290

Phone: (603) 895-3031
info@nhparks.state.nh.us
www.nhparks.state.nh.us/parkpages/wentworthcoolidge/wentcoolhom.html

Location: Although the boulder field is in a state park, it's not easy to find. Take a four-wheel drive vehicle if you have the option, as roads are rocky. Going east from the town of Deerfield on Deerfield Road, turn right into Pawtuck- away State Park at Tavern Hill and drive up the dirt road as far as you can until you see a good-sized pond (Round Pond) on your left. Park the car and continue straight (westward) on a foot trail until you see the boulders. The boulders follow a brook toward the eastern side of North Mountain, and Devil's Den is at the mountain's easternmost edge. You may be able to pick up an unreliable map from the park's welcome center. We did, and it almost got us lost. In any event, bring a compass (or better yet, a guide). Don't forget the bug repellent (New Hampshire mosquitoes can be fierce). And allow plenty of sunlight; you don't want to get lost in these hills.

NOTE: For years, Churchill Rock was thought to be the largest glacial erratic of all until someone discovered the Madison boulder, a massive stone edifice which stands by itself. See *Shock Rock* under Madison, New Hampshire.

Free admission.

Sacrifice on Mount Shaw

If you like treasure hunts and are prepared for a wild goose chase, this may be of interest. On the Moultonborough side of Mount Shaw there is a stone relic, facing west so the sun hits it, said to be identical to the sacrificial stone at America's Stonehenge (see Salem, New Hampshire). One theory is that it—and others yet undiscovered—was carved by pilgrim Carthaginians who, like the English Puritan separatists two thousand years later, sought the new world to pursue religious freedom—in the Carthaginians' case, freedom to sacrifice the occasional human. Quite possibly magician Aleister Crowley, "the wickedest man in the world," used the stone (for what, we're not sure) during his 1918 New Hampshire magical retreat, mentioned in his *Confessions*. He says he visited "Lake Pasquany," but since there is no such place in this dimension, he may well have meant Lake Winnipesaukee, which is nearby. The stone was well known in 1918, and was considered one of the area's curiosities. Then, following a forest fire in 1955, the stone was lost; new growth covered the terrain, disguising its location. Even people who'd seen it were unable to relocate it. Since the area is reputed to be seething with rattlesnakes, expeditions to rediscover Mount Shaw's Sacrificial Stone have been few. Happy hunting!

Location: Mt. Shaw is about seven miles west of Center Ossipee. It is in Tuftonboro, on the border of Moultonborough. To get there, find the Pine Hill Road turnoff between West Ossipee and Center Ossipee. Going west, you'll pass Conner Pond (the center of a volcanic ring and reputedly so deep that no one has ever found the bottom). Keep driving until the road ends. Mount Shaw (elevation 2,975 feet) is straight ahead.

For only the most intrepid of hikers. Even if you find Mount Shaw, it's no guarantee you'll find the sacrificial stone.

The Man Who Got Ahead

Beside Academy Road, near the venerable Pembroke Academy, there is a solitary stone monument commemorating an unimaginably ghastly event. An event that generated lurid headlines nationwide: a murder that was so astonishingly brutal, it has never been equaled in New Hampshire's annals of crime.

On the morning of October 4, 1875, a much-loved seventeen-year-old girl, Josie Langmaid, was on her way to school. Normally she would be with a group of friends, but this morning she was late . . . and alone. Josie never made it to the academy. Someone waited for her on the well-traveled shortcut through Gile Swamp. Perhaps, just for a moment, Josie saw the unfamiliar man watching her. He was not big, but stocky, strong looking, presenting a grim, unnatural appearance. His face was haloed by a tangle of black, unkempt hair and beard. Deep sockets with unusually dark, bushy eyebrows gave his eyes the appearance of terrifying jet black orbs. He was Joseph LaPage, a forty-two-year-old French-Canadian woodchopper from St. Albans, Vermont. Without pausing for conversation or explanation, he raced at her from the shadows. No one knows exactly what happened next. One can only speculate based on the ruined condition of the young woman's body. Mr. LaPage had done his work with a club, an ax, and a knife. His apparent smattering of anatomical knowledge made the result all the more chilling. After the man whom newspapers called "the demon from the bottomless pit" was finally brought to justice, the citizens of Pembroke erected the marker to insure that Josie would never be forgotten. It marks the spot where the horror began, then gives direction to two additional markers. The first, just ninety feet north, identifies the place where Josie's body was found. The second, eighty-two rods away, shows where her head was discovered. The inscription fails to explain what the monster was doing with her head as he carried it over a thousand feet from the ravaged torso.

Location: Follow Route 3 (not 3A) south out of Concord into Pembroke. After the town hall and Congregational church, turn left at the lights. The road takes a dip. There, on the right, is the entrance to the Three Rivers School. Across the street is the granite marker showing the place of Josie Langmaid's death. The first marker will direct you to the other two.

Pittsburg, New Hampshire–Chartierville, Quebec

Anti-gravity?

We're taking liberties with international borders here, but if you make it all the way up north to Pittsburg, you might as well take a few extra minutes, drive a few extra miles, and play around with an unusual phenomenon—a magnetic hill. Is it anti-gravity? Is it an optical illusion? Is it magic? Who knows? All we can say for sure is that it is fun, strange, and effective. You'll sense powerful unknown forces dragging your car uphill . . . with you in it! Here's how it works: You park at the bottom of a hill, put it in neutral, make sure your foot's off the brake. Then wait. Soon—against all logic and laws of gravity—you will find yourself rolling upwards. It is mysterious and almost funny, truly anti-gravity. "Magnetic hills" such as this are rare, and this one is especially convincing. It's well worth going a little out of your way for, and you're already out of your way if you've come to Pittsburg.

Location: The spot is very easy to find because it's almost in the United States. It's just across the line on the Canadian side. As you follow Route 3 north, you'll cross the border at Pittsburg, the only crossing in New Hampshire. You'll have to stop at the Canadian customs booth anyway, so ask the officer where to find the magnetic hill. He (or she) is used to the question and won't think you're nuts. The officer will then point to a nearby sign that marks the spot and gives instructions. Bon Voyage!

No Man's Land

After the Webster-Ashburton Treaty of 1842 was signed, Americans and Canadians finally had to stop squabbling over who owned what. To resolve the vagaries of a 5,525 mile international boundary, two surveying crews, one American, one Canadian, began working from opposite ends of the continent, moving toward the center. The two groups met at what is now New Hampshire's only international border crossing. But at the meeting point there was a discrepancy—an eighteen-inch overlap. Not bad, considering the distance they had to survey. But it's still a foot and a half gap that neither country could claim, and neither would give up.

After many attempts at agreement, they set up two boundary markers that have remained in place for more than 150 years. This created an interesting anomaly. Who owns the eighteen inches in between? Border officials won't say it's a "no-man's-land"; you have to be in one country or the other. But if you stand between the two markers it simply cannot be determined just which country you're in.

Because the double marker (numbers 483 and 484) has always been seen as a local landmark, the two monuments were eventually reset in a single concrete base and assigned a single number—484.

Location: Marker 484 is enclosed in a metal crib beside the road between the ports of entry to Pittsburg and Chartierville.

Glow Stone

People in Portsmouth have a mystery among them—a baffling phenomenon that may be unique to this New England city. It seems that a light can reliably be seen in the South Street cemetery. It's not a floating orb, a luminescent specter, or the lantern of a ghostly caretaker making his eternal rounds. It is, in fact, a glowing tombstone. Three nearly identical markers stand in a row—but only the middle one lights up. Locals have been aware of it for ten or fifteen years, many have seen it for themselves, but no one can explain it. It's visible only at night and weather conditions seem to have little to do with it. No matter if the air is foggy or clear, it shines. Photos show it glowing amidst its darkened neighbors—a subtle luminescence, but undoubtedly there. Is it natural, or supernatural? Both sides have their proponents. Nay-sayers maintain it's a reflection from a traffic light, the nearby pond, or a street light on Miller Avenue. Even skeptics admit it can't be the moon, for the stone glows even on moonless nights. Local writer George Hosker says, "I'm always amazed that people who doubt the glow have no trouble accepting that light can bounce two hundred yards from the street, reflect off the pond, and hit one particular tombstone." So why does it glow? Some say it's supernatural, that it's the grave of a murderer. Or a murder victim. Others prefer a "scientific" explanation. Maybe the stone contains luminescent particles, maybe even uranium. But whatever the reason, we find it interesting that with such a mysterious phenomenon in their midst, the people of Portsmouth haven't come up with a good, chilling legend to explain it.

Location: South Street Cemetery is in downtown Portsmouth, not far from the river approximately where South Street, Sagamore Street, and Miller

Avenue intersect. Take the South Street entrance to the cemetery and walk down the descending path to the pond (on your right). Look across the pond. The stone is in the middle of three old, squarish stones in a row. Its shine can be seen from at least two hundred yards away.

Portsmouth, New Hampshire

Secret Passageway

The Wentworth-Coolidge Mansion is what you might call a glimpse of the good life, circa 1755. It was the home of Benning Wentworth (1696–1770), New Hampshire's first Royal Governor. It is a rambling abode with more than forty rooms, and it has a secret passageway leading from the upstairs mantelpiece to a tiny window, where the governor could peer out unseen to find out who was knocking on the door. Governor Wentworth had plenty of reasons to keep looking over both shoulders. To start with, he was loyal to the British Crown at a time when revolutionary passions were growing. He was also shipping timber and livestock to the Spanish Caribbean in flagrant violation of British law. And he had thirteen siblings, each after a piece of the pie. As if that weren't enough, the portly Harvard graduate scandalized the town in 1760 by marrying his house-keeper, a woman thirty years his junior, when his first wife was but a short time in the grave. The old rogue burst forth with his intentions during a party at the mansion and ordered that a minister marry them on the spot. The house is as quirky as its former owner—bright yellow siding and wide floorboards on the inside, a cellar big enough to conceal thirty horses, and a grill-style "stewing kitchen" built at the request of his French chef. Whether patriot or scoundrel, he must have done something right. Two "Benningtons" are named after him, and he served longer than any other governor in U.S. history: twenty-six years.

The Wentworth-Coolidge Mansion
Little Harbor Rd.
Portsmouth, NH 03801

Phone: (603) 436-6607
nhparks@dred.state.nh.us
www.nhparks.state.nh.us/parkops/parks/wcmansion.html

Location: Going south on Route 1A from Portsmouth, head east on Little Harbor Road until you see the sign. The secret window is inside a tiny cubbyhole accessible through a door next to the wooden mantelpiece upstairs.

Hours: Open for tours June 1–October 1, Tuesdays, Thursdays, Fridays, and Saturdays, 10 A.M.–3 P.M., Sundays, noon–5 P.M.

Admission charged.

Rye, New Hampshire

Brackett Lane Massacre Site

It's an eerie little graveyard, just a few humble rocks in the trees near a salt marsh. Even on the brightest day there's something oddly somber about the place, something that makes you want to talk in whispers. At times you can almost feel the tragedy that happened here on a beautiful September day in 1691. The settlers were going about their business, feeding the animals, tending the fields, perhaps talking in clusters. No one was mindful that the French and Indian War was getting closer to home, moving inexorably toward them along the coast from York, Maine. A band of about thirty Indians landed quietly on the shore. They knew enough to stay clear of the armed garrison houses and slipped invisibly into the settlers' homes while their owners were busy cutting hay. Soon they had set fire to all the houses and launched an attack. When it was over, twelve villagers lay dead, another three had been burned alive in their homes. Seven were taken captive, all of them the children of Anthony Brackett and his wife, who'd been killed in the attack. Today the only reminder is this haunting roadside burial ground. The Brackett homestead, which was just across the street, was burned to the ground. The cemetery's makeshift appearance suggests that the victims were buried hastily, using whatever stones were at hand. Most were left unmarked. It is a cheerless sight, a silent reminder that mass violence has been part of the American experience from the very beginning.

Location: Heading east from the fire station in the town center, veer right when the road splits. Brackett Lane is about three miles away, the second road on the left (the first is Long John Road). The cemetery is on the right, opposite house number 605.

Salem, New Hampshire

America's Stonehenge

A true American mystery. While Old England may have its Stonehenge, New England won't be outdone. The Granite State's claim to megalithic fame is comparably ancient, equally enigmatic, and so weird that H. P. Lovecraft used it in his story "The Dunwich Horror." For years this thirty-acre hilltop complex was referred to as "Mystery Hill." The name should have stuck; no one knows who built the structures, when, or why. The perplexing series of stone walls contains shaped standing stones, primitive cave-like buildings, and a system of baffling tunnels. An enormous flat stone, called the "Sacrificial Stone," may have been used for just that. Beneath it, an eight-foot shaft leads to an eerie underground chamber from which a concealed priest could have uttered predictions, commands, and curses. The unknown builders were well-versed in astronomy. The site is an accurate astronomical calendar that can be used to calculate solar and lunar events. As to its age: clearly it was built long before Columbus arrived. Tested pottery fragments date back to

1000 B.C. Radiocarbon dated charcoal from a fire pit was found to be four thousand years old. Presumably the builders were either an unknown indigenous culture, or a migrant European population. We may never solve the mystery of Mystery Hill, but one thing's for sure: It is probably the oldest man-made construction in the United States. And perhaps the most puzzling.

America's Stonehenge
105 Haverhill Road
Salem, NH 03079
Mailing address: P.O. Box 84, N. Salem, NH 03073

Phone: (603) 893-8300
amstonehenge@worldnet.att.net
www.stonehengeusa.com/

Location: From Interstate 93, exit 3, take Route 111 east to Island Pond and Haverhill Roads (about five miles). Follow Haverhill Road south to the America's Stonehenge entrance.

Hours: Open February 1–June 19, 9 A.M.–5 P.M. daily; June 22–September 2, 9 A.M.–5 P.M. daily; September 3–October 31, 9 A.M.–5 P.M. daily; October 31–February 1, 9 A.M.–4 P.M. daily.

Admission charged.

Sandown, New Hampshire

Slave Pews

Northerners feeling smug about the South should bear in mind that New Englanders also kept slaves. James Garvin of New Hampshire's Office of Historic Preservation points out that before the American Revolution, Portsmouth merchants were active in the slave trade, sometimes bringing them directly from Africa or the Caribbean to live with local families. Some of the proof is evident in the old Puritan meeting houses, where church attendance was universal and obligatory for slave and slavemaster alike. Sandown is a good example. Built in 1773, it is largely in its original condition, with unpainted pews and an elevated tulip-shaped pulpit. Upstairs in the two facing galleries, or balconies, are "sheep-pen pews": square enclosures with a gate. Hard, narrow benches line their inside perimeters. It was here that slaves, indentured servants, and other unfortunates were relegated to sit out the tedious, interminable sermons, women in one balcony, men in the other. Often such pews were identified by the initials "B.W." for black women and "B.M." for black men. Unruly boys were exiled here as punishment. In later years the gallery pews would be occupied by the choir, although it would take another century before the back-aching planks were tempered by cushions, making church services marginally more tolerable.

The Old Meeting House
Fremont Rd.
Sandown, NH 03873

Phone: (603) 887-3453

Location: The church is just north of the town center on the east side of Route 121A where it joins Fremont Road, which leads up to the Meeting House.

Hours: By appointment only during daylight hours. You can also attend the Methodist service here held once a year at 11 A.M. on the second Sunday in August.

NOTE: The nearby town of Danville also has an eighteenth-century meeting house with gallery pews for indentured servants, although town records make no mention of slaves.

Admission: donation.

Wheelchair accessible on the ground floor.

Stark, New Hampshire

Stalag Stark

The tiny village of Stark, with its covered bridge and white-steepled church, is the quintessential image of New England serenity. But such icons are rarely what they seem. Dig a little deeper and you discover the town played an important but largely unnoticed role in American history. For two years during World War II it housed New Hampshire's only prisoner-of-war camp. Two hundred fifty German and Austrian soldiers— Nazis, anti-Nazis, and communists—were incarcerated about two miles upriver in an abandoned Civilian Conservation Corps camp converted into five wooden barracks, a mess hall, a recreation hall, and four watchtowers, all of it encircled with barbed wire. The prisoners were put to work cutting pulpwood and picking crops on local farms. Surprisingly, friendships, even romances, bloomed between prisoners and citizens. Security got so lax that Stark became the easiest of America's five hundred POW camps to escape from. Most escapees were eventually apprehended; their heads were shaved and they were placed in the stockade on a diet of bread and water for up to two weeks. However, some forty years later the prisoners returned willingly. Stark held a German-American friendship day hosting inmates and guards alike. A second reunion was held a few years later to visit the camp's remains and lay wreaths. In some ways peace was more thoroughly established in the camps than on the battlefields.

Location: Head northeast out of town on Route 110 for two miles. The commemorative plaque is on the right. The stone remaining from one watchtower is nearby in the trees, and a second is set back behind it. A path leads to the site.

Tamworth, New Hampshire

Preacher's Rock

Also known as "Pastor's Rock," this is one of those oddities that sounds boring on paper, but holds a peculiar fascination when seen for real. There is not a lot to be said about it, really. It is simply an enormous rock with a stone access stairway leading to its top. The story is that the Reverend Samuel Hidden was ordained as pastor of the local Congregational church on September 12, 1792. Trouble was, the town of Tamworth was still pretty much a wilderness area and had no church. So they held the ceremony on top of the biggest rock around. The giant boulder served as Reverend Hidden's proxy pulpit for some time until the church was built. Years later, a stone monument was placed atop the rock to commemorate the event. Reverend Hidden served the town for forty-six years. In a sense his church really was built on a rock.

Location: The rock is on Route 113 in town center near the cemetery.

NOTE: The rock is not far from the summer home of Grover Cleveland. And while you're in town, you might want to visit the Remick Country Doctor Museum and Farm. There, they say, you can experience early New England life from the point of view of a country doctor, from tending his farm to tending his patients throughout the hills of Tamworth and beyond.

Warner, New Hampshire

Slave Killer

Don't think colonial settlers were the only ones to have slaves. Indians had them too, especially in the Northwest. They were usually members of enemy tribes, but of course they captured the occasional Englishman as well. Indian slaveowners concocted a special device to keep their slaves in line. Called "slave killers," they were carved wooden clubs, rounded at one end, used to whack anyone who disobeyed. The Mount Kearsarge Indian Museum in Warner, New Hampshire (not far from Lake Sunapee), has a ferocious looking one; the rounded part has eyes and teeth inlaid with abalone. Located across from the buffalo, it's in a case with bows and arrows, at the beginning of the Plains Indians section. In this same case is a buffalo stomach made into a bottle to transport liquids, a buffalo bladder that children would blow up and deflate like a balloon, and dried buffalo dung, a prized material used for starting fires. Elsewhere in the exhibit is a man's chest plate, sort of a suit of armor protecting the chest, that is decorated with bits of human hair.

Mt. Kearsarge Indian Museum
Kearsarge Mountain Rd.
P.O. Box 142
Warner, NH 03278

Phone: (603) 456-2600 or (603) 456-3244
mkim@conknet.com
www.indianmuseum.org

Location: The Museum is twenty minutes northwest of Concord on I-89. From the south, take exit 8, go into the village, take a right onto Kearsarge Mountain Road, and the museum is on the right after one mile. From the north, take exit 9, go to the village, take a left onto Kearsarge Mountain Road, and the museum is on the right one mile away.

Hours: May–October, Monday–Saturday, 10 A.M.–5 P.M., Sundays, noon–5 P.M.

Admission charged.

Wheelchair accessible.

Warren, New Hampshire

Warren's Rocket

Imagine you're stepping into an old-time science fiction movie. It begins this way: You're driving into the sleepy little town of Warren, nestled in the green countryside of rural New Hampshire. You feel good, as you would approaching any picturesque small New England village. You're charged with nostalgia. There's an aspect of quaintness in the dignified old buildings—storefronts and restaurants—on the outskirts of town. Then, getting closer, you see white colonial buildings scattered among the lush foliage. And, poking through lofty treetops, you see the pointed tips of stark white church steeples against the blue sky.

But wait! Something's wrong!

One of those steeples isn't a steeple at all. It's the nosecone of a rocket. Have the aliens touched down in Warren? Though you can hardly believe your eyes, you study the massive spire. It's not alien; it's one of ours! Is Warren's village green defended by a seventy-foot missile? Maybe this "Live Free or Die" business has gone a little too far. But it's a fact. There's a Jupiter-C rocket on Warren's postcard perfect town green. Although it's identical to the one that catapulted New Hampshirite Alan Shepard into outer space in 1961, Warren's rocket has nothing to do with the astronaut. It has to do with Mr. Ted Asselin who, in 1971, was stationed at the Redstone Ballistic Missile site in Huntsville, Alabama. That's where disused Redstone missiles were stored. Apparently authorities gave Mr. Asselin permission to cart off his oversized souvenir. Town authorities were delighted to let him position it at ground zero, right in the middle of Warren's picturesque common. After all, most towns had to settle for a Civil War cannon or a statue of their founder. Today, curious observers and space junkies can admire the giant pillar of 1950s-style

A Jupiter-C rocket commands the town green in Warren, New Hampshire.
Photo: Joe Citro

space junk; it is on permanent public display. Don't worry, it won't fall on you. As the on-site marker explains, "The eight-ton missile is secured in the common in an eight-foot deep foundation with five huge steel I-beams set in cement."

And it won't fire accidentally; it isn't even loaded.

Location: The rocket is on the common in the middle of Warren. The Warren Historical Society (open Sundays, 1–4 P.M.) is in a building next to the common. There you can find a letter from Astronaut Shepard along with pictures and artifacts, clippings and brochures.

Washington, New Hampshire

A Grave Place

The town cemetery in Washington seems to have more than its share of entertaining gravestones. Now, we're not sure how proper it is to find amusement in such things, but we can't help but think the creator of this first marker could not have been entirely serious.

1. One Foot in the Grave: This is the grave of a leg. Captain Samuel Jones lost it in a construction accident and—so the story goes—gave it a dignified burial, complete with a funeral and its own head-foot?-stone. It reads, "Capt. Samuel Jones Leg which was amputated July 7, 1804." When the rest of him died a few years later, he was buried in Boston, Massachusetts. You might say Mr. Jones is buried in two states.

2. The Washington Globe: Look up from Mr. Jones's leg's final resting place and you'll see, near the top of the hill, a perfect sphere. Nothing funny about that, at least not until you read the family name: "Ball." Was the humor intentional?

3. An Unusual Insignia: There is nothing funny about this third grave, but it is a real rarity, especially in this part of

the world. Locate what is just about the biggest stone in the cemetery. A closer look will reveal that it proudly displays the Soviet hammer and sickle. It marks the final resting place of Fred and Elba Chase, who died in 1933 and 1967, respectively. They're remembered as "courageous and devoted fighters in the class struggle." This is the only tombstone in the Northeast bearing such an insignia and epitaph. Perhaps the town is not too happy about it. The day we visited, the Chase grave seemed more overgrown and hidden than the rest.

Captain Samuel Jones's amputated leg in its Washington, New Hampshire grave. Photo: Joe Citro

Location: From Route 31 in Washington, go west a short distance on Faxen Hill Road. Before you get to Millen Pond Road, you will find two cemeteries, one on either side of the road. Both are interesting, but you want the newer cemetery on the right-hand side.

Webster, New Hampshire

Covered Bridge House

As further evidence that life can exist anywhere, consider this odd abode—perhaps the only one of its kind in New England. Webster's "Covered Bridge House" is not a house situated near a covered bridge; it's a house *in* a covered bridge. And it's one of the most unusual examples of recycling in recent history.

Originally the 120-foot bridge spanned the Blackwater River at Swett's Mills. It had been there over a century, but, in 1909, was condemned for traffic. Jessie Pearson, whose family had owned the bridge originally, could have had it demolished. Instead she hired a crew to haul it to a choice spot on the top of a nearby hill. She had one end covered with a stone fireplace, added two lofts inside, and finished the exterior with a window, porches and a balcony. Voila! It was ready to move into! The Covered Bridge House has been in the Pearson family ever since. And vice-versa.

Location: From I-89, take exit 9. Go through town of Warner. Take a left onto White Plains Road and follow it until you are on the north side of Lake Winnepocket. Take a right onto Lake Shore Road and drive until you reach a stop sign. The house is ahead, on what turns into Bridge House Road.

NOTE: The bridge-to-house transformation was thorough, so it might not be easy to identify. In any case, it's a private residence, so a drive-by viewing is recommended.

Whitefield, New Hampshire

The Mysterious Finger

Even seasoned headstone hunters are baffled by this one. It is no secret that during the 1860s and '70s it was fashionable to have gravestones bearing carved hands with a finger pointing skyward. The meaning is obvious: The finger points toward Heaven because the deceased is "Going home," "Going up," or "Gone above." But the Methodist Cemetery in Whitefield offers something unsettlingly different. Check out the headstone of Ira Bowles, who died January 10, 1863, at age sixty-two. The pointing finger is there, all right. But it's not pointing up; it's pointing down. What does it mean? Nobody—neither expert nor amateur—seems to know. Why would anyone want a finger pointing downward over their final resting place? And what circumstances surrounding a death could prompt a family to purchase such a stone? Was the interred a suicide? Or perhaps guilty of some foul crime? It is hard to believe that bereaved parents would spend a considerable sum on a marker celebrating their son's presumed damnation. Then again, maybe the strange symbol has occult meaning, perhaps something Masonic? In the final analysis it remains a mystery. And while you're pondering that particular puzzle, here's another one: Apparently no other New England town has such a thing, but a *second* such stone stands in Whitefield's Pine Street cemetery. So why here and nowhere else? People who concern themselves with such things are waiting for an answer.

Location: In the Methodist Cemetery, see the stone of Ira Bowles. In the Pine Street Cemetery, see Henry A. Lane who died on September 17, 1866, at the age of twenty-two. The graves are not too difficult to find; each one stands out like a sore thumb.

Whitefield, New Hampshire

Tree-Hugging Boulder

While you're in Whitefield puzzling over downward-pointing fingers, you might enjoy checking out a newly-discovered oddity that illustrates, as the magazine *COOS* notes, "the tenacious will of a sapling to keep growing in the face of all odds." It's a yellow birch tree that has perched itself atop a large boulder and grown-up remarkably tall by winding its tentacle-like roots around the stone and down to the earth, where, miraculously, it grabs hold and survives. It looks like a giant talon that has reached out of the sky and grabbed the boulder. Admittedly, this is not the only one of its kind in these parts, but certainly it's the most eye-catching. Don't bother to seek it out in winter; it will be covered in snow.

Location: Get on Route 116 heading from Littleton toward Whitefield. About five miles before the village, you'll see the sign for Kimball Hill Road on the right. A quarter of a mile further, partway down a steep hill, the tree sits in a clearing on the right, not far from the road. In the back is a barn-shaped house and a few small buildings. If you go too far, you'll come to a building on the left with a sign that says "Construction Material Testing."

Wolfeboro, New Hampshire

Dr. Libby's Marvels

Tucked away in picturesque Wolfeboro, America's oldest resort town, is a monument to human curiosity, the Libby Museum. On the outside it looks more like a mausoleum, but don't let that deter you. Inside it's alive with nineteenth-century marvels. Dr. Henry Forrest Libby (1850–1933) was a dentist and socialite with a variety of academic interests. The invention of a gypsum plaster useful in dentistry and other scientific applications allowed him the leisure to pursue a personal hobby, natural history. By age forty he was spending almost all his time collecting New England wildlife. He went on a hunting trip to Maine and stayed nine years. Soon he had filled his Wolfeboro cottage and boathouse on Mirror Lake with hooves, hair, and horns, so Dr. Libby clear-cut some of his property, sold the wood, and in 1912, erected the museum. By the looks of it, there is some attempt to make the displays educational. One case compares skeletons, demonstrating how close humans are to orangutans, bears, and catamounts. There

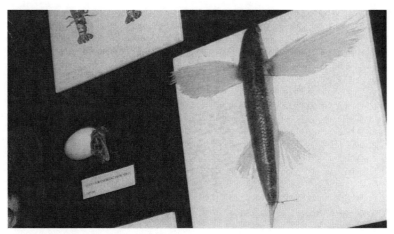

A flying fish and egg, species unknown, is one of the Libby Museum's many oddities in Wolfeboro, New Hampshire. Photo: Joe Citro

are meticulously labeled rocks, minerals, and numerous stuffed animals. But what makes the collection special is its unabashed recognition of oddities. At the far right, labeled "Unusuals," is a group that today's less courageous curators would have banished long ago: a two-inch-long human fingernail, a monkey-tooth necklace, bovine fur balls, two blackened mummy hands, and an alligator emerging from its egg. We don't want to spoil all the surprises, but be careful not to miss the "hair snake," a grasshopper parasite that looks like a piece of thread. If it was curious, Dr. Libby acquired it, down to his smallest specimen: a cootie mailed to him in 1918. We only wish he hadn't forgotten to display the greatest curiosity of all, himself. But you never know—that might be him next to the orangutan.

The Libby Museum
P.O. Box 629
Route 109
Wolfeboro, NH 03894

Phone: (603) 569-1035
www.wolfeboroonline.com/libby

Location: The museum is about three miles from downtown Wolfeboro on Route 109 (Center Street), on the right-hand side. Parking is in the rear.

Hours: Open June 1–mid-September every day except Monday; Tuesday–Saturday, 10 A.M.–4 P.M., Sundays, noon–4 P.M.

Admission charged.

Wheelchair accessible.

Wolfeboro, New Hampshire

Wright Museum of American Enterprise

To see a World War II American tank smashing through the side of an American brick building is a little startling—especially in peaceful Wolfeboro, New Hampshire. But as long as it has your attention, you might as well see what it's all about. This fascinating little museum's focus is not strictly "military." Instead, it celebrates American life during the Second World War, the cooperative and sacrificing spirit of the home front. Those of us born later than, say, 1950, can get an idea of what things were like here from 1939 to 1945 and glimpse the role civilians played in the war effort: blackout preparation, gas and food rationing, meatless meals, metal recycling campaigns ("Bring in your scrap and cook a jap"), and the dramatic cultural shift of men into uniform and women into the workplace. The museum's details are precise and evocative. There are eerie dioramas depicting full scale scenes frozen forever in the early 1940s and populated by motionless mannequins. See the soda shop, the drug store, the dentist's office, and the living room in an era before TVs, VCRs, and home computers. This is a total immersion experience; you feel as if a time machine dropped you in the middle of the war years—and everything is unsettlingly still. To us, these motionless tableaus are among the museum's most chilling displays because they perfectly symbolize the uncertainty of that time. Each depicts a frozen moment. It could be the moment that we've all seen in the end-of-the-world movies, when everything stops just before the big bomb drops. Or it could be the moment that chain-reacts into peace.

But nostalgic as all this domestic ambiance may be, don't forget: Not far away there's a war going on—right in the next building, to be exact. A re-created Victory Garden connects the "Home Front" with "the War Room." It is here veterans and small boys can delight in the machinery of defense and destruction. There are many fascinating exhibits—a classic jeep, a genuine Pershing tank, a WC-7 Command Car,

A U.S. Army tank forever blasts through the wall of the E. Stanley Wright Museum of American Enterprise in Wolfeboro, New Hampshire. Photo: Joe Citro

an armored vehicle, even some airplanes—but for us the real oddity was the contraption used for training pilots—a vintage 1939 flight simulator.

Before leaving, if you'd like to put things back in perspective, you can stop in the gift shop and buy a chocolate tank. That must symbolize something, too.

E. Stanley Wright Museum
77 Center St.
Wolfeboro, NH 03894
Phone: (603) 569-1212

wrmuseum@aol.com

www.wrightmuseum.org

Location: The museum is easy to find in downtown Wolfeboro.

Hours: Open May 1–October 30, Monday–Saturday, 10 A.M.–4 P.M., Sundays, noon–4 P.M., Off season, open weekends: Saturday, 10 A.M.–4 P.M., Sunday, noon–4 P.M. Closed December–March, except during February school vacation weeks.

Admission charged.

Wheelchair accessible.

RHODE ISLAND

Woonsocket

Chepachet

Foster

North
Scituate

Cranston

Providence

Apponaug

Coventry

Tiverton

Portsmouth

Bristol

South
Portsmouth

Middletown

Exeter

Adamsville

Newport

Narragansett

Richmond

Tower of Revenge

It's right in the middle of town, guaranteed to catch the eye and pique the curiosity. Since its construction in the 1800s, this puzzling, white, three-story structure has been called "Spite Tower." Allegedly, it was built with the sole purpose of frustrating someone's line of sight. Just whose, at least today, is a matter of conjecture. The varied stories about the tower share one common thread: the Manchester family. Abe Manchester and his sister Debbie worked in their father's store, which is still standing. Just like his father Ebenezer, Abe slept nights at the store while Debbie stayed with their sister Lizzie at the house. According to Borden Tripp, whose explanation appears in *Historic Adamsville,* a doctor named John Hathaway built Spite Tower after having a falling out with Abe. Allegedly, he wanted to cut off Abe's view of the house so the storekeeper couldn't see his sister signaling him to come home at mealtime. More romantic explanations involve unrequited love. One holds that Dr. Hathaway built the tower to wreak revenge against the Manchester family because Debbie spurned his advances. But, applying Occam's Razor, perhaps the best explanation is that it's simply a water tower. After all, it's built directly over a well. At one time the owner used a contraption involving a steam boiler to heat well water, forcing it through pipes to the tank at the top. Gravity would then deliver it to the house. The tower may simply have disguised the whole unsightly mess.

Location: Easy to spot if you can find your way to Adamsville; it's where Routes 81 and 179 meet. Spite Tower is right in the center of town.

Drum Rock

In the world of tourism, tastes can change. For example, we no longer flock to mineral water spas the way we did prior to the Civil War. But oddities seem to hold continual fascination. Early nineteenth-century tourists who read Pease and Niles's *Gazetteer of Connecticut and Rhode Island* (1819) must have been captivated by their description of a primitive communications device known as Drum Rock. They wrote:

> Within a mile from the village of Apponaug, may be seen a huge rock, so completely balanced upon another, and its equilibrium so exact, that a boy fourteen years of age may set it in such motion that the contact or collision caused thereby, produces a sound somewhat like that of a drum, but more sonorous, which in a still evening may be heard a distance of six or eight miles. Hence, from time immemorial, it has gone by the name of the Drum Rock. From the ponderous weight of that part which is thus nicely balanced, it is generally believed, that no other than the hand of nature ever could have done it. Yet some are inclined to believe, that it was thus placed by the Herculean labor of some tribe of the natives. There remains no doubt, but that this was a place of their resort or encampment; and that the Drum Rock served them either to give an alarm in case of danger, or to call the tribe together from their daily avocations. This rock is considered a great curiosity, excites much attention, and consequently is at the present day a place of much resort, particularly in the pleasant season of the year.

Certainly there are other "Drum Rocks," but this, apparently, is the biggest one in the United States. You can see it, but, sadly, you won't be able to hear it. Somewhere along—after thousands of years of drumming—some municipal do-gooder got it into his head that "someone could get hurt." Drum Rock has been silenced forever.

Location: Drum Rock is in the Apponaug section of Warwick, Rhode Island. From the one-mile stretch of Route 117 that's between I-95 and Route 1, turn south on to Gilbane Street. Drive to the end and turn right. Park near Apartment Complex 16. Next to the Speed Limit 15 sign is a path leading through a break in a stone wall. Drum Rock is there, although vandals have made off with its plaque.

Bristol, Rhode Island

DeWolf Cemetery

An oddity amid the splendor of this historically prosperous town involves the events surrounding the DeWolf family cemetery, particularly the grave of Captain James DeWolf (1764–1837), who made a fortune in the slave trade. He had a deer park built at the southern tip of the city, a place so peaceful that he decided to make it into a private burying ground. An earthen mound was piled up twenty feet high. This was to be his grave and that of his wife, Nancy. According to historian George Howe, "Captain Jim" added an iron door that could be opened so family members could look into the crypt, telling his children, "As long as any of you are around, you'll see my gold teeth, even when the rest of us is dust." On Christmas Eve of 1837, Captain DeWolf died at his palatial home, dubbed "the Mount." His wife was inconsolable, refused to leave her room, and within a week, followed him to the hereafter. They were interred in the family plot (dubbed "the mound"?), leaving behind an estate worth five million dollars. But he was wrong about one thing: His gold teeth did not outlast him—at least not there. On May 11, 1842, by cover of night, a ne'er-do-well named John Dickinson robbed the grave. He used gunpowder to blast the door open during a storm, the explosion camouflaged by thunder. Alas, the captain hadn't stashed any treasure in the grave with him. All Mr. Dickinson gained for his efforts were a few gold buttons and an engraved coffin-plate. But he did get the captain's gold teeth! The entire hoard netted him a mere $6.52. He paid his dues thirteen years later at the gallows, as the grave robber had committed many misdeeds unrelated to the DeWolf caper. As for the grave mound, it is still there in the family plot, albeit without the door. You'll recognize it by the large tree growing out of its middle. The crypt was last used in 1925 when George DeWolf hid out there to avoid creditors. "The Mount" burned down at the turn of the century. Only the foundation can be seen today at the end of DeWolf Avenue.

Location: The cemetery is on Woodlawn Avenue, a right turn off of Metacom Avenue going south toward the water, about a third of a mile in on the left, near telephone pole number 24. Some thirty-three family members—only a fraction of the huge DeWolf clan—are buried alongside the captain.

NOTE: Of the four DeWolf mansions, only one has survived. It is Linden Place, George DeWolf's home, at 500 Hope Street. It was the setting for the Robert Redford movie, *The Great Gatsby,* and contains numerous treasures, such as a chandelier that hung in Buckingham palace. The mansion can be visited (for a fee) Memorial Day–Columbus Day, Thursday–Saturday, 10 A.M.–4 P.M., Sundays, noon–4 P.M. For more information call (401) 253-0390.

Bristol, Rhode Island

King Philip's Throne

One of the most tumultuous events in early American history occurred near this often overlooked spot. It is where the English captured Wampanoag Chief Metacomet, known as King Philip, in 1676, thus ending the bloodiest Indian-colonial conflict in New England history: King Philip's War. Metacomet spent summers at Montaup, which the English comprehended as Mount Hope. Here his secret roost was a naturally shaped granite "seat" with a spectacular view of Mount Hope Bay.

A long, but weakening peace with the English finally ended in 1675 when a tribesman who was spying for the English was discovered and put to death. In response, the English tried and executed three of Metacomet's warriors. Incensed, the Wampanoags began a series of raids on colonial towns, killing villagers and burning their homes. The English retaliated in kind. Although Metacomet enlisted the aid of neighboring tribes, he was outnumbered and his tribe decimated. After his wife and son were captured, he returned to Montaup where an English posse hunted him down. The Puritans killed him, dismembered his body, and took his head to Plymouth, where it was displayed for twenty years on a pole. Some two hundred years later, as a sort of afterthought, the Rhode Island Historical Society placed a slant-faced stone marker in the Miery Swamp near the spring waters where the great chief died. From Metacomet's granite throne—in effect his seat of government—you can look out over the lands and waters he once ruled. Please keep in mind that this is a religious site still used by the Pokanokets, descendants of the Wampanoags.

Location: The stone marker is on the grounds of the Haffenreffer Museum, which is off Route 136 near the southeastern tip of town. Turn onto Tower Street and drive up to the museum parking lot. Park there and walk around the adjacent barn. Walk in a southerly direction along the paved bikepath that runs parallel to the water and take a right at the fork, going uphill to a granite outcropping in the cliff face. The seat faces the water, and the historic marker is in the woods below it.

NOTE: To see more Native American artifacts, visit the Haffenreffer Museum:
300 Tower St.
Bristol, RI 02809

Phone: (401) 253-8388
www.brown.edu/Facilities/Haffenreffer/index.html.

Hours: Open June–August, Tuesday–Sunday, 11 A.M.–5 P.M. September–May, Saturdays and Sundays, 11 A.M.–5 P.M., or by appointment.

Pet Cemetery

Among Newport's rich and famous, Fido, Fluffy, and Fifi get special treatment when they run off to meet their makers. Their bones are lovingly buried in a graveyard for elite animals—the Bow-Wow Villa. This stone-walled cemetery in front of the Portsmouth-area animal grooming and boarding center is a pride of terminally cute headstones: a bronze boxer, a Great Dane, and more. You'll find the last resting place of parrots, cats, even a few ferrets, some with pet-likenesses carved into their headstones. One monument marks the spot where the Duke and Duchess of Windsor parted with their pooch. Clearly the villa caters to a prestigious clientele. The first burial plot was purchased in 1938, and somehow word spread. Then status clicked in, so the place is still expanding. Some people—those of us who find such extravagance too expensive for our parents, much less our pets—might be interested in walking the grounds to see what sorts of names the area's aristocracy come up with for their pets. And with the dogs sleeping here, you don't even have to watch where you step. Bow-Wow Villa is probably the largest pet cemetery in New England, and certainly the oldest animal hotel.

The Bow-Wow Villa
837 Wapping Rd.
Portsmouth, RI 02871

Location: Follow Route 138 north to the Fall River, Cape Cod exit. Go left there and stay on Route 138 through four traffic lights. Turn left at the first stop sign onto Third Beach Road, about three miles from the Jai Alai fronton. At the first intersection on Third Beach Road, turn right onto Wapping Road. The Bow Wow Villa is about 1.2 miles on the left, adjacent to The Innisfree Farm. The cemetery is in front. Visitors are welcome to walk around at any time, but take care not to block the driveway.

Free admission.

Wheelchair accessible.

Threads of Death

Rhode Island may be the smallest state, but it ran the largest slave trade. Bristol came second only to Newport in the number of ships sent to Africa to load up on human cargo. All told, Rhode Islanders abducted more than one hundred thousand Africans between 1725 and 1807, auctioning them off in the United States, Cuba, and the West Indies. One of the most successful slave barons was the flamboyant Captain James DeWolf (whose burial mound we discuss in a separate entry). While scions did much to conceal inhumanities perpetrated for wealth and high social positions, at least one Bristol resident opted to do just the opposite, and in a rather unorthodox way—through needlework. Never a fan of the DeWolf dynasty, Colonel Ruth Briggs, who served on Eisenhower's staff in World War II, set to work memorializing one of "Captain Jim's" most egregious crimes: he tied a slave woman to a chair and threw her overboard, allegedly to prevent her from infecting the other slaves with smallpox. Ms. Briggs needlework creation was a provocative contribution to the 1976 Bicentennial. However her stitchery fails to mention that Captain DeWolf later reformed. Sort of. He left the country until the drowning incident blew over, then returned to Bristol where, in 1821, he used his connections to be appointed senator (as was the practice in those days). From then on, the Honorable Senator DeWolf joined his peers in denouncing slavery, but as he later proclaimed, "even those who deprecate the evils of slavery" can "sell human flesh with as easy a conscience as they sell other articles"—as long as it is profitable.

The Bristol Historical and Preservation Society Museum
48 Court St.
Bristol, RI 02809

Phone: (401) 253-7223

www.destinationbristol.com/museums

Location: The museum is just west of Mount Hope Park near the city's west-ern shoreline. Take Route 136 south and turn right onto State Street. Go left at Hope Street, then left again onto Court. The museum is half a block up.

Hours: Open year-round Wednesdays and Fridays, 1:00 P.M.–5:00 P.M., and on Sundays, June–August, 1:00 P.M. to 4:00 P.M.

NOTE: The depiction is one of several needlework blocks portraying Bristol his-tory that the historical society has mounted together. It is not generally dis-played, but will be brought out upon request.

Admission: a donation.

Wheelchair accessible.

Chepachet, Rhode Island

Little Bett's Murder

It all started in 1804 when Old Bet, a full-sized African ele-phant, arrived in Boston. Since no one had ever seen such a thing before, you can imagine the range of reactions. Some, from pictures in books, knew exactly what they were seeing. Some thought it was the biggest, most fearsome thing they'd ever laid eyes on. And some, no doubt, believed it was kin to the devil. For a farmer named Hachaliah Bailey, it was love at first sight. He purchased the pachyderm, brought it home, and exhibited it for a few cents a peek. It did so well that he ac-quired a group of admittedly less exotic animals, opened some-thing like a zoo, and eventually took the whole bunch on tour. This was a big mistake. While visiting the town of Alfred, Maine, Big Betty was shot and killed by a no doubt well-intended Christian fanatic who knew sin when he saw it—de-cent people ought to have better things to do with their money than gawk at some infernal monstrosity. So he fired away. Old Bet, also known as Betty the Elephant, died on July 24, 1816.

But Mr. Bailey wasn't to be put off. He purchased another pachyderm and named it Little Bett. He avoided Maine, but should have stayed out of New England altogether.

On May 24, 1826, after the performance, Little Bett and Mr. Bailey were leaving the normally quiet town of Chepachet. As they crossed the bridge, seven men hiding in a nearby gristmill opened fire. A hail of musket balls cut Little Bett down; she died there at just twelve years of age.

No one can really be said to have atoned for the deed. Of the seven murderers, only two were punished: They were kicked out of the Masons. The rest, and everyone else in Chepachet, retreated into silence.

Today you can visit the scene of the crime. In the mid-1960s a plaque commemorating the dark deed was placed on the bridge where Little Bett met her end. The why of it all remains a mystery.

Location: The bridge is the only one leading out of town. It's near an old general store, some antique shops and the post office. Adjacent to the post office you'll find the town hall, in front of which is a Disneyesque elephant effigy. On its back, a plaque spells out the whole elephant saga.

www.chepachet.com

Coventry, Rhode Island

Abandoned Civilizations

The countryside around Coventry would seem a perfect place to set down roots. There's a tranquillity about it, and conditions seem fine for raising livestock and crops. But for reasons unknown, settlements have come and gone. We don't know how many, but there's evidence of at least two—and one is far more mysterious that the other. Follow the trails through this Audubon Society nature preserve and you will come across forlorn remnants of homes and workplaces that were long ago abandoned to the elements. There are tumbled cellar holes, the remains of a sawmill at the intersection of Maple Valley Road and Turkey Meadow Brook, what's left of a charcoal processing site, and endless stone walls. Whoever settled these parts obviously planned to stay—but it didn't turn out that way. This was Coventry Center, a seventeenth-century farming community that is now little more than a ghost town. But where there are ghosts there is mystery. As you continue your walk, look a little deeper into the past. You'll discover the colonials were not the first to abandon this place. Hidden in the woods there's a series of puzzling stone cairns resembling caves. Obviously ancient, somewhat spooky, they have always been an enigma, suggesting forgotten inhabitants of a remote past that's lost to history. Some theorize the structures are the work of pre-Columbian, Phoenician, or Celtic peoples. But the fact is, few clues remain to tell us about their builders or why they were abandoned. Perhaps it was a pandemic, crop failures, or severe weather conditions that drove them away. And perhaps the fate of both these settlements, hundreds, perhaps thousands of years apart, is somehow linked. We'll probably never know.

The George B. Parker Woodland
1670 Maple Valley Rd.
Coventry, RI 02917

Phone: (401) 949-5454
www.asri.org/parker.htm

Location: From Providence, take I-95 south to Route 102 north (exit 5B). Follow 102 north for about ten miles. Turn right (east) onto Maple Valley Road (across 102 on the left is Waterman Hill Road). Turn into the second driveway on the left by the Parker Woodland Wildlife Refuge sign.

Hours: Open dawn until dusk.

Sprague Mansion

During the Civil War, the world's equivalent to Bill Gates was a Rhode Island governor by the name of William Sprague. He was the richest man on earth, yet unlike the ever-smiling Gates, he was sullen, moody, and a drinker. From the cupola on the roof of his twenty-eight-room mansion he would admire his commercial holdings: miles of real estate, a railroad, a bank, a horseshoe company, a reservoir, a race track, and the Cranston Print Works, which to this day is the nation's largest textile printer. Governor Sprague and his beautiful wife Kate often lavishly entertained in the mansion's elegant first floor ballroom. But there was trouble brewing, and it wasn't anti-trust litigation. Something, like a specter from the past, seemed to be catching up with him. The governor's grandfather had died in the mansion from a fishbone caught in his throat. Then his father Amasa, who had continued to build the business, was beaten to death in 1843. The chief suspect, who was executed, was later discovered to be innocent when the suspect's brother confessed to the crime. (In response the state banned capital punishment.) But that wasn't all. Now the governor's own fortunes were dwindling. His daughter was born retarded, his son committed suicide, and his wife sued for divorce. After the Civil War, there was nothing to do but sell the mansion. Governor Sprague moved to Paris, where he died in 1915. Ten years later, strange events began to occur at the old homestead. A spectral figure is occasionally seen descending the grand walnut staircase. A visitor to the wine cellar might feel a hand touching them when no one else is there. Lights turn off and on, footsteps echo in the unsettling "Doll Room," and in the dead of night blankets leap from the beds of slumbering people. Seances held in 1968 revealed the ghosts to be Amasa, the governor's father, and a butler, Charles, whose daughter had been jilted by her lover in the 1880s. Unexplained sightings continue to this day; as recently as the summer of 2000, a man reported seeing a ghostly figure on the back steps. The mansion's haunted spots are worth a look; who knows what you might see there. And the parlor has been restored to the former splendor of Governor Sprague's time. The only thing missing is a family curse to explain generations of misfortune.

The Sprague Mansion
  1351 Cranston St.
  Cranston, RI 02920

Phone: (401) 944-9226
  rilydia@ix.netcom.com
  www.geocities.com/rilydia/mansion.html

Location: The mansion is on the corner of Dyer and Cranston Streets in Cranston. The Cranston Historical Society is housed in same building.

Hours: Open year-round by appointment only.

Admission charged.

Wheelchair accessible.

Exeter, Rhode Island

The Vampire's Tomb

If you want to see a vampire's grave you don't have to travel to Transylvania. Mercy Lenna Brown, New England's most celebrated vampire, rests in pieces in the cemetery behind the Chestnut Hill Baptist Church. Mercy died in January, 1892, at age nineteen. Hers was the Brown family's third death in rapid succession. Everyone knew that something was amiss—and wondered if a vampire was in their midst. In an effort to protect those still living, the Browns and their friends dug up their fallen relatives. The first two were skeletons. But then they exhumed Mercy. Townsfolk were horrified to discover that she was still in pretty good shape. And she had moved within the coffin! A hastily performed graveside autopsy revealed "fresh blood" in her veins and heart. Mystery solved: Mercy was the vampire. Her heart was burned on the spot and the ashes were concocted into a gruesome remedy for the survivors to ingest. Perhaps the cure worked; there seem to be no more vampires around. But occasionally folks in the area still see a fleeting white ball of light hovering around Mercy's tomb or floating among the ancient gravestones.

Location: Mercy's grave is in Historical Cemetery number 22, behind Exeter's Chestnut Hill Baptist Church on Route 102. The Browns' graves are clearly marked. Mercy's is right behind Mrs. Mary E. Brown's. The tomb where the bodies were housed before internment is nearby.

Foster, Rhode Island

Rams Tail Ruins

If you are looking for an "official" haunted spot, this is it. The state of Rhode Island said so in its 1885 State Census. What's more, this may be a true ghost town. You can poke around in the ruins, explore the graveyard and, if you dare, wait until dark when chances are above average that you'll encounter a spirit.

Early in the nineteenth century this was a busy factory town with several houses, a warehouse, offices, and a mill for spinning and weaving cloth powered by the Ponagansett River. William Potter managed the factory by day, his partner Peleg Walker served as night watchman. He'd walk the grounds, checking building after building, then he'd ring the factory bell in the morning to summon the workers. A falling out put an end to the partnership when Peleg—by murder or suicide—was found one morning hanging from the bell rope. After he was buried in the nearby cemetery, the haunting began almost immediately. The bell rang on its own. They removed the rope; the bell still rang. For several nights workers were awakened by the mechanical clatter of the mill running all by itself. When they saw the giant mill wheel running against the current, many decided to leave. At night, those who remained soon started seeing the dimly glowing ghost of Peleg Walker, carrying his lantern from building to building. By the mid nineteenth century the factory had closed. Foster historical records attributes it to Peleg's ghost. By the end of the century the whole place had burned down. But Peleg's ghost still walks the ruins, dutifully making his eternal rounds. Maybe you can see him for yourself. If not, at least you can explore this eerie ghost town in the Rhode Island woods.

Location: From Providence, take Route 6 west until you come to South Foster. From there, take Rams Tail Road, heading south until it ends, forming a "T" with Central Pike. Turn left. Drive ³⁄₁₀ to ⁷⁄₁₀ of a mile. On the left you'll see an orange railing and a path. Park and proceed on foot. After about half a mile you'll start seeing signs of the ruins.

Middletown, Rhode Island

Butterfly Zoo

This is the only place we've found in New England where you can enter a hot, muggy rain forest—complete with lizards, tree frogs, and a trained turtle—and have your picture taken with a moth. With luck, a White Peacock will perch on your shoulder (not the bird, the butterfly). And, thanks to the resident lepidopterist (no, not a type of dinosaur), you'll get a crash course in the dark side of butterflies. Why, those little devils can really carry on! They mate for hours with the female on top! While the male—the little rogue—is in a total swoon.

Though the Butterfly Zoo is one of New England's oddest menageries, it isn't really X-rated. Still, the flittery little critters have their dark secrets: The Giant Swallowtail's babies grow up to look like oversized bird poop, and the three-centimeter pupa replicates a dead stick. Other naked pupas disguise themselves as drops of water, dead leaves, and—well, who knows? Most butterflies live about two weeks, but some—the old timers—make it to six months. The world's biggest butterfly is the Goliath Birdwing, with a wingspan of over a foot. You can see one here, however it's dead. But fear not, owner Marc Schenk has over thirty other species to keep you entertained.

All this may be slightly lurid, somewhat surreal, or highly educational, depending on your point of view. But the real kick in visiting the Butterfly Zoo is to get caught up in a colorful cloud of these winged wonders; they'll flutter around you like a multicolored snowstorm. Some even light on you, but behave! There's a strict "hands off" rule. You can watch them eat, drink, spin, and yes . . . mate. Be sure to visit on warm sunny days because that's when the little voluptuaries are out and about. On cold or rainy days they tend to hide, wait for the weather to change, and get into all kinds of mischief. Vladimir Nabokov, an impassioned butterfly collector, would have loved it here. (Maybe that's what inspired *Lolita*.)

Newport Butterfly Farm
 1151 Aquidneck Ave.
 Middletown, RI 02842

Phone: (401) 849-9519
 butterflyzoo@webtv.net

Location: From Fall River, take exit 24 south off of I-95 then exit 1 (Middletown, Newport Beaches). Turn right off the ramp and right at the next light onto East Main Road. When you see the Middletown Dunkin Donuts, turn left onto Aquidneck Avenue. The zoo is three blocks down on the right.

Look for the blue and white striped greenhouse. Turn into Vierra Terrace and park in front of the zoo.

Hours: Open daily mid-May–early September, 11 A.M.–4 P.M., also by appointment. Closed rainy days.

Admission charged.

Wheelchair accessible.

Purgatory Chasm

The devil has left his mark in New England and in some places, he's even left his hoof print. Purgatory Chasm is just such a place. Much evil is said to have occurred here. According to one story, a local lass questioned her lover's devotion. To prove his love to her, she insisted that he leap across "the yawning abyss." He survived the jump but the impact must have knocked some sense into him; he abandoned her there on the rocks. As if her whims weren't devilish enough, Old Nick himself is said to have appeared here to reward an Indian woman for a series of murders she'd committed. Her prize was to be hurled kicking and screaming straight down into the gaping stone mouth. Having planted his feet firmly to extend such an effort, his footprints can still be found imbedded in a rock. His victim is said to have left traces of her blood splattered on both sides of the rocky precipice. Purgatory Chasm itself is not hard to find. It is 10 feet wide, 120 feet long, and at least 50 feet deep. Finding the hoof prints and blood spatterings may be a bit more challenging, as will discovering exactly why it's called "Purgatory Chasm" rather than, say "Hell Hole" or "Perdition Pit."

Location: Purgatory Chasm is amid the rocky outcroppings above Second Beach in Middletown.

Narragansett, Rhode Island

Druid's Dream

In 1884, the wealthy spiritualist Joseph Peace Hazard constructed a 105-foot tower as part of a complex of stone structures on the grounds of his castle, called "Sea Side Farm." Though it is dramatically beautiful and has become a local landmark, the tower wasn't built just to please the eye. Mr. Hazard felt that from its elevated parapet—a good 160 feet above sea level—it would be easier to communicate with the spirits. Maybe he was right. One night while Mr. Hazard slept in his castle an ancient Druid visited him in a dream. The spirit commanded him to rise, leave the house, and walk west. After a certain number of paces the Druid instructed him to construct the curious stone house that Joseph Hazard was to call "Druidsdream." Though Mr. Hazard himself was never to live there, it was intended to be sort of a guest house for visitors— people, forest folk, and spirits. Its architectural eccentricities make it a commanding, if little known, local attraction. Almost directly across from the house is the mysterious "Kendal Green," now an overgrown ruin. Joseph Hazard planned to be buried there, even had a monument erected, then changed his mind. The monument was removed, leaving its base, the surrounding granite pillars, and a number of odd marked stones. The whole area has come to be known as a haunted place about which many spooky tales are told. What's left of the monument is now called "Witches' Altar," for reasons that may become obvious one day. The house still stands, the park decays, and the tower apparently continues to serve as a link with the great beyond. The Roman Catholic Diocese of Providence now owns it as part of the Our Lady of Peace Spiritual Life Center.

Location: Drive to the waterfront and go south past the stone wishing well. Take a sharp right onto Earl's Court. A stone water tower is at the end of the road. Continue to the end of the street and turn left on Gibson Avenue. On the left is the stone house Mr. Hazard named Druidsdream, and across the street is "Witches Altar." Our Lady of Peace Spiritual Life Center is on the shore. Drive north until you see mailbox 507 and follow the driveway in.

NOTE: Druidsdream is private property and should be observed only from the road, but spirit-hunting is permitted in the abandoned park.

Narragansett, Rhode Island

The Towers

This is one of the most imposing and dramatic bits of architecture we've seen in our travels. Although it is definitely haunting, it many not be haunted, and strictly speaking, there is nothing especially weird about it. But the fantasies it ignites in the imagination will surely be a little unusual. The magnificent structure is like a castle or elegant fortress with a colossal stone gate that welcomes you to some magical medieval city. The main road (Route 1A), hugging the Narragansett coast, goes right under the arch—as it might in some European city—although you aren't really entering or leaving anything. Its position by the sea only adds to its extraordinary grandeur. Completed in 1886, The Towers involved the work of forty stonecutters and masons. The building, designed as a casino and an integral part of the seaside resort community, is 490 feet long. The arch is fifty feet high. In 1900, everything burned down around it, leaving the stone survivor standing by itself. Since then it has endured other assaults, including more fires, hurricanes, and relentless northeasters; but it has always stood fast while its neighbors vanished in the elements. Today it is more seen than used, a gift to the imagination. Passing through that arch is like a doorway to Narragansett's never-never land, a grand and gilded era that will never come again.

Location: If you can find your way to Narragansett, you can't miss it.

Belcourt Castle

Our purpose is not to encourage you to ooh and ah over the competitive excesses of America's industrial barons. But if such is your guilty pleasure, Newport is the place to indulge. With names like Cheptow, Chateau-sur-Mer, Rosecliff, and Kingscote, these ostentatious "cottages" allowed the magnates of the gilded age to strut their stuff and forget how their money was actually made. Still, in the presence of such splendor it's hard not to be tempted. So if you decide to surrender just once, the weirdest cottage to visit is Belcourt Castle. Not only is it a wonderful monument to rapaciousness, full of art treasures and antiques, it also contains ghosts, haunted objects, and peculiar paraphernalia. Privately owned since 1958, the resident Tinney family have witnessed a colorful spectrum of supernatural antics. Guests, too, routinely see or experience the same. For example, there is a chair in the gothic ballroom where ladies shouldn't sit. If they pass their hands over its seat, a cool sensation prickles the skin. If they are more brazen and sit down . . . Well, Mrs. Tinney has seen visitors literally catapulted from the chair by an invisible force. And there is a suit of armor whose owner was killed by a sword through the eye. Occasionally, when his spirit returns to the site, guests will hear growls and groans coming from within the armor. Less frequently, people have seen the apparently empty suit moving around like a robot. And then there's the ghostly brown-robed monk who's been spotted in the vicinity of the chapel and near the rude gnome's head carved on a grand stairway. Rebellious workmen put it there after a fickle Mrs. Belmont (the original owner) wanted the whole staircase moved for the fifth time.

For those more materially minded (and who wouldn't be in a place like this?), check out the Italian Banquet Hall with its rose marble floor, and the Russian chandelier made of thirteen thousand hand-cut crystal prisms. The Breakfast Room reminds one of the famous "Hall of Mirrors" at Versailles, and take in the remarkable golden coronation coach. In fact, the whole sixty-room mansion is just crammed with treasures, imitative and original. Ah, go on, have a look. What harm can it do to join the guests . . . and ghosts?

Belcourt Castle
   Bellevue Ave.
   Newport, RI 02840-4288
Phone: (401) 846-0669
   www.belcourtcastle.com
Location: The castle is at the southern end of Bellevue Avenue where it intersects with Lakeview Avenue.
Hours: Open daily, June–October, 9:00 A.M.–5:00 P.M., November–January 1, 10 A.M.–4 P.M., February–March, 10 A.M.–3 P.M., April–May, 10 A.M.–5 P.M.
NOTE: Ghost tours are conducted Thursdays at 5:00 P.M.
Admission charged.
Wheelchair accessible.

Newport, Rhode Island

Beyond Brenton Point

As vexing as some of the ancient megalithic structures may be, there is something even more puzzling: underwater ruins.

One we find especially interesting was discovered off Brenton Point, Rhode Island, in 1935. About a mile offshore, a Navy diver had descended to around forty feet when he saw what appeared to be a stone mound with a masonry top. Suspecting it was the remains of a lighthouse, the diver checked Coast Guard files, concluding it would have to be a fairly modern structure, because only recently have we had the technology to build foundations so far out to sea. However, there were no records of lighthouses, colonial or modern, in the Brenton Reef area. Since then, a number of divers have gone down to investigate. In 1958 Jackson Jenks saw what he described as a conical tower, fifty to sixty feet high, forty to fifty feet in diameter, with the top about forty feet below the surface. He said it was fabricated from quarried stones, each as big as a refrigerator. The top looked like a parapet with what appeared to be a door in it. Since Coast Guard records had already suggested the structure wasn't new, it must therefore be old—pre-colonial at least. And theoretically, if it were several thousand years old, it may have once been above sea level. In the 1960s, what might be a related discovery was made north of Newport. A fisherman, putting out early in the morning during an uncommonly low tide, observed the barnacle-encrusted top of what appeared to be a stone arch jutting out of the sea. These provocative sites have never been marked. Undersea archaeologists and treasure hunters keep exact coordinates secret for obvious reasons. But one wonders if these structures could have been built by the same elusive ancients who constructed the mysterious tower at Newport.

Location: Still a secret, but perhaps one worth pursuing. Brenton Point is at the southernmost tip of Newport.

Jail Hotel

This place has always been easy to get into, but in the old days it was much harder to leave. The Jailhouse Inn, situated amid Newport's jumble of narrow cobblestone streets, is not kidding. The building is a working inn, greeting customers from behind bars. Metal gates jangle at the head of each corridor; windows on the wings and in dormers show where criminals were accommodated. The Georgian-style jail was built in 1772 to replace an earlier facility dating back to 1680. In those days, prisoners were punished through fines or forms of humiliation, such as public whippings or time in the stocks at the center of town. The jail was simply where they put you until they decided your fate. Though imposing, this particular slammer was not very secure. We're told there were several escapes, including one in 1859 by a mason who simply removed the bricks from around the window and made for the hills. Unfortunately it didn't occur to him to cover his tracks in the freshly fallen snow, and the police traced him to the Ocean House Hotel. The jail was enlarged over the years, and housed the Newport Police Department until 1986. The staff seem friendly enough and it certainly looks comfortable, but if you need a place to stay, use caution: Checkout time may be later than you think.

The Jailhouse Inn
 13 Marlborough St.
 Newport, RI 02840

Phone: (401) 847-4638
 vacation@jailhouse.com
 www.jailhouse.com

The Richest Girl in the World

When she was thirteen years old, Doris Duke inherited more than one hundred million dollars from her American Tobacco Company founder father, thus earning her the title that would be with her until she died in 1993 at age eighty. She lived well, married and divorced twice, and had one child who died within twenty-four hours of birth. She was romantically linked with the likes of Errol Flynn, George S. Patton Jr., and others. Her forty-thousand-square-foot Newport house, known as Rough Point, was always an enigma to townsfolk and curious tourists. To insure privacy she commissioned a huge hedge, granite wall, and impenetrable gates, thus making everyone even more curious about what was going on inside its 105 rooms. Today, years after the death of this quirky heiress, her stronghold is open to the public. Things have been kept exactly as they were when she last set foot in the place. If you are so inclined, you can take the tour and see her French cut-glass dressing table, golden toiletry articles, and the five thousand or so paintings displayed here and there. But the real attraction won't cost you an admission ticket. Since 1966, the morbid among us have been examining the area directly in front of the entrance on Bellevue Avenue. It was there that Doris Duke killed Eduardo Tirella. People stare at the spot as if doing so will somehow reveal what happened. Mr. Tirella was Ms. Duke's companion, perhaps lover. She was at the wheel when her station wagon crushed him against the iron entrance gates, dragged him across the street, and slammed him into a tree where he died instantly of head injuries. Ms. Duke and the Newport police chief agreed it was "an unfortunate accident." But within a week, Ms. Duke donated twenty-five thousand dollars to restore Cliff Walk, and cut the deal creating the Newport Restoration Foundation. Perhaps we'll never know what seedy situations led to the death or exactly what transpired that fatal night. But you can go, study the scene of the accident, and try to puzzle it out.

Newport Restoration Foundation
   51 Touro St.
   Newport, RI 02840

Phone: (401) 849-7300
   www.newportrestoration.org/roughpoint.html
   info@newportrestoration.com

Location: Rough Point is at the southern end of Bellevue Avenue.

Hours: Open April through the first week of November. Call (401) 845-9130 or check website for times and accessibility.

Admission charged. Buy tickets at the Gateway Center at the north end of America's Cup Avenue.

Newport, Rhode Island

Tilting at Windmills

In the middle of busy downtown Newport stands what may be the most puzzling structure in the United States. Known variously as the "Old Stone Mill," "The Norse Tower," or "The Viking Tower," this massive stone building has eight columns, two floors, a fireplace with flues, and several double-splayed windows. Controversy has surrounded it for centuries, but the fact is, no one can explain it. It's old; there's evidence it was standing when the first colonists arrived. It's mysterious; no one can determine its purpose. And it's an adopted orphan because its creators are unknown. Some experts think it was built around 1675 by Benedict Arnold's grandfather, Governor Benedict Arnold, to be used as a windmill. However, it appears on a map of Rhode Island dated 1630. Others contend it was constructed far earlier—perhaps during the twelfth century—by Vikings, Portuguese, or seagoing Celts. (If this were the case,

The Viking Tower in Newport, Rhode Island, is one of the city's biggest mysteries. Photo: Joe Citro

Newport could lay claim to the oldest building in America.) Windmill, watch-tower, fort, light-house, or church—numerous theories have been proposed, studied, championed, and dismissed by generations of puzzled professionals. Whatever it may be, it remains a mystery that may never be solved.

Location: The Tower (or whatever it is) is situated off Bellevue Avenue in Touro Park. It is always on view.

NOTE: Excellent web sites include <www.redwood1747.org/tower/millmenu .htm> and <order.mids.org/sinclair/newport_tower.html>.

Backward Church

Not exactly a religious mystery, but a bit of a puzzle nonetheless. Exactly why was this First Congregational Church built in such an unorthodox manner? It is unlike any other church because all the pews are facing in reverse. In other words the pews face the front door, and the minister and the organist face the congregation. The choir sat behind the congregation. Apparently it is nowhere recorded exactly what this strange turnaround is all about. The church was built in 1830, but its design remains a mystery to this day.

Theories about this unique seating arrangement include:

1. The congregation faced the front door in case Indians—or anyone—attacked the church. Facing the doors, they were never in danger of being "surprised."

2. It was a means of applying social pressure on those who might arrive late for church. There was no way to sneak in undetected after the service had begun.

3. The pews are actually positioned correctly. It is the church that was constructed backwards.

The First Congregational Church is no longer operating, and hasn't been for quite a while. But with permission you can visit and see for yourself. Maybe you can figure it out.

First Congregational Church
Main St.
North Scituate, RI 02857

NOTE: You can call the Public Works Department at (401) 647-3366 to make an appointment to see the inside of the church.

Free admission.

Leafy Beasts

If you have ever read Stephen King's *The Shining*, the idea of being attacked by a tree squirrel might not seem so outrageous. But how about a tree dog, rooster, or ostrich? Of course we're not talking about real animals, but rather animals made from trees—a topiary. And not at King's imagined Overlook, but right in semi-rural Rhode Island. We should have known a state that produced the Rhode Island School of Design and H. P. Lovecraft would have a fringe factor, even in gardening. And we would have been right. But, in the daytime at least, there is nothing especially menacing about these animals—a camel, two bears, a giraffe, a lion, a boar, a donkey, even a unicorn—all sculpted from shrubbery. In fact, you'd probably like to hug some of them if they weren't so scratchy. About twenty-seven of the garden's eighty bushes are four-legged, and three cats roam the grounds in the flesh (or fur). There are also abstractly sculpted shrubs, an herb garden, a vegetable garden, and myriad colorful flowers. The Victorian house holds an antique doll collection, which is weird in itself, and a gift shop overlooking Narragansett Bay.

The whole thing was the brainstorm of textile industrialist Thomas E. Brayton and his daughter Alice, who inherited the property. When she died in 1972, everything was left to the non-profit Preservation Society of Newport County, which also oversees the Newport mansions.

Green Animals Topiary Gardens
380 Cory's Lane
Portsmouth, RI 02871

Phone: (401) 683-1267
info@newportmansions.org
www.newportmansions.org/connoisseurs/greenanimals.html

Location: The gardens are off Route 114 between Newport and Portsmouth. From the south, go north on Route 114, pass the Raytheon complex on your left, and after 1.8 miles turn left at the light onto Cory's Lane. Green Animals is half a mile on the left. From the north, Cory's Lane is the first right after Route 24 south ends. At the first set of lights, turn right onto Cory's Lane. Green Animals is half a mile on the left.

Hours: Open daily mid-May–mid-October, 10 A.M.–5 P.M.

Admission charged.

Gardens are wheelchair accessible.

Providence, Rhode Island

African Slave Chains

This black heritage museum in Providence has the shackles, chains, handcuffs, and documents dating back to the time when African slaves were brought in to Rhode Island by the boatload and auctioned off to landowners up and down the coast. One telling warrant issued to the townsfolk alerts them to watch out for a runaway slave. Another is a letter written by a local sheriff proclaiming that the town will take no responsibility for newly freed slaves arriving with the intent of putting down roots. The museum's curator, Bella Texiera, will tell you how some of Providence's most stately mansions were built from the profits of the slave trade. For a time, Rhode Island was the only New England settlement both using slaves and trading them. Their biggest and most brutal slave markets were in Newport and Bristol. In 1765, the Nicholas Brown Company dispatched a ship to Africa for a load, but only 109 of the 167 on board made it back alive. For all the horror and abuses, Rhode Island was also one of the first colonies to legislate an end to slavery, although it took a war to get it enforced.

Rhode Island Black Heritage Society
    At the Arcade, Suite 29
    65 Weybosset Street
    Providence, RI 02903

Phone: (401) 751-3490
    www.providenceri.com/ri_blackheritage/

Hours: Open Monday–Friday, 10 A.M.–3:30 P.M., or by appointment.

Admission: a small donation.

Providence, Rhode Island

Attack of the Fifty-Foot Termite!

With all the adolescent irony of a 1950s sci-fi film, a big blue bug attacks a pesticides factory. But the greater irony is that New England Pest Control thinks they demonstrate their effectiveness by displaying this fifty-eight-foot, two-ton terror. Thought by some to be Rhode Island's strangest landmark, it is without doubt the world's largest scale model of a *Reticulitermes flavipes*—some 920 times life-size. This movie monster's screen credits include *Dumb and Dumber*, the *Oprah Winfrey Show*, and Country Music Television. It measures fifty-eight feet long, nine feet high, six feet in diameter, with wings forty feet long, antennae seven feet high, and legs eleven feet long. The four-thousand-pound monstrosity was created in 1980 for a mere twenty thousand dollars. It is said to be immune to everything, including hurricanes, so if it escapes its rooftop perch there will be no hope for humanity.

Location: The ungodly thing is visible from the highway. Those daring a closer look should take exit 19 off I-95 and proceed to 161 O'Connell Street where it is attacking the New England Pest Control building. The less daring may call (888) BLUE BUG for more information.

Rhode Island † 249

Cannibal Forks

This is foodie central, mecca of everyone in the food business and the richest collection of culinary gadgetry on earth. The museum sprang largely from the personal collection of the late Hungarian-born chef Louis Szathmary, who ran a Chicago restaurant and willed seventeen truckloads of cookbooks, cookware, and exotic paraphernalia to the university. Today, everything imaginable related to food is on display: thirty thousand menus, ancient cookbooks, nineteenth-century stoves, chefs' uniforms, and kitchen utensils galore. Watch for the Disney toaster that imprints Mickey Mouse on each slice and the buffalo sausage press. One display is devoted to presidential appetites (with the possible exception of Clinton's), and another traces the history of American diners, with a replica of one of Providence's most renowned greasy spoons. On her tour, culinary superstar Julia Child even discovered the stove she had learned to cook on when she was growing up. In fact, every detail is present except the most essential . . . there's no one in the kitchen.

Curator Barbara Kuck (whose name is pronounced "cook," naturally) is the person Hollywood calls when they need historically accurate food props. She loaned Steven Spielberg ninety pieces of antique silver for the filming of "Amistad." And there are some five-thousand-year-old cooking utensils awaiting their movie debut.

It's enough to make you hungry, until you stumble on some of Chef Szathmary's original oddities. You may wonder about the chef's appetite when you see the Tibetan skull sawed in half to be used as a goblet by the corpse's descendants. And a real treasure from seventeenth-century Fiji: a cannibal dish and brain-fork. At the end of such a repulsive repast, we wonder what they used as a toothpick.

Culinary Archives and Museum
Johnson and Wales University
315 Harborside Blvd.
Providence, RI 02905

Phone: (401) 598-2805
www.culinary.org

Location: The museum is part of the Harborside campus of Johnson and Wales University, home of the world-famous Culinary Institute. From I-95 South (Route 1), take exit 18 (Thurbers Avenue) and follow signs for Allens Avenue (Route 1A). At the traffic light, turn right onto Allens Avenue and go straight for a mile and a half. Turn left at the Shell gas station onto Northup Street. The museum is the first building on the left.

Hours: By appointment only.

Admission charged.

Wheelchair accessible.

Historic Roots

Stored away in what John Quincy Adams called "the most magnificent and elegant private mansion that I have seen on this continent" is evidence of the strangest grave robbery in American history. The victim is none other than Roger Williams himself. After he died in 1683, Mr. Williams was buried beside his wife on their farm beneath the shade of an old apple tree. Years later a concerned group of citizens decided Rhode Island's founder deserved a far nobler burial site. When the relocation crew opened the graves they received the surprise of their lives. The corpses were missing. In their place were twisted wooden replicas of Mr. and Mrs. Williams. The culprit was the shady apple tree. Somehow its roots had found their way to the coffins and burrowed through the rotting wood. A large root filled the spot formerly occupied by Roger Williams's head. It then penetrated the chest cavity, following the course of the spine to the feet, where it angled upward. A similar process had displaced Mrs. Williams's remains. Today the bloated tubers bear a striking resemblance to recumbent human forms. Talk about historic roots . . .

So that you don't appear to be too much of a ghoul while in the museum, also note the unique glass staircase, the multi-function grandfather clock, the "naked nymphs and satyrs" in the bathroom, and the inventive—though wonderfully quirky—shower installation. But whatever you do, don't eat the apples.

John Brown House Museum
52 Power St.
Providence, RI 02906

Phone: (401)331-8575
leppich@rihs.org
www.rihs.org

Location: The museum is located on the corner of Power and Benefit Streets, 5 blocks south of RISD.

Hours: Open Tuesday–Saturday, 10 A.M.–5 P.M., Sunday, noon–4 P.M. Open some Monday holidays; call for hours.

NOTE: A visit to Mr. and Mrs. Williams is by appointment only.

Admission charged.

Providence, Rhode Island

H. P. Lovecraft

No weird tour of Providence, Rhode Island, or New England, would be complete without a tip of the hat to H. P. Lovecraft. Though there is little to direct you to—other than his papers at the John Hay Library, the houses his family occupied at various times, and the hospital where he died—a stop at his grave would put us in mind of the New England gothic that he almost single-handedly created. Mr. Lovecraft thought his hometown was sufficiently weird to create a complete horrific mythology around it, featuring actual homes, streets, and people. Though his literary output was comparatively large, he is probably best remembered for his tales of the "Cthulhu Mythos," in which the sinister "Old Ones" scheme to repossess the world. Revered by the French, extolled by Stephen King, and, at long last, begrudgingly appreciated by his native Providence, Howard Phillips Lovecraft lives on as the most influential chronicler of the darker side of New England. An introverted Yankee, Mr. Lovecraft was known to walk the dark streets of College Hill, perhaps because at night it was easier to imagine them as part of the gothic colonial era in which he longed to live. Somehow it is fitting that we pay our respects to this often overlooked writer at the bookstore and at his grave.

Location: H. P. Lovecraft is buried at the Swan Point Cemetery. To reach it, head north from Providence on Route 1. Turn right onto Rochambeau Avenue. Follow it till you reach Blackstone Boulevard. Cross Blackstone and you will be on Swan Point. The cemetery is easy to spot, but his grave is not well marked nor easy to find. The best route is to go directly to the cemetery's office and ask directions to the Whipple V. Phillips lot. This is where Mr. Lovecraft and his close relatives lie. He died poor and was buried without a stone to mark his grave (though this was rectified in 1975).

Hours: The cemetery is open during the day. There are many reasons not to go there at night, chief among them is that you will probably be arrested.

NOTE: To get a Lovecraft's eye-view of Providence, we can recommend no better book than Henry L. P. Beckwith Jr.'s *Lovecraft's Providence & Adjacent Parts* (Donald M. Grant, 1979).

Providence, Rhode Island

Silver Desk

As you would expect, the Rhode Island School of Design's art museum is artsy to the core, packed with the most extravagant paintings, porcelain, and furniture imaginable. We weren't surprised to see mahogany, walnut, and ivory. But what stopped us in our tracks was the desk made of silver—yes, gleaming, polished silver. It's a lady's writing table with a matching chair, cast about 1904 from almost fifty pounds of the treasured metal. Although it seemed a little extravagant to us, it all started to make sense when we found out that Providence is the home of Gorham, of silverware fame. The company produced the desk to attract attention at the 1904 Louisiana Purchase Exhibition in St. Louis. And it succeeded. The opulent little desk required 2,153 hours of silversmithing and another nineteen weeks just to produce the models from which to cast its components. Between the silver are segments in mother-of-pearl, walnut, mahogany, ebony, ivory, redwood, and thuya wood. The drawers are lined with velvet. It is definitely an original, although for the 1900 Paris Exposition, Gorham produced a similar desk, which now resides in the Dallas Museum of Art.

The RISD Art Museum
224 Benefit St.
Providence, RI 02903

Phone: (401) 454-6500
www.risd.edu/museum.cfm

Location: The Museum is located at 224 Benefit Street on the edge of downtown Providence. There are two entrances, including a ramp into the Farago Wing.

Hours: Open Tuesday–Sunday, 10 A.M.–5 P.M., and every third Thursday monthly until 9 P.M.

NOTE: The Metropark lot at the corner of North Main and Steeple Streets offers half-price parking to Museum visitors. Bring your parking stub to the museum's front desk for validation.

Admission charged.

Wheelchair accessible.

Smallpox Book

It was in Providence's Athenaeum, with its classic white columns, that Edgar Allen Poe courted Sarah Helen Whitman between the stacks, reading her poetry by gaslight. What drew him there, besides Miss Whitman, might have been this little-known trinket: *The Small Pox Treatise*, an 1837 publication from Siam. More a public health warning than a medical text, it explains in archaic Siamese script the way the disease ravages the human body. Unlike any ordinary book, it folds like a fan, measuring about four by eighteen inches when closed. To read it, you stretch it open like an accordion. Inside are pen and ink illustrations of smallpox pustules on mythical, androgynous individuals with crowns on their heads and wispy, flying hair, as if to underscore their passage into the spirit world. The book was brought to the library in 1840 by a ship's captain. Its label says it documents the "standard of present knowledge and practice in Siam."

Miss Whitman accepted Mr. Poe's marriage proposal provided he abstain from liquor. But he could not, and she called the wedding off. A year later Poe was picked up drunk in a Baltimore street gutter, and he died a few years after. A portrait of Sarah Helen Whitman still hangs in the Athenaeum's Art Room, and an anonymous Poe poem that appeared in *The American Whig Review* in 1848, which he had pulled off the shelf to sign in her presence, is in the rare book collection. We don't know for sure if Mr. Poe ever saw the smallpox book, but we're certain he would have loved it.

The Providence Athenaeum
  251 Benefit St.
  Providence, RI 02903

Phone: (401) 421-6970
  www.providenceathenaeum.org

Location: The Providence Athenaeum is diagonally across from the Rhode Island School of Design on the corner of College and Benefit Streets. *The Small Pox Treatise* is in the rare book room on the shelf.

Hours: Open Monday–Thursday, 9 A.M.–7 P.M.; Friday, 9 A.M.–5 P.M.; Saturday, 9 A.M.–1 P.M.; closed Sunday.

Free admission.

Providence, Rhode Island

Tattooed Head

If you're planning a visit to the Roger Williams Park Zoo and Planetarium, don't miss the second floor of the natural history museum. There, in the Circle of the Sea exhibit, is a treasure-trove of eclectic exotica, including a Hawaiian necklace made from eight hundred thousand feet of braided human hair complete with a dangling whalebone pendant. Not far away is a wooden cannibal fork with long, narrow tines used to pick flesh from human bones, although the museum—trying not to offend—has it labeled only "fork." Nearby are weapons made from sharks' teeth and three unusual pieces from Easter Island (though you'll have to go to Waterbury, Connecticut's Timexpo Museum to see a giant head). These Easter Island artifacts are small wooden figurines of mysterious origin and inspiration. One is free-standing, another is a humanoid in a crouching position, and the third is half-lizard, half-man. But perhaps the museum's most exotic holding is an early-nineteenth-century tattooed head from New Zealand. Not a mock-up, not a mask, not a shrunken head—a real mummified Maori. Alas, it's too fragile to put on display, so it's represented with a photograph. Nonetheless, you can still discern the black, curvilinear patterns painted with a soot mixture over its entire face. Tattooing was a Maori tradition, designating a person's rank and family associations by the design and its location on the face. If you miss it, don't despair. There is one other option: You can go to New Zealand and see it on the Maori people—face tattooing is making a resurgence there as part of a revival of Maori culture.

Museum of Natural History and Planetarium
Roger Williams Park
Providence, RI 02905

Phone: (401) 785-9450, weekends and evenings (401) 785-9457
museum@osfn.org
www.osfn.org/museum/

Location: The park's 435 acres include woods, ponds, and historical attractions in addition to the museum, zoo, and planetarium. From Providence, take I-95 south to exit 17 (Elmwood Avenue). Turn left at the light. The park entrance is the second left. From the south, take exit 16 off I-95, go right off the exit ramp, then turn left at the light. Drive half of a block, and the park entrance is on the right.

Hours: Open daily 10 A.M.–5 P.M., year-round except Thanksgiving, Christmas, and New Year's Day.

Admission charged.

Wheelchair accessible.

                                              Richmond, Rhode Island

The UFO Lab

What first appears to be an unassuming storefront in an ordinary shopping plaza, is, in reality, the UFO Lab Museum! It is the only one of its kind in Rhode Island, New England, and maybe even the universe. Here, through exhibits, narrative, and an impressive cache of UFO-related kitsch, Dennis and Ann Bossack offer "proof" that "we are not alone." You enter the museum via a UFO gift shop that is full of fun fantasy articles we had never seen before (but that doesn't prove they're of alien origin). However, these can wait; we've got more important business to do here. Go directly into the museum, which is like entering a spacecraft. Flashing lights. Celestial music. And a wonderful array of extraterrestrial oddities. Check out the library. Examine photos of real UFOs. Consider evidence, including soil samples, that a UFO crashed in Roswell, New Mexico, back in 1947. Then inspect the incubated alien. And before you leave, try to translate the alien writing on the wall. Per-

UFO Lab, a museum of alien encounters, set up shop in a Richmond, Rhode Island, shopping mall. Photo: Joe Citro

haps more sobering is the information about Ann's father, Richard Clayton Harris Jr., who was accounting and finance officer at Roswell in 1947. He knew about the crash and participated in the cover-up, but never spoke about it until 1997 when he admitted it was, in fact, a spaceship. Shortly afterward he was murdered in his home. If there really are spaceships, gray lightbulb-headed aliens, and sinister government conspiracies, you'll feel very close to them here. This site is well worth the trip, no matter how many light years you have to travel.

UFO Lab Museum
   Ocean State Job Lot Plaza
   Richmond, RI
Phone: (401) 539-9626 or 1-888-414-2830
   dennis@ufolabri.com
   www.ufolabri.com
Location: Take Exit 3A off of I-95; the museum is behind the McDonalds.
Hours: Abducted and gone forever.

Mound House

Rhode Island is awash in spectacular architecture, especially in Newport, with its scores of mansions. But the house that really caught our eye was just north of Newport in the town of South Portsmouth. No marble or Corinthian columns here, just a heap of dirt. The house in fact is a human anthill, covered in grass, with nothing showing but a door. When we drove by, there was a goat grazing on it. Ironically, it belongs to a carpenter who built it himself, perhaps looking to make something relatively maintenance-free.

Location: The mound house is at 219 Braman's Lane in Portsmouth. Going north from Newport on 138, turn right onto Braman's Lane, just south of South Portsmouth.

NOTE: What is it about Rhode Island that makes people want to dig in? There's an underground house built into a hill in nearby Middletown, at 144 3rd Beach Road, off of Trout Drive. We're told there is another near Ocean Drive. Since all of these dwellings are private, viewing is best done from the car.

Corvair Gravestone

When eighty-four-year-old retired police matron Rose Martin died in 1998, she left a very unusual request. She wanted to be buried inside her car. Perhaps if it had been a Rolls Royce or Ferrari we could understand, but a 1962 Corvair? We thought those were dead and buried long ago. Anyway, Rose, for whatever reason, had loved the car and, miraculously, she drove it around for thirty-six years. Six police officers acting as pallbearers slid Rose's wooden coffin through an opening in the rear of the Corvair, where its engine had once been. The entire vehicle, passenger, casket, and all were then lowered into the ground with a crane. The small car, which in life had required less than a single parking place, took up four burial plots. Rose's husband rests beside her, though he is not well represented on the tombstone. It shows a picture of Rose and her beloved car. His mug shot is missing.

Location: Rose Martin's grave is in the Pocasset Hill cemetery, which is on the main drag of Tiverton (Route 77). From the town center go north on 77 until you see the post office. (If you reach the Massachusetts border you've gone about one and a half miles too far.) Pocasset Hill cemetery is alongside the post office. Go in the cemetery's front entrance, take the first left. About three quarters of the way down on the left in the second row you'll find a big book-like stone—possibly intended to be a Bible—with "Martin" written on it. That is Rose's permanent parking place.

Hours: The cemetery is open twenty-four hours a day year round.

Woonsocket, Rhode Island

Little Rose

The circumstances surrounding Marie Rose Farron were sufficiently strange for renowned anomalist Charles Fort to discuss them in his 1932 book, *Wild Talents*. Since then, Rose has passed on, but, depending on your point of view, a miracle or a mystery remains. As far as we know, she is the only stigmatic that New England has ever produced. Beginning on March 17, 1916, wounds spontaneously opened on her hands, feet, and forehead, wounds said to replicate those of Jesus Christ. Apparently she was also a mystic, visionary, and so-called "victim soul." The process may have begun when Little Rose, at an early age, was cured of a leg problem by Brother Andre, a noted Catholic healer from Montreal. At the time of her death at age 33 on May 11, 1936, part of her crown of thorns stigmata was still visible and was photographed. She had acquired a devoted following who considered her a candidate for sainthood. Bishop Russell J. McVinney undertook two investigations, both of which concluded there was nothing extraordinary about her life. But believers attested to an array of miracles attributable to her and, eleven years after her death, when her remains were exhumed, she was found to be incorrupt—her body had not decayed. Little Rose still has a number of followers who meet periodically in the family home. The case for her sainthood continues to this day. You can visit her garden, her chapel (where many relics are on display), and her grave at Precious Blood Cemetery. In Canadian-French her gravestone reads: "The Little Rose / Victim of her Jesus / Marie Rose Ferron / Stigmatist / Born: May 24, 1902 / Died: May 11, 1936 / At the Age of 33 Years."

Little Rose Family Chapel
Little Rose's Garden
302 Providence St.
Woonsocket, RI 02895

Hours: The chapel is open on the first Sunday of each month from 2:00 P.M. onward.

NOTE: This was the Farron family house after Rose died. They were living across the street at 271 Providence Street when her earthly death occurred. Today Rose rests in Woonsocket's Precious Blood Cemetery.

Precious Blood Cemetery is at the Intersection of Rathbun Street and Route 114 in Woonsocket. Immediately after passing through the cemetery gate, bear right. Follow the road to the next small intersection. The tomb of Little Rose is on the left-hand side of the road, two plots from this intersection.

VERMONT

Mercie's Curse

As long as the Hayden house stands in Albany it will be a reminder of one of Vermont's most dramatic run-ins with the supernatural, for the story of Hayden House is the story of a family's destruction, and of a curse that took three generations to run its unalterable course. In 1823, the dying Mercie Dale cursed the well-to-do Hayden family: They would die out in poverty in three generations. Strangely, they did. The last Hayden, Mamie, died in 1927, poverty-stricken and utterly alone. But the story doesn't end there, for something lives on in that old house. What else would account for slamming doors, moving lights, and orchestral music playing in what was once a ballroom? And on the grounds outside there are . . . disturbances. During prosperous times, William Hayden Jr., had allegedly smuggled Chinese workers into the United States to build his railroad. As the illegal laborers died, they were buried in the fields behind the three barns. Sometimes at night people still see the bobbing of lantern lights out there, as if someone is forever patrolling, or perhaps digging graves . . .

Location: Follow Route 14 north towards Albany. The Hayden house is on the left, a mile south of the village. It is brick, noticeable for its circular drive and cement platform in front.

NOTE: The Hayden house is now a private residence. Please view from the road.

Fort Blunder

It's an imposing ruin, a great stone castle, but it may be a stretch of the imagination to say Fort Blunder is in Vermont.

Then again, location has always been part of its problem. Clearly there was good reason for the Americans to build a fort on this spot: It's a strategic point at which New York, Vermont, Lake Champlain, and Canada all come together. During the Revolutionary War, the British moved troops down from Canada at this point. During the War of 1812 they again headed south on the lake. So in 1816, America decided to erect a fifty-cannon fort before England got any more ideas. It was to be called Fort Montgomery.

Construction began and was well underway, when, in 1819, a land survey of the forty-fifth parallel revealed—much to the chagrin of the War Department—that America had built its fort in Canada. Historically, no battles were ever fought at Fort Montgomery, but the British took it without firing a shot. Since then—and with good reason—everyone has been calling it "Fort Blunder." In 1842, the Webster-Ashburton Treaty restored it to the United States, but by then we didn't need it.

Location: This spooky-looking fortress is clearly visible from Vermont as you cross the Rouses Point Bridge from Alburg into New York state on Route 2.

Barre, Vermont

Grave Art

When a wave of Italian immigrants made their way to America in the nineteenth century, many stonecutters came to Barre to work in the vast granite quarries, the world's largest. Some were masterful carvers, as is evident in the number of marble sculptures scattered throughout town (although an errant Scot among them managed to stick in a statue of Robert Burns). For a time, you could go to Barre and hear Italian spoken on the street. The craftsmen, with names like Guiseppe Donati, Lambruno Sarzanini, Antonio Soprano, and Guliano

Cecchinelli, passed their skills down through the generations. But despite their numbers, Barre was rooted firmly in American soil. Artists or not, they couldn't transform this hill town of clapboard houses and grange halls into the cobblestoned gems of the old country. Yet, Italy's legacy lives on in one part of town—the cemetery. A walk through it is the closest you'll get to the Uffizi in Vermont. With its lyrical inscriptions and gleaming marble statuary (including a replica of Michelangelo's Pieta), the Hope Cemetery ranks among America's finest. It is also one of the strangest, spanning the continuum from classical art to pop culture. Where else can you find a married couple holding hands in bed, a half-sized stock car etched from white granite, or a rendering of the tractor-trailer that Uncle Nat drove up and down I-89? The oddities are all the more remarkable for their superb execution. Wander around the newer section close to the entrance and you'll find a basketball, an armchair, a Civil Air Patrol plane, and a perfect cube poised on its corner, each in some way emblematic of the life they represent. On sunny days the place is full of strollers, and it's clear that most of the visitors are not there to lay flowers. They're art lovers in a country where aesthetics are not top priority, and this display, as the cemetery's name might suggest, is a reason for hope.

Hope Cemetery
    Route 14
    Barre, VT 05406

Phone: (802) 476-6245
    www.central-vt.com/visit/cemetery/
    www.oldbones.net/html_java/johns2text.htm

Location: Take the Barre exit off of I-89 and go straight on Route 14 as you enter town, past the worker statue. When the road winds to the right, you'll see Hope Cemetery on the left with its marble-carved gates.

NOTE: Wonder where all this granite came from? On the southeast of town, you can still watch workers cut gigantic blocks out of the earth at the Rock of Ages quarry. (Open May–October, Monday–Saturday, 8:30 A.M.–5 P.M. Sunday, noon–5 P.M.)

Hetty's Couch

Can't get enough of Hetty Green? Her green (of course) fainting couch and the gate to her garden path (up which she led more than one person) are in the Bellows Falls Library, along with a few personal effects, postcards, and pictures of the house. Why can't you see the house itself? Hetty's daughter Sylvia donated the Green property to the town in the 1950s on the condition that it would tear the mansion to the ground. It did.

The Rockingham Free Public Library
   65 Westminster St.
   Bellows Falls, VT 05101

Phone: (802) 463-4270

Hours: Open Monday, Wednesday, Thursday, 1–8 P.M., Tuesday, 9 A.M.–8 P.M., Friday, 9 A.M.–5 P.M., Saturday, 9 A.M.–noon.

NOTE: For more on Hetty, see entry for the *Queen of Cupidity* under New Bedford, Massachusetts.

Stoned Indians

No one really knows who made them or exactly what they are supposed to be, but these odd, round "heads" staring out of the rocks have been vexing Vermonters since before the state was founded. The petroglyphic portraits seem to depict life-size oval or round faces with distinct characteristics, presumably eyes and mouths. Generally suspected to be the work of Native Americans, the faces are adorned with appendages resembling feathers. But something about these rock images looks vaguely otherworldly. Until we know for sure what they are and who made them, the "Humanoid Pe-troglyphs" are open to all kinds of speculation. Perhaps the "feathers" are actually "horns"? And the round heads? Some people have guessed they are the helmets of spacemen, com-plete with antennae.

Location: Just east of downtown Bellows Falls, on the road that leads to Al-stead, New Hampshire, there is a bridge crossing the Connecticut River— Vilas Bridge. Stand on the Vermont side of the bridge, but not in the road. From the right-hand side, look straight down at the rocks below. Keep look-ing. The petroglyphs are a little hard to spot.

NOTE: There are two clusters of "heads" to contemplate: eight nearest the bridge, sixteen more about twenty feet to the south.

Brattleboro, Vermont

James Fisk Monument

Another of Vermont's larger than life characters was James Fisk, born on April Fool's Day, 1834. Though his beginnings were humble, his appetites were grand. A natural salesman, he was like P. T. Barnum in his gumption and flamboyance. Early in his career he did a brief stint with the circus, during which he learned much about human nature and how to manipulate it. When he returned to Brattleboro he purchased a wagon, painted it as garishly as possible, and set out selling things. Dressed like a ringmaster, he began the shrewd wheeling and dealing that would eventually land him on Wall Street. There his fortune expanded along with his waistline. In 1869, he teamed up with the infamous financier Jay Gould. They tried to corner the New York City gold market. This brazen attempt to consolidate all wealth in the hands of two men brought about the so-called "Black Friday," the financial panic of 1869. His greed, cunning, and audacity led to a licentious lifestyle that culminated in Fisk's murder by his mistress's lover. He died at age thirty-eight on the staircase of the Broadway Central Hotel in New York City. Today his ostentatious gravestone can be seen in Prospect Hill Cemetery. It too is larger than life and in questionable taste. It's a tall marble shaft on a base where his bust is displayed. Around him, on each corner of the monument, eight more busts are displayed, two on each of four life-sized statues of naked ladies. Apparently each figure represents a specific aspect of Jim Fisk's career—railroads, steamboats, commerce, and the stage. The monument, like Fisk himself, is in dramatic contrast with Vermont Puritanism and is our only R-rated entry.

Location: From I-91, take exit 1 and go straight until you come to Pine Street, which is opposite the hospital. Turn right onto Pine and go to the end. The Prospect Hill Cemetery is right there. The grave is not hard to find as it is one of the largest.

Brookline, Vermont

Lookout Schoolhouse

There's no arguing that it is a curiosity—the only round schoolhouse in the country. It was built in 1822, designed by its founding teacher and part-time physician, Dr. John Wilson. Constructed from brick, with windows all around, it's a unique piece of Vermont architecture . . . but there's nothing weird about that. What's weird is its architect, Dr. Wilson, a genuine "man of mystery." Locals couldn't figure out why their aristocratic educator would accept a position as a lowly schoolteacher. And why in such an out-of-the-way town? They mused about the inspiration for his unconventional academy, but above all, they wondered about his behavior. Why wouldn't he talk about his past in the British Isles? Why did he occasionally walk with a noticeable limp? Why did he always wear high

collars or thick scarves? And why did he seem so charming yet
. . . unsociable? The answers didn't come until Dr. Wilson's
death in 1847. The undertaker discovered that his heel had
been shot away, he bore the scar of a musket ball on his leg, and
his neck was horribly disfigured. Someone discovered a stiletto
concealed in the cane he carried. An examination of his home
revealed a cache of swords, guns, and ammunition. Eventually
some mathematician—a former student, perhaps—put two and
two together and realized their reclusive schoolmaster was in
reality a famous British highwayman, the notorious "Captain
Thunderbolt." For more than a decade he and his partner "Mr.
Lightfoot" had terrorized the Irish countryside and the
England-Scotland border. Renowned as a dashing rogue of the
Robin Hood variety, he allegedly stole from the rich, gave to
the poor, and stashed enough away to vanish to America.
There he hid out in Brookline, Vermont, warily peering out in
all directions from the windows of his lookout, Brookline's
round schoolhouse.

Location: Brookline is a little tricky to find. Get onto Route 9 running from
Brattleboro to Dummerston to Newfane. Pass through Newfane and take
the first right north of town onto Putney Mountain Road. It will cross a
bridge over West River. Continue past Hill Road on the left. Cross another
bridge and turn left onto Grassy Brook Road. Continue for roughly three
miles. The schoolhouse is on your left. Captain Thunderbolt's attraction to
the area will be quite evident.

NOTE: The old round schoolhouse is not normally open to the public. Those
wishing to go inside should speak to the town clerk whose office is directly
across the street and is open Mondays, 9 A.M.–3 P.M.

ALSO NOTE: The story of Captain Thunderbolt is complex and fascinating. It
will become more real if you stop in the Brooks Library in Brattleboro,
where some of Dr. Wilson's possessions, recovered after his death, are on
display. Among them are his false heel, his medical instruments, a daguerreotype, and his intriguing sword cane.

An Enigmatic Edifice

This massive and mysterious stone building, now used as the Orleans County Historical Society, is nowhere near as immense as the Egyptian pyramids, but in many ways it is just as puzzling. Here Reverend Alexander Twilight, the first black graduate of an American college (Middlebury, 1823), founded his own school, Brownington Academy. The remarkable thing is that this dedicated educator apparently built the entire sixty-foot-long, four-story structure all by himself—in just three years! Then he dubbed it "Athenian Hall." The mystery is obvious: How could one man alone erect such a mammoth edifice? Check it out; you'll see what we mean. Some of the stones are eight feet long and weigh more than eleven hundred pounds. How did he quarry them? How did he move them? But most mysterious of all, how did he single-handedly lift them into place? No one knows. While you're pondering these imponderables, be sure to visit the historical society exhibits inside. Don't miss the fur-bearing trout and the face that is slowly and mysteriously emerging from a painting that should have been completed a century ago.

Orleans County Historical Society and Old Stone Museum
28 Old Stone House Rd.
Brownington, VT 05860

Phone: (802) 754-2022
osh@together.net
www.oldstonehousemuseum.org

Location: From Orleans head east on Route 58 and watch for signs to Brownington (roughly three miles). Once there, you can't miss Athenian Hall.

Hours: Open daily, July and August, 11 A.M.–5 P.M. May 15–June 30 and September 1–October 15, Friday–Tuesday, 11 A.M.–5 P.M.

Admission charged.

First floor is wheelchair accessible.

Cursed Springs

When curiosity-collector Robert Ripley saw them, he called the Brunswick Mineral Springs the eighth wonder of the world. Today the six separate healing springs flowing from a single knoll are a nearly forgotten geological anomaly. Surprisingly, the mineral content of each is apparently different from that of its neighbor. For centuries the waters were freely shared by native peoples. In colonial times, entrepreneurial Europeans killed Abenakis to seize the springs. A retaliatory curse uttered by an Abenaki shaman promised preternatural retribution if the waters were ever used for profit. Subsequently, at least four commercial spas built here inexplicably burned to the ground. Puzzled businessmen gave up and abandoned the site; wilderness—and the Abenaki—reclaimed it. But the ruins and the waters can still be visited. And at night, so it is said, you can still see the ghosts of its Indian protectors guarding the springs or stalking silently across the surface of the pond nearby.

Location: The springs are in the wilds of Brunswick, Vermont, between Route 102 and the Connecticut River. Just follow the trail behind the Town Hall.

NOTE: This is private property and a sacred site of the Abenaki people. When visiting, please show proper respect.

Alien Animals

The city of Burlington tries so hard to be correct and normal that it is difficult to find anything that truly qualifies as weird. However, enough water monster sightings have taken place here that devotees erected a monument to celebrate the fact.

We figured if we poked around we might find a few more curious critters lurking here and there. But let's start with water monsters . . .

Monster Monument

On Perkins Pier there is a granite marker dedicated to Champ, Lake Champlain's own sea monster. Always an elusive little devil, he was first noted by French explorer Samuel de Champlain in 1609, but local Indians knew about him long before that. In 1964, Champ undulated to the surface near a summer camp at Westport, New York, terrifying a group of young swimmers. In 1970, he put in an appearance near the Isle La Motte bridge according to eight witnesses who were fishing at the time. On July 30, 1984, the largest Champ sighting on record took place on a tourist boat called *The Spirit of Ethan Allen,* with eighty-six people aboard. Champ has often been spotted from the bridge at Crown Point, Vermont, which affords a panoramic view of the lake at a relatively narrow point. Probably the best site for champ-watching is near Split Rock on the New York side across from Basin Harbor in Ferrisburgh, where a four-hundred-foot trough is thought to be the deepest point in the lake. Some folks think Champ lives there. But wherever he may reside, there have been hundreds of sightings—reported and unreported—over the years. So don't read the monument; watch the lake!

Location: To reach Perkins Pier: Take exit 14W off I-89, and follow the main road (Main Street) until you are in front of One Main Street, which is Union Station. Turn left onto Battery Street and take your second right onto Maple Street, which leads the short distance down to a parking area by the lake. The pier is a small spit of grassy park bordered with benches. The plaque is on a rock at the left.

Winged Monkeys

From Perkins Pier you can walk north along the bike path until you come to the old Union Station, at the bottom of Main Street. Perched atop its roof you'll see a pair of life-sized metal monsters that look like a hybrid of those screeching terrors from "The Wizard of Oz" and that unforgettable gremlin on "The Twilight Zone," who tears apart an airplane while a horrified William Shatner watches from inside. The monster-monkeys look as if they're preparing to spring at you, but don't worry. They never move.

Rhinoceros

From there go straight up Main Street and turn right on Pine. A few blocks down on the left is number 266, an old mill complex housing a variety of businesses. The blue building closest to the sidewalk is the home of Conant Custom Brass. No, it's not a safari outfitter, although you might think so from looking up. Bursting through the wall on the second floor is a hoary rhinoceros, seemingly stuck for eternity in an effort to escape. Evidently his body was too wide to follow his neck through the planks. Then again, he may have attempted the breakout during the winter and changed his mind.

Whale Tails

Vermont boasts a fair number of moose, deer, and skunks, but being New England's only land-locked state, its whale population is relatively sparse. Apparently feeling deprived, the locals supplied their own. On a popular stretch of I-89 between exits 12 and 13, a pair of whale tails appears on a knoll, looking every bit as if they had breached the surface, flipped in the air, and dove into the grassy field. The cetaceans are actually the work of Randolph sculptor Jim Sardonis, and are officially called "Reverence" to symbolize the planet's fragility. If you miss them, sign up for a whale-watching tour on Lake Champlain; an Essex Junction couple is providing them in response to the many whale-watch requests the state tourist office receives from outsiders.

www.furrs.org/whales/default.htm

Tale of a Whale

If these sculpted tails don't turn you on, there is a real whale to be seen—or at least what's left of him (or her). It was discovered in 1849 by a crew of railroad laborers in the town of Charlotte, some twelve miles south of Burlington. At first it was thought to be a horse. Then a water monster. Finally naturalist Zadock Thompson determined the bones were of an animal that normally inhabits arctic and subarctic marine waters—a beluga whale. Such "white whales" were common in this area just eleven thousand years ago when everything was under the Champlain Sea. Today you can view the skeleton at the Perkins Geology Museum, which operates on a self-serve basis: Visitors are urged to turn the lights on when they come and off when they leave. While there, don't miss the vertical hanging pane of transparent glass that lights up into a life-sized three-dimensional T-Rex hologram when you flick on the light and look at it from the right spot about three feet away. This surprising little museum also has dinosaur footprints, and the tusk of a native Vermont mastodon.

Perkins Museum of Geology
  Perkins Hall
  University of Vermont

Phone: (802) 656-8694
  bdoolan@moose.uvm.edu
  geology.uvm.edu/museumwww/intropage.html

Location: From the road to the north of the University of Vermont campus (Colchester Avenue), turn up the drive for the Fletcher Allen Hospital. Bear right at the stop sign and take two immediate rights. You'll be in the small Fleming Museum parking lot. The Perkins Science Museum is the brick building just beyond the Fleming. The entrance is on the side away from the street.

Hours: Monday–Friday, 8 A.M.–5 P.M., weekends and holidays, 9 A.M.–5 P.M.

Free admission.

Wheelchair accessible.

Burlington, Vermont

Brautigan Library

Author Richard Brautigan is given credit for conceiving the idea, but we bet it has crossed the mind of anyone who has written a book—and failed to sell it. A library of unpublished works. Based on the notion articulated in Mr. Brautigan's *The Abortion: An Historical Romance,* Vermonter Todd Lockwood made fiction a reality in the early 1990s by setting up a home for unsold books—books of every description but published. For whatever reason—lack of funds, lack of interest, lack of space—Mr. Lockwood closed the library in 1996. Certainly it was not from lack of manuscripts. The collection is now housed in Burlington's Fletcher Free Library, where it can be examined. Various bits of Brautigan memorabilia are also on display, including his eyeglasses, his typewriter, foreign editions of his work, and plenty of mayonnaise jars (need we explain?). Brautigan fans will love it. The rest of us will wonder why the originator's own manuscripts are not on display. We feel they should be.

Brautigan Library
Fletcher Free Library
235 College St.
Burlington, VT 05401

Phone: (802) 865-7225

Location: The Fletcher Free Library is in downtown Burlington, just down the hill from the green at the University of Vermont. The Brautigan Library is on the top floor.

Hours: Open Monday–Friday, 8:30 A.M.–6 P.M., Wednesday, 8:30 A.M.–9 P.M. Saturday, 9 A.M.–5 P.M., Sunday, noon–6 P.M.

NOTE: The Brautigan Library has no website, no email address, and its phone was disconnected years ago. It is no longer accepting manuscripts.

Free admission.

Wheelchair accessible.

Burlington, Vermont

An Itch for Kitsch?

What is art? We don't know, but we sure recognize kitsch when we see it: plastic space aliens, barefoot boys with fishing poles, tasteless religious icons, and pop tunes that lodge in the head like a tickle in the throat. It's that unmistakable hybrid of commercialism, cliché, and mass production that turns culture into crap. A few years ago its insipid artlessness inspired art professor Ed Owre to create WHAMKA (the Williams Hall Art Museum of Kitsch Art) that now fills a small hallway on the main floor of the art department at the University of Vermont. Items include rubber duckies, water-filled paperweights, hula hoops, souvenirs, dolphins, trolls, cake decorations, and an impressive collection of PEZ dispensers, all interspersed with tacky renditions of The Last Supper. There's a special section devoted to Elvis. The museum has been so successful that a nearby closet will soon become its western annex.

Museum of Kitsch Art
  Art Department
  Williams Hall
  University of Vermont
  Burlington, VT 05405

Phone: (802) 656-2014
  eowre@zoo.uvm.edu

Location: Enter through the front door of Williams Hall, an ornate brick building on University Place next to the university green. Turn right and go straight into the hallway.

Hours: Open seven days a week, 9 A.M.–9 P.M. Closed on holidays.

Free admission. Kitsch donations are enthusiastically accepted.

Wheelchair access is through the back door: Take the elevator up one flight.

Burlington/Waterbury, Vermont

Register of Horror

After the battle of Gettysburg, a Vermont physician, Dr. Henry Janes, took charge of the wounded. His job was to oversee the hospitalization of over twenty thousand Union and Confederate soldiers, many of whom faced amputations and worse without anesthesia or sterilized surgical instruments. In 1864, he returned to Vermont to run the Sloan Army Hospital in Montpelier, and it was there that he took up a curious pastime. Dr. Janes started a painstaking register of the most "interesting" medical cases relating to Gettysburg, entering each according to the wound's position on the body. Some were meticulous descriptions of how the patient was shot, dragged from the battlefield, and treated. A large 375-page leather journal records the minutest of details in his feathery handwriting on long, yellowing pages. "The entrance wound was healed but the wound of exit was discharging about 2 oz. of pus a day," reads a sentence on page thirty-one. Elsewhere, "Frothy blood issued from the wound and he expectorated blood." Accompanying the entries are photographs of the men displaying their injuries some five years later, each subject posed on the same upholstered chair. One furtively lifts his shirt to show abdominal damage, another with a lifeless eye, stares blankly—maybe blindly—into the camera. Many lift pant legs to show missing feet or legs. A few stand almost naked, their bodies scarred from deep gashes, possibly hasty surgical incisions. One can imagine the scene: Men trying not to move, while the photographer, bending under his black cloth, pops the smoking flash with a loud whoosh! Dr. Janes left his horror register to a colleague, who donated it to the University of Vermont. He willed everything else to the town of Waterbury, some thirty miles southeast. His ancestral house, which doubled as his office, is now the village library. Upstairs are glass cases full of his Civil War mementos: his navy uniform and high leather boots, tiny ointment bottles, his medical bag and its contents, a long knife used for amputations, and a skull with its upper portion sliced off. The pain that Dr. Janes observed is demonstrated in a display of bullets used during operations: Some still bear tooth marks.

Bailey-Howe Library
Special Collections
The University of Vermont
Burlington, VT 05405

Phone: (802) 656-1493
sageunix.uvm.edu/

Location: UVM's Bailey Library is located behind The Old Mill off of University Place, midway between Main and Pearl Streets. Dr. Janes's Register is downstairs in Special Collections; the librarian on duty will bring it out to you.

Hours: Special Collections is open Monday–Friday, 9 A.M.–5 P.M. Closed Saturdays, Sundays, and major holidays.

Wheelchair accessible.

Waterbury Village Library
28 North Main St.
Waterbury, VT 05676

Phone: (802) 244-7036

Location: Take exit 12 from I-89 and follow signs to the village. Turn left under the train overpass. The library is the house on the right after the baseball field.

Hours: The museum is open when the library is, Monday and Tuesday, 10 A.M.–8 P.M., Wednesday, 10 A.M.–9 P.M., Thursday and Friday, 10 A.M.– 5 P.M., Saturdays, 9 A.M.–2 P.M. . Closed Sundays. Ask the circulation desk to let you into the museum.

NOTE: When you've overdosed on Civil War memorabilia, take a look at the elaborate hair wreath framed under glass in the cabinet facing the back of the house. It was made by the daughter of Waterbury's first merchant, Amasa Pride.

Castleton, Vermont

Ancient Vermont Exhibit

The late Dr. Warren Cook, who for years taught history and anthropology at Castleton State College, went against the grain when he began to explore the possibility of pre-Columbian settlement of Vermont. More than anyone else, Dr. Cook led the way in collecting evidence and artifacts and identifying ancient structures that he believed were here long before any conventional European settlement. He suspected the state was widely inhabited by seagoing copper seekers—possibly bronze-age Celts—who mined and exported Vermont's vast supplies of copper. Here, in the college library, is a memorial to Dr. Cook and his work. Among the exhibits and photographs you can see many of Vermont's ancient structures, examples of Ogam writing, carved stones including phalluses (which we are sure were not made by our Puritan grandfathers or grandmothers), and a statue of the genital area of a female torso. There are other anomalies, too: a stone ax found in Vermont, with Greek letters on it; two Byzantine coins from around 1200 A.D. (perhaps used to date the structure in which they were discovered). It is all fascinating and thought-provoking, but one tends to feel a little disappointed. Not so much in the exhibits but in the apparent lack of enthusiasm. It is as if the college can't decide whether to endorse or be embarrassed by Dr. Cook's courageous studies.

Calvin Coolidge Library
  Castleton State College
  Castleton, VT 05735

Phone: (802) 468-1255
  www.csc.vsc.edu/library/

Location: From Main Street turn onto Seminary. Follow it uphill until you see the library on the right. The Ancient Vermont Exhibit is on the second floor.

Hours: Open during library hours, which vary. Check library homepage for up-to-date information.

Free admission.

Wheelchair accessible.

Cuttingsville, Vermont

Bowman Mausoleum

Is that a ghost on the steps of the tomb? No, it's a marble statue . . . and one of New England's most melancholy monuments to the dead. Laurel Hall, the spooky old Victorian mansion across the street, was to have been the summer home for the John P. Bowman family. Sadly, Mr. Bowman's wife and two daughters died before construction was finished. Mr. Bowman moved in alone, had the tomb built to shelter his family, and lived out his years in seclusion. Every morning until his death he'd look out his front windows and see the eerie white apparition of himself, frozen in stone, forever kneeling at the door to the mausoleum. Local legend says he pursued occult secrets to bring his family, and eventually himself, back from the dead.

Supposedly his will provided for the place's upkeep after he died and for fresh meals every night, in case one of the deceased Bowmans were to show up unannounced . . . and hungry. There are also stories of ghostly children, hidden treasures, and moving statues. But the neo-Egyptian mausoleum is a real and observable wonder. This incredible crypt, involving over a year's work by 125 craftsmen, cost a staggering seventy-five thousand dollars, nearly a million and a half in today's dollars. It's made of seven hundred fifty tons of granite, fifty tons of marble, over twenty thousand bricks and more than one hundred loads of sand. Strangely, looking through the barred entrance reveals an interior far larger than outside dimensions suggest. This magic is done with mirrors, an ingenious illusion. It is easy to forget the real Bowman bodies are nearby, resting forever on "A Couch of Dreamless Sleep." In the foreground, statues detail exactly how everyone had looked during the brief bloom of life.

Location: Laurel Hall and Mausoleum are in Cuttingsville, about eight miles east from the intersection of Routes 103 and 7, just south of Rutland.

Fair Haven, Vermont/Low Hampton, New York

William Miller Farm

William Miller was a prophet, and the power of his prophesy threw the whole nation into turmoil . . . *three times*! Through years of Bible study he became convinced that the end of the world was near and that Christ was on his way. In 1831, he preached that the world would end sometime between March 1843 and March 1844. Then he calculated the exact date: April 3, 1843. He was convinced and convincing. Through tireless writing, preaching, and proselytizing, the number of his followers grew. Dramatic coincidental phenomena—earthquakes, wars, meteor showers—seemed to back him up. Joined by other clerics, the number of followers climbed from fifty thousand to one hundred thousand, all preparing to meet their maker. When April 3 passed, Reverend Miller figured he had miscalculated. But followers recalled his original estimation: The world would end *on or before* March 1844. Again the faithful assembled on the final date. Again nothing happened. Meanwhile Reverend Miller had discovered his error. He reset the date of the Second Coming to October 22, 1844. This time for sure. Thousands of people sold their belongings and headed for the hilltops so they'd be closer to Heaven when the moment came. To their utter disillusionment nothing happened. After three failed prophesies, scores left the Miller fold, abandoning him to a handful of diehard followers. He lived out his days where it all began, on his Low Hampton farm. There he studied the Bible, preached at his little chapel, and wondered what had gone wrong. Even today Seventh Day Adventists refer to the day the world was supposed to end as "The Great Disappointment."

William Miller Farm and Chapel
Low Hampton, NY 12887

Phone: (518) 282–9617
www.adventistheritage.org/miller.html

Location: Go west on Route 4 from Fair Haven and enter New York by crossing the Poultney River. Watch for a barn and a silo quickly coming up on the left. Across from the barn and silo, take the right on the opposite side of Route 4. Continue straight. Soon you'll pass a cemetery on the left. Reverend Miller is buried there. After that the road comes immediately to a "T." Go left and watch on your left for the Miller Home, Miller Chapel, and Ascension Rock.

Hours: Tours are available year-round. Call in advance for group reservations, information, and further directions.

NOTE: Okay, so New York is not in New England. But Reverend Miller was very active in nearby Poultney and Fair Haven, and his home was too close to omit. The property is beautifully maintained by the Seventh Day Adventist Church. But remember, they don't see William Miller quite the way we do.

Here Mermaids Dwell

There is no seacoast in this area. No major rivers, either. So how should we account for the occasional mermaid sightings? You can see one for yourself at 186 Townshend Road in Grafton. It is a hideous little creature, half fish, half something else that, in the delirium of a nightmare, might be mistaken for partly human. Its nasty teeth and claws look like they could fend off Lake Champlain's monster. In true New England gothic fashion, the owners keep the deformed little demon locked away in the basement, so discerning how it came into their possession is a bit of a mystery. We suspect its parentage is similar to that of P. T. Barnum's "Feejee Mermaid" (see *The Barnum Institute* in Bridgeport, Connecticut). Historically, these "mermaids" originated in Indonesia where inhabitants synthesized them from monkey tops and fish bottoms, presumably as talismans to insure successful fishing. Later, the aquatic trolls became a source of revenue when they were sold to curiosity-seeking European seafarers. In the nineteenth century, the ancestor of all American mermaids resided at the Boston Museum under the care of Moses Kimball. It was adopted by P. T. Barnum in 1842. Together, man and mermaid earned a fortune. Imitators sprang up all over the country and one poor orphan apparently found its way to Grafton, where you can visit it today at the Nature Museum. If grotesque marine hybrids aren't your cup of tea, ask to see the dueling frogs, a real whimsical bit of nineteenth century stuff and nonsense. Though the rest of this wonderful little museum may be a bit more down to earth, there are plenty of natural wonders to be seen, including live honeybees at work, fascinating fossils, a crawl-through tunnel, and even Vermont's own mystery cat, the catamount.

The Nature Museum of Grafton
186 Townshend Rd.
Grafton, VT 05146

Phone: (802) 843-2111
info@nature-museum.org
www.nature-museum.org

Location: Head south on Townshend Road in front of the Grafton Inn. The museum is a quarter of a mile from the intersection, on the right.

Hours: Open year round, Saturdays, 10 A.M.–4 P.M. Memorial Day–mid-October open weekends and holidays, 10 A.M.–4 P.M., or by appointment.

Hartland, Vermont

Nature Club

If you happen to be anywhere near Hartland, Vermont, on the Fourth of July, make a beeline for the Nature Club. Time has stopped here. The place has never been updated or modernized, maintaining the ambiance of a Victorian men's club. Stuffed animals, some of them a little worse for wear, adorn the walls. Dozens of old-fashioned narrow drawers contain perfectly mounted butterflies, insects, minerals, birds' eggs, and other delights, all dating back almost a century. This is typical of the little museums that, back in the good old days, private individuals would set up in a backroom or shed, and slightly wealthier people, or associations, would establish and maintain with a charming formality. The Hartland Nature Club preserves the latter tradition. But just because it preserves relics doesn't mean it is one. The club still functions, holding nature walks, lectures, and meetings.

The Hartland Nature Club
Damon Hall
Hartland, VT 05048

Phone: (802) 436-2043

Location: Right in the middle of downtown Hartland, located with the town offices in Damon Hall, a conspicuous red brick building.

Hours: Open one day a year on July 4, or by appointment.

Free admission.

The Hungry Gorge

If there is a cursed spot in Vermont, this is it. It looks like a perfect place to swim, bucolic and beautiful, but Huntington's "Killer Gorge" seems to have an appetite for human beings. Since 1950 it has gorged itself on at least eighteen people, all of whom lost their lives by drowning. The victims include three would-be rescuers, among them one heroic state policeman who had jumped in to save a drowning victim. In spite of warning signs and a plaque that serves as a kind of memorial to the dead, swimmers keep sacrificing themselves to the killer currents. In 1976, local citizens tried to stem the flow of victims by blasting away an underwater chute in which people could easily get trapped. Although this dangerous rock formation was removed, the gorge continues to take its death toll. Many people who concern themselves with such things consider it the most dangerous river gorge in all of New England. Predictably, ghost stories have arisen, either as a preternatural consequence of dying or as a contrived method of scaring people away. But even without the supernatural, young thrill-seekers keep falling victim to this scenic site's fatal charms.

Location: From I-89 take exit 10 for Waterbury/Stowe. Get on Route 100 toward Waterbury. At the stop sign, turn right onto Route 2 west, a two-lane highway that parallels I-89 and the Winooski River. Follow it for ten miles until you enter Jonesville. Take a left onto West White Hill Road, which takes you over a green steel bridge. Follow the road to a second, smaller bridge. Take a left onto Dugway Road. Park in any of the several pull-offs. Several paths lead down to the gorge.

NOTE: Wherever you park, make sure that all four wheels are off the road. And prudes beware, the gorge is a popular spot for nude bathers.

WARNING: Don't go in the water.

Irasburg, Vermont

Wilderness Castle

Vermont's northern woods are rife with hidden secrets. One of them reveals itself as you drive south from Irasburg. Suddenly, without warning, you'll see the stone turrets of a fifteenth-century castle rising among the treetops. Is it Brigadoon? A vision from *The Wizard of Oz*? A hallucination? No, it's a castle—a real one—though it's not medieval. This is the

The Castle Shoppe and Café, Irasburg, Vermont. Photo: Joe Citro

home of Harv and Sara Gregoire, who were married in a European castle during the ten years they lived in Germany. Though enchanted with castles in general, one particular Bavarian hunting lodge seemed absolutely perfect. So they sketched it and decided that when they retired, this would be their home. The Gregoires settled in Vermont largely because of its stones. Then they bought a pile of how-to books and got to work. In 1996, after six years of stone-hauling and complex masonry, their masterpiece was complete. They had created it entirely by themselves and totally by hand—a castle in the wilderness. Inside, it has an open living space with a separate kitchen, a library, and about eight other modestly-sized rooms. Outside, seven round towers rise at different heights under conical roofs. The Gregoires also built a patio in the back which they've turned into an antique shop with a European-style cafe. During the summer you can sip coffee under oversized umbrellas while gazing into the countryside. If it rains, you can go inside where the stone walls are covered with medieval prints alongside the mounted heads of wild boar, goats, and deer.

The Castle Shoppe and Cafe
　4887 Burton Hill Rd.
　Irasburg, VT 05845

Phone: (802) 754-2057
　skysport@sover.net

Location: Take exit 26 from I-91 and head for Irasburg, which is four miles away. Turn off the town green next to the white church. In another hundred yards you'll come to another white church on the left. Go left there at the "Y" onto Burton Hill Road. The castle is about a mile from the village on the right as you descend the hill.

Hours: In the summer, the cafe is open Saturdays and Sundays, 11 A.M.–5 P.M., or when the "Open" flag is flying. Call for winter hours.

Wheelchair accessible.

A View of the Past

The Mystery: Isle La Motte, in the northern waters of Lake Champlain, is no tropical island, so why should it contain a coral reef? In fact, why should these occasionally arctic acres contain the oldest exposed fossilized coral reef in the *world*—dating back some 480 million years? Called the Chazian Reef, this geological time machine covers the entire southern third of the island, more than one thousand acres. Outcroppings are visible here and there. One outcropping, in a field near the historical society, looks exactly like black stones, until you look closely. Nearby, the "Fisk Quarry," a wetland and wildlife habitat, busy with birds, fish, and a profusion of colorful wildflowers, is a perfect place to see a snapshot of the world as it was half a billion years ago. Critters like stromatoporoids (extinct sponges), solitary tube coral, and crinoids (ancestors of starfish) can still be seen, forever frozen like a primitive statuary. But why?

The Solution: In the remote past the land that is now Vermont was beneath a tropical sea some twenty degrees south of the equator. The earth's crust shifted; Vermont migrated north, and eventually limestone moved in, preserving ancient life just as Vesuvius's lava preserved the city of Pompeii.

Location: Isle La Motte is connected by bridge to Alburg on Route 129. Fisk Quarry is on the southwest part of the island. The historical society is clearly marked.

Shooting the Bull

Ancient ruins are one thing, but there's something unsettling about new ones, especially in the northern Vermont wilderness. Stranger still is the story of the Space Research Corporation and its founder, the most brilliant artillery scientist of
the twentieth century, Dr. Gerald Bull. Straddling the
American-Canadian border in the town of Jay is what's left of
the mysterious private compound where Dr. Bull developed
and manufactured his extended-range weaponry. Here in rural
Vermont he maintained his own artillery range, telemetry towers, launch-control buildings, radar tracking station, work-
shops, and machine shops. Privacy was essential as was the
company's strategic position on the border. Because arms-
export laws were different in the two countries, the materials
he needed and the weapons he manufactured could be shipped
in either nation. Dr. Bull's goal was to fire cannon projectiles
from the earth into outer space. Over the years he attempted to
sell his space-cannon design to NATO, the Pentagon, Canada,
China, Israel, and finally, Iraq. That's what got him into trouble. He agreed to make the Iraqis a cannon that could put dozens, perhaps hundreds, of satellites into orbit . . . but only for
surveillance purposes. The Iraqi super-launcher would have a
barrel five hundred feet long, weighing 2,100 tons, with projectiles the size of phone booths. However, such a monster could
also dump a load of nerve gas, or a nuclear bomb, onto any capital in the world. Saddam Hussein was delighted. The Israelis
were not pleased. On March 22, 1990, while in Brussels, Dr.
Bull was shot five times in the back of the head. Today his
compound is deserted. We found windowless buildings and a
structure the size of an airplane hanger. We hoped to find a cannon or two lying in the forest like abandoned sewer mains, but
if they were there we didn't see them.

Location: Jay is approximately in the middle of Vermont's northern boundary. From the town center head north on North Hill Road. Stay straight going directly across the intersection with Route 105. You'll now be on a dirt road called North Jay Road. Keep going until the road takes an extremely sharp right angle. Stop. On your left you should see an aluminum gate with a collapsed guard house behind it. That is the entrance to Bull's compound. We suggest you walk from this point unless you have a four-wheel drive vehicle.

NOTE: These ruins are on private property, although there were no "No Trespassing" signs at the time of our visit. If some have been erected in the interim, please get permission, or enter at your own risk.

Lyndon Center, Vermont

Defiant to the End

Generally inscriptions on New England gravestones are biographical or sentimental. Many are of a religious nature—a last attempt to get in a good word before passing on to the next world. But not always. In this rare case, the stone is used to articulate an irreverent philosophical position. In carving his own monument in Lyndon Center, George F. Spencer was defiant enough to proclaim:

> Beyond the universe there is nothing and within the
> universe the supernatural does not and cannot exist.
> Of all deceivers who have plagued mankind, none are so
> deeply ruinous to human happiness as those impostors who
> pretend to lead by a light above nature.
> Science has never killed or persecuted a single
> person for doubting or denying its teachings, and
> most of these teachings have been true; but religion
> has murdered millions for doubting or denying her
> dogmas, and most of these dogmas have been false.

Not surprisingly, local church members tried to rub the inscription off, but Mr. Spencer seems to have anticipated the action: He had chiseled the words too deeply. If you don't believe it, go see for yourself. But watch out for lightning bolts. . . .

Location: From I-91, take exit 23. Turn right onto Route 5, then left onto 122. The cemetery is across from the Lyndon Center post office by the high school. Enter the cemetery and go right. The grave is next to the road and has a sleeping babe on top. It reads "G. F. Spencer."

Middlebury, Vermont

The Mummy's Tomb

In West Cemetery, beyond the grave of Charlotte Moody, and just before Caroline Mead's, there is a strangely marked headstone. If you look closely, you'll see that the grave's occupant died in 1883—B.C.! A slip of the stonecutter's chisel, perhaps? No, this is the grave of Vermont's only royalty, Amun-Her-Khepesh-Ef, the two-year-old son of an ancient Egyptian king. So how did an Egyptian mummy come to be buried in Middlebury, Vermont? More than a century ago Henry Sheldon, a local oddities collector, bought the child-mummy from a New York dealer. After Mr. Sheldon's death, the museum that now bears his name stored the mummy until 1945, when the curator rediscovered it. George Mead, president of the museum's board of directors, decided to give the little prince a proper Christian burial. He had the mummy cremated and buried the ashes in his own family plot—sort of a post-mortem adoption.

Location: Take Route 30 out of Middlebury heading toward Cornwall. West Cemetery is on the right. Drive in through the main entrance and watch for Daniel Chipman's gravestone on the left at the edge of the road. The mummy is buried in that row. The Cemetery is closed from 9:00 P.M. to 7:00 A.M.—but you wouldn't want to visit at night, anyway.

Stone Boy

Resting peacefully in the Sheldon Museum is a small figure that caused a furor in the late 1800s. Though it is referred to as *The Petrified Indian Boy,* many have suspected it is not an Indian at all; it didn't have the features of an Indian. In 1871, George Parsons unearthed the thing near Turners Falls, Massachusetts. He thought it was a statue depicting a boy of about six to eight years old, perfect in every detail right down to its fingernails and eyebrows. But experts hypothesized that Mr. Parsons might have found a human body that had been in the earth for thousands of years. He had fallen, died, and become petrified. On exhibition, the petrified boy captured the public's imagination and sympathy. Experts argued about its origin. If it wasn't an Indian it must be part of some ancient, unknown race. The debate continued until one shrewd Bostonian dug a fingernail into a crack in the petrified boy's ankle and scraped out . . . plaster of Paris. The petrified Indian boy had been a hoax all along, New England's version of the Cardiff Giant. But mystery still surrounds the little figure: Who perpetrated the hoax? Why? How was the statue produced? When was it placed in the ground? How did it end up at the Sheldon Museum? And why don't they exhibit it regularly?

The Henry Sheldon Museum of Vermont History
   1 Park St.
   Middlebury, VT 05753

Phone: (802) 388-2117
   www.middlebury.edu/~shel-mus/
   info@henrysheldonmuseum.org

Location: The museum is in downtown Middlebury near the river.

NOTE: The "Indian Boy" may not be on exhibition, but a request to see it never hurts.

Nazi Memorabilia

If you enjoy atmospheric incongruity, then Camp Meade is for you. This former Civilian Conservation Corps camp has been transformed into a museum commemorating "The Home Front" from 1929 to 1945. You'll know it when you see it: The sign is mounted on a tank, the buildings are brown, and there is a definite military air about the place. The grounds include nineteen cabins where, for forty-two dollars a night, you can become part of this well-armed anachronism. A 1942 military ambulance transports fresh linen from cabin to cabin. If you like, you can sign up for tours on their amphibious vehicle, dubbed "Noah's Ark." In the yard, there's a bunker complete with mannequins of wounded and dying GI's, an F-86 bomber from the Korean War, and a Stuart tank used in North Africa. Inside the museum are wax replicas of Dwight D. Eisenhower and Douglas MacArthur dressed up in their general regalia. There are Japanese family photos lifted from a Japanese factory on the day they bombed Pearl Harbor. Perhaps most bizarre is the glass case full of swastika-covered Nazi mementos. They even have the leather cover of Hitler's guest book found amid the rubble of his burned out Berchtesgaden chalet. There's also a medal awarded for giving birth to German children at a time when Aryan leaders sought to increase the blond, blue-eyed population. Most grisly of all is a slide used in elementary schools to "educate" children on facial features defining Jewish ancestry. If all this is too much, you can catch your breath at the canteen and snack bar. Or, if Camp Meade is very much to your taste, there's an Army Navy store where, among other things, you can outfit your toddlers in genuine military-style fatigues.

Camp Meade Victory Museum
Route 2
Middlesex, VT 05602

Phone: (802) 223-5537 or (802) 476-7903
www.campmeade.com
campmeade@together.net

Location: From I-89, take exit 9 and follow signs toward Middlesex. The museum is in the center of town.

Hours: Open May–October, Monday–Saturday, 9 A.M.–5 P.M., Sunday, 9 A.M.–3 P.M.

Admission charged.

Wheelchair accessible.

Montpelier, Vermont

Hall of Fumes

One of Vermont's lesser known and tiniest museums is in the capitol city. Known as "The Hall of Fumes," it is housed at the Recreation Department's downtown headquarters. There, within an airtight glass case, you'll find displayed the winners of the department's annual "International Rotten Sneaker Contest"—all twelve pairs and counting. In their battered, torn, and paint-splotched splendor, they are works of art unto themselves. But—for some—it is the fragrance that makes the trip worthwhile. Though the glass case keeps the fumes mercifully under control, department staff will break the seal for those desiring to sample the bouquet.

Montpelier Recreation Dept.
58 Barre St.
Montpelier, VT 05602

Phone: (802) 223-5141
don@co.mps.k12.vt.us.

Location: Take exit 8 off I-89. Go left at the fourth traffic light and over the bridge. Go about a quarter of a mile, then bear right onto Barre Street. Park on the street.

Hours: Open by appointment only.

Free admission.

Grave with a View

Near the front of Evergreen Cemetery there's a peculiar mound of earth that seems like a landscaping error. Walk to its top and you'll see a window embedded in the ground—a window that, depending on your point of view, either looks into the earth or up at the sky. If you were looking down, and if visibility were good, you'd be face-to-face with Timothy Clark Smith. In the 1800s, Mr. Smith was a world traveler with the U.S. foreign service. Because of hideous things he'd heard and seen in his travels, he developed a terrible fear of being buried alive—a reasonable concern in those pre-embalming days. Then in 1893, as if setting up a century's worth of scary stories, Mr. Smith died in Middlebury, Vermont—on Halloween. His corpse was transported to New Haven's Evergreen Cemetery, where a very special grave had been prepared for him—the incongruous grassy mound. Mr. Smith was buried there with his face positioned beneath a cement tube that led to the surface. The tube was covered with a fourteen-by-fourteen-inch-square of plate glass. In the corpse's hand they placed a bell that he could ring should he wake up and find himself the victim of a premature burial. So if you decide to visit the cemetery, keep very quiet . . . and listen.

Location: From the village of New Haven, follow Town Hill Road until Evergreen Cemetery appears on the left. The grave in question is right in the front, between the "Entrance" and "Exit" and easily visible from the road. The cemetery is closed from 8:00 P.M. to 7 A.M.

A Glimpse of Fairyland

In a small shed-like building on the grounds of Norwich's Montshire Museum is a *camera obscura,* one of fewer than two dozen known to exist—some of them quite antique. The name is Latin for "dark room," but what *camera obscura* provides is an alternate way of seeing. As a Victorian frivolity, it was said to offer a glimpse of fairyland and was described in hyperbolic terms like "enchanting" and "wondrous." In reality, it works on the same principle as a photographic camera. Inverted miniature images of the outside world are projected through a lens onto surfaces within the dark room. Although this may sound like no big deal, the moving images are strangely fascinating. People, animals, cars, trees, and flowers move about in a hypnotic silence. It is easy to see why the Victorians said they were seeing fairyland. Buildings were constructed to house *cameras obscura* in public parks and private homes. Before the era of *Candid Camera* and video surveillance, they were employed to see without being seen. They were ideal for voyeurs, while illustrating a scientific principle: Light moves in a straight line, and cannot be diffused or scattered. Although the *camera obscura* at the Montshire Museum is relatively new, it works in exactly the same way as its ancestors. Before you enter, check out the various knobs, strings, and signs with the door open so you will know what to do when it's dark. Then shut the door and let your eyes grow accustomed to the nothingness. A small aperture lets in a tiny ray of light, which when projected, opens up a surreal, slow motion, upside-down panorama of a fantasy world—quite the inverse of our own. (See also the *Giant Eyeball* in Portland, Maine.)

The Montshire Museum of Science
Montshire Rd.
Norwich, VT 05055

Phone: (802) 649-2200
   montshire@montshire.org
   www.montshire.net

Location: To get to the museum, take exit 13 off I-91. At the end of the ramp, turn right (toward Hanover, New Hampshire), then another quick right onto Montshire Road. (If you cross the bridge you've gone too far.) The museum is on your left. The *camera obscura* is a small hut in the backyard of the museum and may be visited without entering the museum proper.

Hours: Open daily, 10 A.M.–5 P.M. Closed Thanksgiving, Christmas, and New Year's Day.

Admission charged.

Wheelchair accessible.

Pownal, Vermont

Weeping Rocks

An old-time curiosity that seems to have dribbled out of favor among modern tourists is the weeping rocks. Even the locals can't tell you exactly how to find it, and you'll rarely see it mentioned in a guide or history book. But in times past folks from far and wide made their way to this mysterious spot and uttered phrases like, "I dunno, do you think there could be anything to it?" It seems that in pre-colonial days the resident Indians—probably Mohicans—had long felt secure in their good fortune and entitlement to the land and its bounty. They believed somehow their nation would always prevail and that in any confrontation they would never be conquered "until the rocks weep." Then one day a chieftain happened upon this rock enclosure and looked in terror at what he saw: The rocks were weeping—the fatal prediction had come true. Soon Mohawks fell upon them, and, with little resistance, exterminated the entire tribe. History doesn't necessarily corroborate the story, but the rocks are there, and last time we checked they were still weeping. They're in a shallow cave, set in the hillside at a sharp turn in the Hoosic River. Water drips constantly from overhead, even in times of drought, which contributes to their magical aura. You can see for yourself, but finding them might be a bit of a chore.

Location: Finding the site will be tricky. Take Route 7 south from Pownal toward the Massachusetts border. When you see the grandstands for the Pownal race track on your right, take a steep left up "Cash Place." You are now on a fragment of *old* Route 7, a neglected concrete stretch of road that hugs the cliffs (on the left) and passes behind Joe Tornabene's GMC Auto Sales and Service (on the right). Look left. When you see a conspicuous pile of discarded railroad ties next to the road that's your signal to start looking up the steep bank to the left. Proceed slowly. Soon, about a hundred feet up, you'll see Weeping Rocks, a wet little grotto in an overhanging limestone outcropping. The site is visible from the road. The nearest telephone pole is number 47/132/6.

NOTE: The climb from old Route 7 to Weeping Rocks is difficult. It's steep, rocky, and the ground is likely to be wet and slippery. Approach with caution. If you make it all the way you can sit under a continuous gentle rainfall.

Reading, Vermont

Abduction Stones

Although the markings on these two stones may not be the work of seafaring Egyptians, colonial wizards, or extraterrestrial invaders, their meaning is nonetheless mysterious and perhaps impossible to decipher. But they're worth examining because they are a tangible remnant of an unpleasant colonial phenomenon—Indian abductions—and this is the oldest such monument in the United States. During the French and Indian Wars, Susanna Johnson and her family were abducted in 1754 from Charlestown, New Hampshire. Their captors marched them across Vermont, heading toward Canada. On the banks of Knapps Brook in Cavendish, Mrs. Johnson gave birth to a daughter, but was forced to continue her trek. During their years in captivity her son essentially became Abenaki, while her daughter was adopted into a French family in Montreal. Mrs. Johnson returned home alone. When the three were briefly reunited, they were unable to communicate with each other culturally or linguistically. In 1799, Mrs. Johnson had the stones placed where they are today. True, there is some eighteenth-century English chiseled onto them, but we don't care about that. We're concerned with the odd assortment of pictures carved there, for they are like nothing anywhere else: bows, arrows, people, boxes, trees, rifles, and a number of things unrecognizable. There is a perplexing sequence, design, and coherence to them, suggesting . . . what? Are they a language? A code? Is there some kind of indecipherable message hidden in these peculiar graphics? We'll probably never know.

Location: The Indian stones are on the east side of Route 106 in Reading, right beside the road. Look for them just north of the intersection of 106 and Knapp Brook Road. Park in the turnoff in front of the stones.

Wheelchair accessible.

Richford, Vermont

The Mystery Spot

In northern Vermont, right near the Canadian border, there is a mysterious bit of contrary country where gravitational forces behave in extraordinary ways. Cars, for example, are said to roll uphill, blatantly violating the laws of gravity. Although there's nothing to tip you off, the road winds in and out of Canada, so perhaps there is some confusion about which laws apply. But nowhere should cars roll uphill. A local newspaper, *The County Courier,* reported the phenomenon in 1985, describing a two-ton Dodge and its four passengers moving against gravity at a speed of some 15 miles per hour. However, the newspaper wasn't too specific about exactly which hill it was, and there are several. We've tried to locate it on several occasions, but unsuccessfully. In this case we might take anti-gravity to mean "not serious."

Location: From that small cluster of buildings known as East Richford, turn right immediately before the Canadian border and follow the five mile stretch of gravel road that connects with Route 105. There, somewhere, you'll find Richford's Mystery Spot. Maybe.

Royalton, Vermont

Stone Chambers

There are hundreds of ancient stone chambers hidden deep within New England's glades and forests. Most are igloo-shaped, with massive slab ceilings and enigmatic inscriptions on the walls. Yet through some odd cultural amnesia, we are

One of the many "beehive" stone chambers in Royalton, Vermont.
Photo: Joe Citro

clueless as to who built them, when, and why. The conventional supposition is that they are two-hundred-year-old root cellars, the work of colonial farmers. But if that's the case, why does carbon-dating suggest they were there before the birth of Christ? And Native Americans are as baffled by them as we are. A more plausible explanation—yet one that state archeologists for some reason don't want to consider—is that America was once inhabited by ancient seafaring explorers, possibly Vikings, Phoenicians, or Celts. Similar stone structures in Ireland have been positively identified as Celtic remains. Here such possibilities meet with a deafening silence. In Vermont alone, there are almost two hundred chambers, or "dolmens." In Royalton, there are a half dozen within a mile of each other. They are astounding sights; ancient, solid, and primitive (and sadly, disfigured with modern graffiti). While seeking answers, we ponder the greatest mysteries of all: Why isn't the state attempting to solve the puzzle? And why aren't they protecting these treasures? Some have already succumbed to bulldozers while buildings of far lesser historical importance are meticulously preserved as "historic landmarks." Then again, who are we to question government wisdom?

Location: From I-89, take exit 3 and go east on Route 107 toward Sharon. Turn right on Route 14 going south through South Royalton. Follow the signs for the Joseph Smith Monument; they'll take you left and up a hill. Before you get to the entrance to the Memorial on your right, you'll pass a white house with blue shutters on the left. Park at the rusted yellow metal gate across the road. Continue a ways up the road on foot to the upper edge of the swath of trees stretching perpendicular to the road that separates two open fields on the right. Walk into the field along the trees' edge about one hundred paces, looking in the woods for a huge denuded tree trunk that has fallen to the ground. The dolmen is underneath.

NOTE: Take a flashlight and come pre-sprayed with insect repellent. The dolmen is on private property, so show sensitivity, or you will be thrown off. At least two more chambers are in the hills past McIntosh Pond but they're tricky to find without a guide. To see them, give some thought to contacting the Vermont chapter of the New England Antiquities Research Association (NEARA), which organizes walks to these and similar sites throughout the state. Their local representative's number is (802) 247-3616.

Salisbury, Vermont

Ann's Story

The woman Vermont historians revere for her courage during the Revolutionary War really ought to have won the ribbon for ingenuity. Just think of it. What would you have done if your husband was dead; you had five small children; your log cabin, in the midst of the wilderness, risked nightly Indian and Tory raids during which you could burn to death in your sleep; the British had ordered you off your own land; and it was 1774? What Ann Story decided to do was select an inconspicuous patch of river bank, take a shovel, and dig a cave out of the muck. Miraculously, it worked! Every night it sheltered her, her brood, and another woman with a newborn baby. Also at night, a hodgepodge of Vermont revolutionaries, the Green Mountain Boys, occasionally used Ann's cabin to rest and reconnoiter, taking note of warnings and information she'd leave for them. Each daybreak she loaded the kids into a canoe and emerged from the rushes, a little muddy, but alive. Ann Story's cabin was inevitably torched, and she rebuilt it. Before she died at the age of seventy-five, she had rebuilt it a second time and married twice more. In 1976, to mark the bicentennial, the town transported a log cabin of similar vintage to the spot where hers had stood. It is empty, but, pending a lawsuit to sort out land access rights, it can be visited by the public. A better bet is to find the marker put up in 1914 on the Otter Creek at the site of her secret cave. Though it has long since collapsed, seeing its location gives you an idea of just what Ann was up against. Need is certainly the mother of invention, and names can be self-fulfilling prophecies. This is a good example of both.

Location: The marker is south of Middlebury between Routes 7 and 30 near the covered bridge connecting Cornwall with West Salisbury. Heading west, turn right out of the bridge, leave the car in the parking area on the left, cross the road, and head north on foot for about a mile and a half. The marker is right on the river's edge, half hidden with ferns. Bring the repellent, as the mosquitoes are homicidal.

NOTE: If you must see the cabin, get permission from the Salisbury landowner, Mr. Roger Stone Jr., who may set up a time to meet you. Ann's gravestone is also interesting and can be viewed in the Seeley section of the Middlebury cemetery. She ultimately married a Goodrich and took the name Hannah Goodrich, but the DAR (Daughters of the American Revolution) have added her real identity onto the gravestone.

South Hero, Vermont

Fairyland Kingdoms

Thanks to fantasist Harry Barber's labor of love, South Hero and Providence Island are dotted with castles—fairy tale castles. Hardly bigger than conventional doll houses, they are created with such detail and intricacy that one expects to see the wee folk flitting about; or meet a mini-monarch of the Mad Ludwig variety, whose lilliputian knights are doing battle with Champ, the dragon in the lake. Each stone is positioned with precision, creating peaked facades and tiny

towers with conical roofs. Some have moats, windows with wooden frames, diminutive flower pots, and miniature window curtains. In the old days some had electricity and Swiss watches mounted like clocks in belfries. Although there is a fair number of these minute island kingdoms, they are not easy to spot. But that's what makes them magical. You can discover Harry's handiwork here and there, on lawns, in gardens, or directly on the shore, placed according to no par-

Several of Harry Barber's miniature castles scattered around South Hero, Vermont.
Photos: Joe Citro

ticular design. Some can be spied easily as you drive or bike around the island; some require a bit of hunting. But to discover just one is a delightful experience.

Location. The small kingdoms are on South Hero and Providence Island. The only accessible castles are on South Hero. Have fun finding them; this should be a quest, after all. But if you prefer, the town clerk, library, historical society, or any long-time resident can point the way.

Indian Footprints

Dinosaur tracks are plentiful in New England if you know where to look, but human prints are not—not in stone, anyway. However in South Woodbury, two footprints stare out at you from a boulder at the side of a country road. There are two handprints just above them. They would be monumentally puzzling if the locals hadn't come up with a series of legends to explain them. Around here they're called the Indian Footprints, presumably because no one else would wander these parts barefoot. Bernie Badeau, who grew up in the area, told us his version of the story. He explained that on both sides of the footprints are tall slate cliffs. Thousands of years ago, when the road was a riverbed, these cliffs acted like a gorge. When the water was low, you could walk on the bottom. When it was high, it rose almost to the top of the cliffs. This river acted as a boundary between two rival tribes. Hundreds, maybe thousands of years ago, in a classic Romeo and Juliet scenario, a young man and a girl from the opposing tribes fell in love. They would meet at the opposite sides of the cliff. One day, when the water was high, the girl decided to swim the rapid current to meet her lover. Rushing water swept her away. Though the young man jumped to her rescue, both drowned. His body turned up later in Nelson Pond. The tribesmen were perplexed; he had been a strong swimmer. But when they examined his legs they understood: Both had been broken in the jump. When the river receded, they could see the rock ledge he had landed on. The two chiefs, mourning the loss of their children, came together in peace to carve the commemorative footprints on the stone where the brave had suffered his fatal injury. The prints have been there as long as anyone can remember. And there are many legends to explain them; one even says they were made by angels. In any event, rain and repeated Vermont winters were gradually wearing them away. Tim Hoyt, who lived around the corner, was fearful that the legends would die when the prints vanished. So in 1958, chisel in hand, he incised two clear footprints where they originals had been. No matter which legend we believe, we'd have to agree that the location favors a love story. The trees and cliffs are beautiful, and all around the ponds are brimming with white water lilies.

Location: Take Route 14 north out of downtown Barre until you get to South Woodbury. From there go left (west) onto Foster Hill Road, then right onto King Pond Road. Turn left down Chartier Hill Road, then right at the four-way intersection onto Cranberry Meadow Road. Park the car there and continue on foot for about five minutes. The rock face with the footprints is after telephone pole number 330. It is next to the road on the right, amid the trees, and the prints are about waist high. Look closely, as they are easy to miss but unmistakable. All ten toes are visible, and a foot or so above them, so is the right hand, palm outward.

St. Albans, Vermont

Noted Raid

In 1864, a horrifying event occurred in the northern Vermont town of St. Albans: It was claimed for the Confederacy. In a well-orchestrated terrorist maneuver, twenty-two rebel soldiers wearing disguises inconspicuously placed themselves among the townspeople. At exactly three o'clock on Wednesday, October 19, three precisely coordinated clusters of raiders simultaneously robbed the town's three banks. Meanwhile, other armed southerners were herding surprised citizens onto the village green. The daring conspirators escaped with 208,000 dollars and headed for the Canadian border, later to be apprehended. Today the St. Albans Historical Society Museum commemorates this northernmost Civil War battle by displaying about twenty-one of the actual purloined bills. They are framed under glass, five and twenty dollar notes, donated to the society in 1964 by a private family (we wonder if they were southerners). Interestingly, the federal government wasn't printing money during the Civil War, so instead of "The United States Treasury," the bills say "Franklin County Bank." Until the end of the war, local banks could issue their own currency, but it was only valid locally. To cash in their loot the raiders would have had to exchange it for Canadian dollars, or the whole thing would have been for naught—which turned out to be the case. But the perpetrators might have derived some satisfaction in knowing that within two years all three banks had folded.

St. Albans Historical Society Museum
    P.O. Box 722
    Church St.
    St. Albans, VT 05478

Phone: (802) 527-7933
    don@stalbansmuseum.org
    www.stalbansmuseum.org/

Location: The museum is in downtown St. Albans facing Taylor Park, housed in a three-story 1861 Renaissance Revival–style former school building.

Hours: Open June 15–October 1, Monday–Friday, 1–4 P.M. Also open by appointment.

NOTE: The museum's newest exhibit is an exciting high-tech diorama of the Lake Champlain Basin as it appeared in 1864, the year of the St. Albans Raid. The Raid is its feature story with maps and archival photographs.

Admission charged.

St. Johnsbury, Vermont

Bug Art

Take a step back in time. Visiting the unique Fairbanks Museum is like a tour through the inner sanctum of Franklin

Fairbanks's Victorian "cabinet of curiosities." There are spooky antique dolls, terrifying taxidermic bears, and hummingbirds frozen in flight. But of all the weird sites in this unusual repository, perhaps the strangest are the bizarre creations of self-taught entomologist John Hampson (1836–1923). Though essentially uneducated, Mr. Hampson was a genius who had worked briefly for Thomas Edison. Somehow he recognized the beauty in bugs. In his skilled hands vermin body parts became art. Using the colorful wings, thoraxes, legs, and body hairs of flies, moths, and other creepy crawlers—combined with near-

A Portrait of Abraham Lincoln, made from 6,399 bug parts, at the Fairbanks Museum & Planetarium in St. Johnsbury, Vermont. Photo: Used with permission from the collections of the Fairbanks Museum & Planetarium

limitless quantities of time and patience—he created nine awfully strange examples of his own unique art form, including portraits of American presidents and military men. Each picture contains six thousand to thirteen thousand bugs and each took from three to four years to complete. Hampson willed his bug art to his daughter. When she died the executor of her estate tried to find a museum to house them, but only the Fairbanks would take them. A good thing. These eccentric treasures can be seen and perhaps even appreciated at a museum that is a curiosity in itself. Don't miss the planetarium and weather station.

Fairbanks Museum & Planetarium
 1302 Main St.
 St. Johnsbury, VT 05819-2224

Phone: (802) 748-2372
 fairbanks.museum@connriver.net
 www.fairbanksmuseum.org

Location: The museum is a venerable brownstone building on the elevated part of downtown.

Hours: Open year round, Monday–Saturday, 9 A.M.–5 P.M., Sunday, 1–5 P.M. Closed New Year's Day, Easter, Thanksgiving, and Christmas.

Admission charged.

Wheelchair accessible on main floor.

St. Johnsbury, Vermont

A Chapel Gone to the Dogs

At first glance it might look like an ordinary New England church, circa 1820: white clapboards, lofty steeple, announcement board in front. It's obviously well cared for and the grounds are beautifully maintained. But then things start looking . . . odd. At first, the clues are minor: It seems a little small for a church. And what is it doing way out here, at the end of a dead-end dirt road? Senses heightened now, you begin to understand what's wrong with this picture. Looking up, way at the top of the steeple, there is a winged angel. But wait! That's no ordinary angel. It's a black Labrador retriever with wings! The sign in front provides another clue. It says, "Welcome. All creeds. All breeds. No dogmas allowed." And you finally get it; it's a dog chapel. There are carved dogs out front, carved dogs form the pews, and the interior is illuminated by dog stained-glass windows. And yes, the whole place is built on Dog Mountain.

So what's going on here?

This is the home of dog artist Stephen Huneck, creator of the Dog Chapel. He says it's the largest artwork of his life, that it's intended to reaffirm the connection between art, nature, and spirituality. Certainly it reaffirms the connection between people and dogs. Mr. Huneck created it in appreciation after he survived a near-death experience. A victim of Adult Respiratory Distress Syndrome, he went into a two-month coma and died. Mr. Huneck found the five minutes he wasn't alive to be magical and transforming. Since then he seems to have devoted his life—and art—to dogs. His unusual creations celebrate the spiritual bond we have with our dogs and thanks them for all they give us and for connecting us to nature. If your dog is with you, bring him in; the chapel is open to dogs and people. All this makes one wonder exactly what happened to Mr. Huneck during that near-death experience. Maybe he simply realized that dog is god spelled backward.

Stephen Huneck Gallery at Dog Mountain
  Spaulding Rd.
  St. Johnsbury, VT 05819

Phone: (802) 748-2700
  huneck@aol.com
  www.huneck.com

Location: On Route 2, driving east from St. Johnsbury, turn left on Spaulding Road. Watch for signs for Stephen Huneck.

Free admission.

Emily's Bridge

This is perhaps the most haunted spot in Vermont and apparently the only haunted covered bridge in New England. A whole spectrum of supernatural events are reported here on a regular basis: Lights from nowhere float around inside; electronic equipment fails to function; disembodied voices speak; hats detach from heads and cold spots manifest on warm summer days. Dozens of tourist photographs show mysterious streaks, floating orbs, and wispy female-like forms. Recently a visitor from out-of-state took a picture of the bridge, just because it's pretty. He was alarmed when the finished photo included a girl who, he swears, was not there when he snapped the shutter. The story is that Emily, a teenager in the 1850s, fell in love with a young man who didn't pass muster with her parents. So the headstrong young couple decided to elope, planning a rendezvous on the covered bridge at midnight. Sadly, poor Emily's parents had been right all along—the young man never showed. Too humiliated to go home, and too timid to run off alone, the dejected teenager overreacted: She hanged herself from a rafter. Since then—so the story goes—her troubled spirit has remained on the bridge, waiting, getting angrier as the decades slip away. Of course we can't guarantee you'll have a confrontation with Emily. But we can't guarantee you won't.

Location: Beginning in the Village of Stowe, where Route 108 intersects with Route 100, head south on 100 for 1.8 miles. Just before Route 100 crosses a stream—Gold Brook—turn left onto Gold Brook Road. Continue about a quarter of a mile until you reach a four-way intersection. Keep left and continue on Gold Brook Road for about one mile. When you reach another four-way intersection, Emily's Bridge should be on your left.

Above It All

In the village of Brownsville within the town of West Windsor, there is a remarkable granite mausoleum. Its sole occupant, Daniel Leavens Cady, was a local boy who made good—at least by his own estimation. Long-haired, rotund, and egomaniacal, he did in fact accomplish notable things. He earned an excellent education, married well, and became a prominent lawyer and judge. At age fifty, he retired to pursue a literary career at which he was no less successful. His newspaper column and verse endeared him to many. But those back home knew the truth: Cady was an arrogant, selfish sot. His swan song was the enormous monument he had constructed for himself. Designed to resemble Napoleon's tomb, it is in no cemetery. Rather, it stands all by itself on a prime piece of scenic real estate high atop Strawberry Hill. In addition to his pretentious tomb, he wrote himself a lengthy epitaph, in Latin, two copies of which he had cast into bronze: one outside the mausoleum, the other within. His intent was clear: He planned to occupy the place alone; his wife could find another final resting place. At the end of life's journey Mr. Cady returned to the old hometown to flaunt his success—even in death. His lofty tomb allowed him a spot from which he could spend eternity looking down on his neighbors. He even took a last swipe at everyone with English doggerel on his Latin plaque. It said, in effect, if you can't read Latin, take a hike. But perhaps his neighbors had the last laugh; Daniel Leavens Cady died on April Fool's day, and even the Roman numerals can't disguise that fact.

Location: Heading east from the Brownsville General Store you'll immediately see a left labeled "Strawberry Hill." Go up the hill and stop at the very end. Park and continue on foot until you come to the monument. There should be signs or arrows, but the monument is visible from the end of the road— it's the only one around.

NOTE: Be careful not to use the driveway to the left at the end of the road. It is private property.

The Main Street Museum

It has often been called "the strangest museum in Vermont" and we wouldn't disagree. However, *it* calls *itself* the Main Street Museum . . . or sometimes the Main Street Museum *of Art*. If there is some confusion, that's just part of the package. More accurately, we think, the museum itself is the art. But it's an art of the forgotten, the shunned, the unsettled, and the unsettling. Among whatever-it's-called's many treasures, you can see mink in a bottle, Paul Mangelsdorff's Corn Genetics, Ballantine Ale cans, what's left of the salve applied to Phineas Gage's celebrated head wound, "Modern Art Created by Accident," the preserved carcass of a sea monster allegedly found in the Connecticut River, a wall of taxidermic deer busts, and, for those not easily offended, the infamous half Madonna, half dinosaur "Virgisaurus." Though it was founded by David Fairbanks Ford in 1992, it is an emphatic return to the grand old days of the private museum like those launched by Dr. Henry Forrest Libby and Franklin Fairbanks (mentioned elsewhere in this volume). Where else can you find displays of paintings, sculpture, natural history, mineralogy, Vermontiana, arcana, and "other objects both illuminating and illuminated"?

The eccentric, eclectic holdings illustrate the fickle nature of curating. How do we decide what to save and what to throw away? Objects that once evoked gasps of wonder from our ancestors, might now provoke gasps of horror from our politically correct contemporaries. What are we to make of the head of a

Northern Cardinal preserved in a glass case? Or the illuminated bottle displaying Elvis Presley's gall stones? It doesn't take long to see that as unusual, grim, even macabre as some of these exhibits might be, there is a sense of play and humor about it all, a good-natured confrontation of the arrogance that lies behind any museum's authoritative facade. And if you're not sure if this is your cup of tea, check them out online. They're the only web site we've ever seen with a restroom.

The Main Street Museum
  58 Bridge Street
  White River Junction, VT 05001

Phone: (802) 356-2776
  dff@mainstreetmuseum.org
  www.mainstreetmuseum.org

NOTE: Call for hours, appointments, and directions.
Admission charged.
Wheelchair accessible.

Whitingham, Vermont

Brigham Young Memorial Mystery

A granite marker atop Stimpson Hill has long been shrouded in mystery. It seemed to just materialize there about a hundred years ago while property owner Gerald Wheeler was taking his wife for a buggy ride. When they got back, there it was—the Brigham Young Monument. The second mystery is its meaning. Is it exactly what it seems, a commemorative marker? Or is it a peaceful form of social protest, a gentle criticism of the Mormon stand on polygamy? Interpretation seems to rest on one word: "equipment." Is there some archaic meaning that escapes today's readers? Could it refer to his farm machinery? Anyway, the Mormons were never too fond of the marker and its ambiguity. Which led to the most recent mystery. On Friday, July 30, 1999, the cabin's occupant was surprised by a gaping hole in the ground; the Mormon monument had vanished! A miracle? Probably not. The ragged cavity suggested the memorial—and its cement base—had been ripped from the earth as if by a tractor and chain. The local historical society issued a "Missing Monument" bulletin while suspicion fell immediately on the Mormons themselves. An admission was quickly forthcoming.

To make a long story short, the stone was returned to its hole, the case was quickly closed, the caper ended, and all is well.

If you have any interest in seeing it, better do it quickly before it vanishes again. You can photograph words that are—at least for now—etched in stone. In its entirety, the plaque reads: "Brigham Young, born on this spot (in) 1801—a man of much courage and superb equipment."

Location: The Brigham Young Monument is on the right side of the road as you drive up Stimpson Hill from downtown Whitingham.

Whitingham, Vermont

Floating Island

Nothing very dramatic to see, really, but the true oddity hunter would not want to miss this rare natural phenomenon: a floating island. It consists of twenty-five acres in Sadawga Pond. We can't tell you exactly where to look for it, because it moves around. But it should be easy to spot; it's the largest land mass in the water. And the pond isn't all that big. According to author Robert Pike, if you can catch it, you can build a house on it, and you won't have to pay taxes . . . Now that would be an oddity.

Location: Sadawga Pond is located just south of Lake Whitingham, right next to the village center.

World's First Web Site

Most people think of Vermont as a dairy state, but farmer Will Knight raises creatures far kookier than cows. He grows spiders. Though his herd of arachnids may give some people the creeps, their webs—each as individual as a snowflake—have a strange and delicate beauty. Mr. Knight and his wife have been raising spiders and harvesting webs since 1977. In the spring they collect egg sacks from which baby spiders are soon born. They quickly mature and begin their weaving. Will Knight harvests their handiwork, carefully transferring each web to a dark-colored mount, which acts as a frame. Sometimes Mrs. Knight adds a painted flower or bird to the arachnid's artistry. As of this writing, the Knights have amassed over thir-

Will Knight at his Spider Web Farm in Williamstown, Vermont.
Photo: Courtesy Will Knight

teen thousand webs. A visit to their unusual farm reveals a maze of glassless windows, each in use by its own weaving spider. Like cows, these crawlers do their work in the barn. But that's just as it should be, after all, they're barn spiders.

Spider Web Farm
 124 Spider Web Farm Rd.
 Williamstown, VT 05679-0420

Phone: (802) 433-5568
 webfarm@together.net
 www.spiderwebfarm.com

Location: From I-89, take exit 5, Williamstown, and go east 5 miles to Route 14. Turn right onto Route 14 going south. Go through town and watch for the sign half a mile down on the right.

Hours: Open daily, or whenever the Knights are at home, spring through autumn. Also open by appointment.

Free admission.

Wheelchair accessible.

Windsor, Vermont

Keely's Mystery Machine

A number of mysteries surround this easy-to-overlook exhibit at the American Precision Museum. How did it get to Vermont? How was it identified? And does it—can it—really work? At a glance, it appears to be an elegant bit of Victorian precision machinery—perhaps something connected with H. G. Wells and his time machine. And in truth it is every bit as weird. Called the "Disintegrator," it was made in Philadelphia around 1878 by John Ernst Worrel Keely, who was something of a mystery man. All we know for sure is that he *claimed* he had the answer to the world's energy problems. In Mr. Keely's day the principal sources of power were water and steam, but with the escalating industrialization of America, something more, and hopefully cheaper, was needed. While playing the violin as a child, Mr. Keely had an experience that convinced him that vibrations could unleash the forces of nature. In a fit of genius he contrived "a device which disintegrates the etheric force that controls the atomic constitution of matter." In other words, free energy. With the support of investors he was able to construct his machine and eventually put

on demonstrations that, on different occasions, blasted a one-inch lead ball completely through two heavy oak planks, bent steel rails, and tore giant steel cables to shreds. Observers knew it was a force beyond anything in common use at the time.

Mr. Keely was slow to release the "secret" of his machine, saying such unlimited power would be dangerous in irresponsible hands, but when investors threatened to pull out, he agreed to reveal the workings to one scientist of their choice. They picked Edward Bakel, who was taken into Mr. Keely's confidence and was convinced the device was genuine.

The Keely mystery machine, or Etheric Force "Disintegrator," invented about 1878, in the American Precision Museum, Windsor, Vermont. Photo: Joe Citro

But John Ernst Worrel Keely took the secret of his mysterious "Disintegrator" to the grave. Skeptics claimed posthumously that it was all done with compressed air, but advocates said the air conduits would burst under the enormous pressure Keely's machine had so clearly demonstrated. Still, enough people were convinced he had stumbled on a true secret of the universe that his principles are still being researched today.

Only two Keely machines are known to survive; this is the only one on public display. Much of the original device is gone, used to make parts for subsequent Keely machines.

American Precision Museum
196 Main Street
Windsor, VT 05089

Phone: (802) 674-5781
info@americanprecision.org
www.americanprecision.org/

Location: The museum is located on Route 5 slightly south of the town's center.

Hours: Open Memorial Day–October 31, 7 days a week, 10 A.M.–5 P.M.

Acknowledgments

Many of the items in this publication are by nature obscure and hard to find. We wouldn't have been able to include them had it not been for the astute and daring individuals in New England's libraries, historical societies, educational institutions, and in a few cases, state offices. In a sense this book is a vast collaboration of dozens of people. We want to thank everyone who helped us. We've attempted to show our appreciation in the text or on the following "Cast and Credits" list. Some individuals, by their choice or our failing memories, have been omitted. Our sincere apology to anyone we've forgotten.

In New Hampshire, we received a multitude of pithy tips from Jim Garvin, the state's architectural historian. Folklorist Michael Bell revealed some of Rhode Island's dark secrets. Mary Millard and Ray Battcher at the Bristol, Rhode Island, Historical and Preservation Society were more than generous with time and information. Art Donahue, as usual, was wonderful. And we received important help from Jere Daniell, Chris Woodyard, Paul Grabowski, and Fritz Wetherbee. A special salute to Charlie and Donna Jordan, publishers of the invaluable Northern New Hampshire Magazine.

We're no less grateful to Mary Ahlgren, John E. Alexander, Chris Avila, Eileen Axenroth, Larry Bacon, Bernie Badeau, Patricia Bailey, Anne G. Ball, Rick Bates, Gladys Beals, Melissa Behney, Betsey Bennett, Kay Bell, Steve Bissette, Hazel Blanchard, Nicki Bresnyan, Fred Bridge, John Carney, James Chenoweth, Allison and Brian Citro, Ted Cohen, Shaun Conroy, Al DiMarco, John Dumville, John Dunlap, George Earley, Ben Everware, Bill Faude, Joy Floyd, David Fairbanks Ford, Edith

Foulds, Tammis Fulton, David Gregg and the Haffenreffer Museum of Anthropology, Hank Gruner, Pete Hannah, John Hare, Elliott Hersey, Marvin Hightower, Thom Hindle, George Hosker Jr., Lauren Jarvi and Lenny Gerardi, Brian Johnson, Charles Johnson, Anne Killheffer, Margaret Kish, Barbara Kuck, Greg Laing, Bob Landine, Anita Lavigne, Ken Leidner, Nicole Letourneau, Little Wolf, Suzanne Loder, Steve Lournez, Madeleine Lynn, Karen MacInnis, Carolyn Magnus, Kathleen Maher, Tim Mahoney, Gary Mangiacopra, Philip Masterson, Margot McCain, Thomas Michie, Brenda Milkotsky, John Moore, James Moreira, John Murray, Leon Noel, Linda Pearson, Faye Ringel, Chris Rondino, Louise Roomet, Bernard Ross, Cathy Rowe, Maxine and Pam Scott, Ruth Shapleigh-Brown, Christine Sherren, Jennifer Simonic, Pat Smith, Kay Soldier, John J. Spaulding, Karen Tunney Spaulding, Mariella Squire, Andrea Thorpe, Charles Upton, Ann Vennerbeck, Kate Vivian, Merry Watson, Spencer Welton, Bruce Williams, Jay Williamson, Joan Youngken, and to the many unnamed individuals who helped us along the way.

We have reserved a final and very special salute for Sarah L. Welsch, UPNE's Director of Marketing, who, along with Jessica Stevens and Douglas Tifft, shepherded this book through the updated and illustrated second edition. Thank you all for your vision and generosity.

Index

Page numbers in **bold** indicate photographs; page numbers in *italics* indicate RIP sites—please see p. viii for details.

coral reefs, 290

Cornwall, Vt., 305

corpses, 14, 83, 99, 169, 251–252, 297

Corvair (car), 259–260

"Corvair Gravestone," 259–260

cottages, Newport, 239

Countway Library of Medicine, 100

Coventry, R.I., 229–230

Coventry Center, R.I., 230

"The Cover Story," 66

"Covered Bridge House," 211

Cranston, R.I., 231–232

Cranston Historical Society, 232

Cranston Print Works, 231

"A Crate Place to Visit," 49

Cromwell, Oliver, 50–51

cross. See crucifix,

Crossroads of America, 168

Crotch Island, Maine, 76

Crowley, Aleister, 196

Crown Point, Vt., 274

Crowninshield, George, 150

crucifix, 22, 37, 38, 167, 192

cryptozoologists, 69

Cuba, 227

"Cuff Link Museum," 174

cuff links, 174–175

Culinary Archives and Museum,
250–251

Culinary Institute, 251

"Cursed House," 11

"Cursed Idol," 61

"Cursed Springs," 273

curses, 47, 55, 61, 150, 265, 273, 287

Cushing House Museum and Garden, 142

Custom House Maritime Museum,
142

Cutler, Dr., 107

Cutter, Dr. Calvin and Caroline, 189

Cuttingsville, Vt., 282–283

cymbals, 142–143

D

daguerreotype, 271

Dale, Mercie, 265

Damariscotta, Maine, 51–52

Danforth, Dr. John, 95

Danville, N.H., 205

Daughters of the American Revolution, 305

Dedham, Mass., 114–116

Dedham Community Theater, 116

Dee, John, 23

Deer Island, New Brunswick, 54

Deer Isle (Maine) Granite Museum,
75–76

Deer Mountain, Maine, 79–80

Deerfield, N.H., 194

"Defiant to the End," 292

DeLorme, David, 89

DeLorme Map Company, 88–89

demon-chasers, 19

demons, 285

dentistry, 16, 214

Derby, Conn., 33, 40

Desert of Maine, 55–56

Devil, 236–237

Devil's Den, 195

"Devil's Eye View of the World," 96

Devil's Half Acre, 45

Devil's hoof print, 236

DeWolf, George, 224

DeWolf, Captain James, 223–224,
227

DeWolf, Nancy, 223

DeWolf Cemetery, 223

Dexter, Lord Timothy, 140–142,
170–171

Dick, Jack, 11

"Dick Kemp's Truck Farm," 182

Dickinson, John, 223

Dighton Rock, 95

DiMarco, Al, 73

Helmsley, Harry and Leona, 12
Henniker, N.H., 180–182
Henniker Historical Society, 180–182
Henniker Library, 182
Henry Sheldon Museum of Vermont
  History, 294
Henry's Jewelry Store, 130–131
"Here Mermaids Dwell," 285
Hetty Green Museum, 139
"Hetty's Couch," 268
Heyerdahl, Thor, 38
Hidden, Rev. Samuel, 207
Higgins, John Woodman, 159
Higgins Armory Museum, x,
  159–162, 160
"High Spirits," 179
highway men, 105–106, 271
Hill, Charles and Rubin, 61
Hillsboro, N.H., 182–183
Hinds, Roger, 168
Hiram's Tomb, 113–114
"Historic Roots," 251
Historical Society of Old Newbury,
  141–142
Hitchcock, Alfred, 63
Hitler, Adolf, 295
hoaxes, 95, 126, 294
"Hobo Hotel," 183
Hoffman, Nancy 3, 66–67
"A Hole Man," 98
"The Hole Story,"40
Holmes, Sherlock, 9, 121
hologram, 111, 276
"Holy Land," 37
Holyoke, Mass., 128–129
"The Home Front," 295
Hoosic River, 300
Hoover, Herbert, 146
Hope Cemetery, 267
Hope Diamond, 11
Hopkinton, N.H., 49

Horsford, Professor Eben Norton,
  155, 158
Hosker, George, 200
Hosmer, Rev. Stephen, 20
Houlton, Camp (POW), 56
Houlton, Maine, 56, 56–57
houses: 104; covered bridge, 211–212;
  cursed, 11–12; fairy, 60; haunted,
  116; miniature, 75–76; mound,
  259; skinny, 104–105; sunken, 32;
  underground, 259
Howe, George, 223
Hoyt, Tim, 308
Hudson, Mass., 129–130
Hudson Museum, 62–63
human anthill, 259
Huneck, Stephen, 312
"The Hungry Gorge," 287
Huntington, Vt., 287–288
Huntington Gorge, 287
hurdy-gurdies, 77
Hutchinson, Jesse, 133

I

indentured servants, 205
India, 73, 142, 161
Indian footprints, 307
Indian Museum, 126, 207
Indian Orchard, Mass., 130–131
Indian scalps,169
"Indian Steps," 82, 82–83
Indian Stones, 301
Indian Wars, 78
Indian wordsmithing, 154
Indians, 20, 25, 42, 53, 57, 78, 82, 91,
  95, 125–127, 151, 154–155, 157,
  169, 173, 178, 207–208, 224, 236,
  246, 268, 273, 299, 300–301, 303,
  304, 307
Indonesia, 285

inns, 242
insanity, 153
insects. *See* bugs
instruments: antique, 16; medical,
16–17, 97, 99, 271, 279–280; mu-
sical, 20, 77, 86–87, 121
International Museum of Cryptozo-
ology, **69,** 69–70
International Rotten Sneaker Con-
test, 296
Iraq, 291
Irasburg, Vt., **288,** 288–289
Ireland and the Irish, 180, 271, 303
Isle La Motte, Vt., 274, 290
Israel, 291
Italy and the Italians, 23, 45, 95, 266
"An Itch for Kitsch?" 278

J

Jackalopes, 70
"Jail Hotel," 242
Jailhouse Inn, 242
jails: 91, 185, 241, 242; haunted, 91
James Fisk Monument, 269–270
Janes, Dr. Henry, 279–280
Japan and the Japanese, 177, 295
Jay, Vt., 291–292
Jeanloz, Claude, 174–176
Jenks, Jackson, 241
Jernegan, Prescott F., 58
Jesus, 37, 145, 260, 283
jewels, 61
Johanson, Glenn, 102
John Brown House Museum, 252
John Hay Library, 252
Johnson, Susanna, 300
Jones, Captain Samuel, 210–211
Jonesville, Vt., 287–288
Joseph Smith Monument, 303
"Judges' Cave," 21

Junkermug, Lake, 155
junkyards, 183
Jupiter-C rocket, **209**
Jurassic era, 31, 128

K

kaleidoscope, walk-in, 17–18
Kamuda, Ed, 130–131
Keeler Tavern, 29–30
Keely, John Ernst Worrell, 319–321
"Keely's Mystery Machine,"
319–321, **320**
"Keep Out! The Lock Museum of
America," 35
Kemp, Dick, 182–183
Kendall Whaling Museum, 138–139,
151–152
Kennebunkport, Maine, 57–58
Kennedy, John F., 132
Kilburn Brothers, 187
Killer Gorge, 287–288
Kimball, Moses, 285
kinetic sculptures, 111
King, Stephen, 63, 247, 252–253
"The King of Chester," 170
King Philip, 224–225
"King Philip's Throne," 224
King Philip's War, 224
Kingston, N.H., 183–184
"Kissing Cavalier," 101
Kitty Hawk, N.C., 107
knife antlers, 125–126
Knight, Will, **318,** 318–319
knights, 159–161, **160**
Knowlton, Everett, 76
"Kon Tiki," 38
Konvalinka, Danilo, 86
Korean War, 295
Krass, Hans, 23
Kuck, Barbara, 250

sonic wine glasses, 154
Sonorous Sand, 135
Soubirous, Bernadette, 19
Sound Waters, 6
"The Sounds of Moodus," 20
"Sounds of the Past—The Musical
    Wonder House," 86–87
"Sounds Weird," 153
South America, 7
South Hadley, Mass., 152–153
South Hero, Vt., 305–306, **306**
South Portsmouth, R.I., 259
South Royalton, Vt., 303
South Seas. *See* Pacific Islands
South Woodbury, Vt., 307–308
South Woodstock, Vt., 304
Space Research Corporation, 291
space-cannon, 291
Spanish-American War, 72
Spear, Rev. John Murray, 134
spectral figure, 231. *See also* ghosts
Spencer, George F., 292–293
Spider Web Farm, **318**, 318–319
spiders, **318**
Spielberg, Steven, 250
Spirit of St. Louis (airplane), 49
spirits, 237
Spiritualism, 81, 121, 133, 135, 237
Split Rock, 274
SPNEA, 88
Sprague, Amasa, 231
Sprague, Kate, 231
Sprague, William, 231–232
Sprague Mansion, 231–232
Springfield, Mass., 120, 131
squirrels, albino, 33
St. Albans, Vt., 197, 308–309
St. Albans Historical Society Mu-
    seum, 308–309
St. Johnsbury, Vt., 309–312, **310**
St. Joseph's Roman Catholic Church,
    167

St. Louis, Mo., 254
stairs: carved in rock, **82**; "Flying,"
    87; glass, 252; secret, 123
"Stairway to Nowhere," **82**
"Stalag Stark," 205
Stamford, Conn., 7
Stark, N.H., 205–206
statues, 61, 100; of Hannah Duston,
    126–128, **127,** 169
Stenman, Elis F., 146
Stephen Huneck Gallery at Dog
    Mountain, 311–312
stereoscopes, 187
Stereoscopic View Factory, 187
Steward, Joseph, 15
"Steward's Hartford Museum,"
    15–16
stigmata, 260–261
Stimpson Hill, 316
Stock Market Crash, 191. *See also*
    Great Depression
stocks, 45, 242
Stockton Springs, Maine, 72
"Stone Boy," 294
Stone Brook, 122
Stone, Roger, Jr., 305
stone chambers, **302**
stone relics, 196
stonecutters, 266–267
"Stoned Indians," 268
stones: "Indian" (abduction),
    304–305; mystery, 173–174,
    178–179, 196; sacrificial, 196,
    203–204; standing, 13, 203
Stonington, Maine, 75–76
Story, Ann, 304
Stowe, Vt., 313
Stratford, Conn., 34–35
Strawberry Hill, 314
"Success Cymbal," 142
suicide, 213, 231, 233
sunken house, 32

About the authors

Co-author Joseph A. Citro emerges from Dungeon Rock, Lynn, Massachusetts. Photo: Diane Foulds

Joseph A. Citro is a specialist in New England curiosities. UPNE has published five of his novels on supernatural themes as Hardscrabble Books *(Deus-X, The Gore, Guardian Angels, Lake Monsters,* and *Shadow Child),* as well as his *Vermont Ghost Guide* (2000) and *Green Mountains, Dark Tales* (1999). Mr. Citro has done much to keep the region's history and folklore alive in popular culture. He is a popular lecturer and public radio commentator, and he has appeared on local and national television.

Diane E. Foulds's writing has appeared in numerous publications, including the *Washington Post,* the *Boston Globe,* and the *Christian Science Monitor.* She covered Central Europe for United Press International and was White House and State Department correspondent for Germany's Deutsche Presseagentur. This is her second book.

Co-author Diane E. Foulds emerges from a tree. Photo: Angela Leuker

To contact the authors, please send e-mail to:
stories@burlcol.edu
and visit our website: www.JosephACitro.com

CPSIA information can be obtained at www.ICGtesting.com
Printed in the USA
BVOW02s2214020116

431579BV00001B/1/P